AISLING
BREATH OF THE NEW CREATURE

AISLING
BREATH OF THE NEW CREATURE

A·E· JÜRGENS

atmosphere press

© 2022 A.E. Jürgens

Published by Atmosphere Press

Paperback cover design by A.E. Jürgens
Hardcover design by Ethan Metzler

No part of this book may be reproduced without permission from the author except in brief quotations and in reviews. This is a work of fiction, and any resemblance to real places, persons, or events is entirely coincidental.

Atmospherepress.com

To my parents, who filled my childhood with tales of noble quests and magic, and to my husband, who entertains a wife who never stopped believing in those very stories.

Chapter I

SOME SAY THEY ARRIVED ON DARK CLOUDS, descending towards the earth on ships forged from thunderheads. Some say they emerged from the world beneath the waves, born of the deep—a land where even tyrants could not spread their hands and conquer. And still others believe they were here all along, living parallel to mankind. Between the trees, beneath the mountains, within the wind. Just beyond mortal touch.

To Aisling, it mattered not where the Aos Sí came from, from what abyss the fair folk crawled from. Only that they were savages the Forbidden Lore considered warriors, heroes, ancient deities breathed to life by the blood of the Forge. They were feral, fierce, powerful, a race that defied all that mankind had done to carve itself into the earth.

To Aisling, the Aos Sí were a punishment. Divine retribution for mankind's condemnation of the Forbidden Lore, the tales of creation and the origin of the earth.

"Are you afraid?" Her mother asked, cloaking Aisling's face with a scarlet veil. The torchlight caught the beading of her crimson gown, setting the princess ablaze like a cave of twinkling rubies.

"No," Aisling lied, grateful for the veil shrouding her

expression. Although fear had its uses, the proclamation of it rarely did. Not to mention, Aisling wouldn't give her mother the satisfaction. Clodagh believed she was weak. Believed she was unfit to sacrifice herself for Tilren or the North. A sentiment that mirrored her father's own. Had she not been the only daughter of noble birth in all the Isles of Rinn Dúin, perhaps she wouldn't be here, dressing herself for the unimaginable.

Three knocks sounded against her chamber doors. Before either of the women could grant permission, the door swung open. Four young men entered, only a handful of years Aisling's senior, each dressed in Neimedh tartans and Tilrish finery: Starn, Fergus, Iarbonel, and Annind.

"It's time, sister," Starn, the eldest of her brothers, proclaimed. He swallowed, studying Aisling's dress, her slippers, her sweeping veil, the crown of ebony braids that unraveled like ink down her spine.

Aisling tore her eyes from her brothers, a sharp pain splintering her heart. She didn't look like herself; these were not Tilrish clothes nor styles. And what's more, Starn's gaze was one of mourning, indulging in this fleeting moment, place, person, soon to be a memory. Soon to be forgotten. Soon to be gone.

Aisling nodded, straightening her posture and following her brothers from her quarters. They escorted her through their fortress, a formality, for she'd walked these halls a thousand times, ran through these very corridors as a barefoot child, the cook waving her wooden spoon, chasing her for stealing soda bread before supper. Helping Starn sneak the wolfhound pups into their rooms, naming them after the Tilrish kings of the past, their great grandfathers. Annind shushed her as they hid behind the study's drapes from their father's wrath, their toes peeking out beneath the scarlet trim.

Just beyond Castle Neimedh's threshold, Fergus took Aisling's hand as she climbed into her carriage. This was as far as her brothers would accompany her. Clann Neimedh, her family, all except her father, would travel separately until they arrived and met in neutral land, territory unclaimed by either mortal or fair folk.

But the world outside of Tilren, through the carriage window's smudged pane, was not as Aisling remembered it. The wilderness, the land outside of Clann Neimedh's reach, had grown wilder, more feral, inching towards her carriage, eager to catch a glimpse of her father's generous offering, the Tilrish High King's sacrifice in the name of the North. This unbridled land a direct foil to the scorched and burnt pastures closest to Tilren's walls. And such blackened fields a declaration of mortal authority over the wilds.

But as the trees grew denser, the destriers pulling the carriage whinnied and stomped their hooves restlessly, eyeing the woodlands as if the forest would swallow them whole. A host of tall, thin, wooden sentinels peeping from their beds of needles. Groaning as they extended their spidery fingers and scraped the carriage windows with their branches. And, indeed, the forest had dared to swallow Tilren whole, its creeping vines slithering up their stone terraces, burned again and again by mortal men. As if these leaves, roots, and flowers were another attempt on behalf of the fair folk to reclaim what was never theirs to begin with.

As a child, Aisling roamed these verdant fields, explored the crags that slumbered like mighty giants, danced through these wicked kingdoms of greenwood, oblivious to the perils of fair folk or, at the very least, uncaring. Bewitched by the natural world's beauty and sung from her sleep to inhale its tempestuous opiate. But the violence of war, battle, and conquest had forced Aisling deep behind mortal walls until she was prohibited from ever stepping foot outside Tilren's boundaries lest the sole mortal princess of the Isles be captured by the fair folk.

"No matter what, Aisling, do not forget who you are,"

Nemed told her, sitting on the carriage bench across from her own. Her father was a tall, broad man, handsome if it weren't for the horizontal scar that stretched across the bridge of his nose and both of his cheek bones. As though his head were nearly sliced in half, a mark bestowed by the Aos Sí themselves, a touch of their fury gifted by battle. "Do not forget the world that made you. They will try to deceive you. They will spin lies as easily as they spin their thread. No matter what or how much they take from you, do not let them take who you are or where you come from."

Despite the cold, sweat dappled across Aisling's forehead, her palms, her lower back. She didn't dare respond to her father. Not unless he requested it, gave her permission. She only nodded, glaring out the window once more. She would obey him. For, of course, she would never, could never, forget all she'd ever known: the iron keep and the family that had protected her all her life.

She heard the drums first. And as the night aged, the torchlight in the distance became her beacon in the darkness, a light she dreaded to approach, wishing rather to dissolve into shadow than travel any further. Indeed, Iarbonel had always been the one most afraid of the dark when the siblings were but infants, Aisling, despite her age, comforting her older brother when Nemed snuffed out the candlelight come evening. To Aisling, darkness was pure, whole, all-encompassing, capable of swallowing whatever it desired.

But onward they rode until Aisling could give form to the mass of black interrupted by firelight: crowds of creatures, tents, and blazing stakes nailed to the ground.

The beat of the drums drifted through the evening breeze, echoing off the walls of the cliffs. Great crags surrounding the seemingly endless expanse of wilderness where this ring of fire burned. Stone giants come to witness her fate.

"And remember, Aisling: even in your dying breath, never give them the satisfaction of seeing you wilt, witnessing your fear," Nemed said, his voice low and as formidable as the thumping of the drums, like the heartbeat of the Forge itself. "You represent all of our kind when among them now. Never forget that."

Aisling chewed on the inside of her cheek, sucking in a breath she scarcely possessed the courage to exhale. To release the air from the cage within her.

The carriage stopped. Aisling clutched the seat as the vehicle rocked, settling into place. It was time. They had arrived. Far quicker than the mortal princess would've liked, for even now she considered running, fleeing into the shadowed realm of the wood till she found her iron walls once more.

Outside those thin carriage doors, whispers from the crowd congested the air till Aisling refrained from choking on their sounds. Hundreds of murmuring voices, Aos Sí and mortals alike, awaiting her arrival. But there was another tongue Aisling didn't recognize, hissing amongst the babbling of her own people.

Aisling looked to Nemed for direction. He met her eyes as the door opened, nodding encouragingly as he gestured for her to exit. A glimmer of warmth flashed across the violet eyes they shared, a glimpse of vulnerability, of affection, of love, appearing as swiftly as it vanished.

Her eldest brother, Starn, stood waiting outside the carriage, lips pressed into a thin, hard line. Since Aisling was a child, she'd imagined this day, of all days, unraveling differently: her mother, Clodagh, beaming with pride, Tilrish pipes bellowing in the Northern winds, her brothers' teasing shaking the carriage. But never had she anticipated the glint of fury, as sharp as a blade, in Starn's gaze. The mournful edge to Nemed's usual stony expression.

Nemed offered his daughter his gloved hand as he awkwardly disembarked himself, both legs made of iron prosthetics, another gift from the Aos Sí.

The sea of spectators hushed the moment he emerged.

Aisling swallowed the stone in her throat and accepted her father's gesture. Perhaps the last time, the princess realized, she might hold her father's hand.

The throng of guests continued to murmur wildly, gasping as the princess stepped forth from her carriage and walked through the path of parted attendees. Aisling glared at the grass beneath her slippers, slickened by the dew beading on its blades. She couldn't bring herself to face this foul species. To brave the frightful tales she'd overheard her wetnurses spin when they believed her asleep, ghost stories summoned in the flesh around her.

Nevertheless, even from the corner of her eye, she witnessed how the Aos Sí towered above the mortals among them. Felt the intensity of their unrelenting glares, studying her every step. These fair folk despised her. Loathed every morsel of blood that made her human.

Nemed brought both himself and his daughter to an abrupt stop. Aisling lifted her gaze, fighting the invisible weight pressing her head to the earth. For now, Aisling and her father stood alone at the center of the circle of fire, surrounded by both races. Races who kept their distance, dividing themselves down either side of the circle. Fortunately, the night veiled the Aos Sí's fine features, a small mercy to the princess. She need not lose her resolve now. Not yet.

"As High King of the Isles, I gift my daughter, Aisling of the Clann Neimedh, the sole northern princess," Nemed declared, holding Aisling by the arm with an iron grip.

"There is no greater honor." Aisling fought with herself internally. *"This is your purpose."* That was what Nemed had told her. What her tuath and court branded into her mind over the past several months.

Clodagh and all four of Aisling's brothers, as well as the majority of the Tilrish court, stood frozen on her right-hand side. They were waiting, searching the crowd. Fear flickered across their expressions. Their terror for these wicked beasts near tangible in the shared wind, thick enough to slice. Doubt crept into her brothers' knuckles the more tightly they grasped the hafts of their blades. It was a pointless reflex, Aisling knew. Swords, weapons—even if made of undiluted iron—would bear little consequence against so many Aos Sí gathered in one place. By now, there was nothing to prevent these savages from taking what they wanted.

Through the folds of Aos Sí, three riders emerged. They rode ivory stags, larger and mightier than any steed Aisling had laid eyes on. Dressed in strange armor and crowned by their tangling diadem of antler and bone. But the riders, gilded by the firelight, were plated in sheets of fine metals themselves, armor so slick, so strange Aisling's breath caught at the sight.

A year ago, Aisling never could've imagined laying eyes on a member of the Aos Sí, these primeval deities imbued with ancient, arcane magic and power. Much less stand before them as she did now. It was enough to stun her. To erase the fear, the nerves, even for a moment. But even fear itself was intoxicating, a perfume Aisling was eager to smell more of. To quicken the pace of her heart and breath, both tempered into strict obedience all her life.

The three riders dismounted and lined themselves before the mortal princess and Nemed. The two flanking fae followed the center rider's example, fae knights, legendary warriors nursed on death's tonic. Mortal children battled in Tilren's thoroughfares with spatulas as swords and cutting boards as shields, the largest among them pretending to be these primeval warriors ambushing Tilren's streets and laying waste to their mortal homes, claiming their wives, and devouring their babes. Reenacting the stories they'd all been taught.

The center rider removed his antlered helmet and tossed it to the side. Through her veil of scarlet, Aisling willed herself to meet his eyes. Her hands may have trembled at her sides and her knees weak with fear, but she was no coward. So, with every ounce of will she could muster, she fixed her violet eyes upon him. She knew not his name, but she knew he was the one who would take her. The one who would accept the mortal offering. And against everything and anything she could have imagined, what stood before her was far worse than anything she'd dreaded.

He was remarkable in appearance, stealing her breath the moment their sights connected. His eyes, viridescent, were not the shade of the swaying oaks, the weeping willows, the bristling pines. They *were* the trees, imbued with the spirit of the forest. They were the green of an arcane wood, the blurred portrait of every tree and shrub and flora that bloomed from the earth. The whisper of their leaves in spring's gale.

That was not all that left Aisling's stomach in knots. His dark hair swept his fine cheekbones, several strands braided at random. He bore the great fae height for which they were renowned and the pointed ears. Features Aisling often heard described in passing amongst the chambermaids after their shifts in the dungeons. And just above the collar of his armor, Aisling could see his warrior markings trailing the edge of his throat.

He was beautiful. Frighteningly so. All the fair folk were but nothing like the creature that stood before her, indulging her as she did him. His armor was the most intricate, artfully forged as if by the supple fingers of the rivers themselves. And as he stood before them all, the mortals, the forest, the crags, and even the Aos Sí held a collective breath, in either veneration or fear, Aisling couldn't tell. Perhaps both.

Aisling dared a glance at her father then at her tuath standing to the side, to see if they felt as overwhelmed, as struck and dumbfounded as she did herself. For these fair folk were not the ghoulish monsters they'd been described as, those hunched creatures who lurked in the wilds eager to steal mortal land and women alike. Ugly, demonic entities that shied away from the light.

"*Perhaps this was an enchantment,*" Aisling realized. The Aos Sí were known for their mischief, capable of wielding unnatural powers.

"*They will try to deceive you. They will spin lies as easily as they spin their thread.*" Aisling repeated what her father had told her, rehearsing it till it grew stale in her mind.

The princess struggled to catch her breath. Obviously, she'd never laid eyes on one of the Aos Sí before. Much less one of their kings. She'd seen illustrations, drawn her own conclusions based on the tales she'd been taught since she bore the capacity to sit still long enough to enjoy them. But this noble fair folk who towered over her was beyond anything her imagination was capable of conjuring even if they'd been described correctly. A savage, yes. A barbarian, yes. Something touched by an Otherworldly hand. But there was more. More than she'd anticipated but couldn't quite articulate.

And just as she studied this Fae King, he studied her, exploring her like a predator appraises its prey. His glare burned where it met her skin. Herself, flinching under his scrutiny, his disgust, his disapproval potent in the air between them.

Once he had his fill, he smiled wickedly, flashing two finely pointed canines. The very fangs that had disemboweled hundreds before her, the princess imagined. Innocent mortals who'd wandered too far from their homes. From the man-made world.

This wasn't as it should have been. Aisling should've been gazing into another's eyes, reassured by mutual love, trust, excitement for the future and all the Northern Isles. Another should have stood before her, her mother by her side, her brothers laughing, her father swallowing mead with the King of Roktling in celebration.

Aisling shivered and her skin grew cold the nearer these

beasts approached. These creatures could slay the princess and her clann on a whim. With the flick of their wrists. With curses, they hissed beneath their breath. But her father had known the dangers and organized this trade regardless.

The Fae King gestured to the riders beside him. At his silent command, each unsheathed their greatswords and the metal screeched against their scabbards. All but the knight furthest to the right, who instead, unsheathed one of two twin axes.

Aisling recoiled, reaching for her father but Nemed remained still, chin held high before his enemies. Never had the High King wilted before a threat and Aisling didn't believe he'd start now, even if in the presence of these strange creatures.

The rest of the humans, on the other hand, matched the princess' shock, gasping. Her brothers took a step forward instinctively. The Aos Sí laughed, their chatter rippling through the mass of spectators. Strange voices, nearly ethereal. Like the gentle chime of bells ringing in a soft wind.

Lifting their fae weapons above their heads, Aisling held her breath. Would Nemed truly stand here and watch them slay her in cold blood without so much as a protest? Starn cursed beneath his breath, holding Iarbonel back by the arm. Her mother whimpered but remained stunned, unmoving. The princess wrenched her eyes shut, swallowing the stone lodged in her throat.

The Fae King and his two riders staked their blades into the earth, a line of weapons standing at attention. Aisling opened one eye, then the other. She exhaled a sigh of relief, hoping none had seen her flinch. Perhaps the veil had shielded her expression.

All three riders then turned their attention to Nemed and his daughter, waiting for a response. Aisling looked to her mortal High King, but he appeared just as bewildered as she. All these years at war and still, they knew so little about the

Aos Sí. Even their language was as foreign as it had been the day these demons arrived centuries ago.

Her youngest brother and nearest in age to herself, Annind, stepped forward from the crowd and leaned close to her ear.

"You are to choose the correct blade, Ash," Annind whispered, "only one belongs to the Fae King and it is not necessarily the one with which he has unsheathed from his own back." Annind had studied the fair folk for as long as Aisling could remember. What began as a curiosity for the enemy of mortal man, grew into fascination and eventually a means to communicate, translate, and aid in such exchanges between the races. A knowledge and expertise to which Aisling was now eternally grateful.

The princess regarded the three weapons, each as unique and as strange as the wielders themselves. Aisling knew little of swords or axes or weapons. As princess of Tilren, she trained alongside her brothers, but never did she demonstrate any proficiency; her arrows never stuck their target, her kicks never formed the correct arc, and her muscles never carried more than a shortsword. And so, she'd lost interest in combat, preferring to ride and ride quickly, her only skill amongst a family bearing deadly talents. Talents she envied for their knowledge of such practices made them great and her lack thereof made her weak. A fact that bred fire in her bones.

Staked before her now, the sword on the left bore a pommel embellished with sapphires. The sword in the center boasted a braided, golden haft with a fuller engraved in what Aisling could only imagine was fae. And the axe to the right wore an elegant, knotted wooden haft followed by a wide, black head speckled with etchings and nicks. Metal, leafy vines wrapping around each.

Although the three riders appeared only a handful of years older than Aisling herself, she knew it to be a deception. The Aos Sí lived for centuries and while mankind rotted in the earth these strange warriors maintained their youth and strength. And a king, one of the descendants of the twelve fae monarchs, would have lived the longest, had likely wielded his blades since the mythic destruction of the Forge.

So, Aisling approached the axe on the right, a weapon whose hilt was pressed with mild indentations from ages of being gripped by the same hands.

The princess' stomach fluttered as her eyes met the Fae King's. Despite the veil, he watched her, an invisible tether tangling between them, growing more taught the longer he glared. His eyes narrowed as she neared the axe on the right. There was a flicker of something—dread? surprise?—flashing across his emerald eyes. But it vanished as quickly as it appeared, leaving his expression a solid wall of ice. Nothing that revealed the nature of Aisling's soon-to-be choice.

She swallowed, ignoring the mortal whispers clouding behind her. They knew as little as she, but they could make their own guesses. By the sound of their hushed protests, Aisling knew they believed her to be wrong. That her instinct was misguiding her. For now, she was standing before the axe on the right, her hand hovering over the pommel. The oldest, most ancient among them. Aged and certainly not fit for a king.

Aisling met the Fae King's eyes and placed her hand on the blade to the right.

Silence. His face didn't budge from its scowl but his eyes glimmered with ... something Aisling didn't understand. The rest of the fair folk didn't so much as twitch. It felt in that moment as if their breath was caught in their fair folk chests; the air was thick and oily with their anticipation.

"If that is your choice, Ash, then you must unstake it from the earth," Annind elaborated from behind. His voice grated against the silence.

Aisling glanced at her clann. Clodagh, her brothers, Nemed, all patiently awaiting her decision. What would become of her if she chose wrong? They returned her glance, exchanging a life of memories lived until now. Memories that were at times, warm and friendly, laced with children's laughter. Others were cold, distant, and lonely.

Nemed slowly met his daughter's stare, his scar seemingly redder, deeper, as if agitated in the presence of its makers. The glazed, violet eyes only she and him shared, sparkling with grief.

The princess wrapped her fingers around the hilt and pulled. The axe didn't budge, heavier than Aisling could've ever anticipated. The crowds of Aos Sí snickered, their resentment for the mortal princess now only matched by their amusement.

Aisling clenched her jaw, heat flushing her cheeks and nose.

Some legends claimed the bones of the Aos Sí were carved from the same rock the Forge built the mountains with, affording them divine strength. Aisling didn't doubt it for the blade she attempted to lift was immovable.

The Fae King approached her then. Aisling's stomach twisted and her heart thrashed, willing herself to hold steady as he stood behind her and knelt to his knees. Her joints stiffened and her chest tightened, growing numb from his sheer proximity. The weight of his nearness pressed through the lace, hovering above her exposed flesh.

From this position, the Fae King wrapped his arms around the princess, taking hold of her hands. His fingers and palms were rough, calloused, burning where his skin grazed her own. The princess gasped. She'd never been touched by a man outside her immediate family but, of course, she needn't remind herself that these were savages. They paid no mind to the customs of civility or propriety.

Together, they slid the blade from the grass beneath them.

Relief swept over Aisling as the king raised the axe from the ground and held it above their heads, still gripping the axe's haft and Aisling's hands.

The crowd cheered and the music burst into rhythm once again. The fair folk banged their weapons against their shields, stomped their feet against the earth, and shouted words Aisling couldn't understand. But despite their newfound fervor, their excitement, their anger still radiated their resentment, their confusion written across their ancient faces.

Aisling had chosen correctly. Selected the weapon that belonged to the Fae King.

Cringing at the sudden burst of commotion, she forced herself to stand tall, to not hesitate before either the Aos Sí, her tuath, or the mortals of the North. And meanwhile, the Fae King stood from where he'd kneeled behind her, releasing her hands.

Aisling, against her own volition, turned to study his reaction. His brow was furrowed but his interest in the mortal princess had peaked, regarding her as though she were a riddle breathed into human form.

But the ceremony was not yet complete.

The two riders, the ones who'd entered on either side of the Fae King, approached the princess and their sovereign.

"*Atrealia de mer*," the dark-haired fae said, holding his own hand before him, palm facing the night sky. Aisling looked to Annind, standing a few paces away.

"Give him your hand," her brother instructed, more confidently than Aisling knew he felt.

Reluctantly, Aisling did as he said, extending her hand and mirroring the fae knight and king beside her, their arms distorted reflections of one another. One sleeved in crimson jewels, lace, and velvet. The other, bound by thick fae markings, armor, and leather.

The second knight handed the first a ribbon, a ribbon braided with ivory florals and owl feathers. The Fae King knotted his fingers through Aisling's own. Aisling's toes curled at the gesture, palm to palm. Flesh to flesh.

The dark-haired knight wrapped their hands together with the ribbon. The thorns of the flowers scratched Aisling's skin but she didn't protest. This was why she'd come. Why her clann had offered her to the fair folk.

"*De réig can bhriollú, gallian duic,*" the Fae King began, wrapping the ribbon one, two, three times, "*an chéar ghlal eng mo chuig fola.*" Four, five, six loops.

Aisling's chest burned the longer they were bound together, something stirring wildly in her gut. She snuck a glance at the strange king, but he appeared unaffected, rather distantly studying the mortal princess and her efforts to remain still despite the pressure of the moment.

"By the Forge, I vow to you the first cut of my heart," Annind translated for the sake of the mortals observing the ceremony, "the first taste of my blood, and the last words from my lips."

And just like that, they were handfasted.

Her whole life, Aisling had imagined standing in Castle Neimedh, wearing a white gown, bowing before her father with the Prince of Roktling at her side. Instead, she stood in the wilderness, in a circle of fire, bound to a Fae King. A barbarian. An enemy. The antithesis to the world from which she was born and bred. An immense death took place in her heart for the life taken from her.

The second rider, the one whose hair lit like flames, drew a dagger from his belt and cut his king's palm. Aisling winced. From there, the first rider lifted a goblet of wine to which the Fae King offered his own blood. He squeezed his hand into a fist, so the blood oozed from the wound and dripped into the goblet itself.

Aisling knew what was to come next. They gestured for Aisling's hand once more. The princess hesitated, daring a glance over her shoulder at the clann that stood behind her. Aisling's brothers each swallowed, their muscles tightening beneath their woolen cloaks. Her mother shied away from her glance, unable or unwilling to meet her eyes, her father shifting where he stood.

The princess raised her hand. She inhaled sharply as the dagger sliced her flesh and stole the blood from her veins. It hurt, an acute pain that was thankfully brief. No worse than the nicks and scars she'd received escaping Castle Neimedh to secretly climb the trees outside the city walls or exploring Tilren's narrow passages at night.

Drop by drop, her blood was poured into the goblet, the same as had the king's.

The Fae Lord drank first. He tipped the glass back and Aisling couldn't help but stare as his throat bobbed in the gesture, skin glimmering in the firelight. Then it was Aisling's turn. The king angled their bodies so he could lift her veil, their other hands still tangled in the rope. Aisling caught his glare. There was not a breath that passed where their eyes unlocked from the other, as he folded the veil over her crown of braids, witnessing the bare flesh of her cheeks, her pale complexion, her violet eyes. She felt nude before him. Heart hammering against her chest. More vulnerable than ever before. For he appraised her unapologetically, exploring her expression and the fear that no doubt ran rampant across her Tilrish features.

The Fae King brought the goblet to her lips, and she drank. It tasted of iron as it slid across and stained her tongue. But such a flavor morphed into something else entirely, transformed into a sweet syrup lighting her belly with fire. Something Aisling could've drunk for hours and never tired of it. Like the sap the Tilrish kitchens would boil over the hearth when highland temperatures dropped, filling the city thoroughfare with spice and sugar. A memory Aisling now realized was nothing more than that, a memory never to be lived again.

As soon as she swallowed, the crowd erupted once more. The beat of their drums thrummed through her core, awaking a wild excitement she hadn't realized she'd harbored until now.

    The Aos Sí stomped their feet and banged their weapons against their shields. The mortals clapped and at last her father beamed wildly, masking the cold anger burning behind his violet eyes. The unsatiated rage her brothers ground into their teeth. For now, she was both married and a Queen of the Aos Sí.

Chapter II

THE FAIR FOLK DRANK AND DANCED WILDLY. Aisling blushed at the sight of the females twirling barefoot in the fields, much of their skin exposed to the brisk evening air. Their hair hung loose, weaved through with satin ribbons, flowers, nuts, and pinecones. Flora that resembled jewels rather than scraps from the forest.

The fae males removed their armor and danced alongside them, singing, flirting, sparring playfully. They grabbed one another's hands and formed a circle, twirling to the beat of the drum and the melody of the flute. They were the heathens Nemed had always described them to be, their flesh glimmering with sweat and the intricate tattoos said to describe their conquests, the countless human lives they'd stolen and left piled on battlefields.

The mortals, on the other hand, sat proudly at their tables, too afraid or too disgusted by the Aos Sí to participate in the revelry Aisling was unsure of.

Clann Neimedh were not the only mortals in attendance. So too had the nobles of the other Northern mortal kingdoms—Kinbreggan, Aithirn, and Roktling—travelled to attend the union of the Fae King and mortal princess. Kings, chieftains, their brides, and queens. The countries comprising the

Northern Isles known as Rinn Dúin. Even Dagfin, the Prince of Roktling, once intended to marry Aisling when she came of age, was here. But war had changed such negotiations. War had changed everything.

Nemed and Clodagh had stuck close to Aisling until now, shoulder to shoulder, soaking in their last moments with their daughter. Of course, neither said more than a few words. The silence was heavy and cruel. For her mother and father bereaved their daughter's still-beating heart, a Tilrish heart of iron and stone traded into the hands of the fae. But such proximity was short-lived for every mortal monarch of the Isles wished to speak with their High King and Queen. And so Nemed and Clodagh obliged. Aisling was accustomed to such duty; it was, after all, for all of the mortal sovereigns, all of the North, all of mankind, that Aisling had wed the Fae King.

"I ensured a means for you to write while you're … away," Iarbonel said, taking their father's place beside his sister at the dining tables. Annind settled into his mother's seat. Both Starn and Fergus, on the other hand, stood a pace away from the circle of fae dancers, studying the fair folk for Fergus had scarcely seen the enemy up close. Starn was the only one amongst her siblings who accompanied Nemed on all his expeditions, dangerous or otherwise.

Aisling didn't blame her brothers' fascination. As wild as the Aos Sí may be, they were undoubtedly lovely. Still, no mortals dared join in the revelry. They either sat or stood stiff-backed, fearing for their lives should they inhale too deeply.

"Thank you" was all Aisling could think to respond, her words more clipped than she'd intended.

"It doesn't need to be said but I'll say it regardless: you're doing a courageous thing, Ash. For Clann Neimedh and all the North. Perhaps beyond," Iarbonel continued, his eyes flicking to Nemed. Iarbonel was the third eldest son and perhaps the kindest of the three. "Here. Consider this a wedding gift from Starn, Fergus, Annind, and myself. But don't show Father," he said, a familiar mischief lacing his words. Her brother pulled from a strap across his tunic an iron dagger with a twisted onyx hilt, embellished with a pommel in the shape of a fist gripping a single, large ruby.

Aisling gasped at the sight of it. Iarbonel had taught Aisling how to use a dagger when they were children. All weapons forged in Tilren and in the mortal kingdom were done so with undiluted iron, the only substance known to wound or kill a member of the fair folk.

"Where did you get that?" Aisling said, perhaps too loud, for Annind nervously shushed her, watching Nemed and Clodagh from the corner of his eye as he'd done a thousand times before, while they snuck coins from their father's desk drawers, let the wolfhounds loose during Clodagh's tea, or stayed up past their bedtimes reciting outlandish and inappropriate tavern songs beneath their covers.

"Fergus borrowed it from Father's weapons chamber," Iarbonel said. Aisling took the dagger, inspecting it just below the table. Low enough that none could see but herself and her brothers. "He'll hardly notice it's missing."

At that Annind scoffed, crossing his arms. Hardly a mouse skittered through Castle Neimedh that Nemed wasn't aware of.

Aisling admired the pommel, stroking the ruby enclosed in the fist. It was a symbol for mankind. The crest of the mortals. An image that described how man, in the beginning of all things, had been born of nothing, had made themselves from nothing, had carved themselves into the earth from nothing. The ruby was the fire with which they did so, a fire firmly clutched in the hands of mankind. There were no Gods or religion. Only man and man alone had risen of their own strength and of their own power. This symbol was a rejection of the lies spewed by the Forbidden Lore. Of the beliefs of the Aos Sí. Even if some of their myths and legends still snuck their way into modern man's fireside tales.

"I hope you won't need it but, just in case, we thought you might make use of it. If nothing other than to remind you of home," Iarbonel said, closing Aisling's hand over the hilt. His voice shook in the slightest. Aisling didn't need to meet his eyes to know he was afraid for her. Who knew what would become of her now that she belonged to the fae? There wasn't an aspect of this agreement that didn't endanger Aisling, but it was a sacrifice all of the North, her clann, and her family was eager to make if it meant sparing their people from further conflict.

"I can't thank you enough," Aisling said, steadying the weight in her own voice.

"It's best you keep it a secret," Iarbonel added, and Aisling understood. She couldn't imagine solid iron was welcomed amongst the Aos Sí, especially when wielded by a mortal.

"Even from your"—Iarbonel tripped over his tongue, swallowing whatever twisted his tongue"—your husband."

Husband. Aisling's eyes drifted towards the Fae King. Her stomach flipped at the sight of him, forcing herself to clench her fists around the hilt of the dagger lest they begin to shake. And as if he had sensed her attention, their eyes met. His lips parted, those green irises glimmering in the starlight like Clodagh's drawers of polished jade jewels. He'd removed much of his armor, but his axes remained strapped against his back. Those primordial blades perhaps cast in the Forge of Creation itself if such a myth were anything more than that, a myth.

"What would've become of me?" Aisling blurted. Iarbonel and Annind shifted in their seats on either side of her. "What would've become of me if I'd selected the wrong weapon? During the ceremony?"

Annind followed her gaze and found the Fae King across the way, his axes winking back.

"It's an ancient fae tradition," Annind began, his voice hesitant, "all unions of their kind participate in a similar test."

Yes, Aisling already assumed all of that.

"But what would've occurred had I failed?" Aisling insisted. Annind clenched his jaw, shaking his head slightly as if convincing himself and failing to tell his sister no more.

"If you chose the wrong blade, you'd have been beheaded," Annind said, clearing his throat and averting his gaze. "Normally, if the fair folk bride fails, they engage in combat to the death. In your case, considering you are mortal and bear no ability to duel, you would've been executed near instantly."

"It never would've come to that," Iarbonel spat, shooting daggers at his brother with his crow-like gaze. An onyx hue each of the brothers had stolen from Clodagh upon birth.

Annind ignored him, cursing beneath his breath.

"The Aos Sí believe their sword or weapon of choice is similar to a limb but not a corporeal one. A limb of the soul. True mates can identify their partner's soul based on the weapons they wield, said to be inextricably tethered to their heart. For a king, the practice is taken more seriously," Annind attempted to clarify. To justify.

"It's nothing more than superstition. Even us mortals have traditions we follow out of habit rather than pure belief. Primitive really," Iarbonel said, running his fingers through his dark hair. Hair as black as Aisling's.

"Did Father know?" Aisling asked, turning to face Iarbonel. Her brother avoided her glare, instead exchanging glances with Annind. But that was answer enough. Aisling knew Nemed and Clodagh would place the North above all else, even their children, but to experience such fealty firsthand was more painful than she'd anticipated.

And as if prompted by her thoughts, Nemed stood from his seat and raised a goblet. The Fae King, aware of the gesture, quieted his people without so much as a word, and the celebration dissolved into silence, all eyes pinned to the mortal High King of the Isles of Rinn Dúin, as well as the Sovereign of Tilren.

"I speak for each of the mortal Northern lords when I say we are honored to have participated in the first union between the Aos Sí and our kind. May such a marriage lead to peace between our races in the North," Nemed glared at the Fae King, narrowing his eyes. "May we set an example to the rest of the world."

Perhaps only Aisling, who noted her father's strange intonation as he spoke those last words, recognized his toast as the threat that it was. She found the Fae King in the crowd, a cool smile spread across his face, either unfazed or unaware of her father's passive aggression. But she shouldn't be surprised. The Aos Sí and mortals were natural enemies. Not even a political union could change that.

The kings and queens, chieftains and chiefesses, lords and ladies of Kinbreggan, Aithirn, and Roktling stood from their seats and raised their goblets. Some more capable of hiding their fear than others, steadying their hands and willing the wine not to leap over the brim.

"To the end of bloodshed!" The Bregganite King shouted, tipping back his goblet and downing its contents. He was the eldest mortal sovereign, all his sons having died of a disease born from the lack of fresh food and the increasingly squalid state of the mortal world after centuries of ongoing war with the Aos Sí. Even the mortal kingdoms still standing strong feared venturing too far into the wilderness to hunt or gather lest they be set upon by fair folk. For this reason, Tilren struggled to bring in enough meat, grains, fruits, and vegetables for the entirety of the kingdom to eat their fill. That was why Nemed had begun spreading his walls, claiming more and more of the wilderness, burning trees, laying waste to the wilds. So that he could harbor more cattle and farmland within the protection of mortal walls. A gesture met with the fair folk's fury.

The Fae King and his warriors raised their goblets before he tipped his head to the mortal monarchs. Grinning, he drank. His feral subjects followed his lead, the music prompting their continued debauchery. After all, both the Aos Sí and mortals had thoroughly inspected all wines, meads, and foods present at the festivities for poison or mischief of any sort. Even the grounds were finely combed through for traps should either race choose to take back their word.

But Aisling's mind drifted elsewhere.

For a warlord, the Fae King was beloved by his subjects. Beloved and feared. Aisling had seen firsthand the sort of power her father collected through a similar sort of fear, a merciless ruling hand. Ruthless yet effective. But Nemed wielded such authority through the instillment of obedience, cultivating a civilization of order, efficiency, and harmony. Nothing like these anarchic barbarians. Wild, ages-old beasts in the form of breathtaking men and women, Aisling now realized.

But the Fae King's knights also talked freely around and to him, addressing him like a friend. A comrade. One who had fought battles by his warriors' sides, a strange fae practice Aisling was realizing for in the mortal realm, kings strategized from their castles, their camps, dueling only when necessary to protect the crown and royal legacy. Especially those with iron legs.

The Fae King matched his subjects' energy, laughing and drinking alongside them. Indulging, far more than was proper of a nobleman much less a king. And even from a distance, even over the roar of the drums and the music, Aisling could hear his laugh, drawing her back to him. She studied the fine lines of his jaw, his markings wrapped around his forearms like serpents, disappearing under the white of his shirt. By now, he'd stripped away his armor, revealing the tall, slender yet muscular form of him. Every one of his movements, despite the countless bottles of wine he'd unstoppered, was performed with a grace-like elegance Aisling envied.

It went without saying, he was not the brute Aisling had

anticipated physically. Not the monstrous abomination she'd heard in the tales before bed. But those were the most dangerous sort of creatures, the lovely ones.

Just as Aisling intended to turn away, she'd realized the Fae King had caught her staring. The princess' heart stuttered. His sage-green eyes watched her, a roguish grin sweeping his handsome features. There was something about the shadows in his eyes, the way he undressed her body and soul. Herself, the sole subject of his gaze. A feral devil intrigued by the perfume of her cold fear, her hot blood, the sweat pearling across her skin.

"Aisling," a familiar voice sounded from behind, tearing her from her reverie, "I've caught you at last." Dagfin, Prince of Roktling, greeted the princess with a bow. Her heart twisted the moment their eyes met, a combination of guilt and relief washing over her. The mere sight of the prince disarming the spell the Fae King had woven. A gesture for which Aisling was eternally grateful.

Iarbonel and Annind exchanged knowing glances before standing from their chairs and taking their leave, allowing Dagfin and Aisling some privacy. But Aisling knew this was also an excuse for them to join the rest of her brothers, observing the festivities more closely.

"For the moment," Aisling said, gesturing for Dagfin to sit beside her. Already, Aisling noticed the prince had changed since they were children, sneaking from their rooms in the dead of night. For indeed it had been several years since she'd last seen the prince. Although, he still bore that boyish tousle of locks, thick dark brows, and a scar along his knuckles, a result of Aisling attempting to practice Iarbonel's lessons on her only friend. He was taller now, his shoulders broader, his features more pronounced. No longer was he the boy that tugged at her braids when she'd fallen asleep during their lessons.

"How are you faring, Ash?" He hesitated, uncertainty

clouding his expression, "I suppose I should address you differently now, *Your Majesty*," he said, tilting his head forward.

Aisling smiled, "Nonsense, I preferred it when you called me a spoilt child all those years ago."

"That name suited you then as this new title suits you now." He watched her closely. He'd always glared at her like that; as though she were an uncharted sea, waiting to be explored. That was Dagfin's nature. Perpetually in pursuit of an adventure to whisk him away from his princely duties. To distract him from the crown that would inevitably sit on his head.

Nevertheless, Dagfin had matured since she'd last laid eyes on him. Last held his hand and cried when he'd left for Roktling once more. He'd been nothing more than a boy then. Not the man that sat beside her now. A man whose eyes had darkened, something strange skewing the curve of his smile.

"I'm not your queen," Aisling said, her smile fading as she shifted her attention to the throng of fair folk celebrating with renewed energy, stomping their feet, singing wildly, hollering, cheering, dancing like animals. Their bodies pressed so near together, Aisling's hands grew slick around her dagger, folded away in her skirts. "I'm theirs," she said, meeting the prince's eyes.

A muscle flickered across Dagfin's jaw. That unfamiliar, untapped anger swimming in the oceans of his eyes. Eyes that never strayed from Aisling's own, searching her with an intensity she'd never grow accustomed to.

"You shouldn't be." And, although he hadn't fully expressed it, Aisling knew what he meant: she should be his queen. A Queen of Roktling, ruling over the coastal kingdom when the day came for Dagfin to inherit his own father's throne. Their marriage would've been prompted by politics, just as the one she'd now underwent had been. Nevertheless, there'd been a comfort in knowing she'd one day marry an old friend and now guilt that they hadn't. That she'd wed another before his very eyes. Perhaps Dagfin felt similarly.

"Your father is wrong for this." He'd said it so abruptly, Aisling straightened, startled.

"You shouldn't speak that way about Nemed. Not here. Not anywhere. It doesn't matter if you've sailed the eleven seas, he'd punish you for such a tongue."

"I'm not worried about Nemed. Because of this"—Dagfin gestured towards the celebration spinning around them—"he can burn in the Forge for all I care."

Out of habit, Aisling's eyes darted towards her father, afraid he might overhear their conversation. Thankfully he was far enough away, their voices cloaked by the revelry and music. Still, Aisling was well aware Nemed bore eyes and ears in all corners. Even if one believed themselves to be entirely alone.

"And you, Aisling," Dagfin continued, "the days of running from your father's scoldings are done and gone. He'll pale in comparison to your enemies going forward. You mustn't hesitate to defend yourself, protect yourself, find ways to survive amongst them."

"The peace contract ensures my safety—"

"Enough of contracts, of peace treaties, of political alliances. Your journey from here on out cannot rely on the words of kings written in the name of power." Dagfin moved closer to her, anger carving out every inflection. "I've spent this last year searching for a way out of this for you, and in this effort I've failed you."

"Fin—"

"If you ever feel you're in danger, if ever you need an escape, Ash, write to me. I'll find a way. I offered to run away with you once and you denied me; that offer still stands, will always stand."

Aisling glared at her friend, searching for what she knew not. These words were blasphemous to Tilren, to Nemed, to all of the North, and any effort to spare Aisling from committing this sacrifice was an effort in vain.

And despite all the thoughts, feelings—rage, regret she'd never consciously acknowledge—drowning Aisling's lungs, all she managed was "This is my duty, Fin."

And indeed, it was her duty, her purpose, to ensure the union between fair folk and mankind remained intact until the day she died. The marriage hadn't been her choice, but this was the circumstance with which she'd been dealt. She could— she would make her tuath proud and all of Rinn Duínn. Dagfin's expression twisted as if Aisling had cursed his name. As though she'd rebuked him and all their experiences lived together thus far. An urge to reach out to him, to cradle his cheek with the palm of her hand, tugged at her heart but she sat still. Arms suddenly as heavy as the monoliths that surrounded them.

"So be it," Dagfin said, his voice frosted over like the Roktan shores come winter. Cold enough to send a shiver down Aisling's spine.

Before she could respond, Dagfin looked past the princess. His eyes narrowed, expression darkening as he considered a figure approaching from behind. Somehow angrier than it had been moments before. The Fae King was nearing, pacing forward like a wolf pads across the forest floor. He ignored the prince, his knowing eyes searching Aisling's own then dropping to the little space left between herself and Dagfin.

Instinctively, Aisling leaned away from the Roktan prince. Was such nearness just as inappropriate amongst the Aos Sí as it was amongst the mortals? Dagfin and Aisling were only friends, childhood playmates. They'd even held hands since they were toddlers, but the Fae King wasn't aware of such history.

Before Aisling could utter a word, Dagfin was standing. Aisling's stomach plummeted. He placed his body between the Fae King and Aisling, sheltering her from the barbarian stepping any nearer.

The Fae King dragged his eyes from Aisling's to Dagfin's, the corners of his lips curling in amusement. And as they stood face to face, the attention of the surrounding fair folk as well as Starn, Iarbonel, Annind, and Fergus slowly gravitated towards the Roktan Prince and Fae King.

"Step aside, princeling." The Fae King's voice was deep, every word dripping with his fae accent. Aisling considered this demon more closely. The queen assumed the Aos Sí knew little if not nothing of her language. A barrier she'd dreaded until now. But she'd been wrong. The Fae King spoke her tongue confidently, even more beautifully than herself.

Dagfin didn't waver. Rather held the Fae King's gaze as he spoke: "Save your commands. You're no king in these parts and certainly no king of mine."

The Fae King's emerald eyes glittered with mischief, his mouth tearing into a sardonic grin. The sight of which unnerved Aisling, the image of a wolf baring its fangs.

"It wouldn't take a title to bring you to your knees, princeling," the Fae King replied, the axes crossed behind his back glinting with promise.

The surrounding fae knights as well as Starn, Iarbonel, Fergus, and Annind inched closer, hands drifting towards the hafts of their weapons. Their rising anxiety was palpable in the evening wind. As for Dagfin, he may have outwardly appeared unfazed, but Aisling knew the signs of his cleverly masked fury, the slow closing and opening of his hands at his sides. A gesture followed by many of a fight with the boys who'd teased Aisling as a child for her height, her lack of strength, her temper.

"M'Lord," Aisling interjected, rising to her feet and stepping forward. She now stood a shoulder before Dagfin, her friend's reluctance to allow her to do so thick in the silence that lingered after she'd spoken.

Immediately, all eyes shifted towards the mortal queen.

The fae knights. Aisling's brothers. She'd addressed the Fae King, bowing her head so her crown of braids glittered in the firelight overhead. The demon considered her with those gleaming eyes.

Aisling's pulse quickened, hands slick despite the cool evening breeze. For without another glance at the Roktan Prince, the Fae King closed the distance between himself and her. Every step nearer, testing Dagfin's impulsive will to fight. But he couldn't stop this union from occurring nor proceeding. No one could. Their marriage sealed in the blood they'd shared from a single goblet.

"*Rá an t-amt ragtha done lúra a raoire a thógáil!*" A member of the fair folk shouted across the celebration, gesturing towards the Fae King and Aisling now positioned at the head of the dining table.

"It's time for our king and queen to take their leave," Annind translated for the mortal guests. The bitterness in his voice matched the expressions of her brothers. But nothing compared to the intemperate storm gathering behind the glint in Dagfin's eyes.

At the very least, both her brothers' hands and those of the nearby fair folk had lowered from their weapons, now hanging at their sides, bottled anger curling their fingers into fists.

Aisling willed herself steady, for her knees not to quiver, accepting the Fae King's outstretched hand. She winced as their flesh made contact, nevertheless, allowing him to guide her from the tent, spilling with fair folk and mortals alike. Tucking the dagger Iarbonel had gifted her into her sleeve and stifling her fear.

Aisling dared not glance back at her old friend, but she could feel the pressure of Dagfin's regard as she lengthened the distance between them. Had he expected her to say goodbye? To match his fury and provoke the savage lord she'd been traded to? Aisling knew this wasn't wise, yet her heart stretched and cleaved in two the moment she stepped away from Dagfin and didn't look back.

The rest of the Aos Sí cheered, banging their fists atop the tables. Stomping their feet and shaking the foundation of the tent in which they all stood.

"*Rabhair aoidhre dúinn!*" The Aos Sí shouted, growing louder the longer they sang. A musicality to their tongue Aisling's mortal language couldn't boast.

Against her own volition, Aisling sought out Annind for a translation, but he shied away from her glance. If that was the case, perhaps she was better off not knowing.

The Fae King led his new queen towards the cluster of smaller tents and away from the hordes of people. He laughed and waved at his subjects, but Aisling wanted nothing less than to meet either Nemed or Clodagh's gaze for fear of what she might find. Not even her brothers. Grief, sorrow, fury would do little to save the Northern Isles. So, she turned her back to the festivities and allowed the king to tear her away from the rest of the world, from the life she'd lived thus far. For even if he hadn't devoured her physical body, he'd gutted her, heart and soul.

Chapter III

IF THE AOS SÍ PUBLICLY BEHEADED THEIR lovers as a marital custom, what did they do to their wives in private? Of course, if the Fae King wanted Aisling dead, he could've already done so. They were far enough away from any mortal that none could hear her scream nor find her body if the Fae King wished it.

Still, that didn't rule out torture.

Aisling shivered, shaking away the thoughts.

"Are you cold?" The Fae King leaned down to whisper against her ear lest the wandering revelers overhear their conversation. His breath scalded the nape of her neck. But it was welcomed, warming her frozen skin and sending chills down the rest of her body.

Aisling, startled, turned towards the king.

"Aren't you?" She asked the king in return for he wore less than she, dressed in nothing more than a loose-fitted shirt, trousers, and his axes. Improper for a gentleman much less a king.

He grinned and exhaled a soft laugh.

"My kind rarely grows cold," he began. "I've forgotten how weak humans can be."

"Weak?" Aisling growled, "It is weak to complain of it. Not

to bear that which we have no say."

"Perhaps fragile is a better word then?" He said, flashing his pointed canines like a wolf.

"The most valuable things are," Aisling huffed, relieved her voice bore the confidence she didn't yet feel.

They approached the largest tent at the center of the fae camp. Sentries stood guard at all four corners, their armor flashing with orange in the torchlight. But Aisling bore no illusions that the Fae King couldn't defend himself if necessary. Could not slay a horde of humans if he so desired. As soon as she thought it, the images followed shortly after, accompanying the horror of her assertions. The queen's tongue turned to ash that she forced herself to swallow.

The king spread apart the curtains and gestured for Aisling to enter. The queen held her head high, but she'd dreaded this more than the wedding itself.

The scent of freshly plucked pine needles greeted the queen first, then the miraculous heat of its interior.

Where Aisling had expected dirt and filth, the tent was adorned with rich, luxurious quilts and comforters, plump pillows, hand-woven rugs, and opulent animal pelts, skinned to perfection. How the fair folk had not only parceled and lugged such luxury across the Northern landscape but also prepared it so charmingly, was a shock to the mortal queen. All and every piece was fabricated by fae hands. Mortal fingers couldn't design nor use such rare and luxurious materials. Spider silk too delicate to weave, maiden's moss too spongy to thread, and pale oak too susceptible to splintering to carve.

A bed large enough for three was placed at the center of the room, crowned with garlands bubbling over with plump buds and blooming wildflowers. But some of the flora stole Aisling's attention, shimmering with soft light, the flowers lit the room, casting a warm, hazy glow throughout the tent's interior. Their glittering pollen floating in the midnight breeze. A wind stealthy enough to slip inside the moment

Aisling had.

Within this tent, the air itself must have been enchanted, filled with some unspoken lullaby. A muffled melody that soothed even the mortal queen as she stood soaking in the canvassed chamber. Was this the magic the fair folk were known to practice? The wielding of powers they believed to be bestowed by the Gods themselves?

"The Aos Sí say their magic comes from the Gods. There are no Gods. Whatever abilities they wield are aberrations. Perversities of nature. As they are themselves. Do not let them convince you otherwise." One of Nemed's many lectures she'd received since her marriage was signed and sealed by all mortal and fae sovereigns from the north and elsewhere. Words that she knew she'd do well to remember, aware she'd soon learn the extent of such fae abilities.

The Fae King brushed past her and shrugged off his weapons. Weapons she hadn't yet seen, belted against his trousers, in his pockets, behind his shirt, around his calf. Except for his axes. The only possessions he tucked neatly beneath his pillow as if afraid to part from them even in his sleep.

Aisling had overheard tales of warriors unable to find rest without first preparing themselves for an attack even if years had passed since their last battle. This was what war did to man, death crouched on their shoulders long after the ground puddled with blood. If they survived. Was this what afflicted even a barbarian king? Aisling swatted away the thought, these were beasts. Not men. They bore no such vulnerabilities. Emotions. Hauntings.

Without hesitation, he next removed his shirt. Aisling stifled a gasp, covering her mouth before she could utter a sound. She'd never laid eyes on a male so undressed, even if he still wore his trousers. But Aisling knew this was not what most men looked like; the Fae King was tall, muscled, lean, and painted with complex fae tattoos that disappeared below his narrow waist. Black coils, symbols, knots, and braids that followed the curves of his broad shoulders, his neck, his hands, and Aisling assumed, everything she could not see.

The queen cursed herself silently for having indulged in those nightmarish tales, fireside stories that warned mortal women to resist fae charms lest they be taken how fae males took their own females against their will. No, Aisling couldn't afford to think of such stories now, lest she surrender the courage she'd thus far fought to preserve. Even if said courage was nothing more than the scraps of what it once was back in Tilren.

For the longer she stood frozen at the foot of the bed, the more she lost feeling in her legs, her knees, her feet. Her palms and back beading in a cold sweat. She was a virgin, after all, primed and prepared to one day consummate her marriage with Dagfin, with a mortal man. Not the Fae Lord before her; to touch the body of he who'd used every muscle, every limb, every ounce of will in his accursed form to maim her kin for sport.

"You will escort your betrothed to your bed the night of your union. This evening will be the first of many in your journey to gift him an heir. It will hurt and you will most likely bleed. But fret not, this act is not one of passion or pleasure. Rather your noble obligation to the North."

Aisling clenched her fists at her sides, her mother's words echoing between the wild thrashing of her heart. She'd agreed to this, to happily, willingly allow her father to sacrifice her to the fair folk in exchange for peace. She knew the risks, the responsibility to fulfill her duty to Tilren and all of Rinn Dúin even if it meant marrying for a political alliance. Even if it meant sleeping beside this lethal stranger. Sleeping *with* this Fae King. She'd serve her clann, her race, at whatever cost.

"Will you sleep in your gown?" He asked, flicking his eyes towards her dress. Aisling ran nervous fingers down its bodice, swallowing hard.

Sleep? Sleep was a distant concern in Aisling's mind, and she'd assumed the king's as well. In fact, she hadn't even considered the Fae King slept at all, a mythic warlord burdened by the same exhaustions as mortal man.

"I have none of my belongings to change into," she said.

"Your belongings are being delivered to Annwyn as we speak," he said.

Annwyn. Was this what they called the territory the Aos Sí stole from Nemed?

"It's often assumed a bride needs no belongings the night of her union," he continued, before a single flower's glow suddenly extinguished. Then another. Descending the room into darkness. Flower buds dimming, untouched by either breath or wind or flesh.

Their floral perfume smoked the tent. Aisling turned in time to witness the Fae King open his palm and close it once more. And in pace with the gesture, another flower faded till the ember of light within dissolved into shadow. It was then, Aisling realized, that it was the Fae King's doing, stifling the light of the flora, without touch or contact of any kind. Was it magic? An unholy warping of the laws of nature as Nemed would claim? Where she thought such abilities would strike fear in her, she found herself more curious than afraid.

Aisling inhaled, her chest tightening as the room grew dark. The first night would be the most difficult. She knew this.

"Do not scream when he takes you, M'Lady," her chambermaid had advised in the weeks preparing her for this night. *"Nor should you let your blood run freely too long, menstruating or otherwise. It will only encourage a demon such as he."* At the time, Aisling had merely nodded her head, mindlessly soaking in the instructions the whirlwind of advisors gave her over the past several months, educating her on the nature of sex and pregnancy. But never had such lessons felt more tangible, more petrifying, than they did now. This otherwise-

customary female education was perverted by the circumstances in which she found herself. The thought of the Fae King touching her, seeing her, impregnating her was enough to knock the wind from her lungs.

The mortal queen untangled her braids till the windswept torrents dripped down her spine, spilling against her back in garlands of black.

The Fae King turned to face her, only a single flower left to be lulled to sleep. Enough to gild the queen in its ocherous light, shadows dancing across her undone locks.

He considered Aisling, tilting his head like a fox considers a mouse. With unrelenting focus. No man had ever seen her with her hair undone. A part of her missed the veil she'd worn before, and another part was eager to know what thoughts stirred in his fae mind. What those predatory eyes beheld and thought. Aisling only saw anger, conflict, and perhaps even grief vibrant in his irises. Of course, this was most likely a projection of Aisling's own feelings rather than an accurate reading of the Fae King, the mortal queen knew. Her own horror reflected in his sage orbs.

And as though dread had made her a disembodied spirit pressed against the steepled ceiling of the tent, Aisling watched herself unclasp her dress from above. She slipped its weighted, scarlet layers from her arms, her bodice, her waist, her legs. Her fingers moving of their own accord, fueled by terror, by expectation, by duty. And as the dress pooled around her ankles, her dagger's fall was cushioned in the skirts.

All that remained was her cotton chemise, cinched together by a whale-bone corset. A thin layer hugging the supple contours of her form. And if none had seen her with her hair undone, certainly none had seen her so undressed. But where she'd expected mere embarrassment on this evening if wedded to Dagfin, nothing compared to the distress she felt now, bundling each of her muscles till they cramped and brought tears to her eyes.

Aisling flushed, her skin simmering as if lit with the fire from a blackened wick, writhing in a pool of wax.

The Fae King's face was unreadable now. He stood watching her, studying what mortal flesh was left exposed. They were now bound by law, recognized by the North in both mortal and fae eyes. Man and wife. No. *Aos Sí* and wife. Still, Aisling couldn't shake the feeling she was somehow engaging in something deeply forbidden. This was a violation, a ritual void of the trust, security, and familiarity she'd come to look forward to, without knowing, all these years anticipating a marriage to Dagfin.

It occurred to Aisling then that the Fae King had likely never laid eyes on a mortal this way. A wonder, a strange curiosity she herself felt for the creature before her that for a mere moment was hungry enough to sprout amidst the fear.

The queen quieted her trembling fingers, gently tugging her corset strings. Clumsily, she untied them. The Fae King watched; his cat-like eyes locked onto every slip of the strings as they came undone.

She'd had little experience undressing herself. A result of the countless handmaidens whose sole purpose was to assist the northern princess in all her passing whims since she was old enough to remember.

"*You'll undress yourself for your betrothed this night: a symbol of your surrendering your body to not only him but to all of mankind. An offer of 'good faith' for the treaty freshly sealed*," her mother had attempted to encourage, to contextualize this atrocity. Her words nudged Aisling onward.

But just as Aisling made to loosen the last row of tethers, dropping her petticoat, the Fae King extinguished the last flower, shrouding them both in darkness. Had Aisling blinked, she would've missed the Fae King's breath catching in his broad chest. A flicker of torment flashed across his eyes.

"What's wrong?" Aisling asked, her pupils dilating madly in the shadows.

"You must be tired," he said. Submerged in shadow, the Fae King left Aisling to find her own way through the dark and towards the bed. Untouched.

Chapter IV

THE FOLLOWING MORNING, THE TENTS WERE packed, the fair folk's stags saddled, and every trace of the mortal monarchs gone. Once the sun had peeked its gilded head over the Brimdurn mountains, Aisling had searched for her tuath. But they'd already vanished. Swept away like a leaf in the wind.

The queen had awoken alone, greeted only by a tunic, trousers, and leather boots cut to fit a female's body. Thankfully, a fae handmaiden arrived moments later to help the queen dress and prepare her for the journey ahead.

Somehow, Aisling felt different. And while the mortal queen wouldn't have been surprised at this foreign sensation blooming within, its emergence owed nothing to her virginity.

"*You must be tired.*"

An immeasurable weight had lifted from Aisling's shoulders at the Fae Lord's words. Her incorporeal self, beholding her would-be ruination from above, snapping back into her body, near knocking her off her feet. Nude in the blackness, entirely vulnerable, Aisling couldn't shake the feeling that perhaps she'd done something wrong. Her chambermaids, advisors, and Clodagh had all groomed her for that night. Braced her for the pain, the terror, the indefinable and unavoidable loss of her virginity at the hands of a beast. A ritual of soul-scarring importance, and yet here she was, still a virgin. Unfulfilled in her attempts to uphold her duty for the sake of the North. Her thoughts warring between bewilderment, indescribable relief, and immeasurable guilt.

No. This bizarre feeling was something else entirely. Aisling awoke that morning, hearing and *feeling* the radiance of the sun humming to the tune of the songbirds' chirps, all this despite being sheltered by the tent. She felt the pang of morning's hunger, heard the animals sifting through the trees, and their anxiety as so many visitors lined the forest's edge. Potential predators. Feelings, sensations, sounds, voices that were not her own. As though she were experiencing the thoughts of someone or something else. Even the rustle of the trees was louder, more coherent than it ever had been before.

Aisling rode on her own stag at the center of the fae cavalcade. She blended well amidst their ivory and gold banners, caparisons, flags, and steel armor. A single tree was embroidered at the center of their crest, a tree shadowing the wide stance of a hart beneath its knot of limbs.

Fifteen of the king's knights surrounded their new queen as they cut through the wilderness. The land this far from Tilren was wilder than any place Aisling had laid eyes on before. As if the queen could blink and the mountains would roll, adjusting their slumbering positions like hibernating bears. As if the trees would pick up their roots and dance or the caves would snap their mouths shut after years of yawning.

The rest of the Fae King's men trailed behind, carrying their supplies and belongings. As for the fae subjects, they'd already departed at dawn, beginning the trek back to Annwyn.

Against her own will, Aisling found herself searching her surroundings for the Fae King. He rode fiercely, at times leading their fae procession, other times flanking the wings, surveying from behind, challenging the great hart beneath him to keep his pace. The queen had never witnessed anything like it. Nemed would have ridden beside Aisling at the center of the cavalcade, well-protected by his knights should an enemy, an Aos Sí, threaten his life. The Fae King paid no mind to such precautions. And why should he? He was just as much a part of the forest as it was a part of him. This enemy land was *his* land.

Although each of the knights wore similar armor, the Fae King stood out like the first autumn tree turning at equinox. Not only was he revered by his subjects, their heads turning as he passed, his helmet was embellished with a stag's antlers, bone-white and large like a mighty, thorned diadem.

At times, their eyes met. Always briefly, fleeting like a spark leaping from the flames.

"How long is the journey to Annwyn?" Aisling asked the knight riding nearest, hoping he understood her tongue as the Fae King had. She'd recognized him from the night prior; One of the riders who'd presented his sword during the ceremony.

"We'll arrive within two days' time, *mo Lúra*," the rider said, pulling his hart closer to Aisling's. The queen breathed a sigh of relief. Now there were two members of the Aos Sí she could rely on to understand her. In fact, this rider was one of the few fair folk who regarded the queen kindly. The rest of the Aos Sí studied her through narrowed eyes as if expecting her to transform into some mortal deception at a moment's notice. She didn't blame them. Had a fae princess married either Starn, Fergus, Iarbonel, or Annind, Aisling would've regarded them similarly.

"What does that mean?"

"*Mo Lúra?*" The rider asked and Aisling nodded in response. He considered for a moment, removing his helmet to reveal a collection of hair braided like ropes. He was handsome, as all Aos Sí likely were, but Aisling would need to grow accustomed to their wild, unruly dress and styles. In Tilren, it was uncivilized for a man's hair to surpass the tops of his ears, much less spiral down his back in beaded plaits.

"*Lúra na Bryveth*, Bride of the Forest."

"I don't understand."

"Since the Age of the Forge, the Queen of Annwyn has answered to this title. For the moment any bride is handfast to our sovereign, the moment you handfasted the Fae King, his and your soul are tethered to the forest."

Aisling blinked, doing her best to conceal her surprise. By marriage, by position, she supposed she was queen, but never did she believe the fair folk would consider her so. And perhaps they didn't. Perhaps this rider followed custom, fought to maintain the illusion of peace this union symbolized. As for tethering her soul to the forest, it was nothing more than an odd manifestation of these people's beliefs.

"You may call me Aisling," she said, straightening herself. Fighting to uphold her own illusion of strength amongst these barbarians. The rider smiled, a warm expression framed by dimples. If it weren't for his being an Aos Sí, Aisling would've believed him to bear a kind heart for his cobalt eyes sparkled with a tender sort of reassurance. Surely it was magic that made the Aos Sí so lovely. Made them so attractive, alluring, easy to trust so they could coax innocents into the wilds.

"And you may call me Galad." The rider bowed his head, readjusting his grip on the reigns of his stag.

"Are you faring well?" Galad continued, riding closer to the mortal queen so he could better hear her over the whipping of the stubborn winds. He gestured towards her stag and how she rode the great beast, for indeed this many hours on a mount were bound to chafe and gnaw at the muscles of the undisciplined.

Aisling nodded, "I enjoy riding." Throughout her childhood, the world outside of Tilren's walls was forbidden unless the princess was receiving riding lessons. Aisling grew to treasure those hours spent on horseback, breathing in the mountains, the fields, the cliffs, the forests that the great gates of Tilren eclipsed with stone.

"You're naturally skilled for a mortal," he said, admiring her posture, "the sign of a good rider is their beast."

"And what signs does this beast tell?"

"Saoirse is our most obedient mount, she'd placate even a child who'd never ridden before," Galad said. "I can't say the same for the rest of our beasts."

"I see," Aisling stroked Saoirse's broad neck, disappointed that the stag's deference wasn't the result of her own riding.

"But I can see in the twitch of her muscles, the angle of her ears, her willful gait, she wants to ride faster, quicker, harder"—he considered Aisling—"she's inheriting that spirit from you, *mo Lúra*, and a rider who inspires their stag is a formidable one indeed."

Aisling held back a grin. Was it possible an animal could interpret, sense so much of its rider? Or that the fair folk beside her could identify such a connection?

"Then I quite like this stag," Aisling said, proudly running her fingers through Saoirse's silken hide, a contrast to the destriers in Tilren whose hair was as stiff as the straw they ate. Saoirse shook with delight, leaning into Aisling's palm.

"She's yours," Galad said, much to Aisling's surprise. "Whatever you covet, Lir will give you."

Aisling's smile faded, averting her eyes and searching her surroundings for the Fae King. She found him weaving in and out of the trees that bordered the field in which they rode. Stopping only to remove the gloves from his hands and press his palm against the bark of the pines. His mount danced nervously each time its hooves crossed into the shadows of the wood. The Fae King peered into its depths nevertheless, his great axes strapped to his back as if they could and would be used at a moment's notice.

Once the Fae King was satisfied with whatever he'd been searching for, his attention redirected to the procession. But before his glare could meet her own, Aisling quickly turned away, straightening her gaze up ahead.

He'd scarcely spoken a word to her since the evening prior. It seemed unlikely he wanted anything to do with her, married or not. Aisling wasn't certain what she'd expected, to be eaten? To be tortured? Raped? Burned alive? But certainly not left alone. For this was no normal arrangement. They were not truly man and wife, or in this case, Aos Sí and wife. Especially since they hadn't consummated the marriage. This was nothing more than a symbolic union, a matter of politics. The Fae King owed her nothing. Wedding or no wedding, by blood, they were born to loathe one another.

Between two snowcapped mountains, their procession came to a stop. It took five knights to set up Aisling's tent, an unexpected gesture she was most grateful for. As much as the prospect of sleeping beneath the stars titillated her curiosity, she doubted the hard ground or wet grass would be conducive to a good night's rest.

Nevertheless, she found herself unable to sleep, glaring at the ceiling of her tent and fighting off tears shed for her family as well as dreams—nightmares of being hunted, eaten alive, and cooked over the fire the Aos Sí sat around. There were no females in their procession any longer. It was only males that surrounded Aisling now, a variable that struck more fear in Aisling than she would've liked. The only men the mortal queen had ever been allowed to be alone with were her brothers, her father, certain members of the tuath, and at times Dagfin. Now, here, she was, surrounded by the enemies of her kind, great bestial males capable of grinding her bones between their teeth. Of transforming her into a mouse or roasting her over a spit.

Aisling wrenched her eyes shut, forcing herself to focus on

the songs they sang just outside her tent, sitting around the flames. They sang lullabies, strange lullabies Aisling had never heard before. But they were sung with a particular enunciation, suggesting they were not merely fanciful or lyrical melodies but rather keepers of greater narratives. Tales from their ancient past.

It shouldn't have come as a surprise to Aisling that these savages had also collected centuries of tradition, of culture, of folklore to spread and enjoy when the moon leaned closer to listen. Nevertheless, Aisling allowed her ears to drink in their beauty, every lilt of their male voices intoxicating and softening the rage in her belly. The sorrow.

When they weren't singing, they laughed, startling Aisling with their boisterous guffaws, all of it foreign and incomprehensible. Another thick, impenetrable barrier that alienated herself from her newfound subjects. Subjects that no doubt despised her as much as she despised them. Perhaps one day she'd learn to speak Fae, shrinking the vast void that lay between herself and these beings.

Without warning, the curtains peeled open, the flapping of the canvas against the valley's wind echoing into the tent. Aisling bolted upright, peering through the darkness. A large shadow stood at the entrance. Immediately she identified him by his great height and smell—fresh pine, wet leaves, smoke from the fire outside.

"You must be hungry," The Fae King said, padding further into the tent, soundlessly. Aisling shivered at the rumble of his voice; smooth and deep and inexplicably lovely. "There's food prepared outside."

Aisling could smell it, the succulent scent of meat cooked over the flame, the musk of charred edges and smoke. Against her own volition, her stomach growled. She'd eaten nearly every hour since the morning she'd bid Tilren farewell, but never did it appear to slake her newfound appetite. Even when offered fae food.

Silence spread between them, Aisling appraising his outstretched hand. Even in the darkness, she saw how large his hands were but to her surprise, they were elegant—long, slender fingers coiled in a primordial tongue better left forgotten.

"My knights won't hurt you," he assured, interpreting her hesitation as fear. Nevertheless, he took a step nearer, approaching as if Aisling were a bird prepared to take flight.

Rationally, Aisling knew they wouldn't harm her. Not if they were interested in tearing the peace treaty to shreds and that seemed unlikely considering all they'd done to follow through with the union in the first place. The political tether between the mortals and the fair folk would keep her alive for as long as she was deemed a necessary symbol of their fragile unity. But fear was rarely rational.

"Unless you run," he added.

Aisling swallowed, paralyzed in the darkness. Aisling had been prepared, groomed, and trained for the days leading up to their union, the union itself and the consummation to take place that night. But no one, not her handmaids, not her clann, not her mother, none had prepared her for the following day, the life that would follow that evening.

"My name is Lir." His eyes twinkled, glowing like a wolf's amidst the tent's dark cavity.

Lir. She'd never heard the name before Galad had said it. She repeated it in her mind till she'd memorized it on her lips, wordlessly pronouncing it.

Names had power. Even mortals knew that. *Ensorcellment*, some called it. An ability of the fae to enslave those who'd freely given their names to the fair folk.

"Aisling," the mortal queen replied, more confidently than she felt. For Aisling knew, *ensorcellment* or not, she was already bound to this fae. "You may call me Aisling."

One way or another she'd need to find the courage to walk amongst them. To not live her life in terror. Or at the very least, learn to cope with the terror. This was her purpose after all, her sacrifice to Tilren, and she wouldn't disappoint her family.

Aisling ignored his outstretched hand, making sure to avoid his touch as she brushed past, conceding to the invitation. Behind those piercing eyes, he studied her every move. If he was aware of her efforts to distance herself, he said nothing. Only held up the curtained entrance to the tent, bathing Aisling in his scent.

"Think twice before you consider using that dagger." Aisling jolted, startled by the heat of his breath as she passed.

How had he known? Ever since Iarbonel had entrusted Aisling with the blade, she'd done her best to conceal it. Had slipped it into her sleeve the instant the canvassed doors had opened moments before.

"Or any other time for that matter. And if you plan to run, we'll hunt you down quicker than a wolf catches a wounded animal," he added.

"It is because I thought twice that I carry the dagger with me at all," Aisling blurted, perhaps foolishly. It was unwise to provoke an Aos Sí much less a Fae King. Especially one who Aisling was to ... live with? Perhaps they'd keep her as a prisoner unbeknownst to the mortal world. In some rancid dungeon accompanied only by the rats.

Nevertheless, perhaps more unwise than provoking an Aos Sí was walking amongst the enemy unarmed, union or not. She'd thought twice about the dagger as Iarbonel had slipped it between her fingers and realized it was the most sensible way to protect herself. The only way. An ember of hope that she'd survive amongst the fair folk. So, she steeled herself against Lir's warnings, continuing out of the tent, undeterred. After all, it would be Lir who decided whether or not she need use the dagger.

The night was not as dark as she'd anticipated. Stars lit the endless seas of midnight blue with radiant, twinkling light.

She'd never beheld stars so bright nor so many. Above her were rivers of starlight, bathing in the milk of galaxies. The lights in Tilren must have washed them away, dulling their luster before it met their mortal eyes, for Aisling had never beheld the night sky so.

In some ways, she understood why the wilderness and man were destined to stand at opposing ends. Why the wilds were so hostile against the mortals that carved their buildings, raised their cities, paved their roads on the skeletons of what was once an agrestal kingdom. Only appreciating nature when it fed them, sustained them, and burning it when it did not.

Both Lir and Aisling approached the group of knights sitting around the crackling fire, burning some skinned creature knotted to a large beam, an image that matched the sounds she'd been listening to for the past several hours. Like wild dogs feasting on carrion, they tore large strips of meat from the unfortunate beast's bones, washing down each bite with black wine.

Relieved it wasn't some lost human huntsman or shepherd they smoked over the fire, a weight lifted from Aisling's shoulders. Its build suggested it was some sort of pig, most likely a wild boar: an impressive, nearly impossible beast for a mortal to hunt in the amount of time it had taken the Aos Sí to find, kill, and prep the animal for consumption. A pang of anger struck Aisling then, thinking of how many mortal kingdoms starved, wasted away, too afraid to hunt or gather lest the fair folk attack. And yet, here were the Aos Sí with the entirety of the wilderness at their disposal. The greatest predators in any land. But all land was mortal land despite what the Aos Sí staked claim to.

"*Man was born of nothing but nevertheless born first,*" Nemed taught. "*Man grew strong, mastered his own skills, and became great. Then the Aos Sí arrived, stealing man's land. Taking what man had already conquered—the wilderness—and spinning it in their favor.*"

This was all mortal territory and yet, the mortals were caged within their walls as Aisling had been all her life. Hidden away from those who stole and continued to steal what is man's.

Aisling savored the feeling of her dagger pressed against her arm.

Their stags stood beside the mountain's edge, calmly being fed and tended to by one of the fae. However, they were not tethered. Weren't the Aos Sí concerned they'd run? Wander aimlessly into the night? Perhaps they didn't care but Aisling guessed that wasn't the reason either. As Aisling searched for Saiorse, she heard voices erupting from the group of mounts. Not quite voices but murmurings, a rustle of sentient thought. There was a jolt of hunger, of weariness, of rejoicing at the wind against their pelts.

Aisling quickly tore her gaze away as though the sensation had burned her. She needn't dwell on fae unknowns just yet. Fae mysteries that still turned her skin cold.

Meanwhile, eight or so knights prowled the camp, watchfully peering into the creases of the mountain, the valley, and the forests beyond. Aisling didn't see the point. The greatest threat in all the continents were the fair folk. They haunted the wilds, the places even man found too untamable to possibly burn their mortal mark into the earth. Ironically, there was no place safer for Aisling to be than sleeping amongst the monsters themselves. So, who did they fear? Who did they guard against?

Before Lir could say a word, various of his men stood from their spots and made way for the mortal queen, finding openings to wedge themselves into the circle. They glared at her, no doubt whispering about her beneath their breath. Aisling scoffed to herself; it mattered little if they whispered or screamed their disapproval at the peaks of the summit. Either way, Aisling couldn't understand their tongue and thus, their likely spiteful words.

But one glance from their Fae King quieted their musings, quickly snapping whatever sneers they'd brewed into bewildered yet obedient expressions. Aisling quite liked their expressions. They somehow made this strange race more ... human.

Lir leaned forward and tore off a large bone wrapped with meat. He handed it to Aisling and the queen awkwardly accepted it. Aisling hadn't expected silverware, crystal goblets, or pottered plates. Still, eating straight from the bone was strange—unnatural—entirely improper for a gentleman much less a lady, a princess, a queen. But Aisling couldn't deny that she'd often wished she could throw such rules and etiquette at Clodagh's sharp nose, and dive into the feast held within her mortal castle's halls. Eat with her hands and her poor posture even if just a hair from its dignified, erect stance.

"Is it bewitched?" Aisling asked the Fae King, turning it over in her hands. Lir raised his brows, considering her for a moment. Aisling resisted the urge to look away. There was something raw about the glint in his eyes, something unbroken and deadly yet wondrous and inexplicably lovely.

"There will be food, going forward, that is not designed for mortal consumption. But you can trust that whatever I give you is safe to eat," he said, taking a swig from his flask, "but the wine ... never drink the wine." He tapped one of the men beside him; Aisling believed she'd overheard him be called Rian earlier in the day. His red hair was cropped shorter but bore two lines on either side, shaved to the scalp. His fae markings ran around his neck, as if strangling him, before stroking the angles of his jaw.

Rian met Aisling's eyes, standing and starting towards the stags.

"It's enchanted then?" Aisling asked, glaring at the inky brew.

"In a sense but not for the purpose of harming mortals." Lir tilted his chalice so Aisling could see more clearly. "It's simply not made for your kind. Humans are overwhelmed by what they see and experience."

"And what do they experience?" Aisling continued.

"I've heard some say that humans are made vulnerable to the senses of the Sidhe—the way we feel, understand, interpret the world," Lir glanced at the mountains and the forest, the gale sweeping through his dark hair. So, they called themselves the *Sidhe*. Not the Aos Sí. It struck Aisling as odd she'd never been taught that. "They can temporarily see, smell, listen, and touch the way we do."

"And that's too much for a human?" Aisling asked.

"It would appear so," Lir said, taking another drink, watching her from behind thick lashes.

Rian returned, offering Aisling a flask of water. Water taken from the stags' reserves considering they were the only ones, other than Aisling, who did not drink the wine. The queen accepted the flask, setting it on the ground beside her feet, and nodded to the fae knight.

"Eat," Lir said, reminding her of the meat still grasped in her left hand.

A moment passed where Aisling considered it could be a trick—a prank made to make a fool of the human queen should the food be enchanted, spelled to mortals. It was clear none of them wished for her company, but she was hungry, and if she didn't eat she wouldn't have the strength she needed to continue the journey. It was a strange balance she realized she must strike. To trust the Aos Sí enough to live amongst them but all the while maintain enough caution to not be deceived nor harmed by the enemy of her race. To remember who she was and where she came from. To both be apart and a part. Either way, she supposed, she must eat.

So, Aisling dove into the meat. She wondered what Clodagh would make of such manners. Perhaps she'd faint or her skin would flush beet red. At the thought, the corners of Aisling's mouth couldn't help but curl. After all, it was she who proposed Aisling be used as a bargaining chip and traded into the hands of the enemy. Whatever became of Aisling would be Clodagh's fault. A sentiment that burned in Aisling's core no matter how honored she knew she should be. No matter that this was her purpose, Clodagh or not.

Lir exhaled a laugh, watching her with a startled expression.

"Is everything alright?" Aisling asked Lir, noticing various of the fae knights' attention shifting towards her.

"They—*we* haven't been in the close presence of many mortals," the king said, "other than when an iron arrow aims for our heart or a blade for our throats."

Aisling often wondered what they thought of her. Did they smell her and grow hungry? Did they find her weak and brittle? Did their fingers itch to cast an enchantment on such a susceptible, unassuming target? Some of the Aos Sí acted as if they feared her, keeping their distance from her stag as they rode. But that, Aisling realized, was most likely resentment.

Upon arriving, the Aos Sí had hushed their conversation, awkwardly glaring and whispering as she and Lir spoke. Now, their voices had risen once more, too distracted by their own musings to remember the mortal queen was still amongst them. Lir participated in their discussions as well—all of it nothing more than brutish babble to Aisling. Even if she dared to blend amongst them, laughing when they did, cheering when they did, clapping when they did, it would be an obvious if not embarrassing ruse for all knew she didn't understand. Would it always be like this? Aisling felt like a phantom. No, not a phantom. A social pariah, a mouse in a lion's den allowed to live because it did away with numerous pests. Nothing more. She should be happy. She should be grateful they were not tearing her limb from limb, drinking her blood, or using her when and how they liked. Still, Aisling found comfort in the dagger at her waist, its hilt cool against her hip.

All the attention eventually landed on another member of

the Aos Sí, he grinned, pointed ear to pointed ear, baring those sharp canines. But it wasn't a fearsome sight; he was happy, playful, blushing with too much wine as he stood shakily and waved at his comrades to settle.

"Cathan, *eun fir nak fall big!*" they shouted at him. Aisling's gaze darted around the circle wondering what they were coaxing him to do. Although she couldn't translate their words, there were certain tones, gestures, and social context that, the mortal queen realized, transcended race. Unspoken cues that helped Aisling follow along.

"*Eughlig ler mi gag*," they shouted till Cathan, at last, nodded and cleared his throat. The group quieted their excited jeers and silence befell the group, all eyes pinned to Cathan. Several moments passed before he began to sing.

Just like the melodies Aisling had overheard, hiding in her tent, this one was different than anything she'd heard before. For one, she'd never listened to a male sing before. It was a past time designated only to women in Tilren and Aisling assumed, all the mortal world. But these male fair folk sang beautifully. The deep timber of their voices, wildly satisfying to the ears.

"*Never follow the songs you hear in the dead of night or if lost in the wilderness,*" Nemed forewarned Aisling and her brothers. "*The Aos Sí sing with voices so divine, a mortal couldn't resist wandering into pits of unimaginable danger. This is one of many ways the Aos Sí lure innocent humans into the wilds.*"

Aisling had always imagined pale, foul creatures blessed with such an ability. Not the glorious males that sat around her. Perhaps that was another deception Nemed hadn't had time to divulge. To prepare her for. For already so much contradicted what she'd always been taught.

But it appeared as if his lullaby had done more than merely charm Aisling. The entirety of the group had stilled, drinking his tune—gulping as quickly as their ears would allow while also savoring every note. Aisling closed her eyes. She focused on the foreign words, the roll of his tongue, the intonations so unlike her own language. What would Starn, Iarbonel, Annind, or Fergus think of his voice? Of this song? What would they make of all these strange fae customs?

"He chronicles the legend of Ina," Lir whispered, startling the mortal queen. Aisling opened her eyes to find Lir leaning back on his arms, the flames illuminating his markings till they became molten. "She is one of the first of our kind to be cast in the Great Forge of Creation, shaped by the Gods alongside the highlands, the seas, the rain, the sun." He spoke as Cathan's tune unraveled, translating each verse. "When the six Sidhe kings were chosen—Lugh, Bres, Mac Cuill, Delbaeth, Fiacha, and Nuada—so too were the six Sidhe queens—Dagda, Lottie, Niamh, Siofra, Aoibh, and Ina. Each appointed an enchanted weapon by the Gods—a tool unique to only themselves: the mace for Siofra, the spear for Lugh, the axes for Bres, and so on."

Cathan continued to sing, leaving even the stars enraptured by his voice. It felt as if, Aisling believed, the mountains themselves leaned closer to listen. As if the smoke from the fire took shape and gave life to each word, images in grey, wispy tendrils rapidly forming and reforming.

Aisling knew of the Gods and the twelve kings and queens they'd chosen. These fae sovereigns had been the ones to begin the library known to mortals as the Forbidden Lore. But never had these monarchs been given names. Nemed believed it unimportant for all of it was fiction: lies, empty religion, and stories that dulled the mind.

"And what was Ina's weapon?" Aisling asked, her voice heavy, weighted by the stupor of the lullaby. Her eyes pinned to the images the smoke spun.

"She was not given a weapon," Lir said, "Instead, they allowed her to peer into the Forge. A gaze that gave her *sight*, capable of seeing beyond the day in which we live and into the vast realm of another day, the day we might live should we make the choices she anticipates," Lir said, glaring into the flames that danced between the logs.

"But with all great tragedies, she fell in love," Rian piped, meeting Aisling's glare. Lir shifted beside her, his gaze lowering, growing more distant than before. Then it always was. As if he was never truly beside another but in some distant, untouchable realm.

So, Rian could speak Aisling's tongue as well? Could they all speak it and chose not to? Aisling swallowed the bitterness churning in the pit of her stomach. Fought the sneer burning the backs of her eyes.

"Ina was besotted with Bres, a sentiment forbidden amongst the Sidhe kings and queens. For the Gods divided them across the earth, giving them sovereignty of their own share of the land and the wilderness," Rian continued, his accent thicker than his king's.

Aisling bristled. The Aos Sí believed they'd been given divine right to the land? What would Nemed think of such lies? He'd most likely threaten to cut out their tongues and char their land—threats he'd managed to accomplish before, after taking fae hostages. Aisling remembered Nemed, his men, and Starn marching into Tilren's gates, four fair folk bound at the wrists with iron shackles. Wool bags were placed over their heads. It was some years ago, but Aisling could never forget what he did to them before the whole of Tilren.

"It is unfortunate that us mortals were not blessed with the strength or magic the Aos Sí wield, but given enough cleverness anything can be done," Nemed had told Aisling. *"There are no Gods; do not let the religion of the Aos Sí deceive you, plague your mind. This world is an earthly one, designed by mortals and for mortals. The Aos Sí, on the other hand, are intruders, aberrations, a perverse mutation of mankind."*

Aisling chilled at the memory. That day, her father stood atop the great walls surrounding Tilren, lecturing Starn. Had

Aisling not been following her brother around the castle, Nemed wouldn't have bothered to lecture her. To waste his kingly time with a child who would never inherit his throne. His kingdom. His people.

Aisling shook away the thoughts, refocusing her attention.

"The Northern continents went to Bres and Ina, the king and queen of the forests and the mountains," Rian said.

"The forests and the mountains?" Aisling repeated. How could one rule the wilds? The mountains and the forest obeyed no one and no thing. Neither did the rest of the wilderness for that matter.

"Aye, all of the Sidhe belong to a certain court—courts already divided by the natural world."

"And what then is your court?" Aisling asked.

"The forests," Rian said. "Lir inherited the Kingdom of the Greenwood from his father." Rian tipped his head in Lir's direction.

King of the Greenwood, Aisling repeated the title in her mind. Were the trees his subjects so much as the Aos Sí were? Aisling had known the Aos Sí to be vile creatures but never had she realized just how strange they were.

"If the rulers married, however, the Gods feared they'd stray from their own kingdoms, leaving that part of the world unguarded." *Unguarded against who?* Aisling wondered but did not ask, fearing her questions would reveal a certain bias for her own kind, although such a bias would be inevitable. "However, Ina ignored the Gods after having foreseen Bres dying in battle."

A battle against the mortals? Aisling had never heard of this war. Had never learned of it. Perhaps she'd fallen asleep during her lessons. Did Starn, Fergus, Iarbonel, and Annind know or remember this tale? It seemed unlikely considering Cathan's rendition was already blasphemous to the mortal understanding of their collective history.

"Ina raced to Annwyn, the forest court, leaving her

kingdom vulnerable, knowing the outcome. A selfish mistake that cost her her land and countless Sidhe lives alike. And in the end, she was unable to prevent Bres' death. What she'd seen, had come to pass."

Aisling shifted her glare back to the Fae King. Lir's expression had turned cold. Unreadable. A thick wall of ice.

"What became of Ina?" Aisling asked Rian, leaning forward. The fair folk took a large swig of wine, licking his lips after but it was Lir who spoke first:

"She was punished by the Gods; both she and the entirety of her mountain kingdom were cursed for all eternity."

The air was thick, flammable as the silence stretched between them, only Cathan's song easing the tension in Lir's shoulders. The smoke morphed into the form of beautiful creatures below the shadow of the mountain, falling to their knees and writhing in pain as something was taken from them. As they were cursed.

Finally, Rian continued, "An entire kingdom doomed to a damned legacy. But before that, it's said"—Rian hesitated, eyes flicking towards the Fae King—"it's said, she had one last vision. A prophecy she shared with her only son."

Aisling turned to the knight then, her eyes wide. Was Rian implying Ina carried and birthed Bres' son? Aisling opened her mouth, curiosity itching to know what the fortune had been, but she stopped herself short. Lir's expression spoke for itself. Those sage eyes brewing with some intemperate storm. A muscle flashed across his jaw as he stood and walked away. Silent.

Rian said nothing, merely clapped when Cathan finished his song, the world spinning back into motion, momentarily swelled by the tune. But Aisling watched Lir over her shoulder, disappearing into the night, his right-hand clutching one of his twin blades. Blades she never saw him without.

Lir entered their tent a handful of hours before dawn, collapsing into the bed beside Aisling and waking the mortal queen. Aisling said nothing, somehow managing to fall back asleep on her edge of the mattress, listening to his breathing slow into slumber itself. Every one of his breaths reminded Aisling of winds weaving through the trees.

Chapter V

THE NEXT MORNING, THEY CONTINUED THEIR trek across the continent, forming their fae parade once more. The wilderness was veiled with morning fog, cobwebs of dew draped across Aisling's poorly tied braid. She'd never needed to wind her own plait before, for the handmaiden who'd aided the queen the morning after her wedding had travelled separately. To her surprise, Aisling didn't mind. She enjoyed the privacy of dressing herself, especially since Lir was never in their bed come morning. Somehow, even when he'd gone to bed hours after she, the Fae King managed to wake before her and begin organizing his men for the journey. Aisling knew it was, in part, because he was a king, always responsible for one problem or another. But Aisling also knew it was because of her. For the sake of the union, Lir would pretend. Pretend that the union between the mortal and the Aos Sí was normal, good, effective in uniting the races. He needed to lead by example. Otherwise, it would all be for naught. But in private, he didn't need to pretend. He didn't need to spend a moment more than necessary with Aisling. That much had become clear.

"I've brought you breakfast, *mo Lúra*," Galad said, handing her a brown sack. Aisling reached across the space between their stags and peered within. A simple pairing of bread and cheese.

"Thank you," she said, shocked the fae knight had thought of her. Lir had left food for her, resting at the foot of their bed before she woke. She'd devoured it quickly, hungrier than she'd ever felt before. Not to mention, she was in no place to refuse an unwarranted kindness when such hospitality was far and few between.

"So, what does the mortal princess think of the world outside her stone walls?" Galad asked, grinning wolfishly. Aisling wondered if the Aos Sí had ever laid eyes on Tilren before, if he knew which walls had certainly sheltered her for her entire life.

"It's compelling—enticing," she said honestly, "I can imagine it being hard to go back to living without so many stars lighting the night sky."

"And our kind? What do you think of us?" Galad grinned mischievously, boasting his own set of pointed canines. Aisling's eyes flitted towards Lir, surveying the lip of an approaching pine forest.

"The Aos Sí?" Aisling asked, more as a means of stalling than genuine curiosity. But she'd already forgotten what Lir had called their kind; *Sidhe*, she reminded herself.

"Is that what the mortals call us?" The rider mused, a playful expression challenging Aisling's stony one. Aisling opened her mouth to respond but was quickly interrupted.

"Galad, *tá aois éigil da mhaith lirn go freilick*!" Lir called from up ahead.

"Excuse me, *mo Lúra*," Galad bowed his head before kicking his beast and breaking from the cavalcade at the command of his king. The two of them spoke till the rest of the fae knights closed the distance, pointing between the trees. Lir and Galad's stags grew restless, stomping the dirt beneath their hooves, madly pacing within the shadow of the pines. Aisling could sense their nerves, the fear tightening the coils of their muscles, charging their hooves. Pangs of unease radiating from them like a sour smell she could feel, hear, and see.

Aisling had witnessed horses behave this way before, even the masterfully trained Tilrish destriers. But only ever in the presence of a forest, reason enough for her riding instructor to ban the princess from nearing the woodland's edge on horseback or otherwise. A law that made Aisling all the more eager to venture through the trees.

Once they'd finished their conversation, Galad nodded to Lir and returned to the procession slowly approaching, weaving through the knights till he arrived at Aisling's side once more.

"*Mo Lúra*," Galad addressed her. "Lir has requested you share his mount while we cut through the woods." Aisling glanced at the forest ahead, an agrestal fortress of pine and oak and feral creatures, innocently swaying in the Northern winds.

"Are these woods dangerous?" Aisling asked, but Galad didn't stop to respond, reaching for her reins and pulling her towards the Fae King.

"All forests are dangerous," Galad replied at last, bringing Aisling's mount to a stop. But wasn't this Lir's kingdom? His domain? Aisling kept her questions to herself.

Lir leapt from his own stag to aid Aisling in her dismount. He ignored her offered hand, instead reaching for her waist and lifting her effortlessly to the ground. In another moment, Aisling was atop the Fae King's stag. Lir mounted behind Aisling, wrapping his arms around her till his hands found the steed's reins, slender hands tangled in those tribal tattoos that glimmered even in the shade. She was frightened of him still, clenching her jaw, willing herself to quit the trembling that accompanied the Fae King's nearness. Would the fear ever dissipate?

He said nothing to her. Didn't so much as meet her eyes.

Aisling did her best to ignore the press of his body behind her, the smell of him, of pine needles. Of the earth freshly soaked with rain, as he clicked his tongue and the stag obeyed.

The procession tightened its formation, cautiously entering the forest behind the Fae King and their new mortal queen.

As if entering a new world, the pressure of the air thickened. The sun dimmed, cloaked by thick canopies and the smell of damp wood carried in by the morning breeze. A gale that slipped through the labyrinth of greenwood and challenged the cacophony of crunching leaves beneath the stags' hooves. And as these ancient, primordial trees whispered groggily, awoken from their slumber with the groans of a tree trunk swaying in the wind, Aisling couldn't shake the feeling that they were being watched.

The stags nervously whinnied, prancing in place. But what could inspire such fear in the Aos Sí and their mounts? Surely it was not a pack of wolves or a den of bears. The fair folk could do away with such creatures weaponless and continue unscarred.

Nemed had warned Aisling, his tuath, and all the Isles of Rinn Dúin about the forests, the mountains, the wilderness, lest they be captured by the Aos Sí. In her father's stories, this wicked race was the monster lurking beyond their civilized walls. So, what struck caution and fear in the ancient beasts she now accompanied?

"Is something wrong?" Aisling asked Lir.

The Fae King studied their surroundings, peering between the great oaks, his breath as steady, as still as a beast of prey, skulking across the forest floor. He considered for a moment.

"Tell me, what do mortals tell their princesses about the wilderness?" Lir asked, the vibrations in his chest thrumming against Aisling's back.

"That the Aos Sí hide within their depths, eager to kill mortal men, steal their women and devour their children," Aisling said, more honestly than she'd intended. Lir grinned, exposing his sharp canines that never seized to surprise Aisling—even more so than his pointed ears.

"And do you believe those stories?" He asked, his voice low, nearly a purr.

"It's all I've ever known," she replied, considering the horde of Aos Sí that trailed behind them, suspiciously eyeing the trees as though they might leap from their roots and attack in a moment's notice. "Do the Aos Sí forbid their subjects from the wilderness as well?"

"No," Lir said, shaking his head as if it was a ridiculous notion. As if the idea that the mortals did just that disgusted him. "But even the Sidhe must be wary of its depths."

"Is there something out there?" Aisling asked, suddenly more attuned to the eerie silence.

Aisling craned her neck to meet Lir's eyes, feline and green enough to challenge the surrounding woodland. But he hesitated as if considering whether to tell her something.

A branch broke to the right of their procession. Lir tore his gaze from Aisling, expression darkening as he followed the source of the noise.

The stags grunted, stubbornly prancing as the fair folk drew their weapons. But Aisling saw no movement in the forest beyond.

The cavalcade stood frozen for what felt like an eternity.

"*Ar aglaidh aoise coirrigh don fúile are orailt!*" Lir called to his men, shattering the quiet, to which they nodded and, at last, continued.

Before Aisling could ask any more questions Lir spoke in her ear, "At my command, close your eyes."

Aisling opened her mouth to protest but instead, thought better of it, nodding her head in response. Something must be wrong.

Several moments passed, the silence thickening, becoming unbearable as they trudged onward. No one spoke, whistled, or laughed. The world was holding its breath, waiting to exhale. Until Lir bent lower to whisper once more in the queen's ear.

"Close your eyes, Aisling," he said, her name on his lips strangely intoxicating. In the mortal world, only those closest to a lady were permitted to use her first name. His use of it was wickedly inappropriate. Although was it? He was her husband, after all, even if they were strangers and enemies at that.

"Don't open them until I say."

Lir tightened his grip on the reins, one arm reaching for an axe strapped to his back.

Fear rippled through Aisling but she did as he commanded, shutting her eyes. Focusing on the darkness.

The silence persisted, only interrupted by the sound of her beating heart, her racing pulse, rushing through the veins in her ears. And as if they'd stepped into the blackest depths of the sea, the air grew cold. Aisling's ears popped from the pressure, weighing heavily on her shoulders, her head, her legs like an invisible hand threatening to squash her flat.

She focused on her breathing. Her only anchor to the outside world was Lir's embrace, the hardness of his chest against her back, his legs against her own, and the steady gait of their mount.

From the silence, somewhere in the muffled distance, Aisling heard female voices. A swarm of incantations, whispering, humming wildly. Hungrily.

Initially, their song was lovely, alluring, familiar as if inspired by a childhood memory, perverted only in the slightest. She could feel every word as if it had a texture of its own, silky, oily, eager to touch her. Aisling craved to hear the song more clearly, to better understand every note and intonation of their melody.

Lir's breath shortened, his fae heart pacing more quickly.

The symphony of voices rose, screaming, banging against the fortress of silence that surrounded her, a bubble dampening their vile yet wondrous chorus. Aisling had never heard anything like it and a part of her, considered opening her eyes. What damage could be done from one peek?

But in an instant, stepping from that muffled, far-off chamber, the music stopped. The sounds of the world returned, and the birds chirped wildly, flapping their wings. The pressure faded and Aisling's ears, once again, adjusted.

"Open your eyes," Lir commanded.

Lir challenged their stag for the remainder of the trek, urging the beast to ride more quickly. The trees became a blur as the Fae King guided them through the forest, leaping across streams and trunks and gliding down muddy slopes. His knights mirrored his pace, watching the surrounding wood with narrowed eyes. The trees seemed to bend lower, daring to touch one of their newfound guests. Seemed to whisper to one another when they believed no one to be looking.

Aisling found herself both willing and unwilling to peer into the depths of the forest. There was a fear there, a terror brewing within that she might see something she could never unsee. For what could strike such a response from the most lethal predators themselves? Still, her eyes studied the greenwood, unable to unlatch themselves from the shadows lurking between, the moss blanketed boulders or the trees whose trunks were so large, eight men could not wrap their arms around them.

No one spoke or sheathed their weapons for several hours after.

"What happened back there?" Aisling asked, more aware of the shadows that slipped between the trees.

"Dryads," Lir said, his voice distant as though his mind was otherwise occupied. Even his muscles remained taught long after the encounter.

Dryads? Aisling had never heard of such creatures. The only races mortal subjects were made privy to were humans and the Aos Sí. But even the resources written on the fair folk were limited, authored by the mortal monarchs and their respective courts. Endeavoring to find information elsewhere was considered treasonous, to deny the authority of the mortal sovereigns, those who write the pragmatic truth of the beginning of the world and all things after. The beacon of light to the twisting darkness that was the Forbidden Lore. For the only other literature that chronicled the conception and making of the world was the Forbidden Lore, a library of texts written by the original twelve fae kings and queens. Rumor had it that such a collection was commissioned by the Gods themselves. In the eyes of mortals, however, such sources were filled with lies and manipulations unfit to educate mankind.

"In time, you'll learn of all who occupy this world and beyond," Lir said, seeming to sense Aisling's confusion.

All who occupy this world and beyond. There were others? More than just the humans and the Aos Sí? Among them, creatures that startled even the Fae King himself? Aisling's mind spun, throbbed at her temples. The royal tutors, Friseal—the Tilrish court advisor himself— and those who had educated Aisling, Starn, Fergus, Iarbonel, and Annind, had never mentioned such possibilities. Perhaps Lir's words were the lies and manipulations she'd been forewarned of. But she'd heard these dryads herself ... hadn't she?

"They will try to deceive you. They will spin lies as easily as they spin their thread," Nemed had told her in the carriage. One of the last things he spoke to her.

"I'd like to see them. All of them," Aisling said, hardening her voice. Lir whipped his attention towards her, studying her expression.

"In time," he repeated, "there are beings out there even I

deign to face—much less a mortal—"

"You need not coddle me," Aisling growled. If she was to live amongst this primordial race, amongst the enemy of her own kind, she would need to know its dangers. Familiarize herself with the world she'd been sacrificed to.

"I wouldn't dream of it, princess," Lir replied, irritation tightening his expression.

Before Aisling could respond, the Fae King brought their stag to an abrupt stop. Stretched before them was a mighty gorge. Perhaps two hundred men wide. Its walls were dressed in emerald moss and lichen's frothy breath, green giants bathing in the waters. The water gleamed, reflecting the thick canopies and jagged rocks above.

Aisling gasped, eyes wide as Lir lifted her from the beast and onto the ground. He gestured for her to follow him towards the water's edge where a single boat bobbed. It was small, large enough for only a handful of passengers, and wonderfully carved with imaginative reliefs. A scaled serpent crowning the bow of the craft.

"The stags, the others, how will they cross the waters?" Aisling asked, eyes still pinned to the gorge. Surely their entire procession wouldn't wait upon a single boat to carry them up and down the gorge.

"They'll travel another route," Galad called from behind, exchanging positions with Lir to escort Aisling onto the craft. The Fae King, meanwhile, handed their mount to Rian to care for the beast in Lir's stead. "There's a quicker path through the rock itself, a natural tunnel where the stags can pass."

"And why do we not travel with them?" Aisling continued.

"Lir wished to show you Annwyn from the front entrance," Galad explained. "There's no better view of Annwyn than from the water."

Aisling found it odd the Fae King's knight had referred to him by his primary name. She cringed, imagining Nemed's response to such behavior. Her father would've considered such informality disrespectful and worthy of swift punishment. She'd witnessed it before.

Galad crouched to sit beside Aisling in the boat just as Lir approached, prepared now to depart into the gorge. But before the Fae King boarded the craft, he stepped into the waters, drenching his trousers to the thigh. He rolled up his sleeves and pushed the boat, setting Aisling and Galad adrift before leaping aboard himself. Aisling averted her eyes, lest she witness his trousers sticking to his waist and legs as the water ran down his lower half and soaked the bottom of the boat.

Aisling had never travelled by vessel. The craft floated like one of the lily-pads elegantly sitting atop the water's surface. It was strange yet wonderful. Fearsome yet thrilling. The steady rock from side to side. The sound of the water curling beneath the wooden serpent, leading their craft further into the gorge.

The blush-bellied wrens heralded their arrival around every bend and the rush of frothing water, slapping stones as it spilled over the moss-cloaked boulders, grew nearer the longer they travelled. Aisling had not realized—had never known that such natural beauty existed. That the wild was more capable of building, carving, fostering monuments and empires far greater than any complex mortal man attempted. Aisling bit her own tongue. For such thoughts, Nemed would whip her if he knew what she'd spoken into existence even if only to herself.

The mortal queen leaned over the edge of the vessel to peer into the waters below. The water rippled like liquid sea glass. And, if Aisling moved any further, she might've fallen in. The idea delighted her. Titilated her. Just as had the lake slumbering beside Tilren's eastern wall.

Amid her reverie, Aisling witnessed something swim past. Its scaled body reflected the light percolating through the canopies overhead, before slithering farther below. It was large, perhaps even giant. Surely it could not be a fish. But it moved like one, snaking through the gorge's undercurrents, daring to catch a glimpse of its new guests.

"*Mo Lúra*," Galad said, startling Aisling and releasing her from the water's spell. "We're here."

Further down the gorge, cut from the rock itself, stood a colossal cave. Like the mouth of some mythic god, the cavern stood agape, framed by statues of females carved into the stone. Nude maidens bedizened by elegant, wasp-like wings. They were frozen in time, as if spell-bound by a bygone curse, guardians to the threshold draped in sheets of water from the cascades above, interrupted only by hanging, flowered vines whose buds were swiftly pollinated by a variety of winged creatures.

Lir steered the boat so that as they crossed, the water misted above them instead of pummeling and capsizing their vessel.

However, Aisling hardly noticed the spray of the waterfall's breath as they dove into the blackness of the cave. Her eyes struggled to adjust, focusing on the monoliths standing tall and wide within the waters of the cavern. So large and formidable they appeared nearly sentient, protecting this cave and its black cauldron of waters. The sort of cavity Aisling imagined all Aos Sí resided in, hunched over and feeding on mortal flesh. Was this where she was to live out her remaining years? Driven mad by the eternal, hollow patter of streams dripping from the cave's ceilings and onto the stony surfaces below?

After several moments of silence, an opening appeared in the distance, its light blinding Aisling as it flashed into view. Fresh forest air greeted Aisling along with the distinct smell of food—cooked meats and baked breads, controlled fires burning, and smoke billowing. Then came the distant chatter, the clanking of metal, the moans of cattle, and the plucking of music—sounds of a heavily populated city, Aisling realized.

And sure enough, just beyond that wondrous hole of light,

rested a hollow of gargantuan trees, cradling a kingdom larger than any Aisling had laid eyes on. More magnificent than the mud pit she'd anticipated or the cavern from which they emerged, artfully woven into the forest itself; a glowing city nestled below a stone-faced castle carved into the side of a mountain.

The waters they sailed bubbled with soap, remnants of the fae females labor as they scrubbed their clothes upon the water's shore. Once they caught sight of their Fae King aboard the vessel, they leapt from their knees and raced along the water's edge, alerting the kingdom of their sovereign's arrival.

By now, twilight was spilling across the North, darkening the sky, and speckling its deep hues with starlight. The surface of the water reflected the warm glow of the city lights, illuminating the hollow in an orange, firelit luster.

Aisling was left breathless.

"This is your home now," Lir said.

The queen turned to meet the Fae King's eyes only to find him studying her, watching her. She too would've been curious to see her expression. to witness the reaction of any mortal who beheld this fae land. Perhaps she was the first.

"This is Annwyn."

Chapter VI

LIR'S CAVALCADE OF FAE KNIGHTS GREETED Aisling, Galad, and the Fae King himself on the other side of the waters. Aisling rode, once again, on Lir's stag as they entered Annwyn's corridors. The Fae King held the queen's waist with one arm and the reins with another. A gesture, a physical contact that heated every inch of Aisling's skin. It was a performance. A showcase of their political union.

The streets spilled over with fae subjects, each craning their elegant necks to catch a glimpse of the mortal queen. Males, females, few children, large and mighty and beautiful. Tangled in black, knotted runes, braids, and symbols tattooed into their iridescent dark or gold, pink or pale skin. So unlike the ghoulish aberrations she'd anticipated. In fact, it was difficult to believe mortals lived under the same grey-clad sky as this preternatural civilization. That they shared the North's breath. It's wistful sighs and verdant earth.

And just as the cave's threshold implied, many of Lir's subjects bore wings. Large, nearly translucent appendages, resembling those of a wasp. But these wings bore no color of their own, rather reflected the light around them as the fair folk danced barefoot, sang sweet tunes, puffed clouds of pollen, carpeted the flagstone streets with thistles, heathers, and frosty avens.

"How many of you are there?" Aisling asked Lir, waving at a female who'd called him by name. A female whose long tresses arrived at her hips, braided through with bluebells. Or perhaps the bluebells *were* her hair, sprouting from her scalp. Her angled cheekbones shelving a kaleidoscope of butterflies.

Lir was silent for a long moment, leading Aisling to believe he'd never respond until he, at last, spoke: "A couple thousand here in Annwyn."

Aisling surveyed the crowds, the fair folk filling the glistening streets, pouring from the strange shops and houses, running through the surrounding forest, peering from their homes in the treetops. To Aisling, it seemed there were so few. Nothing compared to Tilren's overflowing thoroughfares where peasants and commoners burst at the seams of their Northern kingdom. Where commonfolk trampled one another to navigate the cobbled paths.

In addition to the fair folk, there were other creatures who populated this city; animals that interrupted Aisling's beating heart. Furry beasts the queen recognized whether it be their likeness on parchment or over Tilren's walls: Badgers, foxes, rabbits, bears who, here in Annwyn, did not crawl or growl but stood and walked on two feet, clapping their paws and speaking through their muzzles. Magic. As distilled and potent as the fog rolling in from the highland peaks.

Aisling did her best not to gawk, instead averting her attention to the stores lining every corridor, the same sort of shops and services one would encounter in mortal territory—tailors, smiths, bakeries, homes—but somehow laced with fae taste, skill and culture. Apples, peaches, plums, and berries bubbled from the vines and cloaks of green that smothered everything in their reach. In fact, many of the cottages were carved into the trees themselves, spindly, spiral staircases winding around the girthy trunks and into the canopies. The highest branches braided in colorful ribbons and cylindrical chimes that sang with every passing breeze. A breeze that smelled of hogweed seeds, ramson capers, powdered peppery bolete, spignel leaf, and scarlet incense. Nothing like the rot vegetating in Tilren, a product of mass waste from overpopulation.

Some cheered as the royal procession entered. Screamed their king's name. Most scowled at Aisling, regarding her with disgust and contempt. Even loathing, tightening their fists around their weapons or at their sides as if they'd like nothing more than to harm the mortal invading this stolen ground. As the procession passed, they were no doubt already dreaming of the ways they'd nail her head to a pike to avenge what the mortals had stolen after years of warring. But said reaction was perhaps the only aspect of the fair folk and Annwyn that Aisling had accurately predicted. For everything else, left her speechless, searching for words.

One Aos Sí, in particular, caught her attention, a male bent below the awning of a silversmith. He tempered a thin stretch of metal, pausing only to follow the crowd's gaze to the royal procession. His blonde hair was braided away from his face. It lay across his broad back like a fox's tail, revealing an ugly scar that cut diagonally across his seething expression. The wound had removed his right eye, leaving an angry, knotted lesion. But that was not the only injury he bore. His left arm had been severed at the elbow, a wound to match his lost eye. Both were marked by crimson, expanding like an open hand till the wounds dissolved further up his appendage and across his nose.

Was this what iron did to fae flesh? Were these the marks iron left if such blows didn't kill them in the first place?

Suddenly Iarbonel's dagger, hidden away within Aisling's sleeve, felt heavier. It weighed heavy on her arm, threatening to fling her to the ground and off Saoirse's back. The fae smithy's knuckles grew white, clenching his tools as his glare deepened. Aisling knew he wished her dead. Nemed was right.

Here in this odd world, Aisling represented all of mankind and in so doing, bore all the fault for the crimes of mortals, in fae eyes at least. Every morsel of their hatred was now concentrated into a single person, Aisling. A queen who was the newfound symbol of their enemy, prancing into Annwyn.

Aisling didn't blame the Aos Sí for their blatant disregard. Her father had slaughtered hundreds of their kind, tactfully finding ways to rid his land of the fair folk without engaging in direct combat, for mortals would sooner perish than claim victory on a battlefield, face-to-face with the Aos Sí. But Aisling had seen Starn return, his clothes covered in soot and ash, a day spent paving the earth for mortal expansion. Nemed was clever. Although he couldn't match their strength or power in direct combat, he could outsmart them. Which is exactly what he and all the mortal kings and chieftains before him had done for centuries.

And now, a mortal girl arrived to rule them. All in the name of peace. But that was a mere illusion. Aisling had no power here. Only the appearance of it. She was more a slave than a queen amongst the Aos Sí and she would always be considered as such. To think otherwise would be foolish.

Aisling swallowed her sympathy, reminding herself that the Aos Sí had laid claim to Clann Neimedh's land, built this fae civilization on stolen Northern territory, forced mankind from the rivers and highlands and groves to hide behind their iron walls. Nemed and the other mortal sovereigns had protected their race. Generously, gallantly sheltered humans from the fury of this savage, barbaric fair folk whose nature was to reap violence.

"*They will try to deceive you. They will spin lies as easily as they spin their thread*," Aisling repeated to herself, savoring the memory of her father's voice.

The architecture in Annwyn differed from anything she'd experienced in the mortal lands, each beam and pillar and vaulted roof, carved with elegant detail, flowers, animals, fae faces etched into the pale oak or stone. And the waddle and daub homes that lined the periphery of Tilren were nowhere to be found here. Only the work and materials fae fingers could both manipulate and craft, Aisling was realizing. Perhaps through magic and magic alone.

Through the hollowed-out trees, atop the undulating flagstone paths, beneath the trickling waterfalls and lined with buckets for freshwater collection, the procession wove itself up the mountain and towards the castle, admiring its kingdom below. Moss, algae, roots, and other flora clung to every surface of the summit like a lovely, sentient disease, infecting everything it beheld. Not even the altitude nor the chilled northern air could strike fear in these forests, growing as strongly, as potently as they had below.

Lir was sovereign to an immense dominion, so much larger than Tilren. A society occupying even the canopies of the trees—limitless space and freedom. So unlike the mortal lands spilling over with man, woman, and child; kingdoms whose subjects lived atop one another in narrow, congested alleys, spreading diseases like wildfire.

Lir's castle itself was sculpted from the summit. A mountain cutting through the greenwood, white stone notched into turrets whose peaks were blanketed either by clouds or prehistoric elms, covered parapet walks suspended in the air, a steepled chapel whose stained-glass windows glittered in the evening light, and walls dressed in vines and flowers.

Six sentinels stood guard on either side of the drawbridge to the castle. A drawbridge that connected the mountain to the forest earth, separated by a steep drop where frothing rapids swam far below. But these sentinels were no fae. They were great, bipedal bears, strapped with fae armor and equipped with greatswords and shields, bowing to Lir as he approached in near-perfect unison. What did they protect the castle from, Aisling wondered? Were the Aos Sí a threat also to themselves?

"Are these sentinels from your military?" Aisling asked over the clack of the stag's hooves on stone, surveying their intricate yet elegant armor, armor that matched the knights surrounding her, their thick, umber coats, their long muzzles snapped shut to hide a collection of razor-sharp teeth, Aisling had no doubt. Did her father know of these animals? These familiar creatures that stood and acted like men?

"They're trained soldiers, yes, but our military comprises all of Annwyn," Galad replied before Lir, nodding to the sentries as their procession passed.

"You mean even the"—Aisling hesitated, unsure what to call these strange beasts—"*commoners* fight?" Aisling asked, aware that perhaps these were not the most appropriate of questions considering her position. Nevertheless, if she were to live here, she would want to understand how their society worked. To understand the fae themselves.

"Aye, the commoners, the noble people. Everyone, save for the children," Galad said. Aisling considered the fae knight, meeting his sapphire eyes. The mortal queen had never heard of such a society, one where every member was born for battle. What had she expected? The fair folk were savage. A folk the Forbidden Lore was said to describe as a tribe of legendary heroes. Warriors Forged in enchantments, curses, and the bending of the elements.

"Where do you think their markings come from?" Galad asked rhetorically, turning to face the castle.

The doors to the fortress were perhaps fifty men tall, embellished with enormous stag-head door knockers, whose muzzles gripped the rings. Such rings were not needed, however, for the threshold opened of its own accord, revealing the inside of both the mountain and the castle itself.

Aisling gasped as they entered the fae bastion for even the interior of the castle burst with wildlife, a forest growing from within the heart of the fortress despite the immaculately polished floors and gilded ornamentation. The walls were masterfully sculpted with large, epic narratives. Pots bubbling over with flowers sat on glass tables, on staircase steps, along the walls, from the ceilings. In fact, large pillars molded into the image of winged fae females held up such ceilings. Bluebirds and sparrows fluttering from pillar to pillar, foxes skittering up the winding staircases on two feet and chasing rabbit tails. A room cast in the breath of the woods. Hardly the bestial den or monstrous cavern she'd imagined a day prior. No, this was something different. A palace spun on a spindle of dreams and enchantment.

Once Aisling, Lir, Galad, and several other knights had stepped inside the castle, the knights dispersed themselves, melting into the colossal fortress either tending to duties unbeknownst to Aisling or enjoying some rest after their travels. They slipped into the corridors, travelled up the numerous staircases, or spoke to one another. The Fae King was one of them. For nearly the moment their group stepped into the fortress, Lir was abruptly requested by one of his court advisors—Aisling assumed the role based on the Aos Sí's dress—leaving Galad to accompany the mortal queen. Perhaps, Aisling thought to herself, the urgency with which the advisor had pulled Lir from Aisling's side was related to the dryads they'd encountered passing through the forest.

Still, the queen found herself staring after the Fae King, watching as he vanished further into the castle without a word or glance in her direction. She was glad for it. He, more than all the rest combined, unsettled her. Struck fear into her core, a fear that inspired both dread and a bizarre sort of thrill she knew was best stifled and not entertained.

As Galad guided Aisling through the castle, they passed several fae servants, what appeared to be cooks, musicians, masons, and falconers, among others, cursing the mortal queen beneath their breath. All taking the form of those strange, bipedal animals she'd seen loitering about Annwyn before. And they were each lovely, dressed in finely sewn servant attire draped neatly over their gleaming pelts or feathers. Nothing like the faded robes and frocks the help wore in Tilren.

"*Ba hadith rekka dú fuile a lur*," Galad addressed the staff as they swept by, gesturing between Aisling and the bestial servants around them. They bowed as he did so, eyeing their new sovereign beneath hateful expressions.

"This is the primary staff for the castle," Galad explained. Aisling schooled her expression but within she was shocked there weren't more. Castle Neimedh was half the size of this enormous bastion, and yet their servants tripled what Lir possessed here. "In time you'll become familiar with both their names and their individual responsibilities. For now, know they are all eager and willing to serve you."

Galad glared at each of them as he said the last words. None dared counter his statement nor did they have time as the fae knight travelled further into the keep with Aisling following shortly behind.

There was seldom a moment Aisling forgot about the pointed canines hiding behind both the fair folk's and these bipedal animal's calculated, smiling lips. Fangs that could rip out her windpipes at a moment's notice. Not to mention their Otherworldly strength. Even the fae commoners she'd seen in the streets. Aisling was a fly in a spider's nest, offered by her own tuath.

"This is Gilrel," Galad said at last, gesturing to an obscenely large—large for its species—pine marten crouched on the floor as they rounded another corner. Its paws were cushioned in clouds of bubbles as the beast wiped the checkered floors in consistent, shapely circles. By the looks of it, the marten had already buffed an entire hall, the marble glossy enough to witness one's own reflection. But it was not alone. Kestrels fluttered high above, making use of their wings to sponge the highest panels of stained glass while the squirrels dusted the rafters, and swabbed the vaulted ceilings.

"She will be your handmaiden. Your comfort and all that you require is Gilrel's concern." Aisling hid her surprise. So, she would not spend her remaining years in whatever loathsome pit they called their dungeons after all. Even if that meant being waited upon by a furry little beast like the one who glowered at her now.

The marten unfurled herself, standing tall before curtsying, her small apron wet with suds. She was hardly the nervous chambermaid Aisling had employed in Tilren, as lovely as a marten could be and adorned with the same tribal markings all the fair folk sported beneath their clothes, brandished solely on her paws and ears. As well as scars and nicks, Aisling could spot from where she stood a slender scrape along her jugular, a cut across the bridge of her muzzle, and a jagged line across the back of her paw. Memories of violence whittled into her skin.

"Does she speak my tongue?" Aisling asked Galad.

"I'm fluent in most mortal dialects as well as, of course, my mother tongue, *Rún,* also known as the 'divine language,'" Gilrel said, her voice as lovely as a songbird, perverted by her bitter disapproval of the human woman before her. Aisling audibly gasped, stepping back instinctively. If their ability to walk and behave like people weren't enough, the clarity with which this beast spoke was enough to send Aisling to her grave in fright.

Aisling cleared her throat, doing her best and failing to cloak her surprise; for other than the obvious enchantments performed before her eyes, it was not common, at least in mortal society, for a servant to be so educated. Perhaps it was their lengthy lifespans that awarded them centuries to acquire the knowledge an educated mortal gained in one measly lifetime. In fact, these Aos Sí most likely lived various lives between the time of their birth and the date of their death. Did these strange bipedal beasts live so long as well? The marten handmaid had obviously, based on what Galad had said about all citizens of the Aos Sí serving in their armies as well as her scars, fought in several wars. This chambermaid had more experience, knowledge, than Aisling could begin to imagine. And yet, she would serve a human. One whose only education and experience were that which her court advisor deigned to provide her.

"Gilrel is an honored member of the staff, *mo Lúra*. You'll be well taken care of," Galad encouraged, perhaps sensing the tension vegetating in the air between them.

"Very well," Aisling huffed, refusing to wilt before a servant and an animal one at that for Gilrel still shot daggers from her beady black eyes. That's what her father would want. Had asked of her. "Will you show me to my chambers? I'm in desperate need of a meal and good rest."

Gilrel nodded, her brow furrowing.

"This way, *mo Lúra.*" The handmaiden acridly gestured for Aisling to follow, waddling up ahead on her two paws.

The queen glanced once more at Galad, already immersed in a conversation with another servant. One of the many creatures busily scuttling in every direction, carrying bundles of roses and strawberries in baskets hooked into the crooks of their arms, piles of freshly laundered drapes, and delegating order after order. They were preparing for something. Aisling knew the signs of an approaching royal event.

"Is there a reason you don't use fire to light your passages?" Aisling ducked beneath various flowering ramblers reaching for the crown of her head. Florets glowed with warm bulbs at the heart of their gown of petals. The same breed of plump buds responsible for illuminating Aisling's tent the night of her wedding.

Gilrel's gaze sharpened. "We prefer no flames in our

interiors."

Aisling nodded her head but she already knew this. Had already noticed the absence of flame when inside any fae dwelling. Aisling was rather concerned with *why* that was, but Gilrel was clearly in no mood to answer, her furry face taut with resentment, making Aisling all the more curious.

"Have you ever gotten lost in these halls?" Aisling continued, admiring the complex labyrinth that was this fae palace. A bastion Aisling would've believed, days prior, to exist only in her most wild machinations.

"Not for many centuries, no," Gilrel said, considering the castle herself as they travelled through its passages.

"Perhaps when you were young?" Aisling wondered if the servant had indeed lived in Annwyn when she was young. The queen knew the Aos Sí had arrived centuries prior to the day she herself was born, but no one knew the exact year or date. Only that since this strange race stepped foot on mortal land, the humans and Aos Sí had been at constant war; Nemed was one mortal king among hundreds before him who served to protect mankind. To protect the mortal world from these abominations. Imposters. Fair folk. So perhaps their furry fiends lived equally as long.

"I've not been a child for quite some time," Gilrel said, her gaze growing distant. How old could the marten handmaid possibly be? It was strange to think the young marten before her, appearing no older than Aisling herself, was ages old.

"And when did you learn to speak?" Aisling bit her tongue for she knew the question was a risk. Perhaps it was rude to ask but she wanted to know.

The corner of Gilrel's lips curled.

"You mean to ask me: 'how can a lowly beast speak your mortal tongue?'"

"That's a bold assumption." Aisling stiffened.

"But a true one," Gilrel lifted her muzzle triumphantly. "Sidhe territory is imbued with the same power that once stirred in the Forge. Ancient, archaic forces vibrating through even the marrow of the Sidhe. An energy that has blessed those beasts born during the Forging of these lands, with the ability to speak, walk, communicate, sing, even fight as do the Sidhe. And the longer we live, the more civilized we become."

Aisling's mind spun as she considered all of this. Question after question bloomed within her mind as she debated which to query next. But none of the boisterous musings ever left her lips. It became clear that the information she would acquire would be given gradually and not all at once. After all, she had a lifetime to understand all these strange creatures.

As soon as Gilrel pushed open the doors to the mortal queen's chamber, Aisling's mouth fell open. The room was exquisite; opulently furnished and decorated with precious metals and stones, polished marble floors, and a rounded balcony floating amidst the plush, emerald canopies of the surrounding forest, the same wood that hugged the mountain in which the castle was carved.

This was so unlike her home in Tilren—a gothic fortress of stone and iron, an impressive bastion by mortal standards. But this, this fae palace was not the barbaric pigsty she'd always imagined. Aisling didn't know what to make of it or if she'd ever come to believe it truly existed. For it felt more like a dream, a hallucination, an enchantment than anything she'd laid eyes on before. This world was certainly made of magic but not the twisted and wicked charms she'd anticipated.

"Your belongings arrived before you and have already been unpacked and stowed away in these cupboards," Gilrel opened two large wardrobes, filled to the brim. Flocks of mint green moths burst forth from cabinets, richly cloaked in opulent garments fit for nobility. A fragrant, sweet, and powdery cloud followed in their wake, dusting Aisling's clothes.

"The other end of the chamber houses all your *caera*'s belongings." Aisling assumed that meant Lir's possessions.

She hadn't even considered the possibility that she and the Fae King would share quarters. Nemed and Clodagh had always slept separately in opposing wings of their Tilrish fortress.

"What does that word mean?" Aisling asked, cautiously stepping further into the room.

"*Caera?*" Gilrel's brow pinched, thinking of an explanation, "in mortal terms, I believe you call them husbands. Spouses, perhaps. But it is more to us. All mates in our culture are only wed if they are *caera*. Soulmates, in your tongue. The bonding of two hearts in the Forge."

How superstitious these fae creatures were.

"This applies to even political unions?" Aisling asked, biting her tongue as soon as the words slipped from her mouth. Perhaps she shouldn't speak of such things with just anyone much less a commoner. She needed to remember to trust no one. No one and no thing. These creatures were beasts and her enemy despite their beauty, despite their attempts at hospitality.

"The Sidhe cannot wed if they are not *caera*," Gilrel insisted. "You wouldn't have been capable of choosing the correct blade otherwise." Aisling remembered the test the night of her union, the three blades staked into the earth before her. Two swords and an axe. Logically, there was a one-out-of-three possibility to select the correct blade. Unless, Aisling realized, Gilrel was implying enchantment was involved. The mortal queen laughed at the thought. Iarbonel had claimed such a marital custom meant nothing. In fact, he'd insisted it was no more than a ritual and she'd no reason to trust a member of the fair folk over her own brother.

"And had I chosen wrong? What would've become of the peace treaty between our kind?" Aisling pushed, focusing on Gilrel's reaction. This, considering Aisling would've been forced to duel Lir to the death and been executed as a result.

"I'm merely a handmaiden, *mo Lúra*. I'm not privy to such discussions. However, having served beneath the king for several centuries, I can confidently say Lir would risk a great deal for a chance to protect the Sidhe. If the mortals requested a political union, Lir would stop at nothing to achieve his ends."

In another world, another reality, Aisling had chosen the wrong weapon the night of her union and had been beheaded by Lir. The mortals and this savage race were still at war, battling atop the ground where Aisling's blood ran deep. All for a silly, fae superstition. Superstition fostered by childish fireside tales and unfounded religion. A religion with no logical bearing. Although, what logical bearing did a talking marten boast as it stood before her now?

Had Nemed known of any of these customs before agreeing to the union? Before trading his daughter for peace? Had he known the risks to her life? Of course, he had. But Aisling knew as well as he that her life was nothing in comparison to the thousands that would be spared as a result of her sacrifice.

As for Lir, Aisling expected no less. If anything, it was a relief knowing he was as wicked as she'd always imagined. As her father had always described.

"*He is the worst of them, ruthless, merciless, no more than a depraved fiend driven by hunger, need, and power. But, unlike the wolf, he is insatiable. Never let your guard down around him, Aisling. Never give him an opportunity to choose between you and what he covets.*"

Nemed's words echoed in her mind, hardening her resolve. Her purpose here.

Aisling wandered towards the vanity facing the four-poster bed.

"This is to be your gown for the *Snaidhm* tomorrow afternoon."

Gilrel hung an embroidered gown beside Aisling's new wardrobe. A gown woven with leaves like chips of emeralds and threaded with strings of pearls.

"*Snaidhm?*" Aisling asked.

"It is customary in our culture to host an event the day following a union. However, for obvious reasons, the event has been postponed until tomorrow."

"An occasion to celebrate an occasion?" Aisling turned her back to Gilrel, allowing, although reluctantly, the handmaid to pull the muddied and wind-hardened frock over her head and dispose of the trousers now steeped in the scent of stag's pelt. For nothing pricked Aisling's nerves more than the thought of the marten's calloused paws or weather-worn claws stroking her bare flesh.

"A wedding celebrates the union. The *Snaidhm* celebrates the consummation of said union," Gilrel said, untangling Aisling's coronet with impressive skill, careful to avoid tugging at her scalp or splitting strands of hair. The result of centuries as a handmaid, Aisling assumed, or perhaps the benefits of finely pointed claws in the place of blunted mortal fingers.

The mortal queen blushed, immediately reminded of her wedding night. Shame or perhaps embarrassment washed over Aisling at the thought, for she had not yet fulfilled her promise to Rinn Dúin. As far as Clann Neimedh would be concerned, she was not yet queen if the marriage hadn't been consummated. And if a consummation was as important in fae tradition as it was in mortal tradition, Aisling's suspicions had been correct. Lir barely deigned to speak to her, much less touch her. Perhaps there was something to be grateful for there. The lack of consummation would be their secret, for Lir was bound to uphold the image of their marriage as much as Aisling was.

"Fret not, *mo Lúra*," Gilrel said, misinterpreting Aisling's palpable anxiety. "It is merely a day to bid the *caera* good fortune in producing an heir."

A murder of silver-eyed ravens let loose in Aisling's stomach. Clodagh had warned Aisling of this responsibility for Clodagh too had borne a similar duty upon her union with

Nemed.

"Eventually, you will be expected to gift your betrothed an heir. Do it quickly lest he uses you till your belly is swollen and the responsibility completed. That is, if he's willing to settle for a child of mixed race. Your father would rather forsake such a bairn than dub it his heir, but perhaps the Aos Sí do not hold themselves to such pureblooded standards."

Aisling did her best to swallow but her mouth was dry and her tongue brittle. She could almost see Clodagh's black braids tightly spun into a low bun, her spidery fingers adorned with iron rings smoothing out the skirts on her lap.

"Quite a fuss over an inevitability," Aisling mused, avoiding Gilrel's beady eyes as Gilrel slipped a dressing gown over the queen's shoulders, only possible if Aisling lowered herself enough to be within reach of the little beast.

"A mortal mentality," Gilrel snarled, spitting the word "mortal" as if it were a curse. However, the servant quickly and wisely softened her tone before continuing. "To the Sidhe, children are rare. A thousand years may pass between a female's first pregnancy and her second. That is, if she's capable of bearing a child at all. Most of us are not. For that reason, Sidhe children are precious."

This made sense to Aisling considering there were far fewer Aos Sí than there were humans despite their long lifespans. While the mortals continued to overpopulate their towns and expand their walls, the Aos Sí were dwindling, made worse by the casualties of war. At least, that's what she'd overheard her father's counselors discussing while she finished her tutoring, proven true by what she'd already seen of Annwyn.

"And what of a mortal bearing a fae—a *Sidhe* child?" Aisling asked. Gilrel considered, brushing Aisling's cloud of onyx spirals. A hue that separated Aisling, if she was not already different enough, from the fair folk and their gilded coloring. Even those who bore darker locks and complexions still glittered like marvelous, deep gold in the sunlight. Aisling's on the other hand was so black it was nearly blue in direct light.

"As far as I'm aware, such a union has never been. The Forge be willing, you will be the first *caera* to bear a mixed-race heir, *mo Lúra*."

Chapter VII

Even when the sun was swathed in black, come evening, or bathed in pink, come morning, Lir never returned to their quarters.

Aisling picked at the breakfast Gilrel had fetched for her. As with all else fae, their food was impressive: artfully knotted pastries, colorful sweet cakes, emerald gelatins, potent teas steeped with strange leaves. Spoons who stirred sugar into her teacup of their own accord and teacups that resembled large foxglove flowers. The teapot was a bundle of cabbage with a handle, lid, and spout, one the hare skipping across the room eyed hungrily. All of which intrigued the queen to no end. Aisling didn't believe she'd ever become accustomed to this world. Not fully.

Aisling was ravenous, as she found she always was in this new world. But she missed the taste of the milk in Tilren even if it was sourer, the hard breads, the fire crackling in the corner of her chamber, the familiarity of her old home. For every corridor, every room, every stairwell of this castle was imbued with the Northern chill, the fae refusing to warm their walls with flame.

Aisling wondered what her brothers would make of this world; would they be equally as impressed or more capable of seeing past the fae deception that Aisling was too naive to detect? For more and more Aisling found herself guiltily enjoying the quirks of this fae land. Whatever the case, Fergus certainly would enjoy the food. Even if the tales claimed fae fruit, meats, and wines were all bewitched.

"Is there something wrong with your meal, *mo Lúra?*" Gilrel asked, sorting through a pile of silk, chiffon, and organza with the help of several magpies fluttering enthusiastically around her paws.

"Legends claim men have gone mad after having tasted a single peach from your gardens, plagued with an insatiable hunger till the day they met their end." Even if Lir had promised the food would be safe for her, she couldn't help but doubt. In fact, she'd be a fool to trust the fair folk and whatever pleasantries they sweetened the air with.

Gilrel laughed. "You believe this is an enchantment? I've seen for myself the men you speak of. It is nothing more than humans struck with a pleasure they'd yet to experience. It is not the Sidhe's fault mortals are easily seduced by bodily pleasure," Gilrel smirked, mumbling something beneath her breath in Fae.

Aisling considered the tray of food for a moment, "But you are capable of magic? Spells, enchantments, curses?" Had that part of her education been true? Lir had, after all, extinguished all the floral light in their wedding tent, bud by bud. Even the sentient spoon before her, and Gilrel herself and the animals that frolicked so near to the Aos Sí, so unlike the infinite chasm that lie between man and beast in the mortal world.

"Aye, the Sidhe do possess a certain ability or power. Mortals may refer to such a spirit as *magic* but to us it is essential to our being, a part of our making."

"It is in your blood then?" Aisling stood from the cloud of quilts to stretch her legs.

"No," Gilrel said, "just as humans reap their breath from the trees around them, so too do the Sidhe obtain and inhale their '*magic*,' as mortals would understand it. Just as the air fills your lungs, gives you breath to live, magic nourishes the Sidhe, passes through us, in us, for us."

Aisling considered asking her marten to demonstrate such abilities but thought better of it. It would be wise of the mortal queen to establish certain boundaries between herself and the fair folk, especially those who washed her clothes, prepared her food, and accompanied her throughout the day. Aisling didn't and perhaps never would fully understand the Aos Sí and their abilities. And despite her curiosity, she shouldn't lick the blade she feared.

"You are dangerous creatures," Aisling said, padding barefoot towards her private balcony.

"Mortals would do well to remember it, lest they fancy themselves thieves or trespassers again," the handmaiden sneered.

"That's enough, Gilrel," Aisling snapped, holding her beasty gaze. Gilrel stilled, her lips pressing into a thin line of contempt. Whiskers startled straight.

"And remember, Aisling: even in your dying breath, never give them the satisfaction of seeing you wilt, witnessing your fear."

The memory of Nemed's words was all that kept Aisling from relenting. From not appeasing the handmaid even if this creature could drink her blood from the floors.

Had Aisling not been stunned by the view from her terrace, she might've been tempted to further counter her handmaiden's claims. After all, the fair folk had been the ones to steal Northern land and trespass on mortal territory, a world that was not theirs to begin with.

But standing on the balcony was like floating amongst the trees, suspended hundreds of feet in the air in the tangle of flowers and branches and leaves like chips of Connemara. Out here, it smelled of sweet sap, fresh pines, and the Northern wind. Aisling could see all of Annwyn from this vantage point;

the edge of the castle and its winged statues admiring the lovely kingdom knitted into the forest, the gorge where Aisling had entered, and the great expanse of woodland, cliff, and mountain.

And just as Aisling leaned her head against her palm, she spotted movement, a crowd fussing over a group of armor-clad men entering Annwyn.

The mortal queen perked up, leaning over the terrace to catch a better glimpse of the commotion.

Fifteen fae knights, perhaps more, travelled through and up Annwyn towards the castle. At the center of their cluster, two knights were cautiously carried by their comrades. One appeared well enough to hang from another's shoulder, limply trudging on. The other was unconscious, carried by his comrades soaked through with red.

"Gilrel," Aisling called, "what's happened?"

The chambermaid dropped whatever she'd been busied with, the magpies leaping into the air startled, and joined the woman atop the balcony.

Gilrel inhaled sharply. "It appears there's been another attack."

Attack? But there was peace between the mortals and the Aos Sí, as far as both races were concerned. Aisling's marriage to a Fae King was evidence of that. Who would possibly launch an offense two days post a political union?

And, as if sensing her thoughts, Gilrel spoke: "This is no mortal attack. I can smell their blood from here and their wounds reek of Unseelie."

Unseelie.

Aisling blinked.

Gilrel, understanding Aisling's confusion, continued, "the *Unseelie* are all the creatures inhabiting the feywilds, the forests belonging to the Sidhe. They are like the Sidhe, Forged alongside them, but far more chaotic in nature. This includes great monsters and—"

"The dryads?" Aisling interrupted, remembering her encounter in the forest.

"Aye, the dryads, among others," Gilrel said.

Aisling bit her bottom lip. Why had she never heard of these *Unseelie*? Why had her tutors, Friseal, her father never spoken of these creatures? Perhaps they were unaware of such dangers, in which case, someone must warn them. Warn all of mankind of these other races, beings that could harm the fair folk themselves. Even fae knights. And the possibility that Nemed, her tuath, the Northern kings, chieftains, and tiarnas had known of the Unseelie and kept it a secret ... such a possibility was unimaginable. What reason was there to lie to the Northern people? To Aisling herself?

The knights raced up the steps to the castle's front entrance, near enough that Aisling caught sight of Galad and Lir among the flurry of fae warriors. Even from this distance, Aisling could see the dents in the Fae King's armor, the dirt caking his joints, the scarlet bleeding across his hands and neck. Was it his own, the blood of his men, or the blood of his enemy?

Had they gone chasing after the dryads? Or some other *Unseelie* Aisling didn't yet know of? If Lir and his knights had gone in pursuit of such creatures, it could only mean they were a direct threat to the fair folk and their land. In which case, mortals hardly stood a chance against such enemies. They needed to be warned. Aisling shook away the thoughts of Starn, Fergus, Iarbonel, or Annind stumbling upon such demons. They would be defenseless, doomed before they'd realized what unknown threats lie just outside Tilren's walls.

"Come, *mo Lúra,*" Gilrel said, shattering Aisling's trance, "You'd do well not to dwell on it. We must prepare you for the *Snaidhm.*"

Aisling sat before her vanity alone.

Gilrel had dressed Aisling in that emerald gown, trimmed with white forget-me-nots, a point of contention between the mortal queen and her marten for the fair folk dressed so differently than the mortals. Humans were forbidden to wear color lest they draw too much attention to themselves when near the wilds. But here in Annwyn, among the Aos Sí, it was normal if not expected.

That morning, Gilrel had done her best to encourage Aisling to wear her hair undone but the mortal queen required more time to adopt their customs. Even wearing these sparkling, jewel-tone gowns with their flowers and leaves had been a leap of courage. Aisling wasn't yet prepared to unpin her hair in public. Not yet.

It had been several hours since the chambermaid had said she'd return. This was after a mouse had come squeaking about a broken cage. Gilrel had appeared reluctant to leave Aisling alone, especially before the *Snaidhm* but had done so regardless to address whatever the small rodent was alarmed with. So now Aisling sat in silence, listening to the soft chirping of the songbirds hovering around her head at Gilrel's command. It was becoming more and more clear Aisling wasn't trusted.

But the door to her chambers whispered her name as the sun's crown turned gold, inviting her to explore Castle Annwyn. To prowl around its seemingly infinite spiral stairwells as she'd done as a child in Castle Neimedh. After all, these nighttime explorations had been just as forbidden then as they appeared to be now. The only difference was Dagfin at her side, encouraging her mischief as she encouraged his. Not to mention, the vast and darkly enchanted corridors that awaited her here in Annwyn.

"*Castle Annwyn was not designed for humans to traverse unaccompanied,*" Gilrel had once said when Aisling had inquired why she wasn't allowed to leave her rooms without an escort. The thought bothered her, fanning the embers of her curiosity.

So, Aisling abruptly stood from the vanity, grabbed Iarbonel's dagger, and slid it beneath her corset. She rushed towards her chamber doors, shutting the heavy threshold as quickly as she was able, so as to trap the magpies in her rooms. Three slipped through a small crevice in the nick of time, refusing to allow her the privacy she craved. Aisling cursed them beneath her breath, straightening herself and continuing down a corridor.

The halls were narrow but crowded with glowing flower bulbs. Silence grew potently here, interrupted only by the whispers of the wind slipping through the castle or the fluttering wings of the magpies clouding around Aisling's head. Of course, no servants or guards or fair folk traversed these halls now. Most likely were they already at the *Snaidhm* awaiting her arrival.

Aisling travelled through the castle, tempted by every bolted door, every poorly lit chamber, every portrait rotting away beneath the oppressive vines. Leaves that curled in her direction, inspecting their mortal passerby.

And just as Aisling made to return to her rooms, unamused by the endless winding of Castle Annwyn's passages, did something slither by in her periphery.

An onyx serpent glided across the stone floors, lifting its head as though in greeting. Its amethyst eyes locked onto her own, before proceeding through the window of an arched doorway, a wooden threshold whose knob was whittled into the shape of a hand, poised to shake palms with whosoever wished to enter.

The magpies, still tweeting nervously, pulled on Aisling's braids in the direction she'd come, unravelling Gilrel's handiwork till curls framed her face.

Aisling ignored the birds, instead tugging on the strange knob.

The door groaned opened easily, presenting several dim chambers, each smelling of mildew, of duchess fungi, of dust left to settle.

So, Aisling followed the sinuous shape of the serpent as it continued on, glancing backwards as though ensuring the mortal queen indeed followed. It wasn't until they both entered a round chamber that Aisling diverted her attention, setting eyes on a large fountain pressed against the far wall. A forest of thorns and bone ivy clung to the structure, climbing up the wings of fair folk molded by stone. Creatures who, frozen in time, all strained to reach an owl at the apex of the sculpture. The owl's three eyes inlaid with twinkling jewels and wings outstretched.

The snake journeyed up the fountain before disappearing into the gaping mouth of the owl, reflected in the inky waters below.

Aisling shivered. The owl's opalescent orbs gleamed as if studying her, the sensation of meeting another for the first time and forming a first impression. An eeriness capable enough to spin Aisling on her heels and shuffle her out of the room. But as she turned, she collided face to face with another.

Two emerald eyes glared down at her. Aisling staggered back in surprise, nearly losing her footing. The magpies knocked into one another in their attempts to flee.

"A princess and a thief," the Fae King said, already closing the distance between them. "Who taught you to bypass our locks?"

Aisling shook her head. If he was referencing the arched threshold from the corridor, it bore no lock she was aware of.

"The entrance was left open," Aisling managed, forcing herself to meet his glare, as potent as touch itself and as intimate as a stroke of the finger on bare skin. That was what his gaze felt like. Deeply personal. Like the heat of the sun warming and dying the canopies of the forest gold.

Unconvinced, he pushed on. "What is it you wish to take,

little thief?" His clouds of breath mingled with her own as a result of the cool, damp room.

Aisling swallowed, her mind clawing for an explanation. For this was the first time the Fae King's voice was not the soft ripple of milk, cream, or silk it usually embodied. It was sharper now. A sonorous growl that chilled Aisling's core.

"I took to exploring the castle and grew lost," she lied. Aisling wasn't certain why she'd refused to divulge her experience with the small serpent. The way it guided her to this very room and vanished into the mouth of the owl frozen midflight behind them.

Lir considered her. His Otherworldly features reminded Aisling who stood before her now: he, the muse of the nightmarish legends that haunted her kind.

"You should already be at the *Snaidhm*." At last, he released her from the sage grip his eyes held and ambled past her.

He'd stripped himself of his armor, instead donning finely tailored leathers, gilded chains around his neck, and the twin axes across his back, the very blade she'd pulled from the earth at their union. His hair was damp, and the blood she'd witnessed from her terrace cleaned up as though it had never been.

"Very well, m'Lord," she said, bowing her head. She took this moment as an excuse to leave as swiftly as she was capable and lengthen the distance between herself and this wicked lord.

But the Fae King stopped her in her tracks, "I'd prefer you call me by my name."

Aisling turned to find him standing beside the fountain, dipping his fingers in its murky depths. Seemingly satisfied with her excuse for finding her there at all.

The mortal queen nodded silently in response, held captive by his attention.

"Tell me, do names bear power in mortal tradition?"

Aisling watched the fountain waters slip between his fingers, hurrying back into the pool from which it came.

"Symbolically, yes. But, from what little I know of your religion, they do not enslave the one who gives it as they do in your culture."

Lir's eyes flashed with mischief.

"You believe yourself enslaved to me?"

"Would you prefer I call it imprisonment? Most marriages wouldn't seclude their brides to their rooms lest accompanied by another, never free to explore her new home unguarded or unwatched."

The corners of Lir's lips curled, the edge of his fangs glinting in the reflection of the owl's jeweled eyes. Aisling's stomach knotted, tightening the intangible cord that lie between them, a reminder of the bloodthirsty monster his beauty would have her believe he wasn't.

"Tonight, at the *Snaidhm*, do not be frightened," he continued, his voice a purr, rubbing against the shadows that clung to him, "For there will be moments where you question your safety amongst the Sidhe. But I implore you to never surrender to such fear. When danger abounds, understand it is powerless while in my presence. There is little in this realm or the next that isn't within my control."

Aisling, disoriented by the change in topic, struggled to regroup her thoughts. The magpies buzzing around her head, a mirror to what warred within her. After all, there wasn't a moment Aisling hadn't questioned her safety amongst the Aos Sí.

"A name given freely and another received in return is not to enslave but to bind. The Sidhe call this *ensorcellment*. I am as much linked to you as you are to me."

Aisling bundled her trembling hands into fists, hoping the terror, the uncertainty she felt now didn't betray her efforts to steel herself. If the Fae King was implying that she should trust him ... the thought was inconceivable.

"Come," the Fae King said, at last, shattering the momentary silence, "the *Snaidhm* awaits."

Aisling and Lir rode their stags as two sentries walked alongside them. Bear sentries whose names Aisling learned were Duibhin and Alastair, titles gifted to them by the fair folk after the creation of all things by the Forge. Guards tasked to protect the mortal queen, she surmised, from the rest of Annwyn. From they who wished her harm. From those too angry to care of treason or peace between the races. Aisling could feel their hatred. Feel it as if it were a tangible flock of hands, clawing at her skin.

Afternoon was quickly dissolving into evening, blanketing Annwyn in a feverish firelit glow. Aisling was beginning to realize that the fair folk were most alive at night, running barefoot atop the flagstones, swimming in the waters of the gorge nearly nude, and going about their strange chores.

Most, if not all, stopped what they were doing to watch the mortal queen pass. Their faces twisted with palpable disdain. Aisling fought the urge to shift on the saddle, to squirm beneath the heat of their regard. She wouldn't give them the satisfaction.

A large clearing sat a stroll's distance from Annwyn, lodged into the forest among its mighty trees. Trees that, as with all the forest thus far, seemed to bear a life of their own. As though they studied her. Waiting to see what she would do next. Whispering to one another the moment she came into view.

Within the approaching glade, torchlight gleamed, tents were erected, music flavored the air and flags billowed. The smell of broiled meat, freshly baked bread, and sparkling wines wafting in the breeze. Aisling could spot, even from a distance, the dream-like dances of the fair folk, twirling barefoot in the grass. It was a vision. a hazy, stupor of a celebration, a pyretic gathering where the fireflies lit the clearing with hundreds of small bulbs of light, floating aimlessly.

Aisling, the Fae King, and the guards slowed their stags' gait, indulging the view of the *Snaidhm* beneath an overcast sky. A great, colorful festival filled to the brim with bipedal beasts, fae nobles and commoners alike, intermingling casually, an oddity in Aisling's mortal eyes. Such neglect for class and the hierarchy such classes naturally demanded was strange. Aisling didn't believe she'd ever spoken to a commoner other than her chambermaid. The more Aisling saw of these fae people, the more she understood how different her life had been from the one she was embarking on now. Her mortal life—the life pent up between Tilren's walls, the one she wept over when she believed none to hear or see her tears—felt like a distant dream as she stepped into another.

To one side of the glade, stood an arena whose seats were already being filled. A stadium Aisling had only ever witnessed be used for jousting or sparring. One where spectators lined the seats to behold whatever competition took place at its center.

This was no ball, Aisling realized.

The Aos Sí parted as Aisling and the Fae King entered the clearing. Aisling heard their whispers, the snickering from the fae people around them, but even when she was in ear-shot, she couldn't understand their fae tongue. *Rún*, Gilrel had called it.

Duibhin and Alastair guided Aisling towards a large, raised box, positioned for perfect viewing of whatever spectacle they'd be witnessing at the center of the arena. Aisling sat in the throne to the left of a much larger, empty seat. A space clearly designed for the King of Annwyn and the Greenwood.

And to Aisling's surprise, Gilrel was already making herself comfortable in the little chair beside Aisling's, politely nodding to the other nobles placed in the box.

As soon as her eyes fell upon the mortal queen, her muzzle

wrinkled, eyes narrowing. Aisling knew the pine marten would be more than vexed she'd run off into the castle on her own, but it had hardly deterred the mortal queen. Let the furry chambermaid stew in her own anger, Aisling thought to herself.

Twelve or so other lords and ladies occupied their box, accompanied by their animal servants, sitting either behind or beside the thrones designed for the king and queen. They wore gold, ivory, crimson, violets, emerald greens, and vibrant oranges, tunics and gowns embroidered with gleaming threads of every hue, lace so delicate Aisling believed it would tear at the slightest of stretches, and chiffon so resplendent perhaps it would dissolve in water. Fluttering wings mirrored the colorful palettes of their dress. But despite their breathtaking attire, it was clear from their palpable disdain that none were too eager for a mortal, an enemy, to sit at the highest position of honor only second to the king.

Aisling and Lir took their seats, the Fae King quietly, arrogantly soaking in his subjects' praise. He smiled at her. A radiant beam that threatened to ignite the world around them. But Aisling knew it wasn't truly intended for her. It was for them. For his people. For riding into Annwyn on his stag and even his grin now was a performance for all the Aos Sí to behold. So that they knew the mortals and the fair folk were no longer at war. So that they felt safe. Aisling knew this. Understood this even as Lir took the mortal queen's hand and kissed the back of her palm. As cold as a river glazing the rocks in a woodland stream.

Chills ran down Aisling's spine as she willed herself to stay put. To not snatch back her hand and rub away his touch.

Once the Aos Sí decided where and how they'd like to enjoy their viewing, squirming amongst one another in the common rafters, Galad stood from where he sat on Lir's right-hand side and cleared his throat.

"*Is lócáid an-áragh minniu!*" the knight shouted, capturing the animals and Aos Sí's attention. Graciously, Gilrel translated Galad's words for Aisling:

"Today, we celebrate a joyous occasion! The Sidhe welcomes our new queen, and we pray to the Gods for the arrival of an heir!" The fair folk roared, stomping their feet, pounding their fists, and shaking the rafters, the air igniting with their excitement.

"The union of our beloved king is not only the marriage between two *caeras* but the union between the Sidhe and the mortals. An end to centuries of rivalry, bloodshed, and the spite with which mortals have haunted our kind."

At that, Aisling whipped her attention to Galad. The rest of his speech was blurred by the anger smoking in her gut. Had he truly claimed it was the mortals that reaped violence on the Aos Sí? Haunted *their* race? As if the mortals held a single flame against the wildfire that was the fair folk.

Aisling bit her bottom lip. She wouldn't stand for any disrespect against her kind even if she were surrounded by these creatures, a race she would do well not to forget were the devils her father had claimed them to be.

"*A member of the Aos Sí could devour a little girl like you whole if it so desired,*" Nemed had told her once after she'd been caught trying to escape Tilren's city gates, "*An Aos Sí wouldn't hesitate to skin you alive and bathe in your blood if it had the opportunity.*"

The Aos Sí cheered again, inevitably shaking the entire arena with their excited fervor. Galad finished his speech and took his place on Lir's right-hand side once more.

From the corner of her eye, Aisling was aware of Lir's persistent gaze. His need to study her, to watch her, exploring every curve of her expression.

"Does it make you angry?" Lir whispered, tipping his head down to address her. Even seated beside one another he was vastly taller.

"I am already angry. It simply awakens such rage." Aisling

simmered, scowling at the Fae King behind her thick lashes. These words were unwise, dangerous, lest Aisling have a death wish. But, in that moment, the mortal queen cared not for her own neck.

"I could have you hanged for such confessions," he said coolly, smiling like a wolf grins at a cornered hare.

"Not eaten? Disemboweled? Roasted over a spit? Or do you prefer mortal flesh raw?" Aisling quipped, her voice raising above a whisper. He was a savage after all.

Lir laughed darkly, leaning closer till they were nearly nose to nose, "I prefer to toy with my mortal princesses first: chase them, play with them, and only then are they satisfying to eat."

The Fae King bit the air between them. Aisling willed herself still. She couldn't flinch. Couldn't expose the rapid beating of her heart, her pulse drumming around her throat. It was an empty threat she knew, his own desire to watch her squirm. To intimidate her. To ridicule her. She wouldn't give him the satisfaction.

"And you?" Aisling challenged in return, lifting her chin and steeling herself before this barbarian king, "what makes the King of the Greenwood angry?" Her voice was steadier than she anticipated.

Lir ran his fingers through his tousle of hair, avoiding the braided strands. His hair was shorter than most of the Aos Sí, curling around his ears thanks to the sheets of mist gathering in the clearing.

"You," he said. There was a tightness in his voice, repressed, tempered anger. Aisling knew the tone well enough. "Everything about your kind, your blood, your bones, your spirits." His eyes flickered towards the neckline of Aisling's gown before flitting back to meet her eyes. "Your hearts."

Aisling swallowed the stone in her throat. But where she thought her anger would grow, swell, and expand to its full capacity, she found herself unable to unlatch her eyes from his own. Ancient jadeite eyes that struck fear in her. A fear she wished to explore. To know. To master. After all, he had more reason than most to despise mankind; he was ultimately responsible for the casualties dealt by the mortals after centuries of warring. A king was always responsible for the death of his men even if by the hands of the enemy. Even Nemed couldn't claim to have experienced such loss in his comparatively short lifespan. Aisling didn't blame him for his prejudice against her kind, nor did she expect him to blame her for hers.

"You are all the same," Lir added. Aisling considered him, the press of his lips where his fangs scraped on occasion. The way his brows shadowed those emerald eyes. The posture of his head, his hands lazily settled on either arm of his throne.

"He is the worst of them, ruthless, merciless, no more than a beast driven by hunger, need, and power. But, unlike the wolf, he is insatiable. Never let your guard down around him, Aisling. Never give him an opportunity to choose between you and what he covets."

Abruptly, silence befell the arena and Aisling held her breath, unsure what to expect from these fae customs. But it was also a relief, a reprieve from that tangled, tightened cord pulling her away and towards Lir simultaneously.

To her surprise, thirty or so fae females swept into the arena. Dressed in pale lilac, pink, tea, and cerulean gowns—one made of owl's feathers, another thistle, and another snap pea—they arranged themselves at the center of the grass. Sparkling circlets framed their brows, cinching clouds of wild, loose curls where berries clung to each ringlet. And from their backs sprouted wings. Bewitching, translucent wings like spring beetles.

Music arrived with the rain, showering the festival with a sound so lovely, Aisling's heart was struck with an ache-like longing. And despite the cloudburst, the torches were not extinguished, the fae people did not shrink away nor flee, and the women at the center of the arena began their dance.

Aisling forgot about the cloudburst that soaked through her gown, the chill of the Northern air, the hordes of fair folk surrounding her.

"This is an ancient fertility ceremony," Gilrel whispered into Aisling's ear, startling the mortal queen and tickling her ears with her whiskers, "they've summoned the rain to bless your womb." At that, Aisling looked to the groaning sky above, flashing with lightning. The crack of each bolt was as much a part of the music as the beat of the drum or the blow of the flute.

Aisling had danced in the rain once before. Alongside Dagfin, she'd climbed the stairwells of her fortress in Tilren. Fergus was the first to find them, reprimanding them for their carelessness, their stupidity. But the exhilaration was an opiate Aisling struggled to resist.

The dancers took one another's hands and formed a circle. Like this, they twirled, rotating in an endless loop around the arena, never dizzying, never falling.

And as they moved the earth began to shift. The high risen flags quivered, the stands shook, the tents flapped, the forest moaned, as something at the center of the arena began to ... grow. Aisling leaned forward, squinting and rubbing her eyes to ensure she wasn't hallucinating. Wasn't dreaming up the leaves, the bubbling flowers, the thorns rising from the earth in great, miraculous hedges. Large bushes bejeweled with roses perfuming the arena till the badgers sneezed and the bumblebees hummed excitedly.

Aisling inhaled sharply. This was impossible and yet here it all was. This magic, this forbidden, ages-old magic mortals considered wicked and perverse and wrong. All of it was more breathtaking than Aisling could've ever imagined. For within the span of a few heartbeats, the hedges had grown into a labyrinth at the center of the arena.

Just as abruptly as the dance, the music, and the rain had begun, it stopped. Aisling watched the fae performers curtsy before the noble box and take their leave. Her eyes followed them as they dissolved into the crowds of spectators praising the performance. It was sorcery. All of it. Everything. Everyone here. And Aisling should hate such sorcery. Despise it as much as Nemed.

As the mortal queen whispered in her handmaiden's ear, Aisling was caught off guard by various fae entering the arena. But these were unlike the dancers who'd just performed. No, these female Aos Sí were strapped in fae armor, leather, and more weapons than Aisling could count. They stood with lethal poise. Their immaculate sheets of armor and twinkling chainmail, flattering their Otherworldly forms. One among them, more impressive than the rest.

She was a vision: her hair the hue of autumn's climax, framing her delicate face, a face embellished with suns for eyes and full, rounded lips. Drenched by the recent rain, she maintained her mighty glamor, her feminine strength, and grace-like ease. Even her fae markings wove airily around her long, distinguished form, like a flower's roots or trails of a passing comet. But her regard was cold if not cruel as she and the other fae ladies drew their weapons.

"That is Peitho," Gilrel whispered, following Aisling's line of sight. Peitho leaned into another lady's ear and gestured towards the private box. Both their feline eyes flicked towards the mortal queen before erupting into hushed chatter.

"Who is she?" Aisling asked, straightening her posture.

"She is a princess from one of the Sidhe territories in the Southern continents."

"Then why is she here? In the North?"

Gilrel hesitated, brushing invisible lint from her furry shoulder before replying, "she was betrothed to Lir, *mo Lúra*."

Against her own volition, Aisling's eyes spun to the Fae King, waiting patiently for whatever these female warriors would eventually perform. It hadn't occurred to Aisling that just as she'd been intended for Dagfin, Lir had been intended for another as well.

"Then it was my union that interrupted their affairs?" Aisling continued as three, enormous bipedal hedgehogs took their places before the fae females, one in front of the other. Oranges delicately balanced between each of their ears. Peitho tested the weight of her sword in her hands, swinging her arms in preparation for whatever was to take place.

"Aye," Gilrel nodded "It is my understanding that once your father suggested a union, the first of the mortal kings on any continent to offer such a treaty, there were many councils held over whether the Sidhe would agree to such an arrangement and if they did, which of the six Sidhe kings would volunteer. The risks were great for if the king and the mortal bride were not *caera*, beheading her would only exacerbate the feud between mortal and Sidhe."

"And Lir volunteered?" Aisling asked.

"Once the Sidhe had agreed to take the risk, to satiate your father's demands, it only made sense that the Northern mortal princess would unite with the Northern Sidhe king." Gilrel clapped for the warriors on cue.

"But if you claim myself and Lir to be *caera*, how could Lir have ever married Peitho?"

"Centuries ago, they were raised together. Peitho's father, the fourth Sidhe king, believed them *caera*. Most of us did. Not to mention, the Sidhe have inter-political strife of their own to sort through. Their marriage would've been a unique alliance all its own. One Peitho was desperate to seal," Gilrel said.

Peitho laughed at one of her comrade's comments, tossing her glossy locks over her shoulder. Strands braided through with orange poppies and yellow buttercups.

"Can Sidhe have more than one *caera* in a lifetime?" Aisling asked.

"Some claim it to be possible. Others do not. However, I suppose those who insisted the latter have already been proven wrong." Gilrel sat up straighter, a smile spreading across her features.

"Watch, *mo Lúra*; you'll want to prepare yourself for what's to come next."

Aisling turned her attention back towards the arena, avoiding Peitho's daggers for eyes, burning into her flesh. But it was not Aisling that Peitho watched now. It was Lir she regarded from the corner of her eye as she pulled back her blade and launched it towards the hedgehogs. Her arms and legs rippled with muscle, visible even beneath her leather garments.

The tip of the sword flew like a sparrow, straight and true, puncturing the three oranges sitting atop the beasts' heads. Juice exploding and spraying the nearest spectators with its citrus blood.

Aisling swallowed. She'd never witnessed such skill before. Deadly skills she'd practiced all her life yet never bore the talent to perform.

Each of Lir's knights stepped onto the field, positioning themselves to one side of the great labyrinth the dancers summoned. They wore their armor, strapped with blades and shields, and contraptions Aisling knew not the name of, raising their arms and baiting the crowd to cheer more wildly.

"What are they doing?" Aisling eyed them warily, familiar with their many faces after having journeyed with them once before.

Gilrel's muzzle stretched into a thin smile.

"It's tradition. The male *caera* will fight to prove he is worthy of you and the strongest among his circle."

Aisling blanched for there were twenty nights to one. The task appeared impossible. But before she could respond, Lir was standing, the fair folk bursting into wild praises, chanting the king's name to the beat of their stomps as he held out his hand, gesturing for Aisling to take it.

Chapter VIII

AISLING RELUCTANTLY TOOK THE FAE LORD'S hand. After all, what choice did she have?

A knight, one Aisling had not yet met, stepped into the center of the field, before the great labyrinth, to announce each of his comrades. He raised their arms above their heads and the spectators clamored with increased fervor. Yevhen, Aedh, Tyr, Hagre, Einri, Rian, Galad, and Cathan were among the names Aisling remembered. All sported fae braids, shaved sides, or beading in their hair. Scars speckled their bare skin, a testament to centuries of warring and protecting their kind.

Next came Lir's introduction to which the *Snaidhm* exploded with their chants. Already he guided her down the staircase of their private box and onto the arena's pitch.

"*Damh Bán!*" The crowds repeated, the sheer volume of their shouts vibrating through the box, the arena, the earth beneath them, surely waking every worm and rodent if any still slept down below.

"What are they saying?" Aisling asked the Fae King. The rest of Lir's knights formed a line to the right of the hedge, but the Fae King led Aisling to the left where a single pillar stood.

"It means the 'White Stag,'" he explained, "a moniker given to the King of Annwyn and the Greenwood, protector of the feywilds."

She stumbled clumsily after the Fae King, her skirts absorbing the mud dampening the field.

"And what becomes of the male *caera* who fails to outdo all these competitors?"

"I don't fail." Lir flicked his eyes towards her, measuring her response. But Aisling was unamused, becoming increasingly suspicious of what was unraveling around her.

Lir brought her to an abrupt stop, halting before the wooden pillar nailed into the ground, glaring down the rosy labyrinth towering before her.

"Do you trust me?" Lir asked, unable to wick away the devilry curling the corners of his lips. The question echoed in her mind as Aisling spotted a cage lifted above the fae crowds' heads by four black boars approaching the arena steadily from the Western entrance. Made of carved wood and dark metals, its door was bolted shut lest the mad creature within, shaking the bars of its prison, be set free.

Aisling's tongue turned to ash as she beheld the—the *thing*. Her palms were wet with sweat as she backed into the pillar.

The Fae King followed the mortal queen's line of sight, landing on the approaching cage. A cage rattling with the fury of its captive.

"Is my trust contingent on anything to do with that?" Aisling asked, nodding her head in the cage's direction.

"That, princess, is a *trow*."

Aisling mouthed its name breathlessly, unable to look away from the nightmarish fiend floating nearer and nearer. The smell of it drowning out the freshness of the rain, the roses, replacing such perfume with a putrid stench. But the boars carrying the creature appeared unfazed by its attempts to break free from its prison, its grotesque appearance, or its unbearable smell. So, the bestial sentinels placed the enormous cage on the opposing side of the labyrinth where Aisling could no longer see. A few yards from where Lir's knights readied themselves.

"A species of Unseelie. Wicked creatures with insatiable appetites despite their short stature. Dull, square teeth that ensure their prey are all the more reluctant to be caught. Usually, rabbits or mice or even foxes but today, I'm sure this trow is just ravenous enough for a princess." Lir's smile widened, boasting his pearly collection of teeth and fangs.

"You intend to feed me to it?!" Aisling managed to spit out, willing her teeth to stop their chattering. What was this—this *thing*? This aberration of all that was good and right. Did Nemed know this creature existed? Did the mortals? Had Aisling forgotten some vital teaching she was intended to remember? No, no, no. She would've remembered tales of this.

There was nowhere to run, to hide, to escape. Not when she was surrounded by hordes of Aos Sí. Hordes who hollered around the arena, laughing, cheering, dancing, strumming their fiddles, and beating their drums.

"You wound me, princess," Lir feigned offense. "So long as I'm near, the trow won't manage a taste much less a bite. I'm a jealous king," he teased. But the Fae King's words did little to reassure her for as soon as Aisling spotted the tether in his hands, she staggered back. A rope to bind her.

Aisling knew this instinct to run was fruitless. Lir was quicker, stronger, imbued with a magic Aisling knew not the limits of.

"My knights tell me to tether you to this column lest you attempt and escape," he said, unhooking a single axe from his back.

"And you? What does the *Damh Bán* say?"

Lir considered her for a moment, their audience growing more impatient by the moment.

"I believe trust a more formidable tether than a rope." He threw the rope into the mud where it lay like a snake, pelted by the rain.

"I will not stand here as bait," Aisling growled, balling her hands into fists.

"The choice is yours," Lir said, "run from what frightens you or challenge yourself to be a part of our world. Either way, no harm will befall you so long as I'm concerned."

The audience began banging their fists and paws against the rafters, eager for the tournament to begin. Their animal faces, their fair folk expressions howling into the magic imbued winds of Annwyn. Fury coiled inside Aisling's belly, a fire burning through her gut and rising with every chant.

"If there is a Forge, may you all burn in it," Aisling hissed, planting her feet in the mud. She'd stand and wait for Lir to finish his fair folk games. For, a part of what Lir said was true: she'd been sent here to be a part of this world. Had sacrificed all she'd known, her clann, her brothers, Dagfin, to join a world she knew was bloodthirsty long before the union. Nevertheless, her bones burned with rage and terror alike.

Lir smiled triumphantly, sage eyes flashing beneath the overcast sky.

"And you allow it a head start?" Aisling's voice cracked, tears pricking the backs of her eyes. For indeed, Aisling, judging by where the cage had disappeared behind the lofty labyrinth of hedge and rose and leaf, could assume they'd given the trow an advantage. An opportunity to race ahead of the knights.

"The trow is blind. Its only way of navigating the labyrinth is to sniff you out."

Aisling glared at the trow across the field, paling at the sight of the beast.

"Fret not, princess," Lir continued, "you're braver than you give yourself credit for."

The Fae King watched Aisling, lingering before at last, lengthening the distance between himself and Aisling. She was left alone beside the column, facing down the trow now rattling the cage with increased fervor the longer it smelled the mortal queen. Knew she was just a maze away, helpless. Unable to run quickly enough or fight hard enough.

Aisling cringed at the memory of the fiend already burned into her mind's eye: it was short in comparison to the Aos Sí, viciously ugly with two beady, pale eyes, a grossly wide, gummy smile shadowed by an even larger, drooping nose. Its legs were thin and boney, knobby knees knocking against one another as it thrust its fat body against the bars of the prison, reaching its rough, large, spidery fingers towards Aisling. Its sharpened, serrated nails clawing at the air.

This. This was the creature inspired by the mortal tales of the Aos Sí, this nightmare born in the flesh.

Unseelie.

"By the Forge," Aisling whispered beneath her breath, low enough so only she could hear. She didn't know why she said it. There were no Gods and certainly the ones the fair folk believed in wouldn't save her now. No, she was helpless. Not strong enough. Agile enough. Skilled enough to break loose or escape such fate. Sold first by her family then doomed by her captors. Forsaken to glare down this abomination as it made its way to devour her.

Her only salvation, he who she loathed the most.

Once the hollow horn was blown, Aedh was the first knight to spring forward, racing towards Aisling with the others on his heels. In the same moment, the trow was released, the cage breaking apart and the creature staggering forward on his slender legs, panting with insatiable lust for the princess. The trow and each knight following Aedh, sinking into the maze where Aisling could no longer see.

Aisling sucked in a breath and held it, the roar of every spectator thrumming through her and rendering her numb.

"Mine, mine, mine," she heard the trow growl amidst the hedges.

The Aos Sí jeered, leaning over the banisters and shaking their fists as mud splattered across their ethereal faces. Badgers carved the railing with their claws, wolves standing on their hind legs as they howled into the air. Barbarians. Brutish savages. Excited at the prospect of Aisling alone at one end of the arena, staring down the hobbling trow as it emerged from the labyrinth first.

And with every painful, passing moment the beast hobbled closer and closer, her blood and flesh its only guide. The reality of the trow biting into Aisling becoming more real, chewing on her skin a more tangible future.

And although short in comparison to the Aos Sí, the trow was the same height as Aisling. Its bizarre proportions on full display: its head thrice as large, its abdomen short and wide, while its legs stood tall and thin on wobbly knees.

Aisling opened her mouth to scream but found the sound caught in her throat. Dread seeping into her bones. Had she been more skilled in combat, prepared to stare down her foes or defend herself, perhaps she wouldn't feel as helpless as she did now. Aisling had never felt more pathetic. More *furious*.

The trow closed the final distance between itself and Aisling, sniffing both her sweat and terror with deep, exaggerated inhales. Aisling hiked up her shoulders, as she braced for what was to come next.

"Sweet, sweet, sweet," the creature rasped, licking its teeth and laughing wickedly to itself. Inhaling so deeply Aisling believed it might fall backwards. So, the mortal queen allowed her rage to guide her. She reached for her dagger, lodged in her corset, and drew it the way she'd imagined Starn would, waving it before the trow. A gesture that inspired a slew of gasps from her audience.

"Naughty, naughty, naughty," it said, stepping back and narrowing its eyes before it lunged for Aisling once more. Now

Aisling did manage to scream, her voice rising above the roar of the spectators and perhaps all of Rinn Dúin.

Just as the trow's teeth were to skim the naked flesh on Aisling's neck, an arrow struck its enormous ear, the shaft of the reed protruding from either side. The trow screeched, a sound that nearly ripped Aisling's eardrums in two. And from behind the beast, Rian emerged from the labyrinth, bow in hand.

Aisling's heart leapt at the sight of him, of anyone. It mattered not that Lir was nowhere to be seen. But anger still pooled within her chest that she need wait upon anyone at all. That Lir had placed her here and requested her trust.

The trow tore the arrow from its ear, splattering Aisling's face.

Rian raced forward, aiming the bow to strike again. He placed the arrow upon the hard edge of the bow's rest, pulling back on the string till it could no longer budge. And just before his fingers released the reed, an axe spun through the air like a winding sparrow, slicing the string and destroying the bow. The arrow struck the trow's shoulder instead of its heart.

Aisling's stomach dropped the moment she saw Lir. The king raised his second axe and swung for Rian. The trow grinned, delighted that the king and his knight battled blade to blade behind him. For Rian's two shots had merely deterred the beast, not killed it.

Tears ran down Aisling's cheeks, interrupting the hot, smelly lines of Unseelie blood speckling her face. Watching the trow rip the second arrow from its shoulder. And why she did not run, she didn't know.

"By the Forge," Aisling cursed beneath her breath again, wrenching her eyes shut till darkness enveloped her. For the darkness would be what she encountered next. The nothing after death. Deepest shadow and nothing more. But where she thought, upon closing her violet eyes, she'd be alone in the darkest pits of her thoughts before death... she wasn't.

There was something else. A creature that hadn't been there before. Something hiding in the abyss of herself. In the chasm of her soul. A sentient being that looked back at Aisling with a curiosity that matched her own.

The trow shrieked once more, forcing Aisling out of her reverie. The mortal queen opened her eyes in time to witness ropes swinging around the thing's arms, yanking it back and away from the mortal queen. Aisling gasped, her chest rising and falling violently as she beheld the trow squirming on the floor, tangled in those thick, dark, ropes. No—not ropes. Vines. Roots risen from the earth like serpents, snapping at the demon with sentient rage. The trow shrieked an unearthly bellow, biting at the ramblers, digging its nails into their thick flesh. But where one split, two more grew. The roots coiling around the trow, a great leaf-ridden squid pinning the monster to the mud.

The trow did its best to set itself free but it was futile. And now, what captured Aisling's attention most of all was what stood behind the tangle of vine and trow.

Lir.

Painted in blood and mud, he watched the trow coolly, eyes as still and dark as the shadowed depths of the forest, where no man dared wander, lest he sing death to his door. A monstrous glint illuminating those orbs. And behind him, lay Rian, bloodied and defeated, falling in and out of consciousness atop the emerald grass.

The *Snaidhm* erupted with excitement. Lir lifted his eyes to Aisling. The only knight to defeat both their comrades and the trow alike in order to reach Aisling. A competition, the mortal queen now realized, between monsters. For he who saved her from the trow was no better than this foul beast screeching for its breath and pinned to the earth. Perhaps worse. Much, much worse, Aisling recognized to her own dread. So now, after all was said and done, she realized she could indeed trust Lir, entrust the Fae King to be the nightmarish legend for which he was renowned.

"*Damh Bán!*" They chanted, their voices rising into the rain-heavy clouds above, the spidering of lightning illuminating Lir's lovely, lethal expression.

Aisling believed the entire forest and all of Annwyn to tremble beneath the spectator's cheers, their stomping, the shaking of the rafters, tents, and seats around them.

Then the Aos Sí's voices melted from "*Damh Bán!*" to "*Krie grae!*" Their shouts grew louder, matching the beat of their fists against the railing.

Aisling bore little idea what the audience screamed, flicking her attention to Gilrel out of instinct. The one who answered her questions, gave her guidance. But she too beamed amongst the spectators, yelling alongside the rest and leaning her furry form over the banister.

Aisling bit her bottom lip, redirecting her attention back to Lir.

Not bothering to wipe the blood from his face, he approached steadily. That invisible cord between them snapping to attention and tugging at her chest.

But despite the mud and sweat and crimson that washed over his lean muscles, his fae markings shone beneath, wrapping around his corded arms and abdomen. Aisling did her best to keep his gaze; there was no reason for her to wilt as he shortened the distance between them. The smell of him, of the forest, enveloping her, drowning out the outside world like a sweet drug.

Lir ran his blood-soaked fingers through his hair, tipping his chin down to meet her violet orbs.

"You see?" Lir unlatched one of his axes from his back, swinging it by the haft artfully. "Nothing to fear."

"Your arrogance precedes your success. The creature still lives," Aisling snarled, her fear of the Fae King only rivalled by her rage, a rage that could set fire to this arena. Take back what had been taken from her. For indeed, the trow still struggled to free itself from his magic.

"*Krie grae!*" the Aos Sí called, lifting the Fae King's attention to the pit of demons surrounding them. Watching their king's and her every interaction.

Lir flashed his fangs, amused. "They want you to kiss me."

Aisling blinked. She searched for the words that caught in her throat. Heat rising to her blood-soaked cheeks. Rage, horror, embarrassment mixing in the pit of her stomach till she believed she might be rendered ill there and then.

"But don't get too excited just yet, princess," Lir said, flipping the axe between his fingers, having understood the horror on her expression, "you're right; the game isn't yet finished." He released Aisling's arm, handing her the hilt of his axe.

Aisling glared at the weapon. That knotted haft slick with blood and rain and mud, his tattooed fingers still coiled around it. She'd touched this axe before. The night of her wedding. Hadn't been able to lift it on her own. Not without his help.

Lir tilted his head towards the trow, still squealing like an angry pig in the mud.

"Kill it," he commanded. His voice was cold. Steeped in shadows of blackest tar. Sending shivers down her spine as shock rippled through her.

"I—" Aisling managed, her mind racing quicker than she could speak. "I can't."

"You can," he commanded, his grin fading from his lips but remaining in his jadeite eyes. "And you will. Its intention was to tear you limb from limb," Lir interjected, his voice the only coherent sound amidst the discord, "that's what it means to survive outside your iron walls."

Aisling took a cautious step back.

"Or do you prefer when someone else kills for you?" He stepped towards her.

Aisling's eyes darted towards the trow. Its pale, slimy skin now painted purple, it strained against the roots holding it in place. The trow squealed more loudly and the audience grew impatient.

Aisling couldn't deny she wanted the thing dead. A dark creature within herself delighted at the sight of the beast in pain. Had looked forward to Lir slaying the blight. But Aisling didn't have it in her. She was no warrior. No soldier. No king.

Aisling tightened her fists at her sides, grinding her jaw harder.

"You're wicked," Aisling spat but Lir only exhaled a laugh.

"Do you claim to stand against such beastly sins when practiced by your own kind then?" Lir challenged, his expression darkening the longer he spoke, "or did you defend the Sidhe when your father slaughtered our villages? You see there are none who are fully wicked nor fully pure. Only those hungry enough to be powerful."

"You describe the world as if they are nothing more than beasts."

"Most of us are."

Aisling shook her head, balling her hands into fists, a rejection of the blade Lir still held before her, eager for her to take.

Lir's expression grew smugger, narrowing his eyes. "We are all slaves to desire. And right now, princess, all that separates you from that trow's desire is me," he grinned like a wolf, deadly and handsome all at once. "You can change that," he continued, "you can take what he wished to take from you. Take and not be taken from."

Aisling's eyes flicked towards the axe before her, glinting marvelously. Encouraging her to come closer. To touch its haft. Wrap her fingers around the wooden hilt, the braided designs. To paint her hands in red.

"The choice is yours: predator or prey," the Fae King purred.

Aisling met Lir's eyes, careful not to lose herself in their

Connemara glen. Holding onto the edge of reality as she glared deeply into those murderous depths, her mind spun faster with each passing moment. Her stomach twisting more tightly. Her knees wobbling, about to buckle beneath the pressure. The screams of the surrounding audience vibrated through her bones.

"You wish to corrupt me," Aisling surmised in barely a whisper.

His smile widened then, those fangs winking back at Aisling. An expression that seized her heart, dared her to look away. The cord between them groaning, nearly snapping.

"No," he said, "I wish to show you, you already are."

Aisling couldn't halt the shivering of her shoulders in the cold. Couldn't help but to swallow the stone lodged in her throat. For by now, she could no longer feel her legs. Her hands. She was numb, adrenaline coursing through her veins. And perhaps it was adrenaline that unfolded her fists. Perhaps it was adrenaline that raised her arm and gripped the haft of the axe, raising it with both hands with all her might. Perhaps it was adrenaline that turned her towards the helpless trow and raised the axe above her head. Perhaps it was adrenaline that made her enjoy what she was to do next.

Chapter IX

AFTERNOON BLED INTO EVENING. ONLY THE moon and the stars and the firelight illuminated the night, a night that seemed to never end. The Aos Sí had yet to exhaust their energy, dancing to rhythmic, feverish music till Aisling believed their feet bruised beyond recognition—perhaps if they were mortals this would be the case.

Resisting the smells of the feasts spilling over the dining tables beneath the tents, the mortal queen followed the engorged squirrel scampering over every plate. Aisling considered allowing herself to indulge in such delights with Gilrel as her guide. Some foods were more dangerous to humans than others, more likely to form an insatiable addiction amongst her mortal kind. But despite her insatiable appetite, anger fueled her, the memory of their games burned into her mind. And where Aisling believed she'd be scarred, tormented, traumatized by the act of slaying the trow, she was not. The strange sensation of the axe beheading the trow was indeed now ingrained in her mind. The immediate gratification of power she garnered from watching its life slip from its blind eyes. Sweet vengeance a lingering taste on her tongue.

And for the most part, the fair folk continued to avoid Aisling as she did them, watching her warily from a distance.

Aisling's slaying of the trow garnering her no approval from the Aos Sí.

As for Lir, all Annwyn was eager to catch a moment of his attention. He obliged, spinning around the *Snaidhm* effortlessly. He didn't rule from a distance as did Nemed. He ruled amongst them. So much so that, Aisling herself believed the respect of this bloodthirsty monarch's subjects to rival her father's own, their fear of their king to rival Nemed's.

"Have you tried the wine?" A female voice piped from across the width of the dining table. Aisling lifted her gaze to find one of the fae glaring back, her expression feline. Cornellian beetles lining her throat like precious gems and the crisp smell of autumn blooming in the air as she spoke. Peitho.

She'd peeled off her armor, instead, sporting a gown of sparkling ginger, honey, and marigold cobwebs.

"I've been told it's unwise." Aisling softened her tone, relaxing her shoulders despite the stress bundling each of her muscles. Such pain only worsened her fury for the fair folk. Her resentment a bitter fog circling her every conscious thought.

"For mortals, it is indeed," Peitho purred. Aisling made to walk away, to continue her perusal of the feast but Peitho matched her pace, walking parallel to the mortal queen.

"Forgive my manners, *mo Lúra*," the fae princess persisted, "I am Peitho, Princess of Niltaor, a southern Sidhe territory. Have you heard of it?"

"I'm familiar," Aisling said, ignoring the proficiency with which Peitho spoke her tongue.

"It's a pleasure to at last make your acquaintance, *mo Lúra*. For months we've anticipated your arrival. How are you faring? Your display during the tournament today was quite entertaining."

Aisling bit the inside of her cheek. For although she'd successfully beheaded the trow with Lir's axe, her wielding of

Iarbonel's dagger was lackluster at best. Especially when compared to the warrior beside her.

"I'm doing well. Thank you," Aisling replied, glancing over her shoulder to ensure Gilrel was still following closely behind. And indeed, the marten trailed the train of her gown, her tail sweeping the grass below.

"You must be quite frightened. I can only imagine what it must be like for you." Peitho plucked a grape from within a roasted pig's mouth, popping it into her mouth.

"I'm not afraid of your kind." It was a lie, but the queen would rather be fed to a trow than admit the fair folk frightened her more than Aisling understood, including Peitho.

"How brave of you, a mortal amongst all these Sidhe. If it were I, I'd be convinced death waited around every corner. Although, the longing for my home, my own kind, would far outweigh the fear."

"In that case, how fortunate for both our races that it is I who is married to Lir and not yourself," Aisling quipped, aware of the poison that laced her words. Peitho's smug expression wrinkled with annoyance before collecting itself once more.

"May I call upon you one of these days, *mo Lúra*?" Peitho asked, recovering the sweetness in her tone, "Many of the trooping females are simply dying to make your acquaintance and an afternoon together would be an honor."

Aisling hesitated. "'Trooping'?"

Peitho simpered, "Pardon, *mo Lúra*, despite your clear mortality, I've somehow managed to forget how little you know of our world. Much like the humans, the Sidhe are divided by class—what mankind may refer to as the 'aristocratic' class, we refer to as *trooping*."

Aisling swallowed her annoyance. She'd already known, had already witnessed a social hierarchy at work but the moniker was indeed useful.

Trooping, she repeated to herself.

"What do you have in mind?" Aisling asked, turning to face the princess once they'd arrived at the end of the dining table. Peitho towered over Aisling, appraising her like a Manx considers a rat.

"Many of the female Sidhe enjoy archery when our schedules allow for it. I'm aware mortals are far weaker, more *temporary*, so we'll be sure to lessen our enthusiasm in your presence, *mo Lúra*." Peitho tucked her silken mane of ribbons behind a pointed ear, studded with hoops of amber.

Unsolicited, the image of Rian's arrow puncturing the trow flashed violently across her mind's eye.

"I look forward to it," Aisling managed, offering her most polite smile. And this time, it wasn't a lie. For although her skills in combat were embarrassingly absent amongst her family and now the fair folk, she'd rather fall ill than refuse a challenge.

"Till then, *mo Lúra*." The princess at last curtsied before vanishing between the folds of fair folk.

"I'll pad your gowns more thickly before such an outing," Gilrel chimed once Peitho was out of earshot, "perhaps even a petticoat of chainmail will be appropriate."

Gilrel scampered closely behind Aisling's heels as the mortal queen aimlessly navigated through the *Snaidhm*. They weaved through the torchlight, through a sea of gowns made of petals, weeds, animal furs, and feathers, inhaling the cool evening air, air steeped in spells, enchantments, and charms. For the fair folk smoked their pipes, puffing wispy clouds that spun overhead in the shape of winged serpents, screaming mortals, and dancing toads. Smoke that smelled of overripe fruit and syrup. Flyaway bubbles found Aisling's nose and drifted inside.

Aisling had long since tossed off her slippers, thrilled by the texture of the slick grass beneath the soles of her feet.

The queen had little idea what hour it was, only that sleep was a distant dream. She may not have had the stamina of the Aos Sí, but this world was undoubtedly intoxicating. Adrenaline fueled her since her wedding night, yet to run dry. Propelled by the sensation of the axe's blade slipping through the trow's neck, haunting the hollowed realm of her most reluctant yet persistent memories. A phantom winding through the fair folk and their animal friends who danced as if the morning would never arrive, gulping the night like a bottomless chalice of champagne. A spirit bubbling with starlight.

"I wish to be alone," Aisling told the marten. This was a lie. For while half of Aisling longed to be with her family: Starn, Iarbonel, Annind, Fergus, Dagfin; the other part craved absolution, to dissolve into the masses till all that plagued the shadows of her mind vanished like nightmares come dawn.

"It's my honor to accompany you, *mo Lúra*," Gilrel said, longingly witnessing the beginnings of a group dance forming at the center of the *Snaidhm*. Fair folk hand in paw with their animal companions. But Aisling knew it was no honor, rather a duty the marten was obliged to uphold, ensuring Aisling didn't go off exploring as she'd done earlier that day inside Castle Annwyn.

"Go, Gilrel," Aisling encouraged. "I won't shatter from a few moments left alone. Nor should I wander too far while enwreathed by your world."

Gilrel studied the queen's expression, perhaps wondering if indeed the mortal wouldn't fall and break into a thousand irreparable pieces. At last, Gilrel curtsied enthusiastically, hardly capable of walking towards the commotion, small paws prepared to leap into the mischief that awaited.

And once Gilrel's furry form was safely out of sight, Aisling exhaled and relaxed her posture, wandering through the festivities both alone and surrounded by strangers. These predators could tear her limb from limb without hesitation. The very fiends who whittled her childhood dreams into terrors. Who now pared new frights: the image of the trow's head rolling away from its body frosting the joints between her bones. But now, as fate would cruelly have it, these fair folk were her people—by law, not blood. And she'd prefer to walk among them alone than perpetually chaperoned.

Hopefully and given time, the Aos Sí would come to respect Aisling's place in Annwyn. Yet the mortal queen bore no illusions they'd ever revere her as they did their Fae King. Fear her as they did Lir. And so, Aisling couldn't help but wonder what power, influence, had she sacrificed in marrying the Fae King instead of Dagfin?

Aisling tiptoed further into the *Snaidhm*, charmed by the steady beat of the drums. The lightning bugs floated above their heads to the melody of the song. The Aos Sí whirling wildly, moving with an elegance matched only by their ferocity. And not without guilt, Aisling believed this scandalous, sensual dance that transfixed the mortal queen beautiful. The smell of fermented strawberries rendered her dizzy. The kaleidoscope of color showered her, soaking her in a tune whose pace mirrored every lustrous star above. The rhythm was as hungry as it'd been when she'd slain the trow. When the Aos Sí chanted her name. Her skin was warming, as warm as the blood that'd so recently speckled her cheeks.

Aisling followed the music deeper into the hordes. Brushing past pelts, bare skin, silken gowns, and cotton tunics. Stepping on bare feet and paws and tails. She'd never been around so many people, let alone fair folk, in all her life. Unguarded and unwatched. Almost forgetting how many Aos Sí surrounded her. Neglecting that she was at the mercy of these barbarians. She'd never be safe again. Not fully. And the thought of trembling, shivering, perpetually frightened as she'd felt in the presence of the troll, made her angry. Made her want to behead the crown of fear till she was soaked in its black sap.

Aisling clumsily stepped to the tempo. Her movements were ungainly compared to the Aos Sí. Growing more and more engrossed by the purling incense around her, the splashing of wine at her feet, the smell of the fair folk, and their sweat as they twirled. Absorbed until she saw where Gilrel danced. Where a fox grabbed the handmaid's paws and spun her. Where the Aos Sí formed a large circle, the air thickening around them. As dense as syrup. The luminescent flowers humming more brightly. The stars grinning from their bed of black above.

It would be easy, simple, to join them. To leap into their circle and frolic alongside them. In fact, Aisling wanted to do nothing more than just that: to lose herself in the pounding of the sheep skins, the plucking of cords, the hollow breath of the flute, the voices of the Aos Sí singing louder and louder and louder. The glazed eyes of the trow strangling her memory, desperate to be remembered. So just for tonight, she'd forget her heart was made of fire and iron. Dance amongst these beasts. Spin until her feet were bruised and the image of the trow was lost to sweet oblivion. To forget her family and the ache the memory of them elicited. Forget Tilren. Forget she was mortal. Forget how powerless she was. Forget her fear. Forget how it felt to kill. A sensation that confused her. Made her mind tilt along with the dancers.

So, Aisling stepped forward, into the circle of Aos Sí.

Chapter X

A HAND WRAPPED AROUND AISLING'S WRIST. It pulled her back, spinning her towards her captor.

"Aren't there mortal tales of wolves that warn maidens not to wander alone?" A familiar voice said from nearby. Aisling leapt at the sight of him, clutching her chest.

Lir stood before her, his sleeves rolled to his elbows and his pants cuffed above his ankles. Even from where she stood Aisling could smell his cologne of pine, wet leaves, and woodland memories. Sacred, age-old oaks and ashes.

Haloed in firelight, he approached in smoke and the sensual rhythm of the music.

"This maiden wishes to join the wolves' dance," Aisling said, her stupor dampening her anger. Washing away the bitter taste of the day with tea sugars and winter spices. A dense, sparkling cloud muffling every sober thought.

"The choice is yours," he said, stepping nearer still, "but you should know the risks of entering a Sidhe ring."

Aisling glanced over her shoulder at the dance, the feverish haze a muse to their every movement.

"Once a gathering of Sidhe forms a circle, they bond their '*magic*,' forming a cradle of mass enchantment. For a human to step foot in one ... let's say it's unwise."

"Have you seen it before?" Aisling slurred, blinking to readjust her focus.

"A mortal step into a Sidhe circle?"

Aisling nodded in response, doing her best to shake away the haze.

"I've seen mortals dance themselves into their graves, infants stolen by the hands of the Other. For even after the Sidhe have left, the power remains."

Aisling looked down at the fair folk's feet. Mushrooms grew beneath their toes, bubbling from the earth till Aisling believed she heard them giggling. Was this how the dancing Aos Sí had created that labyrinth of hedge and rose at the center of the arena?

"Then why form one if they are indeed so dangerous?" Aisling asked, watching them over her shoulder.

"Dangerous to mortals," Lir clarified, "to the Sidhe, such power and unity are euphoric." The Fae King fixed his eyes upon her. Eyes that cut into her soul, explored her till she felt bare before him. At times, Aisling believed him a figment of her imagination. The muse of grisly fireside tales breathed to life in the flesh. To the mortals, he was a wicked sovereign who sat on a throne of mortal blood and bones. Her betrothed, measuring her as he'd measured so many humans prior to shredding their flesh with fangs now sheathed in wine.

"You're charmed, aren't you?" Lir settled his feline eyes on her own unfocused ones.

"What?"

"The music, the dancing, the circle. Even when you're near to such spells it affects you, doesn't it?"

Aisling's body responded for her, swaying to and fro, violet orbs pooling with black. For the music rippled through her, every note promised bliss. The night gripped her jaw and poured its tonic past her parted lips as the stars cackled.

Aisling's feet picked up once more, the rage still burning a hole at her core. But the music, the lights, the smells. It was all too enticing, too easy to lose herself.

Lir was nothing more than a blur when he spun her towards him, danced with her inside the fae ring. His wicked grin was a mess of pearls and diamonds whirling in the opposite direction the world rotated. The *Snaidhm* a kaleidoscope of glittering dust and laughter till she began to fly. No not fly. Glide through the revelry in the arms of another. Her eyes rolled as she struggled to reply to the oaks hanging their heavy heads to ask her for her name.

Aisling wasn't certain how much time had passed when the debauchery faded into a distant, collective murmur. Only that every step further from the *Snaidhm* made her more aware of how truly alone she was with the Fae King. His heart beating against her right temple. Aisling hadn't believed he bore a heart. Perhaps he'd stolen it.

The mortal queen blinked rapidly. Her internal, lucid self, fighting to regain control. To claw its way out of this slippery stupor and towards sobriety once more. For her feverish, muddy mind was already tearing like gossamer.

Aisling counted Lir's steps as he neared the trees. The great shadows of the forest cloaked them both at its lip. She was one, perhaps two steps away from foregoing one world and entering another. A realm of trees that eyed her warily, arguing back and forth as they leaned forward for a closer look.

Lir set Aisling down on a bed of moss, placing her as far from the *Snaidhm* as possible without entering the shadowed keep of the greenwood. From this distance, the music and uproar of the *Snaidhm* were but a drawl, vibrating through the earth.

These were his feywilds, Aisling repeated in her mind. A

concept she struggled to wrap her mind around. For Aisling had always been taught the forest was wild, untamable, insatiable, ruthless, but not more so than its monarch. The sovereign who knelt beside her now, watching as she inhaled her sanity once more. The way his eyes perused her unsettled her more than she could describe.

And once the lucidity crawled back into her mind, the night air sobering, Aisling clumsily stood, staggering and lengthening the distance between herself and Lir. Closer and closer to the edge of the forest. Away from he whose breath trailed around her still, prickling her skin.

Lir smiled, unfurling himself from his crouch.

"If you knew what lies in those woods, you'd prefer my company to theirs."

Aisling snapped a branch beneath her heel, a reminder of how close she stood from entering the surrounding woodland.

"More trows and dryads?" Aisling quipped, rummaging through her mind for the right words. After all, a thick cloud still blanketed her thoughts, lifting at a glacial pace, the *Snaidhm*'s residual enchantment that'd transformed her bones to glass and her limbs to jelly.

"Aye, and other fiends of the feywild."

Aisling glared at the forest over her shoulder. The instinct to avoid the woodland tugging at her conscience lest she be punished, for the wilderness had always been forbidden. Until now. There was no Clodagh to reprimand her, no Nemed to raise his hand to her, no brothers to ridicule her. She could do what she liked here. Even stand with the enemy at the woodland's edge, the forest himself.

And perhaps it was still the *Snaidhm*'s charms that made it appear as though the forest spoke amongst one another like a great counsel. The groaning of their trunks in the evening gale, the rustling leaves, the murmuring insects, the hoots of an owl, all were sentient. All alive and eager to see her. Touch her. Know her. Ancient and feral and unpredictable. Inhospitable to all they reject.

Lir held out his hand to her. "You're not in your right mind. I brought you here only to diminish the effects of the *Snaidhm* before continuing on. Return with me to Annwyn. From that distance, the sorcery of the *Snaidhm* should entirely—"

"I'm fine," Aisling interrupted, holding his gaze.

"You lie easily and quickly, is this a mortal trait?" He asked.

"A dreadful habit of my kind," Aisling quipped, "although, perhaps more characteristic of your blood than mine." Nemed had indeed always said the mouths of the Aos Sí were designed to spew lies and speak deception, incapable of being honest lest their tongues burn.

"You believe we lie?" Lir scoffed. "To tell a mistruth requires great concentration and even then, it is poorly told," he said, the ghost of a smile tugging at his lips. "Believe me, I tried when I was a child." How long ago that must've been. What was it like to carry centuries of memories? For one's childhood to be lost in some distant, ancient past?

Aisling stifled her surprise. If what he said was true, how could her father have been so wrong? Perhaps the Fae King was deceiving her even now but there'd already been a great deal Nemed had chronicled poorly. The way the fair folk looked, for example. Aisling had never known her father to be wrong about anything. Although, she realized, pent up in Castle Neimedh, there'd never been another to disprove his claims.

"So would say a liar."

He laughed, eyes glinting like a rogue. "I don't need to lie to you."

Aisling clenched her fists at her sides, her fear of the fair folk only rivalled by her rage. Her resentment. The bitter taste of an upbringing stoked by her race's rivalry with these brutes.

"Do you know how to wield that dagger?" Lir's attention

shifted between her corset and her face, devilry widening his smile.

Aisling slid the knife from her bodice, careful not to reveal herself in the process. She bore no intention of using it on the Fae King but was rather comforted by the sensation of it in her hands.

"You'll have to draw it more quickly if you wish to take me off guard," the king continued, moving closer. So close, Aisling needed to tilt her head up to meet his lowered gaze.

"Who says I have any intention of using it?" Aisling growled. For the mortal queen would be foolish to consider jeopardizing all her clann had sacrificed. And attempting a strike on the Fae King was among the fruitless errors that would find her executed by either the Aos Sí or the mortals themselves.

"It's written in all that you do: your strange, violet eyes perpetually glancing over your shoulder, how you recklessly clutch your dagger even while you dream, the flickering of the muscles in your hands each time I near you, the tension in your jaw each time I look at you," Lir's eyes flicked to Aisling's mouth, quickly returning to her eyes. "I know you want to use it. But I also know you won't. You and I both know the risks of presenting this union as anything other than a joyous pairing."

Horror ambushed Aisling, her throat running dry. Lir had noticed more of the mortal queen than Aisling anticipated. His sage eyes were more watchful than she thought possible, capable of dissecting her behavior with an accuracy that chilled Aisling's spine.

"Regardless," Lir began again, "a queen—especially one of the feywilds—should be familiar with her dagger."

"I'm aware how a blade works," Aisling spat, taking a step back, standing on the lip between the forest and the glade. "I use the pointy end and stick it in your heart."

"Show me."

Aisling inhaled, trapping the breath inside her chest. If he wanted to provoke her, then provoke her he would. For he inspired something reckless within her, the sensation of swimming in an abyss, holding her palm beside a flame, wrestling with a wolf.

So, the mortal queen lunged for the Fae King, waving the dagger the way she remembered Dagfin practicing in the gardens while she read. And in response, the Fae King laughed, a cruel cackle that bred fury all over again in Aisling's veins.

"Had I wished you harm, you'd be dead before the tip of your blade decided upon its direction." Lir smiled broadly. A brief flicker of mirth before he propelled forward. Had Aisling blinked, she would've missed it. The flash of movement as he snatched the dagger from her hand and held her in place by the wrist.

"To draw your weapon, you'll need to be quick. You may be weaker, smaller than most opponents you'll encounter but you can be fast. Drawing your advantage first is half the battle. And if given the opportunity, you should always be the first to strike"—Lir considered her bodice, flushing Aisling's cheeks—"and you'll need something more practical to stow away your dagger than a corset."

"My brother advised to wield only in the name of self-defense," Aisling said, as breathlessly as she felt. Internally, she cursed herself for it.

"Your brother is wrong," Lir said, releasing the queen from both his grip and regard, instead, studying the dagger. "I'm surprised you were allowed such a trinket. My advisors tell me you lacked proficiency with all weaponry."

"It was a gift," Aisling said, regaining the sharpness in her tone.

"From the princeling besotted with you?" Lir's eyes flitted back to Aisling.

The mortal queen blinked, the backs of her lids burning with the memory of Dagfin's face, his voice the song of her childhood: stealing destriers to spend a day at Hannelore's Linn, inventing songs to torment poor Fergus, tickling the sleeping guards with pigeon feathers.

"No," Aisling replied distantly. A word that caught Lir's attention and held it for the briefest of moments.

"An expensive gift, nevertheless," the Fae King resigned, his thumb stroking the ruby enclosed in the pommel's ebony fist. A ruby that dulled in the presence of its dagger's most loathsome enemy.

He tested the dagger's weight, flipping it effortlessly between his fingers. It looked odd in his hands, long fae fingers toying with a mortal blade. So much smaller than it'd appeared in Aisling's own grip.

His fingertips traced the haft, the cross-guard, until they found the iron blade. But once his skin touched the iron, he recoiled, hissing like a wounded animal.

"Don't look so surprised. I'm sure your father made certain the effects of iron on our kind were common creed."

"What does it feel like?" Aisling asked, eyeing the red and purple blister forming on his injured flesh. Skin that didn't, couldn't, recover the way the rest of their body did when exposed to non-iron harm: quickly. Miraculously.

"Like it looks, flame to flesh." So, even fae lords were slaves to iron. Aisling had often wondered if these foreign monarchs were susceptible to the same weaknesses as their subjects. Vulnerabilities Nemed and all the mortal kings before him used to their advantage in the name of the Isles of Rinn Dúin. Of mankind.

"We should return to Annwyn, you shouldn't be this near to the feywilds for so long," he said, tossing Aisling the dagger. "I should've returned you to Annwyn once you woke." The mortal queen caught the knife. And as she sheathed her dagger in her corset once more, she glanced longingly at the forest.

"But isn't this your kingdom?"

"You'd be a fool to believe sovereigns capable of controlling every subject."

"You refer to the Unseelie?" Aisling pushed, her feet planted in place even as he gestured for her to follow.

A muscle flashed across Lir's jaw. "How much do you—"

"Gilrel informed me there were other races, monsters, creatures who roam these forests, the mountains, the waters. I know no details. Only that your kind refers to them as *Unseelie*. As you yourself have intimated before."

Lir exhaled, the muscles in his shoulders slackening in the slightest. "You shouldn't pry into what will only endanger you—a risk to both the Aos Sí and mortals should you die and the treaty be for naught."

"You believe me afraid?" Aisling challenged, moving nearer to the woods.

"No, and that's what concerns me," he replied.

Aisling peered into the forest, a shadowed realm of tree and branch and endless ferality, studying the mortal queen in return. It was lovely the way a whetted blade was lovely. The way a storm ravaged the land it danced across.

Lir exhaled, realizing he'd have to relinquish at least a cent of information if he wished to purchase her compliance. Lest he carry her away himself. And Aisling believed he wanted to touch her as much as she did him. Which was not at all.

"When we passed through the forest, on our way to Annwyn, I veiled you with a glamour. A shield against the dryads," he said, his voice as cool as the mist building around her ankles.

"A glamour?" she turned to face him.

"A protective spell, a cloak that can shroud an entity entirely or change its image briefly."

"You wielded magic then?" Aisling's stomach dropped, realizing she'd been both enchanted and totally unaware. This was unlike the *Snaidhm*: magic that had been accidental, too potent for a nearby human. No, this ... this was different, a crossing of some line she hadn't realized she'd drawn until now. He'd bewitched her. She was both powerless and at the mercy of his tricks.

"I do not wield magic—I breathe it."

Aisling recalled the muffled silence, the pressure popping her ears, the voices slamming against those invisible walls as they trailed through the forest and towards Annwyn.

"Were your knights glamoured as well?" Aisling asked.

"No. Fortunately, that day the Sidhe far outnumbered whatever dryads lurked in that part of the woods. They wouldn't have dared approach our party especially when accompanied by me. But with a human..." Lir hesitated, his eyes meeting Aisling's. "*Unseelie* crave mortal flesh. Had they known you were there, they would've been unable to resist."

Aisling paled.

"*The Aos Sí will not hesitate to devour you with their spells. They will toy with your mind, steal your agency, manipulate your reality. All magic is evil and dark and unnatural,*" Nemed had told her, his voice alive only in memory. Achingly distant.

"The glamour, however, served its purpose. They could smell you but not see you—a good enough disguise to help us pass."

"How do I know you speak the truth? That this is not all some elaborate deception? You've now admitted to using magic to manipulate my reality. How do I know these *Unseelie*, creatures the mortal world has never so much as mentioned, are real?" But even as the words left her lips Aisling knew the answer. The reality of the trow she'd beheaded hours before. Its memory flooding back to her, nearly bringing her to her knees. A sense of guilt, of pleasure she blamed on the Fae King.

"You don't have much of a choice."

He was right and that made Aisling all the more furious.

"Your kind are considered monsters in mortal eyes, ruthless. Cruel. Savages who hunt humans for sport."

"I would've imagined a princess to be educated in the Lore enough to—"

"The *Forbidden* Lore is outlawed," Aisling growled. "*A library of pure deceit.*"

Amusement bent his lips. "I should've realized your father's lies cut deep. What other deceptions did the Fire Hand of the North steep his mortal kin's mind with? He who wears the blood of the forest on his hands?"

"You know not what you speak of," Aisling growled. Nemed had indeed burned the wilds to make room for their overpopulating kingdom. To expand Tilren's walls so the mortals could live comfortably without fear of the Aos Sí. So it was the Aos Sí who preyed upon mankind, forcing them behind walls to eventually spill from the seams of their iron kingdoms. Not Nemed.

Lir laughed but it held no humor.

"It is not I who has been fed on lies and coaxed to sleep in an iron keep." Lir prowled nearer still. "And it is not I who has manipulated reality as you claim. That guilt lies with your father."

"What do you know of my father?" Aisling continued, her heart thrashing against her chest, ears ringing with anger, palms growing hot.

But before Lir could answer, some branch snapped further inside the forest. In an instant, the Fae King's posture changed, his shoulders tightening, eyes gleaming like a wolf's, hands flexing until no longer did the White Stag stand before her but rather a demon of violence. Could he smell something? Sense it? See it even amidst the evening's veil?

"Step away from the forest," he commanded, his voice thicker, lower than it had been moments before.

Aisling glanced over her shoulder. Her vision blurred, her temples throbbed, suddenly consumed by a crashing wave of white noise thick like fuzz. The mortal queen shook her head, but it did little to assuage the popping of her ears or the pressure falling as thickly as the fog. Aisling had felt this sensation before. Had been crippled by a similar energy. Force. Bubble. She could see no further than a few paces before her, the rest a mess of shadow and distant noise. But she could sense it. Whatever *it* was. Angry, hopeful, eager, impatient.

"Take my hand," Lir reached towards her, his palm facing the star-speckled sky. Aisling glared at it, desperately attempting to orient herself within his magic. Somehow, taking his hand was a betrayal of her own kind. The fact she *was* afraid, that she perhaps needed to accept his help in order to survive for the second time in one day, worsened that sensation.

"Aisling."

A growl erupted from behind her.

"Take my hand," Lir ordered, a brief glimpse of panic seizing his expression. But now he wasn't looking at Aisling. He was glaring over the crown of her head and into the forest. At whatever sighed down her neck and pawed closer. Deep, guttural, laced with hunger. Aisling could feel its hot breath on her ankles.

Chapter XI

AISLING SWIVELED, COMING FACE TO FACE with a beast, a spectral hound, washed in shadows of deepest black. As large as one of Nemed's destriers, larger, it wrinkled its muzzle, peeling back its lips to boast an impressive collection of fangs. A snarl so ugly it occurred to Aisling it might be grinning. And as the tentacles of darkness formed and reformed, Aisling peered into the skeletal interior of the hound. Lightest white against darkest black.

The queen couldn't scream. No, her throat was sealed shut. Her muscles were petrified. Even her hearing had resorted to a distant, muffled ring.

Aisling stepped back, snapping a branch beneath her bare heel. The sound, swaddled by white noise, still pulsed through the forest, catching the beast's attention, its ears flicking side to side. Aisling stifled the urge to gasp, realizing the beast wasn't glaring at her but rather past her. At Lir. As though she were invisible.

A glamour.

"Don't run," Lir said, his voice resolute, the only sound that wasn't smothered by the enchantment.

The hound took a step forward, inching towards Aisling. It raised its muzzle, nose to nose with the queen, and inhaled, savoring the warm, fleshy perfume of mortality.

It was too late. Even if she were to run, it already knew she was here. Her presence could no longer be denied even if Lir had glamoured her.

A great force flung Aisling to the side. The queen flew, landing further into the forest on a cushion of leaves and rolling until she collided against a pine. As quickly as she was capable, Aisling staggered to her feet. A brief inspection suggested she suffered no broken bones, fractured limbs, sprained joints, or otherwise serious injuries. Unless the adrenaline was doing a fine job of subsiding the pain.

At the lip of the woods, Lir wrestled the wolf, a knot of vines and shadows.

The beast pinned the Fae King, limiting access to his twin blades, its muzzle chomping at the tip of the Fae King's nose. Nevertheless, Lir managed to free one arm, pushing back the hound's jaws with roots he'd freshly summoned. Roots the creature shredded when they threatened to burst its windpipes, forcing Lir to peer down its gaping throat until he could fling the creature off himself. Strength the Fae King made appear effortless. The wolf collided against the sharp edge of a boulder, lending Aisling clear sight of the beast for the first time since Lir had attacked.

Before she could think twice, Aisling drew Iarbonel's dagger from her corset, tossing the blade as hard as she was capable. To her surprise, the dagger found its target, sticking the beast below its rib cage, a pitiful whimper echoing into the forest.

But it was far from vanquished, instead, reminded of Aisling's potency nearby. For although the wolf couldn't see her, its nose would be guide enough.

The beast abandoned Lir where he stood paces away, racing instead for the woman. More interested in satiating its appetite than encountering its inevitable demise at the hands of the Fae King.

Aisling picked up her feet, heavy beneath the pressure of Lir's glamour, and ran. She leapt over stones, across logs, through icy streams, weaving through the labyrinth. Aisling had never ventured this far into the forest. It was a vast maze of chittering trees, each craning to get a good look at the mortal woman dashing for her life. Aisling felt their sighs, the groans of their primeval bodies waking to the sound of her feet brushing the undergrowth. In other circumstances, Aisling would've enjoyed losing herself in the woodland. A realm of feral enchantment, the antithesis to her father's stone and iron world. But, as it was now, fear charged her. Nourished her race through these feywilds.

The mortal queen ran quickly but her predator was quicker, nipping at her heels with increased fervor. As though the chase rendered it more esurient, more desperate, more capable of 'seeing' her with its nose and appetite than its eyes ever could.

Close enough now, the creature nipped at Aisling's legs, sending the mortal queen tumbling against spidery roots and unforgiving stones. The world was a blur of black, brown, wet and cold, as Aisling slid through slush on the forest floor. So, she clamored to her knees as the wolf sprang for her arm.

Aisling screamed. She'd never felt pain like this before. Never endured anything worse than scratches, scrapes, and bruises. Now, red flowed freely from the wound, dying the sleeve of her emerald gown. A throbbing, blistering pain that, despite Aisling clutching the tender flesh, worsened as the seconds passed. But this monster wasn't finished. The wolf padded nearer to Aisling, savoring the frenzied beat of her heart, the sweat beading against her pale skin, the smell of her blood, and the excited trembling of her hands and knees. After all, she couldn't fight the creature. Couldn't outrun it.

Help, she said wordlessly, recognizing the futility of such a cry. Flames of panic and anger scalding her from the inside out.

The wolf leaned back on its haunches, preparing to lunge forward. And just as it did, a small, black creature snapped between its eyes.

A snake. Not just any snake. The sable serpent that'd guided Aisling through Castle Annwyn, or at the very least the same breed.

It stiffened its neck, belly tightening before striking the monster's eyes. And although this obsidian friend could do little more than deter the hound, the distraction was lifesaving for it afforded Aisling a breath. A single exhalation before a weight tackled the wolf to the ground, skewering its chest to the dirt with a thick, razor-edged branch.

In a flash, Lir was atop the creature, driving a steak into the ghostly spine of the hound. It released a blood-curdling cry. Enough for Aisling's skin to crawl but the mortal queen was unable to pry her eyes from the violence, the puddling beneath the monster's now-limp corpse, the meaty sound of punctured flesh, Lir's eyes void of any morsel of humanity. For in this moment, there was none of the whimsy of the Aos Sí in his expression. It was all barbaric. All savage, come to claim its kill and relish in its death.

The demon still twitched so Lir grabbed the hound's head.

"Close your eyes," Lir said, his voice an Otherworldly growl. But Aisling ignored him, forcing herself to witness this death. A silent agreement sealed between Aisling and Lir as the Fae King nodded, twisting the neck of the beast. Aisling's ears popped in time to hear the crack of the wolf's bones.

The glamour was done. The demon collapsed, heaving one last wicked puff. And its fiery, ruby eyes simmered into nothing more than glassy, black coals.

The next several hours were a blur.

Lir climbed off the corpse, white rage possessing his features, eyes capable of devouring anything and everything they beheld with the wild breath of the wood. The next moment, Aisling and the Fae King were surrounded by Aos Sí, the music and lights of the *Snaidhm* flashing forcibly.

Lir, having carried her from the forest, his hands sticky with her blood, handed her to Galad. They spoke their Rún angrily, voices rising over the commotion, the confusion. Then suddenly, Aisling was in her chambers, busily fussed over by Gilrel, her magpies, and several other nameless creatures Aisling had yet to meet: two hares, an otter, a fox, and a particularly scrupulous hedgehog.

They stripped the queen of her gown and bathed her, washing the mud, dirt, and blood from her hair and skin. But Aisling felt fine. In fact, the pain hadn't settled until the following morning. And when she awoke, the ache in her arm was unbearable, the bite wound cleaned and wrapped tightly, bandages replaced every so often.

Several of her fingers were purpled and swollen while her hands and feet were riddled with flesh wounds. Aisling hadn't recalled receiving those.

"You're in shock, *mo Lúra*," Gilrel said, accepting a teapot from a flock of magpies hovering beside her. "What do you remember?"

To the best of her ability, Aisling chronicled the night to her chambermaid. The images flashed across her mind, recoiling as if having been burned by the memory alone. The sound of the hound's baleful growl vibrating through her body still.

"The Cú Scáth," Gilrel interrupted her tale. Aisling wasn't familiar with its name. How could she be? Clann Neimedh had never once mentioned the *Unseelie*. They either were blissfully unaware *or* they'd pretended they were. Aisling couldn't decide which was worse. Either way, she needed to write to

Nemed and clear this all away. Rid herself of the burden of this knowledge.

Once she finished reciting the memory in its entirety, Gilrel frowned. The room was silent. Even the doors to the balcony had been firmly shut, shunning the morning breeze, the songbirds, the badger that crawled in to feed on Aisling's scraps from time to time. And whatever maids had come to assist Gilrel the night prior were nowhere to be seen, perhaps already having returned to their usual responsibilities throughout the castle.

"You're fortunate your *caera* was there, otherwise ..." Gilrel trailed off but Aisling knew the implication. She'd be dead, half-digested within the belly of that foul beast by now.

But despite her shock, the horror of the memories, Aisling found herself strangely exhilarated. Aisling had scarcely spoken the words to herself, guiltily keeping them at bay. Even so, the queen had never endured anything half so exciting in all her life, confined to the walls of Tilren lest her and Dagfin escape. But now, she'd felt it for herself, experienced it herself.

Aisling repressed such excitement, stuffing it into some cobwebbed corner of her conscious mind. It was foolish to delight in danger. In violence. A lifeforce of its own, pulsing through her as though her bones, her body had been lulled into a hollow sleep. Until she'd dropped the axe on the trow's head and faced the Cú Scáth.

The mortal queen considered the teacup in her hands, tilting the liquid from side to side. It smelled both bitter and of some unfamiliar foreign spice.

"Tears of Leshy." Gilrel set the pot on Aisling's bedside table. "A forest spirit. Drink for it will heal you quickly and efficiently."

"A wraith?"

"Not quite. Leshy is amongst the oldest of trees; his roots said to cut near the center of the earth. Unless he wishes to run, to dance; he travels through the woods. A great guardian to the feywilds."

"And these are his tears?"

"Aye. Leshy is near impossible to find, to chase. To extract his tears is an unthinkable task save for the King of the Greenwood. And such tears are reserved for his knights when targeted by their vulnerabilities. And now his queen."

Aisling swallowed, avoiding Gilrel's glare. So, this was how Lir's knights had miraculously recovered after iron's kiss, for their unique ability to heal swiftly only applied to wounds dealt by non-iron means, this much Aisling knew. And this new knowledge, knowledge of Leshy's power ... well, Aisling only wondered what Nemed would do with such insight, a potion capable of eliminating one of the mortals' only advantages against the fair folk if harvested in great enough quantities.

"Leshy's tears may be somewhat repulsive, even by mortal standards, but it will quicken your recovery. By tomorrow morning, you will feel as if you've been freshly cast in the Forge."

Aisling gagged after her second whiff, its acrid stench trailing through the whipped, billowy puffs of steam atop its milky surface.

Gilrel climbed up the chair beside Aisling's bed and sat, adjusting her tail so it sat neatly beside her. Her scars were caught by the rays of sunlight filtered through the castle's stained-glass windows. There was seldom a moment Aisling didn't wonder how the marten handmaid had received them. Did these familiar beasts fight beside the Aos Sí? Had Gilrel faced her father before? Encountered Starn on the battlefield? Aisling would quite enjoy watching Gilrel wield a sword. In fact, she'd be fascinated to witness these furry beasts fight. How radiant they must be, fully dressed in armor of their own. Perhaps one day she would. After all, even if the Aos Sí and humans no longer opposed one another, it was quickly becoming clear that another threat lurked throughout the wilds.

"Has it always been this way?" Aisling asked abruptly, studying the marten's reaction, "have the Unseelie always been a threat to even the Aos Sí?"

Gilrel met the mortal queen's eyes.

"Yes," she said sharply, stroking her whiskers, "but never like this. They're becoming bolder, stronger, angrier. Our forests weren't always so at odds."

"But the Unseelie are motivated by human flesh?" Aisling thought of what Lir had spoken the night before: *the* Unseelie *hunger for mortals*. A notion that continuously baffled the mortal queen the longer she considered it.

After all these years, how was it possible her own kind was unaware of their most insatiable predator? Had they been so focused, so distracted by the Aos Sí to understand what lurked between the trees? Aisling's fingers twitched, the memory of a quill in her fingers drawing her towards the parchment at her vanity. She must write to her father. Especially if the fair folk bore reason to fear their own woodlands. A world they, the elms, and the ashes staked equal claim to.

"Half a century ago, a member of my litter was maimed by an *Unseelie*," Gilrel said the words so flippantly, Aisling near choked on Leshy's tears, but the marten's expression grew severe.

"My sister was protecting a mortal. A young child she'd found lost in the woods. Nuala was a silk weaver, skilled with sewing rare thread sourced only from a rare *Unseelie* species known as the *Neccakaid*."

Spidersilk, Aisling conjectured. She'd heard tales of the material, its pricelessness, but where or how it was harvested was never if rarely disclosed.

"The Sidhe and the *Unseelie* are indeed rivals," Gilrel continued, "but we've found ways over the centuries to *coexist*. For the most part. Nuala traded mortal trinkets—jewels, clothing, objects manufactured by human hands—in exchange for yards of *Neccakaid* silk. I'd always despised the transactions. Warned her that no good could come of dealings with the *Unseelie*. Obviously, she ignored me and on one unfortunate day, she'd encountered a human boy aimlessly wandering near the Neccakaid caves. Why the mortal child was there, no one knows, but it hardly matters. Nuala wished to warn the boy before the demons caught his scent, but it was too late. They descended upon the mortal child, and instead of fleeing herself Nuala stayed behind"—Gilrel's voice caught in her throat, deepening as she forced herself to continue—"to this day, I can't bring myself to understand why she'd chosen to sacrifice her eternal life for a life so fickle, so sickly, so small." Gilrel laughed a dark, humorless chuckle.

"The child abandoned my sister, left her to die. When Nuala didn't return that night, we went in search of her. We found the mortal boy first, covered in Sidhe blood, running through the trees. A quick interrogation revealed Nuala had indeed slain one of the *Neccakaid* to save the boy. But my sister was dragged along with it into death's hollow."

Gilrel blinked as if batting away the memory. She cleared her throat and shook her head, smoothing out the creases in her apron.

"Lir wouldn't let me kill the boy for abandoning my sister in fears it would only exacerbate the conflicts between Aos Sí and mortals. But there isn't a day I wish I hadn't torn that child to shreds. So, you see, *mo Lúra*, even the Sidhe are not immune to the bloodthirst of the *Unseelie*. You are fortunate to be alive."

Aisling set the cup aside. She could offer her condolences, apologize for Gilrel's loss but none could truly assuage the grief that no doubt swelled within the marten before her. Especially from the lips of a mortal, the same race that had forsaken her sister. Gilrel wouldn't want Aisling's sympathy. So, Aisling sipped her tea, ignoring the burn of its waters on her tongue.

Several moments passed before Aisling set down her cup, its base cushioned by the saucer.

"Perhaps, the mortals and the Sidhe have at last found common ground"—Aisling held Gilrel's gaze—"a common enemy."

Chapter XII

ANOTHER TWO DAYS DISSOLVED IN THE NORTHERN wind and still Lir hadn't returned from wherever he'd vanished after the *Snaidhm*. Aisling hadn't intended to count the days he was away, nor had she intended to peer over her balcony every few hours, awaiting his return. Her idle mind searched for a distraction, anything to halt the endless rehearsal of the past several nights. For she was locked away in this mountain castle with nowhere to explore, save her own mind, a perilous terrain, threatening to unravel her fully as Gilrel insisted she rest, insisted she sleep and eat without distraction so she would recover with the aid of Leshy's tears. But her physical wounds paled in comparison to the mental scars she now bore. Terrors that salted the healing lesions, soaking her thoughts with blood and teeth. And something else. Something far worse that gnawed at Aisling. Made her hungry. Made her lie awake when the sky turned obsidian and the forest whispered her name.

Meanwhile, Galad was tasked with overseeing the mortal princess while Lir was away. He stood outside her door from dusk till dawn. And no others, not even the rest of Lir's knights, were permitted to enter Aisling's chambers.

So, Aisling set to writing at the vanity, an ivory quill poised in hand, made from the feathers of a three-eyed owl, Gilrel explained. The handmaiden fussed over her magpies braiding Aisling's hair too tightly as they weaved through, up, and over one another, curls pinned between their beaks.

Aisling nodded her head vacantly as Gilrel spoke, dipping her pen into the pearly inkpot. Her handwriting, clumsy initially, softened as she scribbled each sentence with utmost concentration. Penmanship was of course one of the many courses offered throughout her tutelage. One she'd find useful before and after political marriage. For she'd already written and re-written this letter several times over, tossing out those with the slightest of imperfections. Had spent her morning either pacing back and forth in her chambers, counting the fish that leapt in the gorge beyond Annwyn, asking Gilrel endless amounts of questions, or ripping sheet after sheet till she resolved to finish a single letter.

Dearest Father,

I hope this letter finds you well. I write to chronicle all that I've seen and experienced. What the Aos Sí are like and not like. What their world is like. But to describe such thoughts would be to fill an opus worth of pages. So instead, I'll tell you the direst of news: during the short time I've spent amongst the Aos Sí, I've become privy to a threat. A threat that jeopardizes the safety of our people despite the treaty. The Aos Sí call them Unseelie, archaic races that live within the wilds, growing more formidable by the day. But do not take the Aos Sí's word for it. Take mine instead. I've seen them. I've—

Aisling hesitated. Paused long enough that the quill bled into the parchment. The mortal queen crossed out the last word, shaking her head and continuing.

I realize the degree of responsibility and change you must be overseeing in the mortal world. But please, write back to me at your earliest convenience so we may discuss this in greater detail. I think often of Tilren. Of Clann Neimedh and of home.

Home.
Aisling's chest tightened.

With Love

—she continued, steadying her hand once more—

Your daughter, Aisling.

Carefully, she folded the letter and slipped the parchment into a parceled envelope: an emerald sleeve sealed with lavender bramblebee wax harvested from fae honeycomb gardens. And hopefully, her letter would arrive swiftly enough to prevent any further tragedies. After all, the mortals believed their only enemy, the Aos Sí, to be bound by a peace treaty. Inevitably, they would relax their guards, potentially venturing into Unseelie-infested feywilds.

Aisling blanched. She could and would protect her own kind. Could prevent tragedy if only the mortals were informed quickly enough. This was her responsibility to bear and none other's. For she alone was able to ensure this information reached the appropriate ears.

Aisling stood from her chair and carried the envelope across the room, the sweeping of stray leaves catching the hem of her gown. And despite her eagerness to deliver the letter as soon as possible, the mortal queen hesitated before opening the chamber doors. For, on the other side, Galad leaned against the stone walls, idly flipping a reed between his fingers.

Aisling steeled herself, lifting her chin and jerking the door open.

"*Mo Lúra*"—the knight straightened lazily—"how are you faring?"

Aisling frowned, biting the inside of her cheek. "I'm afraid I harbor little interest in empty concerns for my welfare."

"What would give you the impression my concerns are empty?" Galad grinned, flashing his canines. His hair was braided differently today, tugged away from his face and beaded with fragments of bone. His sapphire eyes glinting marvelously as he leaned towards the mortal queen.

Aisling bristled. "Need I remind you I was nearly devoured by a Forge forsaken trow and then a Cú Scáth or do the fair folk enjoy misremembering their crimes against mortals?"

"Ah, but you were not actually eaten by the trow nor the Cú Scáth. The only real harm that befell you had nothing to do with what I or any of the Sidhe partook in; the Unseelie can be unpredictable. As for the *Snaidhm*, you were promised someone would reach you before the trow and its intentions. That promise was kept."

"What heroism," Aisling bit, uncertain why she'd chosen this battle with Galad instead of Lir other than the fear she still harbored towards the Fae King, "to place a helpless maiden in danger only to expect praise for releasing her from said perils."

"Helpless?" Galad dipped his head lower so his words were but a shadowed whisper between them. "Am I misremembering, as you claim, or was it you who raised Lir's axe and behead the Unseelie yourself?"

Aisling hesitated, tongue-tied, as the memory of the trow's rolling head resurfaced. The ease with which the blade cut through the beast's bone. Aisling shivered, a wave of nausea rising in her gut, inspired not by shame nor disgust but pride. Aisling wrenched her eyes shut, disgraced by her own gratification. Blinking open and willing such feelings gone.

Gone and away so that the knight before her might not catch a glimmer of such pleasure in her violet eyes.

Galad laughed, still studying her. "Was there something you needed, *mo Lúra*?"

"A letter to be delivered with haste. Gilrel informed me you'd be able to aid me in doing so. If not, I can find—"

"I'm assuming to Tilren?" The knight interrupted, cunning eyes darting towards the envelope folded in Aisling's hands.

The mortal queen hesitated. "Yes, a letter for my father." Father to Aisling. Villain to all the fair folk.

Galad slipped the reed into the quiver strapped against his back.

"I can take care of it for you, but Lir's court advisors will need to read it before it ever leaves Annwyn."

"For what reason?" she asked, but Aisling already knew.

"Despite being *mo Lúra*, your heritage obviously suggests certain blood loyalties. Loyalties, that at least initially, the Sidhe should be wary of. If you write to your tuath, our court advisors will need to inspect more than your penmanship to ensure it doesn't contain any sensitive information. Information that could jeopardize your union with Lir or Annwyn itself. So, any plans to poison your betrothed, steal his axes, exchange incriminating details or the like should be erased now, *mo Lúra*."

"You're suggesting I'm a spy? That my intentions to protect my own kind are not pure?"

"I'm suggesting you *could* be a spy, *mo Lúra*," Galad grinned, not ashamed in the slightest of his accusations implied or not.

"Was this Lir's idea?"

"Aye, it was, and if anyone can understand it should be you. I'm confident your kind would do the same in our position." Aisling didn't disagree. Nevertheless, it remained a nuisance that, each time she corresponded with her family, her words would be sifted through for a betrayal on her behalf.

"If I must comply with your precautions, may I, at the very least, accompany my letter to ensure its hasty delivery?" But Aisling was already closing the door behind herself. Asking for permission was more of a courtesy. She'd follow him whether he agreed to it or not.

"Have you recovered sufficiently?" Galad's eyes darted towards the gauze peeking beneath her sleeve.

"That furry little nightmare may have a fit but I'm in no mood to be stuffed in my chamber for yet another day," the mortal queen huffed. Galad eyed the door firmly shut behind Aisling, where just beyond Gilrel would eventually return in search of her Lady. Would inevitably scold her magpies for not keeping the mortal queen contained for the second time.

"Lir instructed—"

"Tell me, do you always do what you're told?" Aisling interjected, holding the door's wooden knocker tightly between her fingers.

"The better acquainted you become with your *caera*, 'doing what you're told' becomes the more appealing option," he said, gesturing for Aisling to fall into step beside him. "Nevertheless, I don't envy your solitude, especially after last night. Walk within my shadow at all times. The castle is no place for a mortal wandering alone."

At times, travelling through Castle Annwyn felt endless. Rooms, hallways, doorways, staircases were susceptible to moving, shifting, rotating when they believed none to be looking. Ghostly laughter floating on the sails of every passing draft. Paintings that were thrashed, portraits of a great maiden and her three-eyed owl. Chambers whose doors were chained and bolted shut. Yet the corridors smelled of the flowers that hung from their vines and the further they travelled up the mountain, the air grew cold.

The castle's staff scurried past the knight and Aisling, forcing themselves to bow or curtsy while in the queen's presence. Aisling did her best to ignore their ogling, memorizing the names Galad used to address them as they passed by. Back in Tilren, Aisling had only ever bothered to learn a handful of the staff's titles. Those who directly served her. But here in Annwyn, everyone was familiar, a result of centuries of working alongside one another. Surely if Aisling had been ages old, she would know her staff's names. Wouldn't she?

"How much farther are these court advisors?" Aisling asked, breathlessly climbing yet another winding staircase.

"Not much farther, *mo Lúra*," Galad assured, unfazed by the boundless upward trajectory. A trail visited by strange insect-like creatures, some charming and others grotesque, scampering by her slippers as she passed.

"I'm assuming the Aos Sí don't tire of these steps?" Aisling paused to catch her breath. If she'd boasted any stamina or muscle, perhaps this wouldn't strike the mortal queen as such a feat.

"Rarely and those who do, use their wings instead."

Aisling blinked.

"Do all of you bear wings?" Perhaps it was rude to ask but Aisling found her curiosity far outweighed her manners. So, Aisling tilted her head to inspect the knight more closely as he climbed higher. No wings flared from his armor but perhaps they were tucked away somewhere beneath. Somewhere far below his finely forged plating, his artfully braided chainmail, the skinned leather, or his painted skin.

Galad exhaled a laugh, the sound echoing through the tower in which they stood.

"Not all, no. It's a subspecies of Sidhe, some among us born with the ability to bloom wings on a whim."

"Does Lir have them?" Aisling blurted, immediately

wishing she hadn't spoken his name aloud. There was something about those letters on her tongue that felt strangely intimate to let spill from her lips. Perhaps even to think within the privacy of her own mind.

"Shouldn't you already know the answer to that?" Galad asked.

Aisling's stomach dropped. If only she'd kept her mouth shut. Had Aisling and Lir consummated their marriage, were truly husband and wife, she would know. She should know, had they disrobed before one another, seen one another in their full glory. She would know. But alas, Aisling was as ignorant as a passing stranger, for no such ritual had occurred nor did she believe it ever would. A secret she was more than content to share with the fae lord.

"Do you bear them?" Aisling countered, changing the subject as quickly as she was able.

"Yes," he confessed while turning to continue up the staircase, "and so does your *caera*." Aisling nearly tripped on the hem of her gown, awkwardly straightening herself. The thought knotted her stomach as she swatted away the image now invading her most vivid imaginations. But there was no indication, no sign of strange appendages she'd noticed yet. Perhaps they truly could grow them on a whim—another variable that, despite their beauty, made them so cruelly inhuman.

"Why do you conceal them?" Aisling continued, palming the stone wall for balance. Her thighs protesting every step higher.

"Unlike the rest of our bodies, our wings don't heal quite as efficiently. If one were torn or injured, it could never restore itself fully. Even if mended correctly. In which case, for a knight or a king, it's unwise to sport them regularly. To sport any vulnerability regularly."

Aisling didn't doubt it. The wings she'd already spotted amongst the populace appeared as thin and as delicate as a fly's, nearly translucent if it weren't for the way they reflected both light and color.

"They're lovely," Aisling confessed, the words spilling from her tongue before she could intercept such words of flattery.

"Is that a compliment to the Aos Sí, *mo Lúra*?" Galad glanced back, extending a hand to aid the mortal queen climb a series of dilapidated steps. Steps chipped away by the chisel of time.

Aisling ignored both his offer of help and his comment, heaving herself up on her own instead. "Where does such a trait originate?"

"From the Mountain Kingdom, *Iod*, originally ruled by Ina," Galad said, glancing at the mortal queen following shortly behind. Aisling remembered Cathan's song, Rian's translation, and the narrative it described. "At her conception, it's said Ina was Forged with wings, a gene passed on to her original kin. Those of us born of at least one parent of Iod often carry the trait. Although, such unions no longer occur."

"So, both yours and Lir's parents are subjects of both Annwyn and Iod?" Aisling asked, struggling to maintain Galad's pace. "But how can Lir then be king?"

"It's more common than you'd think. So long as the child is the offspring of a monarch belonging to the lineage of one of the original twelve sovereigns, they have claim to the throne. Lir was the first-born son of his father, the last King of Annwyn, so it matters not where or who his mother was."

In that case, the last King of Annwyn bore a child with a subject of Iod, the mountain kingdom, and that union led to Lir. How strange these fae lineages were. Starn, the rightful heir to Tilren, would one day marry a noblewoman. Preferably one of Tilrish nationality for the purposes of birthing pure-blooded Tilrish children. As it'd always been done in the mortal world with few exceptions.

At last, Aisling and Galad arrived at a narrow door, owls

etched into the splintering wood, appraising all who greeted their threshold. The knight pushed open the door, waking the world beyond with the hollow groan of its hinges. A cloud of mildew released from the heart of the dark chamber.

Aisling followed Galad closely, eyes adjusting to the shadows when she spotted the ash tree leaning against the far wall of a lofty stone cathedral. Growing at the core of the mountain, its colossal branches reached for the cross-vaulted ceilings, dripping with jeweled leaves and bulbs of light from the center of blooming elderflowers.

"Those are *Sylphs*," Galad whispered, following Aisling's line of sight. For indeed, wispy creatures, made of mountain fog, flew among the highest branches, stealing bites from bundles of ripe samara.

"Are they Unseelie?"

"Not quite; most claim they're spirits of the mountain, long-since-deceased Sidhe of Iod, searching for Ina in the summits instead of carrying on to the Other."

One Sylph in particular caught Aisling's eye, lounging at the end of a branch. Its wings sparkled against the glow of the elderflowers, fluttering open the moment it spotted Aisling from its perch. Lazily it rose its ivory head, twinkling eyes considering the mortal queen carefully before gesturing for the others to come and inspect Aisling for themselves. As though she were the creature made of magic and not them.

"This way," Galad said, drawing Aisling's attention back towards the task at hand.

At the base of the tree stood a steepled door embellished with a knob carved in the likeness of an outstretched hand. The twin knob to the one Aisling had found while wandering the castle alone, leading to the fountain room, creases at the knuckles and palm, indents where nails should be, a hand large enough for Galad to take hold and press his own palm against the wooden one.

Aisling opened her mouth to speak but before she could

utter a word, the oddest thing occurred: the whittled hand came to life, groaning as it curled its stiff fingers around Galad's own.

Aisling gasped, flummoxed at the spectacle.

Galad, on the other hand, grew still as a windless wood till the whittled hand, satisfied with whatever it intended, retreated, molding back into the lifeless appendage poised to meet its next guest.

And had it not been for the several clicks and the budging of the door, Aisling would've stood there for hours, inspecting the whittled hand beneath the light of the elderflowers.

Aisling cursed under her breath, for the chamber was so silent, it felt intrusive to speak louder than a whisper.

"This ash prefers to make the acquaintance of whosoever passes its threshold, for the sake of ensuring none shall pass who shouldn't be privy to the information or the people beyond this door."

Magic amongst the Aos Sí, Aisling was realizing, was effortless. Indeed, the fair folk seemed to inhale magic and exhale fantasy. All of Annwyn pulsing with this tempestuous opiate. Feeding the enchantment and in return it fed them.

"And what does lie beyond this door?" Aisling continued, cringing as the door shut of its own accord behind her.

"The other side of the mountain." Galad's eyes flashed in her direction, gaging whether his sardonic reply had dampened her curiosity. It hadn't for the more they withheld, the more Aisling couldn't help but pry.

To Galad's credit, the ingress had indeed revealed the other side of the mountain. A steep drop looming on the right of a parapet walkway. And as Aisling searched for whatever land lie far below, she saw none, the earth eclipsed by a sea of clouds.

"And how does the tree recognize your touch from others?" Aisling asked, more so to distract herself from the potential of one fateful misstep than genuine interest.

"Trees are knowledge keepers. They know every ash, rowan, hazel, and willow by name, a title branded into the rings of their trunks. Know more languages than either Sidhe or man are familiar with. Know the faces of all those who enter their woods."

"You speak of them as though they were sentient."

"Because they are. The trees are always watching, listening. Nosy creatures. The eldest, most ancient of trees the most formidable. And the most judgmental."

That was impossible. Not because Aisling doubted its truth—she'd already seen enough to understand how strange the Sidhe world truly was—but because Aisling couldn't fathom what that meant for her father. For her clann. For every chieftain, tiarna, flaith, and king who'd burned, chopped, laid waste to acreages of woodland.

Aisling's tongue turned to ash; hadn't Lir referred to Nemed as the Fire Hand of the North?

"He who wears the blood of the forest on his hands."

Is this what Lir meant? Was the whole of the forest as sentient as Gilrel had described the great Leshy? Aisling's father had burned miles of woodland, creatures as conscious as Aisling was herself. No, that wasn't a fair comparison. These trees, like the fair folk, lived for centuries. How many memories were lost when Nemed charred kingdoms of forest? Starn alongside him, stomping out the ashes of these sentient beings on the tattered old rug by the kitchen entrance in Castle Neimedh.

"He who wears the blood of the forest on his hands."

Aisling, suddenly grateful for the cliff should she fall ill, struggled to abate the nausea. Nemed didn't know. Couldn't know. Wasn't aware of what truly comprised the feywilds. So, she would tell him. Once he replied to her letter, she would help him. Help the north. A thought that sobered her, warming her complexion once more.

Galad paused before the last door on their left, pressed

into a corner of the mountain. The knight knocked three times before the door creaked ajar, revealing a thin, tall chamber. The room was framed by scrolls, parchment, and books. Shelves that seemingly stretched to the tips of the summit, where three tawny hawks perched amongst the highest of tomes. A room that reeked of animal skins, of dried ink and dust, of the birds whose windswept feathers ruffled at the sight of newcomers.

But no aspect of the chamber was quite as interesting as he who sat behind the desk, haloed by the sunlight dyed resplendently in the hues of stained glass.

"Filverel," Galad greeted the fae male.

Filverel lifted his head, peering past the ivory strands, hardening his already angular features. And despite dawning the appearance of one thirty or so years of age, Aisling knew from one glance at the primeval edge in his moonstone eyes that he was much, much older.

"Galad," the Aos Sí replied, grinning broadly. "I'd heard you'd been tasked to guard the mortal queen. But I hadn't expected to see you until Lir returned."

"Has he sent word?" Galad asked.

"Only that he'll be longer than usual this time."

Galad nodded his head. "I anticipated it wouldn't be as simple as it once was."

As *what* once was? Where had Lir gone? Aisling opened her mouth to ask but before she could utter a word, Galad glanced at Aisling over his shoulder.

"Aisling requests to correspond with the—her *father*," Galad said, on the verge of referring to Nemed as something Aisling assumed would only inspire her temper.

"I don't believe I've had the pleasure." Filverel stood from his seat, moving like a ghost and gliding across the carpets with eerie elegance. An impossibly tall, grey-clad phantom. Of course, he didn't sport the usual tunics, inars, trousers, or *léine*, the mortals usually did. No, like all other Sidhe, he wore a far more interesting counterpart, one woven and embroidered masterfully by Sidhe hands. Attractively cut and, at times, imaginatively embellished with all manner of woodland accessories: petals, leaves, pine needles, bugs, stones, feathers, and furs. But as startling as this Aos Sí was, Aisling had already crossed his path twice before. Once the night of her wedding and again at the *Snaidhm*, sitting a few seats over in their private box with the rest of the trooping Sidhe.

"I'm one of Lir's oldest court advisors," he said, bowing and never once releasing Aisling from his gaze. The stench of lavender and thyme, dusting off his robes and clouding the room.

"Pleased to meet you," Aisling said, dawning the etiquette Clodagh had branded into her every muscle, bone, and breath since she bore the wherewithal to eat with a book balanced on her head. "Aisling of Clann Neimedh. the—"

"The almost-beheaded mortal princess." Filverel bared his pointed canines. "Forgive me, I'm still reeling from the reality of it. I was among those opposed to your union, considering it was nearly an execution bound to exacerbate mortal and Sidhe tensions. But alas, here we are. The princess lives."

Aisling snapped her mouth shut, considering her next words carefully. He'd read every thought she'd harbored over the last several days with alarming accuracy but hearing an Aos Sí speak of it as though her human life were as frivolous as a flower to be plucked from the earth, was unnerving, to say the least. A product of their immortality, it shouldn't shock Aisling that her mortal life would indeed be considered insignificant by comparison.

"Aye, nearly headless then and heedful now for, not only did I keep my head, I've added a crown."

"Of course, *mo Lúra*." Filverel hesitated, a flicker of uncertainty flashing across his opalescent orbs, appearing as quickly as it had vanished. The tone with which he said "*mo Lúra*," a knife, gliding across his tongue.

"Aisling's letters need to be revised before they're delivered," Galad interjected, stepping between the mortal queen and advisor.

"Yes, I recall Lir mentioning as much should the princess fancy herself nostalgic. Where's the letter?"

Galad considered Aisling before offering Filverel the envelope.

For what felt like an eternity, this Aos Sí inspected the parchment, combing through each word, dangling the page in varying lights—even over the beams striking through his window—perhaps for some clever ink with which the mortal queen could slip a message.

At last, he set down his magnifying glass and his quill, folding and slipping the parchment back into its parcel.

"As far as secret codes or treasonous slurs go, the princess is innocent," Filverel said, melting the seal anew. "But, *mo Lúra*, I must ask: what gives you the impression your father isn't already aware of the Unseelie?"

Aisling met Filverel's stare, annoyed he'd read her letter at all. For not only had he thoroughly devoured every stroke of her penmanship, but now he'd pried into the content even after determining it innocent.

"He's never mentioned them before. No one in the mortal world, as far as I'm aware, has ever mentioned the Unseelie."

"And you believe that reason enough?" Filverel challenged, narrowing his eyes.

"I have no reason to doubt him."

Nemed was her father. Sovereign to Tilren and High King of all the Isles. He wouldn't deliberately lie to her. Everything and all Nemed had done, however cruel and ruthless it may appear, was done in the name of mankind. In the name of sparing her race from the heathenous dominion of the fair folk.

Filverel touched his slender fingers to his lips, scouring every inch of the mortal queen till she felt nude before him.

His regard was frigid. As though his spirit had once been bespelled and frozen but never fully thawed. Even his fae markings trailed his flesh with caution, thin bands tiptoeing around his lanky frame.

"It was some decades ago that I met your great grandfather. It's been even longer since I met one of your ancestors—Barhan, I believe his name was. The man who built your Castle Neimedh and its walls, stone by stone. One of the first of your kind to scorch the earth, making way for more land than he could possibly do with."

The words hit Aisling like a physical blow. Aisling bore a handful of memories of the fires the mortals lit. She would stand atop Tilren's walls to witness the gilding of the horizon by flame. Breathing in the ash already staining the skies black. Ash that showered the north for several days after, choking her with the dust of all those slaughtered trees.

"Cellach, who bound Sidhe females in iron shackles and forced himself upon them. It was then Finnlug, your great, great, great grandfather who killed fae children for sport. All of these fabled mortal sovereigns, keepers of those violet eyes you yourself have inherited," Filverel leaned forward, as if considering cutting the hue from Aisling's irises. "Tell me, *mo Lúra*, did you also inherit your father's silver tongue?"

"*Est mire lend*," Galad hissed in Rún, taking a step forward.

"She'll learn sooner or later the true nature of her kind, if she doesn't already know. This way will be far less painful than witnessing it for herself."

"You speak as though the Aos Sí are innocent. As though the Aos Sí have not laid waste to mortal villages, terrorized from within the shadows of the wilderness till no mortal dare venture past their settlement walls, even for food for starving children. As though the Aos Sí did not steal, kill, or enchant innocents. As though the Aos Sí have not stolen our land," Aisling said, her pulse quickening with the rage clawing like hands in a tomb for escape. The hawks squawking madly from above, blowing loose sheets of parchment with the flap of their wings.

"You are worse than ignorant. You are foolish," Filverel said, laughing beneath his breath.

"*Coirrigh dol beanga nó,*" Galad snarled but again Filverel ignored him.

"None are innocent in war. But, if a centuries-old Sidhe may impart some wisdom, I suggest you find the truth for yourself instead of parroting the words of your kind. Of your father. All of us claim to know the truth, only some of us do. Find it for yourself before you stake your life and your loyalties on unchallenged lies."

Aisling's face flushed with fury, digging her nails into the palms of her hands. But Galad was already tugging her out the door, pulling her away from Filverel before Aisling could protest.

"Your letter will be delivered before the sun sets...*mo Lúra,*" the corners of Filverel's lips twitched as Galad swung the door shut. The only sound, the hawks screeching madly from their shelves.

Chapter XIII

ANOTHER WEEK PASSED AND STILL NEMED hadn't replied to Aisling's letter. So, she waited each morning for the raven to return, envelope in beak, but with each new day, Galad was forced to awkwardly disappoint Aisling all over again.

More than enough time had already passed for Nemed to have both received and replied to her correspondence. In fact, it was Gilrel who informed Aisling that fae ravens travelled swiftly, capable of delivering a letter as far as the southern continent and return with a reply in no more than a handful of days. Tilren was a fraction of that distance and yet, Aisling felt as though it were on the other side of the earth. A quiet, soundless corner of the earth.

Aisling woke for the second time this night, swathed in furs, glaring at her chamber's coffered ceiling through the canopy above her bed. Lacey drapes weaving through windy wisterias, growing larger each day as if fed by her nightmares.

Idly, her thumb stroked the handle of an ivory dinner knife. A replacement for Iarbonel's dagger, a dagger perhaps still lodged in the Cú Scáth's corpse rotting somewhere in the near forest.

No longer did she weep for her clann. Rather most nights,

she drifted in and out of consciousness, desperately clawing at the terrors that greeted her the moment she closed her eyes. Nightmares that were somehow worse than the conversations she rehearsed in her mind while awake: the trow hobbling towards her, Lir's grin as the creature's head rolled away and his vines relaxed, the Cú Scáth sinking its teeth in her flesh.

"He who wears the blood of the forest on his hands."

"Find the truth for yourself before you stake your life and your loyalties on unchallenged lies."

"The Aos Sí will try to deceive you. They will spin lies as easily as they spin their thread."

Aisling wrenched her eyes shut, pressing the heels of her hands into her lids. Even the distant brush of trees in the midnight gale haunted her. Willows and elms knew just how many of their brothers and sisters her father had burned. Nemed who'd often summoned Tilrish festivals to smell the smoke, ash, and conquest clouding their Northern skies in streaks of black and grey.

If only Nemed would respond. He could clarify all of this. Make sense of everything he'd gotten wrong and defend all that still stood unproven. He could reassure Aisling. So why, Aisling wondered repeatedly, had Nemed not replied?

Each day it became more and more difficult to remember their voices. Starn, Iarbonel, Fergus, Annind. Dagfin. Everything they'd told her in the weeks before her wedding, muffled by time. A reality that made her ache with guilt, for the memories of her home and family were who she was, what made her who she was. And if she no longer had those, could no longer remember, what would become of her in this new, nonsensical world of the Aos Sí? A land of dangerous dances, forbidden wines, lethal tournaments, and knowing trees?

"Do not forget the world that made you. They will try to deceive you. They will spin lies as easily as they spin their thread. No matter what or how much they take from you, do not let them take who you are. Where you come from."

The chamber door creaked open. Followed by the unfurling ribbon of yellow, floral light, spilling into the room. Aisling's mind yelled internally, fighting for the mortal queen to sit upright and ready herself. But Aisling's body refused, weighed down and anchored by fatigue.

A shadow entered her chamber. They were silent, shutting the door behind them before sweeping towards the center of the room. It was obviously a male, impossibly tall, lean, strong, stripping his armor and tossing it across an ottoman. Aisling watched him through the transparent curtains as she feigned sleep. Herself clouded with exhaustion, wading on the brim of consciousness.

Lir entered the room the same way he did in her nightmares, silently, unexpectedly, in the dead of night. She was most likely still dreaming, unaware that she lay trapped in her subconscious. Although in her dreams, the Fae King always climbed over the terrace and skulked towards her bed, wielding the same eyes as the night he'd killed the Cú Scáth. The same feral expression. All beast and bloodthirst. He didn't enter through the door as he did now. He didn't slowly strip off his clothes till nothing remained, save for his trousers. He didn't disappear in the bathing chambers, the sound of running water filling Aisling's ears. He didn't pad across the room and hesitate before the bed, realizing Aisling now lay in his furs as well—as though he had forgotten, didn't watch her for what felt like an eternity as he did now. For he'd been gone for a week, perhaps more—time was different here—doing whatever it was he did in the forest with his knights. And before then, Lir and Aisling had scarcely shared a bed save for their wedding night.

Aisling's eyes fluttered closed, somewhere between feigning and truly being asleep. Nevertheless, dream or not, Aisling heard the sweep of the curtains as Lir peeled apart these cobwebs. The weight of him tilting the edge of the bed. She felt him watch her, his eyes caressing the contours of her face. Drifting down her arms and hands. A regard as potent as physical touch itself. Aisling didn't know for how long he stood there or for how long he watched her. Only that once her eyes fluttered open once more, fighting sleep, some dream-like poison, slumber's tonic, he'd turned away. Setting a knife down on her bedside table.

Iarbonel's dagger.

A knife she'd lost in her tousle with the Cú Scáth. A knife she believed she'd never see again. One he'd also brought a scabbard for, placing it beside the weapon.

The Fae King faced the open terrace. His features lit with the moon's soft glow, rendering his damp skin radiant. His hair was a tumble of black, curling around his ears and pushed away from his forehead. Loose braids retied.

There were new scars now. A trail along his ribcage and three faint lines, like claw marks, dragging between his shoulder blades. Blades that now harbored wings. Only the starlight rendered them visible.

If this was a dream, she could do anything she liked, including touching his wings without fear of the consequences. She needn't be ashamed of wanting anything while in a dream. Even if what she wanted was to touch a member of the fair folk. To see what those wings felt like.

"*He is the worst of them: ruthless, merciless, no more than a beast driven by hunger, need, and power. But, unlike the wolf, he is insatiable.*" Nemed's voice drilled into her chest, opening a bottomless cavern.

While in shadow, Lir was the macabre King of Barbarians her father had always described. And while in light, he was the stag his people knew. So, for the first time, Aisling understood why the Aos Sí dubbed Lir the *Damh Bán:* he the embodiment of the still, silent, and powerful fae stags in this particular dream. A dream painted by the fair folk's gaze. And when she woke, he'd once again bare his fangs, eager for blood.

Beneath his breath, he hummed a haunting tune. One with

which Aisling was familiar, Cathan's song and the legend of Ina. The lullaby threatened to lull Aisling to sleep once again but she craved more. Desired her ears to drink and drink till the sun itself deigned to rise and the world remained a prisoner of the moon. The vibration of his voice, the way the natural world leaned closer, delighted by his song. The wisterias swaying back and forth. The ivy braiding themselves into Aisling's hair.

So, Aisling lay there still, eventually descending once more into deepest slumber. Stolen away, swept into another distant, dark world of dreams and nightmares. Whisked away to another place, another time. But Aisling found herself resisting those new machinations. Reaching rather for that one nightmare of the Fae King and his ivory wings. Just out of reach.

Chapter XIV

WHEN THE MORNING ARRIVED, AISLING WAS seized by the memory of him. Dreams of a winged fae lord sitting at her bedside, humming that song. At the time, there'd been some uncertainty as the memory was nothing more than a sleepy hallucination. But any doubts were quickly put to rest when Aisling was, yet again, alone in her bed, no sign of the Fae King having come or gone. Save for Iarbonel's dagger at her bedside, ruby winking in the morning light.

Aisling paled at the thought of him being so close. The eternal war lord had watched her as she slept.

And just as Aisling padded out of bed, the chamber door burst open. The mortal queen lunged for her dagger before she'd had an opportunity to witness who'd entered.

"Morning, *mo Lúra*," Gilrel said, strolling into the mortal queen's rooms, unfazed by the ebony dagger pointing in her direction. "I'm glad to see you're returning back to normal. Your recovery has gone better than anticipated for a mortal. Miraculous, really."

Aisling lowered the blade, sheepishly fiddling with it between her fingers.

"Apologies, I thought you might be someone else."

"Your *caera*?" Gilrel smiled wryly. Was she not concerned

about Iarbonel's dagger potentially being held at her king? Perhaps she didn't believe Aisling capable of doing any such damage to Lir even if it had been him at the door or perhaps the Aos Sí were warriors, violent savages even in the privacy of their relationships. Immediately, Aisling shook away the thought.

"I've caught word he's returned," Gilrel said, rummaging through Aisling's cupboards.

"Here? To Annwyn?"

"Where else?" the lady's maid retrieved a sleeveless, emerald tunic and various leather accessories to accompany it. Something far too form-fitting for Aisling to ever select herself.

The mortal queen dimmed. She'd known the Fae King would return at some point, but she hadn't been prepared for it to be today. She'd grown comfortable in her solitude despite the aching monotony of being cooped up in her chambers, a sensation that reminded her of life in Tilren and not in a positive way. That was the one change Aisling had been eager for, to wander wherever she liked. These chambers may not have been the dungeon she'd imagined before marrying Lir, but it was certainly a form of imprisonment.

"Come, we must prepare you," Gilrel said, already helping the mortal queen undress from her chemise.

"For what, may I ask?"

"Today is your opportunity to leave the castle's walls," the marten said, as if having read her mind. "Just to the training fields, beside the stables, but it's better than nothing."

Aisling had obviously never ventured towards the fae stables, but she'd seen them from a terrace further inside the castle while navigating the corridors with Galad. The stables stood beside the forest's edge, at the end of a verdant pitch where many of the Aos Sí sparred, wrestled, swung their blades, shot their arrows, and exercised the stags. Trained to slay mortals, Aisling thought bitterly to herself.

Aisling awkwardly slipped her legs into the trousers, aware of how they hugged the curve of her legs. Next, Gilrel tugged the emerald tunic over the queen's head, a vest and skirt of chainmail, all cinched by a leather corset. "The training fields?" The mortal queen swallowed.

"Peitho has requested you join her for the morning and, despite it being Peitho who asked, I thought you'd be delighted to receive some fresh air. As am I." It was then that Aisling realized Gilrel wasn't wearing her usual servant's dress but rather clad in two small shoulder plates, a bandolier, and a tunic of chainmail over her furry belly.

"You'll be joining us?" Aisling asked the chambermaid.

"Only if you allow it, *mo Lúra*. I haven't had the practice in some weeks and figured this would be a good time—"

"Of course," Aisling interrupted her. "I don't think I could handle Peitho on my own regardless." Gilrel did her best to conceal the shock, perhaps even gratitude, flaring across her expression. So, she swiftly redirected her attention to the magpies busily folding Aisling's chemise pooled on the marble floors.

"You underestimate yourself, *mo Lúra*. There is nothing the Lady Peitho despises more than a worthy opponent." Gently, Gilrel swiveled Aisling on her heel till she faced the mirror.

The mortal queen stilled; she didn't recognize her own reflection. Aisling had donned the guise of a warrior. The leather hugged her form, flattering what little muscle she brandished and lengthening her limbs. The chainmail padded her curves, hardening her countenance. Aisling looked as if she could swing a sword, raise a shield, defend herself.

"There's no competition. She's already lost." For if Peitho still resented Aisling's marriage to Lir, it mattered not. One couldn't unseal the treaty Aisling and Lir had already sewn in blood and vows. Never mind the fact they hadn't consummated the alliance, a secret Aisling pledged to protect. And if the southern princess chose to outright threaten their union, she threatened all of mankind. A threat not to be taken kindly by mortal clanns.

Gilrel weaved her paws through Aisling's hair, braiding it tightly.

"And now, *mo Lúra,* you underestimate Peitho."

This early in the morning, the training fields were empty. A long stretch of grass interspersed with round, shooting targets and dummies. Around its edge were the steep walls of the greenwood, standing as straight as sentinels.

Peitho sparred with three trooping females beneath Castle Annwyn's edge. Five stags already saddled and huffing fat clouds into the misty mountain air beside them.

"I'm assuming you've never held a bow before?" Galad said, standing behind both Aisling and Gilrel. The knight had insisted he escort them lest Lir return and catch him neglecting his responsibilities.

"How difficult can it be?" Aisling replied, already starting towards Peitho and swallowing the nerves eager for her to return to the security of her quarters. This considering Peitho moved as lethally as she'd done the afternoon of the *Snaidhm,* defeating those who challenged her with relative ease.

And if her strength weren't enough to inspire doubt, her beauty was; Peitho was autumn incarnate. Flaming hair, the twin spark to the vermillion of her feline eyes.

Peitho, however, wasn't the only striking creature Aisling approached. One bore curls like ice, a jagged scar through her bottom lip. The other seemingly bathed in the southern sun and the last, forged by the supple, umber fingers of the forest's streams. All four were much taller than Aisling, ever more obvious as each needed to tilt their heads to meet her gaze.

"*Mo Lúra*," Peitho purred breathlessly, narrowing her eyes. "I was concerned you wouldn't make it."

"I wouldn't neglect an invitation from the Princess of Niltaor."

"I only assumed because, since you've arrived, we've scarcely had the honor of passing you in the castle corridors or dining alongside Your Grace." Peitho exchanged knowing glances with the others, still breathless from their activity.

Aisling smiled, considering her next words carefully lest she fall victim to Peitho's silver tongue. After all, a lie risked being discovered, but the truth cost richly in embarrassment: to admit that her movement within the castle was limited. Indeed, the Aos Sí's lack of trust trumped the only card she bore against Peitho: that she, a mortal, was queen of the fair folk and the fae princess before her was not. She couldn't forfeit that advantage so easily.

"*Mo Lúra*, has been quite preoccupied with growing accustomed to our way of life since she arrived. Especially considering all the responsibility she's undertaken while the Lir's been away," Gilrel chimed, stepping into place beside Aisling.

The mortal queen stifled her shock, the gratitude rising in her chest, exhaling an inconspicuous sigh of relief. Before now, Aisling couldn't have ever begun to imagine being indebted to Gilrel for her sharp tongue.

"So, it seems," Peitho smirked. "Forgive me, I've been so rude, *mo Lúra*. These are my friends and soon to be yours: Blaine, Deidra, and Noirin." The three fae bowed. "Each from territories in Niltaor, Vulra, and Saryn. As favorites of mine, they accompany me on all my"—she hesitated, eyes flashing with doubt—"political outings."

Aisling nodded, understanding. Blaine, Deidra, and Noirin had likely been the fae selected to stand at Peitho's side during her union with Lir.

"Do you know how to fight, *mo Lúra*?" Noirin asked,

eyeing Iarbonel's dagger strapped to Aisling's thigh. A weapon of mortal making.

"I've had brief experience," Aisling confessed, for it was useless to feign otherwise. She was clearly slimmer and smaller than the Aos Sí before her. She didn't possess their chiseled limbs or stealth-like grace. But Noirin already knew that.

"Will she be able to participate today?" Deidra asked Peitho, as though Aisling weren't perfectly capable of responding herself.

"I'm eager to learn," Aisling interjected.

"Is it wise to teach a mortal, one who sleeps with the king, to fight?" Blaine asked, her expression twisted with obvious derision. "Should anything happen to her ... or him, it would be our heads beneath the axe."

"She already killed the trow, can already stomach the blow at the very least," Deidre added quickly. Aisling cringed at the mention of the trow, at times forgetting all of Annwyn had witnessed her slay the beast at Lir's command.

"Are you suggesting Lir couldn't defend himself against his own *caera*?" Galad piped.

"Most males cannot," Peitho bit, no longer interested in hiding the venom of her tone.

Unamused, Galad gestured towards the stags. "Let's begin if we ever wish to finish."

"Eager to be done with this verbal sparring and onto more physical means of casting blows, Galad?" Noirin grinned.

"If the Battle at Beigarth's Fjord is any indication, Noirin, you need the practice," the knight replied, already turning towards the stags, finished with this conversation.

But the very mention of war sobered Aisling. After all, the Battle at Beigarth's Fjord had been a bloody duel between the Aos Sí and the mortals, her very own clann having participated, Starn and Dagfin among those soldiers. They could've, should they have met more unfortunate ends, been one of the countless Lir, Peitho, Galad or even Gilrel had no doubt slain. The many they'd stained the earth's blood with.

But Aisling knew better than to voice her irritation. She was smarter than that. So, the mortal queen bit her tongue and followed Galad towards one of the prepared stags. A beast who fanned Aisling with an aura of excitement the nearer she approached and eventually mounted. For riding was one skill Aisling did possess.

Its round eyes considered her, tilting its head back. Close enough for the queen to better marvel at the diadem of tangled bone. So, Aisling slid her fingers over the contours of each antler.

"What are we to do?" Aisling asked, straightening her posture atop the mount. Galad retrieved a bow and quiver for her, handing it to his mortal queen.

"You see that dummy at the end of the pitch?" Galad asked, pointing into the distance. Far off stood a humanoid doll, limply nailed to a stake.

"We call it the Fire Hand of the North"—Blaine grinned wickedly—"for inspiration."

Aisling felt her blood boil, heating her skin till she nearly simmered. But losing her temper to these Aos Sí would be a loss. She couldn't allow them to provoke her.

"It's a game we train with. You'll be paired up to race towards the dummy. The first to impale its head wins," Galad explained, draping the quiver over her shoulders.

"Is there a certain distance I'm to shoot from?"

"You can shoot from here if you like. But you only have one arrow so make certain it'll find its target. On the other hand, the longer you wait, the more opportunity you give your opponent to strike the dummy first."

"You'll need to manage your mount, aim your reed, time your shot against the race, and hit the target," Gilrel elaborated, climbing atop her own stag. A funny sight if Aisling were being honest. But although small in form, Gilrel more than compensated with her confidence and unmatched resolve.

"Simple enough." But once the words left her lips, she knew Galad heard the uncertainty inherent within.

"It's not so difficult, *mo Lúra*. Hold the bow with one hand and the arrow between these two fingers"—Galad demonstrated—"set the arrowhead on your fist to steady it. I like to draw an imaginary line, a thread between the tip of my arrow and its target. Then inhale and shoot with the exhale. As for the riding, I'm confident in your abilities."

"No one expects you to master it on your first try, *mo Lúra*," Gilrel said, nudging her hart closer to Aisling's as the rest tested the weight of their arrows against their bows.

"No, we absolutely do not," Deidra added.

Gilrel ignored the trooping Aos Sí. "We've had centuries of practice."

"But by the way you hold that bow, I'm assuming you've had none." Peitho brought her stag beside Aisling's own.

"*An ragairl é fin, a* Peitho?" Galad barked but the fae princess shrugged him off.

"Gilrel and Blaine, why don't you demonstrate first?" Peitho tossed her fiery hair over her shoulder.

"Very well," Blaine replied, eyeing the marten with shards of ice for eyes.

Both warriors commanded their mounts towards the starting line, a band painted across the grass with two torches lit on either side. The rest of their group joined them, spectating a few paces away. But the doll, far in the distance, was a mere speck at the other end of the field.

"What happens if they miss?" Aisling asked.

After all, the challenge they'd described was a feat—at least, Aisling realized, for a mortal.

"We don't miss," Galad said, training his eyes on the dummy up ahead. The mortal queen was on the brink of discovering whether that was true and if it were, she was indeed riding straight into a humiliation she didn't believe

Peitho would soon forget.

"Are you ready?" Peitho asked and in response both Blaine and Gilrel nodded, taking hold of their reins and leaning forward.

"Very well," Peitho continued. "On the count of three."

Gilrel narrowed her beady eyes to the horizon.

The group fell silent, allowing them their concentration. Their stags prancing anxiously beneath them. A punch of energy, of eagerness, of a drive to run, to feel the morning wind in their manes, the ground beneath their hooves, startling Aisling.

"One, two," Peitho counted, "three."

Both Gilrel and Blaine erupted from the starting line, an explosion as they became mere blurs of color in the distance.

They raced wickedly fast. Shrinking with impossible speed as their mounts carried them towards the dummy. Blaine raised her bow first, reaching for the arrow in her quiver and balancing it on her bow. Gilrel pulled ahead, both paws still clasping the reins. Her beast quickened with Gilrel's guidance fully focused on her. Blaine, on the other hand, fell behind, near standing atop her mount. Poised to strike. She demonstrated a savageness Aisling realized was wonderful. A realization met by a familiar guilt.

"What's Gilrel waiting for?" Aisling asked Galad, her heart hammering against her chest. Her hands squeezed the leather stirrups. For still, Gilrel hadn't reached for her bow nor stood from her mount.

"Gilrel is prioritizing speed"—Galad watched intently as he spoke—"she'll come closer to the dummy more quickly if she keeps her attention focused on the stag. It's an easier shot the closer she rides to the dummy, but she risks her opponent succeeding on an early attempt. Blaine, on the other hand, prioritizes the shot. Her approach is more aggressive. If she can make the shot from far enough away, striking first, she wins despite the slowing of her stag."

Aisling held her breath, straining to watch them both in the distance.

By now, Gilrel was far ahead of Blaine, increasing the distance with each of her mount's gaits. But Blaine, indeed, shot first. Releasing the arrow from a way's back. The reed spun like a swallow and cut the fog, brushing past Gilrel's ears. A magnificent attempt. One that put mortal archers to shame. Including those within her own tuath.

But alas, Blaine's risk didn't pay off. The arrow struck just below the dummy's chin, a hair's length from its intended target. Aisling squealed, clenching her hands into fists.

"Does this mean Gilrel's won?" Aisling asked.

"Unless she manages to miss, then yes," Galad said. And sure enough, Gilrel stood atop her stag—a tiny, mighty little creature—raised her bow, placed the reed against the string, pulled and released. The arrow cut across the length of the field, nailing the dummy in the center of the head.

A perfect shot.

Aisling yelled, unable to stifle her excitement. A gesture that summoned Peitho's, Noirin's, and Deidra's twisted expressions.

"Don't be too thrilled just yet, *mo Lúra*. Your turn is coming," Peitho said, ignoring Gilrel's hoots of victory from across the field.

Blaine and the marten plucked their arrows from the dummy and trotted back, Gilrel's bow held above her in victory.

Noirin and Deidra lined up next, readying themselves just as Gilrel and Blaine had. Peitho, once again, counted down until they burst from their positions with equal fervor.

They raced fiercely, challenging their stags. Like twin stars, catapulting towards the earth. They were closer to the target now than either Gilrel or Blaine had been, at last releasing the arrows in nearly the same breath. Noirin's arrow struck first, landing in the dummy's chin. Deidra released her arrow next, puncturing the doll right between the eyes.

"Who's won?" Aisling asked Galad, watching as they both retrieved their arrows from the dummy. "They've both managed to hit it in the head."

"Aye, but Noirin released her arrow first," Galad said, "she wins this round."

The two fae returned to the group. And as they rode, Aisling knew that with every gate closer, time was fleeting before it was her own turn. She, whose skills in archery were only dismally better than her sword fighting, which was saying very little.

Aisling clenched her jaw, willing the flock of crimson-eyed ravens to settle within her stomach.

"Ready, *mo Lúra*?" Peitho asked, already positioning herself before the starting line. "Will you count us down, Galad?"

The pitch stretched on for an eternity. Much larger than it had ever appeared from the terrace in the castle. The dummy was dwarfed by the distance and disguised amongst the landscape of trees that spectated as well.

Aisling's hands grew slick with anger. The mortal queen was expected to fail and fail miserably. For no one expected her to compete against a member of the fair folk, pride unscathed.

Nevertheless, Aisling would rather suffer the loss than surrender. A more humiliating alternative.

"You needn't fret, *mo Lúra*," Peitho whispered beside her, "despite your showing at the *Snaidhm*, all of Annwyn knows you're no fighter. You mortal princesses are best suited for spectating rather than participating. It's best your attentions remain focused on birthing an heir. The Forge knows you'll need it"—Peitho beamed—"especially after what happened with his last *caera*."

Aisling stilled, unable to utter a word without scalding Peitho with her unfiltered thoughts. Too angry, too ambushed by the insinuation of another *caera* to properly organize her thoughts.

"You didn't know, did you? That Lir had another *caera* before you? Obviously, she died, or else you wouldn't be here, now would you? Died during childbirth as did the child. So difficult for us Aos Sí to bear children, you see. Of course, you mortals don't have much issue with that. Like cattle you breed endlessly." Her face twisted with disgust. "I thought I'd be his second *caera*, against all odds. Considering how *close* we were." Aisling sat frozen. "Don't look so shocked. Be grateful I informed you of his past, mo *Lúra*. I don't think anyone else would have."

Aisling struggled to find words.

A second *caera*?

Filverel was right. All the fae had indeed anticipated Aisling's union was nothing more than an execution. For Lir had entered that ceremony prepared to behead her. To go against the political union the mortals believed it to be. Just as Filverel had intimated. After all, Aisling didn't know much about fae customs or traditions, but she knew them well enough to know a second *caera* was unheard of. In which case, Lir hadn't had expected Aisling to survive that night.

But there was another side to Peitho's words. A part of Aisling's heart that weighed heavy for Lir in a way she didn't think was possible for a Fae King. He who'd killed so many of her kind. And yet, she pitied him.

Aisling opened her mouth to speak but before the mortal queen could gather herself, Galad's voice materialized, emerging from the fog.

"Three," he said, "two." Aisling's heart thrashed violently. "One."

Peitho exploded from the starting line, flying down the field. Aisling did her best to shake away the thoughts, her stag bucking, desperately aware of the distance Peitho was increasing by the breath.

"Go, Aisling!" Galad shouted.

Aisling encouraged the mount forward, cutting through the morning air. She pushed the stag, whispering for it to run faster, quicker, harder. She could feel its determination, its fury, its will to win at all costs. She coaxed those feelings in the stag. Allowed the stag to feel her own desire to win, her *need* to claim this one victory.

Peitho was far ahead, already gathering her arrow and pressing its head against the bow's rest.

Aisling clenched her jaw and narrowed her focus on the target. The stag flying beneath her. The ground below its hooves was a mess of color and texture. Aisling had never ridden this quickly. Never been allowed to. It was an opiate. That sweet sense of peril.

Aisling and the creature raced at Peitho's heels. A feat she once believed impossible when she'd seen how far ahead Peitho charged. But the dummy was taking form in the distance and she was running out of time to attempt a strike.

Aisling reached for her bow, releasing the reins in one hand. The gesture alone challenged her balance, nearly catapulting Aisling from the stag and into the mud below. But alas, she managed the bow. Now the reed. Aisling took the arrow from its quiver, squeezing the stag beneath her thighs to keep her balance.

"Set the arrowhead on your fist to steady it. I like to draw an imaginary line, a thread between the tip of my arrow and the target. Then inhale and shoot with the exhale."

Aisling imagined the gesture, then performed it herself. Much, much more difficult done than said. For the arrow continued to fall off her fist, worsened by the rock of the stag beneath her. She couldn't possibly aim under such conditions let alone on her own two feet.

Peitho was beside her now, the string of her bow pulled taut. At any moment, she'd release it, patiently biding her time.

Aisling inhaled and drew the string back—far more difficult than Noirin, Deidre, Blaine or Gilrel had made it seem. Her mortal muscles shook, not quite strong enough to hold the string in place for long. Body aching. All of her was as rigid as a board.

This was it. Aisling couldn't hold the string much longer. So, she set it free. Fired the reed before Peitho.

The reed cut through the air and travelled across the field with wicked speed. Aisling caught Peitho's disbelief as she herself released the string.

But who shot first mattered not, for the mortal queen's arrowhead soared over the dummy and into the feywild beyond.

Not only had Aisling missed the target, she'd done so miserably.

Peitho's reed, on the other hand, nailed the dummy in the mouth.

Clumsily, Aisling's body relaxed, muscles going slack, still burning from sudden exertion.

Peitho brought her mount to a stop elegantly, admiring her work on the dummy before wrenching the reed from its head.

"A pleasure, *mo Lúra*." Peitho grinned, the stag prancing beneath her triumphantly. "Don't take too long searching for your arrow in those woods. I hear the Unseelie are feral these days." And with that, the southern princess frolicked back towards the group, leaving Aisling alone at the brim of the woods.

The mortal queen fumed. Her entire body was charged only by the loathing she felt towards Peitho. A hatred, a jealousy, that thankfully distracted Aisling from all the fae princess had only just told her. It could all be lies. It could be a deception Peitho delighted in. But Aisling, despite her own hopes, knew it wasn't. Peitho had enjoyed spilling those secrets too much for any of it to have been a mistruth.

Aisling approached the woods on her mount, but the stag reared, unwilling to enter the forest.

The mortal queen cursed under her breath.

"Very well, I'll go on my own!" She shouted at her stag, dismounting and marching straight into the greenwood's keep.

The arrow was lost, and Aisling harbored little hope of ever finding it amidst the unruly brush. But Aisling preferred facing some other Unseelie than returning to the group empty-handed. Tangible proof she'd failed so miserably she couldn't find the arrow try as she might.

So, Aisling ventured deeper into the forest, ignoring the fear that brewed within her. Flashes of the Cú Scáth breaking through her courage the longer she searched. But her eyes didn't catch onto an arrow. Only a snake glaring back at her. It was perched upon a low hanging branch, hissing sweetly.

Aisling approached it cautiously, half anticipating it to slither away. But it didn't, rather glared at her through slit pupils, considering the mortal queen as she navigated deeper into the forest. Until someone or something pressed her against a tree. Pinned her to a rowan before she bore enough time to scream.

Chapter XV

"THE MORTAL PRINCESS APPEARS UNABLE TO resist certain peril," Lir purred, his face mere inches from her own, her feet dangling above the ground to meet his great height, "you shouldn't be out here alone. Where's Galad?"

"Let go of me," Aisling squirmed beneath him, but it was fruitless. His grip was impenetrable, one arm around her waist and the other pressed against the bark of the rowan, closer than Aisling had been to any individual much less a male. So, she cursed the simmering of her skin, the fire coiling tightly within her abdomen.

"It's never wise to release prey so panicked," His breath hot against her skin.

"Prey suggests a hunt, My Lord, a comparison mortal women don't take kindly to," Aisling bared her teeth, wrapping her slick palms around her dagger's haft, still strapped to her thigh.

"Because the opposite is often more accurate," Lir said, eyes miraculously bright, even in the morning haze. He caught Aisling's wrist before she could draw Iarbonel's dagger from its scabbard, thwarting her attempts. Aisling cursed beneath her breath. She hadn't planned on harming him. Simply threatening him enough to release her.

Aisling's face flushed with anger.

"You blame the cornered creature for baring its fangs."

Lir breathed another faint laugh. "I hardly think of you as a 'cornered creature' or prey for that matter. There's more that runs in your blood than your people would credit you for."

At last, Lir released her, her feet finding the earth inelegantly. He towered above her once more. The flashing of his eyes implied he'd acknowledged Aisling's fae leathers for the first time, her chainmail, boots, and tunic a stark contrast to her usual floor-length gowns.

Aisling exhaled, still counting each of his breaths should he move too quickly, too violently. This time, Aisling would have the dagger poised to strike the Fae King who filled her thoughts. Thoughts she foolishly attempted to burn over and over again. But always they regrew from the ash, sprouting and taking claim to her every passing whim. And now that he glared down at her, a tangible form to all her terrors, her blood burned. No longer simple words spoken around a fire.

"You speak as though you know my people," Aisling bit.

"I'd wager I've known more mortals than yourself, princess. Enough to convince me you're all the same."

"And yet you don't know me," Aisling spat.

"I know enough," he said, pupils dilated in a sage eclipse. No more was he the dream-spun stag sitting at the edge of her bed. The luminous king even in the shroud of evening. He was once again the wolf. Angry, formidable, ravenous.

"You've been tainted by an upbringing designed to breed hatred towards the Sidhe."

"And I'd bind myself to an enemy a thousand times over for the sake of my clann and my kind. To keep them safe. As would you." For Aisling was not the only one who'd sacrificed something. Lir too had bound himself to the mortal princess for the sake of the fair folk. Or at the very least, had resolved to behead a mortal princess to preserve his kin even if it meant war.

Aisling steeled herself, hardening against all emotion lest she dwell on the fact that the Fae King had borne every intention of severing her neck. And far worse, Aisling batted away the sympathy as quickly as it blossomed. There was no reason for her heart to ache at the thought of Lir's past.

Briefly, his emerald eyes flickered with understanding before collapsing into that thick, impassable wall of contempt. That cool arrogance rippled through his every muscle as he leaned against a nearby tree.

"Your people are still in danger. As are mine," Lir said, some of his amusement vanishing.

"You refer to the Unseelie, don't you?" Aisling surmised, searching his expression for answers. She'd wondered endlessly about the Unseelie. About what Lir was possibly doing in the feywilds all this time. But none seemed willing to impart any information. Not Gilrel nor Galad nor the birds and certainly not any of the other Aos Sí she'd encountered.

"Yes," he confessed.

"And have I endangered Annwyn?" The question was one Aisling had mulled over often. For hadn't it been intimated that Aisling's mortal scent was attracting the Unseelie to Annwyn's borders?

"The Unseelie are a threat regardless of your presence," he said, "they've been worsening for some time."

"That's where you've been, isn't it? Securing Annwyn's perimeter?" Aisling asked in earnest.

Lir grinned. "Concerned for my welfare, princess?"

"Of course"—she held his eyes—"so long as it affects my own." At this, Lir laughed, the sound caressing Aisling's senses.

"Aye, securing Annwyn's perimeter among other things," he continued, "dealing with the Unseelie is complex. They're not a single race. They're many with various lords, chiefs, matriarchs, and leaders. Ranging from pure beast to conscious, intelligent creatures. All chaotic, archaic, opposed to order and governed solely by hunger and need."

"And what of your sovereignty? You're their king are you not?" Aisling asked.

"Aye and we've managed to coexist for many centuries, constantly dancing on the precipice of conflict. For some time, they've questioned the leadership of the Sidhe and now that I've taken a mortal bride, they've grown angrier than ever before."

Aisling wondered why he divulged so much. No members of the fae court, thus far, had deigned to reveal anything so specific to the mortal queen. But Aisling said nothing for fear he would stop. Perhaps fae lords grew lonely just as mortal kings became. She'd seen such loneliness spread within her own father. The way he carried his shoulders, the vacant look in his eyes that Clodagh could never warm. For monarchs were burdened by responsibilities the average man couldn't fathom. And to carry such weight for centuries as did Lir ... Aisling couldn't imagine.

"Galad suggested my scent lures the Unseelie to Annwyn."

"Partially. The Unseelie have always hunted mankind and the Sidhe have allowed them to in exchange for their aid in protecting the feywilds, our kingdoms. This arrangement has proved effective over the centuries. But peace between the Sidhe and the mortals leaves the Unseelie without an incentive for their loyalty."

Aisling bristled, anger abated only by the passing thought that based upon this agreement between the Sidhe and Unseelie, perhaps mankind had mistaken the two fae categories all these years. That would explain the impossibly inaccurate accounts of what the Sidhe truly looked like. How they ate mortal babes in caves and tricked children into rivers. But this by no means exonerated her father. Nemed had fought the Sidhe for decades, captured them, tortured them. He would be well acquainted with his enemy.

Aisling was drawn from her thoughts by the shouting of

her name in the distance. Galad and Gilrel were calling for her.

"You should return to the others," Lir said, pushing off the tree. His voice was both coy and cold, iced, like the evergreens sparkling in the gems only the frost could afford.

"And what of you?" Aisling asked.

Lir eyed the surrounding woodland, and it was only a moment later Aisling heard what the Fae King already had: others approaching. And sure enough, through the trees, Aisling could see the faint shadows of Lir's knights making their way towards the castle.

"I'll meet you tonight," he said, already stepping back, away from her and towards his knights. "And then you can explain to me how a mortal princess learned to ride like that."

Aisling didn't move, only watched as he disappeared into the forest, as wild as a wolf and as elusive as the stag. And despite Galad and Gilrel's calls, she stood there, watching Lir vanish, catching him glance back before disappearing entirely.

It was a snake that at last diverted her attention. The black flame of a creature cautiously approached the mortal queen, abandoning her reed before her boots.

Aisling sunk into the tub. She'd already bathed in the steam, sour pudina, tayberry tea, and suds for the better half of the day with little desire to ever emerge.

But just as he'd promised, a lanky fox knocked on her chamber doors on behalf of the Fae King, requesting Aisling join Lir for supper. And by the time the sun set, Aisling was expected to be sat in the dining hall. A room she hadn't explored much less been invited to. This considering all her meals had been delivered to her chambers. A product of the distrust Aisling didn't blame fair folk for; her tuath only need send word for Aisling to betray her newfound world.

"Come, *mo Lúra,* we must get you dressed," Gilrel said, approaching the basin with a pile of warm towels in tow. Reluctantly, Aisling indulged the handmaid, allowing Gilrel to dry her, brush through her knots, spray her with the winds of Innisfree, and select a gown for the evening.

The dress was sky blue, large, transparent sleeves billowing before cinching at the wrists and elbows. The bodice ribbed like a corset. A foil to the loose, sweeping skirts that spilled from the waist in waves of cerulean. Giant moth's wings Aisling realized, stroking the soft surface and powdering her fingertips.

As with all fae gowns, it was a stark contrast to Tilrish fashion: the countless brown, grey, and black dresses Gilrel had stuffed into some unbothered drawer upon her arrival, her Neimedh tartans the only respite from the drab collection, tartans she cherished, woven in the threads of her ancestry. But Aisling hadn't donned these mortal gowns and fabrics lest she stand out like a beating heart in a graveyard. Or because Gilrel would contest it to no end. But whatever the excuse she gave herself, Aisling knew the true reason: these gowns were far superior to anything mortal hands sewed. No mortal land, township, kingdom, nor village existed where Aisling could sport beetles as jewels and spider webs for skirts, swathe herself in petrified rain, or bloody her neck with cave rubies. So why, Aisling began to ask herself, should she deny herself the guilty pleasure here?

Once Gilrel's magpies had stitched Aisling into the gown, the lady's maid began weaving her fingers through Aisling's hair. She tied it tightly behind her head as she always did. As Aisling always insisted.

"Perhaps, Gilrel," Aisling began, "you may try something different tonight." For Aisling was realizing more and more each day just how much she resembled Clodagh with her hair pressed against the scalp and knotted in a crude bundle.

"A woman's hair is a self-reflection. For that reason, a lady

never wears her hair undone. It is to be safely pinned, as prim as the lady herself. To wear one's tresses loose and wild implies the woman is just as impetuous as her hair suggests," Clodagh would say as she raked a brush through Aisling's locks.

"How would you like it, *mo Lúra?*" Gilrel asked, securing the tethers she'd already placed.

"Undone," Aisling replied. The lady's maid considered the mortal queen before putting herself to work, struggling to hide a satisfied grin as she removed the pins one by one.

"Easily enough done," the chambermaid said, already barking orders at her magpies. Birds who gathered Aisling's hair in their beaks, knotting disheveled braids to complement the loose mane of unkempt black.

The gilded doors parted, and the mortal queen stepped into the dining hall. Barreled ceilings dripped with showers of hanging butterwort, bittercress, bilberries, buttercups, and bogbeans. Chandeliers of waxing wendies hung low, sweeping the heads of the Aos Sí seated at their tables spilling over with chartreuse gelatins, pudding pies, stewed rabbit, tea-toasted buns, and goblets of strawberry wine to name a few. And while several bears stood guard along the periphery of the hall, it appeared the entirety of Annwyn's royal court was in attendance. Violent reds, blues, greens, golds, and silvers dying their tunics, the females' rich Gúnas, their capes, their tailored trousers. Flaunting their attire as winged Aos Sí twirled in the air with their partners, wings tickling the vaulted ceilings and showering the hall in loose petals.

As Aisling entered, the fair folk turned to glare, their feline eyes exploring her gown, her hair, her bare feet padding across the marble floors speckled with leaves and insects.

"Are there always this many Aos Sí attending dinner with

the king?" Aisling asked her handmaid, following shortly behind.

"It's to celebrate Lir's return to Annwyn," Gilrel explained, nudging Aisling forward.

"*And remember, Aisling: even in your dying breath, never give them the satisfaction of seeing you wilt, witnessing your fear. You represent all our kind when among them now. Never forget that.*"

From across the room, through the maze of Aos Sí, Aisling's eyes met Lir's. The Fae King danced amidst the crowd of fair folk, taller than even his fae subjects, stepping to the flutes, fiddles, and bodhrans. That intangible cord between she and Lir growing taut, groaning with every inch Aisling grew nearer.

He was dressed in an ebony tunic embroidered with sage thread, split down the center so Aisling could see the white of his shirt beneath, its undone tethers, the chains he brandished around his neck, and the skin below his collar where fae markings proudly graced.

And if it weren't for his elegant, masterful skill for the dance, Aisling wouldn't have noticed his partner, Peitho, as radiant as the southern sun.

"*Mo Lúra,*" a voice said from nearby, shattering Aisling's trance. The mortal queen whipped her attention towards the source, her stomach instantly plummeting.

Filverel approached her, a sparkling chalice of wine in hand.

"You're looking well," he said, cocking his head to the side and probing her with his opalescent eyes. "I'd ask if you've heard back from your father but I'm already aware of the answer."

Aisling's jaw set, face reddening.

"Any idea why that may be?" He pressed, smiling even as he took a large sip of his wine.

"Have you nothing better to do than concern yourself with

my father?"

"I'm Lir's first court advisor. It's my job to concern myself with the Fire Hand of the North. Especially when he's been so silent. I think you'd agree his sudden if not abrupt tranquility is cause for concern. I can't remember a time the High King of Tilren wasn't clumsily trampling on fae sensitivities."

"Because there's never been a time presaged by a peace treaty. One Nemed proposed." Aisling made a point of peering around Filverel, more interested in concluding this conversation than prolonging it. But Filverel laughed, bearing his pointed canines.

"How naive you are if you believe Nemed to abandon all he covets for the sake of peace."

"If that's what you believe, then why did any of you agree to the union?"

"You may recall my admission that I was among those who advised against it," Filverel said, running his fingers through his silken hair. "Oh, don't look at me like that. I had your best interests in mind, *mo Lúra*. You should be thanking me. It was Lir who believed your head was worth the risk."

Aisling's brows knotted, irritated that in this sense, she agreed with Filverel. Especially after what Peitho had already divulged.

"*He is the worst of them: ruthless, merciless, no more than a beast driven by hunger, need, and power. But, unlike the wolf, he is insatiable.*" Nemed had been right about Lir. Had known and Aisling had never doubted his word. So why now did Aisling feel the prick of a sharp shadow following the truth of Filverel's argument?

"Aisling," his voice called, one Aisling could identify in her sleep. Not because she'd heard it often but because it was a voice that belonged to the Fae Lord.

Lir approached, his cunning eyes fixed on the mortal queen. Peitho was no longer visible amongst the hordes of twirling fair folk.

"You drive me mad waiting."

"You shouldn't claim to wait upon that which you dread," Aisling quipped, shooting daggers at the king from beneath her dark lashes.

His expression lifted in the slightest, the corners of his lips curling.

"Care to dance?"

Aisling hesitated, his eyes fluttering across her every feature. The last time Aisling had partaken in such revelry with the Fae King, she'd been enchanted, on the precipice of her sanity.

"Perhaps the fleshling requires sustenance," Filverel suggested, his empty concern maddening.

Lir considered Aisling again, eventually gesturing towards his throne and the empty seat beside it, "I'll settle for dinner then. But I warn you, a debt to a fae is a perilous debt indeed."

Lir offered his hand to the mortal queen. Aisling glared at it for a moment, the rage and sorrow she felt towards the Fae King collapsing into complete dissonance: Lir's past challenged Aisling's preconceived expectations of him—a nightmare when compared to the waking fantasy, each a blurry truth existing simultaneously. But, to Aisling, it mattered little what she personally felt or thought of the Fae King. What mattered was the treaty, her duty, the strengthening of the mortal world as a result of her union with Lir.

So, Aisling accepted Lir's hand. Her chest tightened at his touch. And if it hadn't been for the muscle flaring in his jaw, the hesitation, Aisling wouldn't have believed he also sensed that strange string curling between them. They'd touched hands once before, when they were handfasted, and even then the sensation had been enough to unbind her. An acute, near painful jolt of energy. The joining of that which grows with that which kills.

Lithely, Lir collected himself, guiding Aisling towards the dining table with both Filverel and Gilrel following shortly behind.

Aisling recognized many of the knights sitting around the table: Galad and Rian were positioned the closest, along with, unfortunately, Filverel. Cathan, Yevhen, Tyr, Einri, Aedh, Hagre among others, sat further down until the knights dissolved into trooping fae Aisling was both familiar with and not. Among those she knew were Peitho, Blaine, Noirin, and Deidra. Aisling intentionally avoided their watchful eyes as Lir led her towards the seat beside his own.

Gilrel sat to the left of Aisling, waiting for the mortal queen to settle before doing so herself.

And as the mortal queen took her seat beside the king, she couldn't help but notice her plate was different from the others, her meal specifically prepared for mortal consumption. Even her chalice was one of water instead of wine. For only demons and monsters could eat poison and live, Aisling thought to herself.

Those seated nearest to the mortal queen, nodded their heads in her direction so Aisling stiffly returned their gestures. Filverel inspecting her every twitch as though she might burst into flames before his very eyes.

It didn't take long for the table to resume their conversation, fae babble to Aisling's untrained ears. They devoured their meals with bare hands, ignoring the ivory utensils set before them. An orchestra of drunken laughter, heated arguments, clumsy songs, and outlandish tales. So unlike Castle Neimedh's suppers, meals to be eaten in silence or idle, soft chatter. No discussion of politics or business, humor or controversy. All rules which Starn, Iarbonel, Fergus, Annind, and Aisling broke on several occasions. Fergus, in particular— for as much as he hated the fair folk—would find enjoyment in meals like these: endless food and the permission to indulge with wild abandon.

Galad turned to Lir then, murmuring something in Fae to which Rian glowered in Galad's direction, pointing his knife at the fae knight. Rian gestured at Aisling next and Lir grinned wolfishly. The mortal queen bristled, eyes darting between the knights as they continued back and forth. Speaking of her as though she were a child and beneath their direct acknowledgment.

"Galad says you can outride most of Lir's knights, including Rian," Gilrel at last translated in Aisling's ear.

"If the mortal queen can outride me, as you say, then Galad would grow dizzy watching the circles she rode around him," Rian bit back, shoving the sapphire-eyed knight in the shoulder.

"If only you were all there to witness her nearly outrace Peitho," Gilrel said, speaking to Cathan and Einri as well now, leaning in to join the conversation.

"She started half a field behind and passed Peitho still," Galad added, daring a glance at the fae princess too far down the table to overhear their conversation amidst the chatter and music of the hall. This despite her incessant glances at Lir and Aisling.

"What stag did she ride?" Einri asked, his hair tied away from his face in a loose bun, exposing sharp cheekbones and deep-set amber eyes.

"Faolan," Galad replied, shoveling another mouthful of pudding pie.

"A stubborn, willful old brute," Rian said, leaning back in his chair and crossing his arms. "That beast listens to no one. Would rather graze than be ridden."

"And how does a mortal queen learn to ride more proficiently than a member of the Sidhe?" Cathan asked, lowering his head to glare at Aisling.

"Forgive me, but I hardly believe it. Galad is known to exaggerate the truth and Gilrel is her lady's maid," Einri waved his hand dismissively before lunging across the table for another loaf of bread.

To Aisling's surprise, both Gilrel and Galad flared in their seats, opening their mouths for the rebuttal.

"I saw it myself," Lir piped first, "She was more spirited than Faolan himself, an energy the beast recognized. Animals respond to fearlessness in their masters; they seek that courage."

Lazily he leaned back in his chair, his body tilted to the side as he stroked the intricately carved arms of his throne. Every lean, elegant finger was bedecked with fine rings.

"Courage to ride a stag?" Cathan scoffed.

"When you're as small a mortal as she, capable of breaking every bone in her body should she lose her dominion over Faolan, fall and be crushed upon impact," Lir growled, "then yes, there's courage in riding a stag."

Cathan and Einri shrank at Lir's tone, tails between their legs, their goblets suddenly quite fascinating.

"Such courage will prove useful in the days to come," Filverel interjected, flashing Aisling a taunting glare.

"In the days to come?" Aisling asked, eyes darting between the fair folk around her.

Lir leaned toward Aisling, the smell of him encouraging Aisling to do the same but she willed herself steady.

"Do you remember what I told you earlier about the Unseelie?" Lir searched her expression.

"Yes, the agreement you struck with their kind, now rendered obsolete by our union, puts Annwyn in jeopardy of their wrath," Aisling summarized, cautiously glaring around the table for some indication as to what this was all about.

"Not just Annwyn. All of the Sidhe," Lir added, petting the stem of his goblet, a gesture that was wildly distracting.

Aisling tore her attention back towards the discussion at hand. "But you've made progress with the Unseelie during this time you've been away?"

Lir exchanged glances with his knights.

"Not quite," he said, licking his lips, "the Unseelie are ... difficult."

"That's putting it mildly," Rian interjected.

"Such creatures don't respond well when they feel slighted," Lir continued, "often they refuse to speak with us and when they do there's little progress to be made."

"Elusive beasts." Galad shook his head.

"Can't you command them? As their king?" Aisling asked, uncertain why they suddenly chose to speak of the Unseelie in her presence but too curious to risk them stopping.

"The same way mortals command the weeds growing in their gardens? No, they simply pluck whatever deigns to acknowledge their self-assigned authority from their path; would you have us do the same with the Unseelie?" Cathan's eyes narrowed, his words designed to cut Aisling where she sat. But she wouldn't give him the satisfaction, so she sat still, unprovoked, unbothered by his misplaced rage.

"Such a strong hand could cause a revolt on their part if it hasn't already," Lir said, tilting his head down to meet her gaze once more. "I can't risk them spilling Sidhe blood to make a point."

"And what of the mortals?" Aisling asked.

"They're equally at risk of the Unseelie's wrath," Filverel said, "if not more so."

So, it was just as she'd feared. If only she could speak with Nemed. If only he'd reply to her letters.

"But fret not, *mo Lúra,*" Filverel said, reading her expression once more, "you're going to help."

Aisling's heart leapt. "What do you mean?"

"We need the Unseelie to acknowledge our attempts at reconciliation and there's nothing the Unseelie respond to better than their own appetites," Filverel continued, his words laced with sadistic delight.

Galad crossed his arms. "You're going to help us negotiate with the Unseelie."

"You've showcased your talents well, a vibrant perfume to the trow and then the Cú Scáth. So, this will be your first opportunity to serve the Sidhe as their new sovereign, luring the Unseelie from their hiding." Filverel beamed. "The perfect bait."

Aisling met Lir's gaze, her chest rising and falling rapidly.

"We leave tonight," Lir said, downing the rest of his wine without another glance in her direction.

Chapter XVI

AISLING PACED BACK AND FORTH IN HER CHAMBERS. Gilrel, on the other hand, busied herself assembling both her own and Aisling's belongings for the journey. She worked alongside a red fox: Liam, he'd said his name was. Lir's first squire who'd be accompanying them on the trip. None of the knights had specified how long they'd be gone but it was evident enough that it wouldn't be for a handful of days. No, they'd implied weeks, perhaps even months depending on how *responsive* the Unseelie were.

Aisling stripped off her gown in the bathing chambers and dawned the leathers she'd worn earlier that day. Already she found herself accustomed to their movement and fit. But none of that could assuage the fear bubbling in her stomach, the fury that the Sidhe would use their own queen as bait, the *excitement* of embarking on such a perilous quest. The latter threatening to implode the mortal queen should she halt her pacing, the beat of her fingers on her thigh or the gnawing of her bottom lip.

The door creaked open, the scent of fresh pine sweeping into the room. Aisling startled at the sound, clutching her chest as she reached for Iarbonel's dagger.

Lir stood at the door, his hands in his pockets, his hair

more ruffled than it'd been before.

Although the mortal queen didn't think it possible, her heart thrashed more heavily against her chest. Blood rushed to her ears.

Lir entered leisurely, as though afraid Aisling might startle should he move too quickly.

"Liam, Gilrel," he addressed his squire and her lady's maid, his voice like mulled wine, "will you give us a moment?"

Liam bowed and Gilrel curtsied, flashing one last glance at Aisling before she brushed past Lir and into the corridors beyond.

It didn't take long for the Fae King to meet Aisling's glare, dragging his feline eyes across the floors swept with leaves, the bed sheathed in gossamer, and the terrace doors strangled by vines, till they landed on the mortal queen. Against her own volition, Aisling shivered.

"You're already dressed," he spoke first, pacing nearer. "Several of my knights will be disappointed to know they've already lost their bets; they believed you'd be scaling the side of the mountain in escape by now."

"How often they forget my duty to my own kingdom"—Aisling opened her terrace doors—"*despite* your savagery, this is my fate, my role to play for my kind."

And with each of Lir's steps forward, Aisling resisted the urge to step away.

"If I'm to die in this plot of yours, then I imagine you'll be swiftly repaid by my father. A variable you aren't unaware of."

Cruelly, Lir grinned, sliding his fangs along his bottom lip.

"Or," Lir purred, the moonlight washing his fine features as he cornered Aisling onto the terrace. "Do you secretly enjoy this?"

The small of Aisling's back bumped against the cool edge of the railing. A railing wrapped in garlands of honeysuckle and baby's breath. A single barrier preventing Aisling from plunging into the surrounding canopies, the oceans of clouds, and the twinkling fae city that lay beneath.

"Enjoy what exactly? Your barbarism? Your foods that would drive my mortal self mad upon consumption? Your people's palpable disdain for me? Or perhaps the fact you so willingly risk my life as though mortal breath means nothing to you? Even your queen's?" But as soon as Aisling said it, she wished she hadn't. *Your* queen. She was no such thing and the flash of mischief that graced his eyes the moment she spoke the word aloud was enough to make Aisling rue it all the more.

"You believe a queen's breath more valuable than a commoner's?" He taunted, caging Aisling on either side of his arms, gripping the railing. He tilted his head down to meet her gaze, forcing her to lift her own lest she appear afraid, withering before the fae lord her body could no longer deny she feared. A terror Lir likely smelled for it attracted him closer, enjoying how her body tensed when in the presence of his own. And the longer Aisling resisted, the greater the game to him.

"In regards to you, it's not the queenship that would make such a breath more valuable. Only that it so happens that the queen, bound to you by political union, breathed it."

"That *would* make you more important to me," he said, "so much so, that I wouldn't risk your mortal life."

"Yet you offer me to the Unseelie?"

"Not an offer," he said, "more like parading you before the Unseelie."

Aisling's temper flared but she wouldn't take the bait. Not if that's what he wanted.

"And that's so much better?"

"You tell me: would you prefer to be offered to the Unseelie so they may do with you as they like, or merely brandished till they crawl from their holes and I can protect you?"

The very mention of such aberrations skulking from their cavernous depths was enough to make Aisling's skin crawl much less dangled before them like a prize pig. But despite herself, Aisling was eager to lay eyes on the Unseelie. To witness them in all their monstrous glory. To behold what demons dwelled in the darkest corners of the wild. To unearth the horrible mysteries she'd shamefully and so secretly obsessed over as a child.

"Neither," Aisling replied and Lir tilted his head curiously. "Another lie."

The Fae King lazily eyed her undone hair. Tresses that gushed down her chest in unruly, raven torrents before studying her eyes. Eyes as violet as Nemed's and all the other mortal sovereigns in her ancestry. What loathing brewed within him each time he met her glare? He must've seen her father, the blood spilt between himself and this mortal adversary. The blades they raised in loathing for the other. The fires that lit the North, stoked by Lir's very forests. Within the Fae King lived untended gardens of hatred for her father, devouring all that was near and fostered by centuries of rivalry. Not only for Nemed but for all the mortal sovereigns before him, all tied to Aisling by blood of iron.

"As much as my people may pray for it, I won't let you be harmed." Lir released Aisling from his gaze, eyes gilded by the glowing city down below. "Despite my own loathing of your kind, not only are we ensorcelled to one another but I also made a vow the night of our union. Perhaps mortals don't treat such vows as sacredly as do the Sidhe, but political treatise or not, I made the decision to speak those promises and I don't intend to break them."

Lir clenched his jaw, an image of a scarred knight, kissed by iron blades and jaded by grief's arrow.

"By the Forge, I vow to you the first cut of my heart, the first taste of my blood, and the last words from my lips," Lir said, repeating the words they'd both sworn that night. A sacrifice they'd both made for the sake of their people. An obligation that weighed heavily on the Fae King, the signs of ache written across his burdened shoulders, as tangible as when Aisling felt them herself. Yet Lir's responsibility to the Aos Sí far outweighed Aisling's own. The mortal queen was a sacrificial lamb. Lir, the axis on which the Aos Sí revolved.

Aisling swallowed, unsure how long she allowed herself to drown in his eyes, dishonorably, guiltily admiring the bestial, primeval king all the mortal Isles feared.

"No harm will befall you," he repeated, stepping back from Aisling and slipping his hands into his pockets once more.

Aisling's brows pinched. Lir still wasn't aware of what Aisling knew, the night of their union hadn't been the only time he'd sworn those vows. There'd been a time in his life when he'd spoken those verses to another, his first *caera*. One he hadn't been forced into speaking those words to for the sake of his kind. Someone he'd attempted to raise a child with. Someone he'd lost and with it, a part of himself. A few weeks ago, Aisling would've thought the fair folk incapable of love or human emotion. But the pain in Lir's eyes was sharp. A shard Aisling could prick herself on should she dwell on it further.

Aisling didn't know how long they stood like that. In silence.

"My father," Aisling began abruptly. "I'm expecting a letter from him. If I do not reply, I fear for my race should negotiations with the Unseelie not fare well."

Lir considered her for a moment, eyes darkening. For each time Nemed was mentioned, a shadow seeped beneath his skin.

"I'll ensure any letter addressed to you will find you even as we travel," he said, turning his back to her.

"That's possible?"

"Our ravens can find a recipient anywhere in the known world. In fact, your father should be in possession of our raven until he responds to your initial correspondence." He started towards her bedroom door. So silently did he move that

Aisling would've believed him already gone if she weren't counting his every step

"And what of it being inspected?" Aisling asked, hoping Filverel wouldn't be joining their mission. The very thought brought bile to her throat.

"If your father does indeed respond, we'll cross that river when we come to it." Lir reached for the crystal knob, turning once and opening the door. The age-old entrance groaned, freeing a pillar of floral light from the corridor beyond.

He turned one last time, meeting Aisling's gaze. His hair curled around his pointed ears, the occasional braid loosely tied and sweeping his cheekbones.

"You may not realize it now, but you can trust me, Aisling."

The mortal queen tilted her head, doing her best to interpret his expression. But, once again, it was unreadable. Schooled into that forest of ice he'd mastered over lifetimes.

At last, she nodded, ignoring the knotting of her stomach the sound of her name on his lips inspired. Something she believed she'd never grow accustomed to. On his tongue, her name didn't belong to her. It sounded wilder, more feral than on her own.

"They will spin lies as easily as they spin their thread."

The mortal queen could and likely never would trust the Fae King. Lir despised her too greatly and she him for any loyalty to bloom between them. He'd protect her on this trip but not because of any vow he'd now pledged twice. Once to her and once to another.

"Never let your guard down around him, Aisling. Never give him an opportunity to choose between you and what he covets."

Lir would protect Aisling to prevent further war with mankind. War, Lir had already gone to great lengths to avoid. Nemed had been right, Aisling reassured herself. A vow would appear sanctimonious enough until there was something that stood between Aisling's life and what the Fae King desired—

needed. For example, negotiating with the Unseelie. All she could do was surrender to the fact that she was now here, amongst the Aos Sí and subject to her husband's will. For this was her purpose. Clann Neimedh would want her to die if it meant protecting the union they'd sacrificed her for. And for a moment, a blame-worthy moment, Aisling allowed herself to consider that perhaps all this—this rationale to willingly join Lir on his quest—was more than an obligation. Perhaps all those years locked within Tilren's walls had driven Aisling mad for now she craved this, this adventure. To place a face to all the horrors she'd lied awake imagining. To encounter magic in all its loathsome form.

And as suddenly as the Fae King had entered, he vanished out her chamber doors, leaving behind the smell of the earth after a storm. A wild perfume was abandoned in his wake. A fragrance that had long called Aisling past the walls of Tilren, across the verdant fields, and into the forbidden forests. A scent that drove her mad long into the nights when she grew restless of years cooped inside an iron keep. Long before she ever met the fae lord. And yet, perhaps her father had been right. Perhaps the fair folk did lure innocent mortal maidens into the wilds. Perhaps Aisling was still drunk on the Fae King's woodland stupor, foolishly dancing into his realm of wicked wonder.

CHAPTER XVII

"WHY DO WE TRAVEL AT NIGHT?" AISLING ASKED Lir. The Fae King seized her waist, lifting the mortal queen onto Saoirse's saddled back. Gilrel, Liam, and the rest of Lir's knights mounted their beasts alongside the mortal queen. As well as, unfortunately, Filverel. One who'd grinned as she'd approached the stables with stags prepped and tethered to their belongings. Mounts prancing eagerly before the lip of the forest as though the rustling of the leaves in the nighttime gale were curses only the beasts could understand.

"Unseelie prefer the night, creatures of shadow and moonlight," Galad interjected, grabbing his saddle's horn and swinging himself atop the mount. "It's said the Gods Forged strange phantoms that climb down from the skies and lace every bite of night with a juice that makes the lips loose, the body wild, and the thoughts feral. And while the diurnal creatures slumber, their nocturnal brethren rise from their dens to stalk the midnight tonic till the sun ascends come dawn"—he grinned devilishly—"the evening fiends reign, beckoning their spirit brothers to drink up the starlight."

For the past several hours, the sky burned with embers of rose, the sun descending and bowing to great summits. Now, the moon took its seat on the starry throne, tilting its head to observe their fae procession.

Aisling peered into the surrounding woods. Her skin grew cold. No longer pressed beneath the light, these forests had abandoned their daylight persona; now, the trees tiptoed in the shadows, humming to the chorus of mating insects. The woodland was watching. Anxious to greet their guests even if this fae cavalcade would forge a trail through its agrestal keep. Did they know Aisling was the daughter of he who burned so many of their kind? He who laid waste to countless trees till nothing but ash carpeted the floors upon which men built their castles?

"*Frell regla ort uirli má téann lú le do guid scéalta*," Hagre chastised, sitting near enough to overhear their conversation. His fae accent was thicker than most. So dense, Aisling couldn't interpret his words even when he spoke her tongue. Hagre was also the largest member of the Aos Sí, head shaved and scarred with countless angry lesions—iron wounds, Aisling realized.

"The mortal queen is not so easily frightened, Hagre," Gilrel quipped, twirling a whisker in her paw. The marten donned countless weapons: daggers, small throwing axes, a custom bow, and a quiver filled to the brim with reeds. Aisling had already witnessed her proficiency with the bow, eager to behold how she made use of the rest.

"We'll see how she fares against the Bocanach then," Filverel winked. The court advisor dressed in combat leathers of his own, throwing knives strapped across his bandolier, and his long hair tied behind his head.

"Try the Fomorians," Aedh added.

"The Fomorians?" Aisling asked, all too aware of the foul taste the word burned onto her tongue.

"One of the more," Rian chimed, nudging his stag nearer to Aisling's, "*vicious* species of Unseelie."

"Some say they were cast from the blackest cauldrons of the great Forge, skin as pale as the light of the moon, fangs carved for ripping their prey to shreds," Aedh said, tossing back a thick flask of fae wine. Aedh bore the loudest laugh of all the fae knights, often cajoling the rest into some wild, misbehaved nonsense.

"And everything they touch, rots," Cathan added. "The personifications of death and darkness and blight."

Aisling averted her eyes from the shadows and yellow-eyed beasts peering back from the abyss beyond.

"You believe you'll find these Fomorians?" She asked.

"With your mortal scent wafting from this edge of the forest to the next, they won't be able to resist crawling from their pits." Aedh offered Aisling a drink from his flask. A flask Gilrel slapped away, hissing a vulgar phrase in Rún.

Aisling swallowed, Aedh's descriptions given life in her imagination. What the beast wanted with her Aisling dare not dwell upon lest she lose the resolve plated against her confidence like armor, the only variable precluding the chattering of her teeth. That and her willingness to remain poised before the fair folk.

Lir secured several more travel sacks onto Saoirse's back, knotting them with a braided thread, a string of silver said to be sourced from starlight itself. Unbreakable save for by blades of gold, Gilrel explained after she'd caught Aisling admiring the embroidery of a freshly sown fae gown. But it was so fine and so lovely, Aisling knew Clodagh would go to great lengths to collect this string for herself, fae or not.

Lir leapt onto Saoirse's back, positioning himself behind Aisling, his arms wrapped around her to grab the reins in his gloved hands.

"I can ride on my own," Aisling hissed in a whisper, her breath catching at the cool touch of his armor against her bare skin. All the knights donned parts of their protective plating, gleaming, expertly cast trappings of metal. However, their bodies were, for the most part, not sheathed in silver but rather swathed in training leathers, strapped with every sort of fae weapon imaginable, only one of their shoulders padded with armor and chainmail around their torsos.

Some wore helmets while others wore hoods. Hoods that veiled their expressions in shadow. Lir's own helmet, embellished with antlers that spread in bone-white wings, hung from the side of Saoirse's saddle while his hood cast a dark band across the top half of his face. But no night was ever dark enough to extinguish the light in his feline eyes. Eyes that never seized to catch her wandering glances.

"Would you prefer to ride unguarded should the Unseelie appear?" He asked, leaning his head down to whisper in her ear. Chills ran down Aisling's spine at the heat of his breath, slithering around her throat until she felt it dissolve within the crater of her clavicle.

"Isn't that the plan?"

"The plan is to lure them. Not feed them."

Aisling huffed, "I'd prefer to be far from this place entirely."

The mortal queen allowed the anger bubbling within to save her from sinking against his chest in search of heat. For despite the warm winds the forest sighed during the day, the dry heaves of nighttime were cold and frigid, eager to be felt.

"But that's not true, is it?" He challenged, commanding Saoirse forward and through the group of stags that surrounded them. "Your body hums with this," he said and at the mention of Aisling's body on his lips, every inch of her indeed heated. She squirmed, unable to sit still beneath the weight of his forwardness. "You're attracted to the peril of it all," he continued, bringing Saoirse to the forefront of their cavalcade.

"Isn't everyone?" Aisling asked genuinely. For isn't that what drove her father? Her brothers? Lir himself gone for days in the forest? Other than their responsibility, of course.

"No," he said, matter-of-factly, "most live in fear."

"Do you?"

Lir hesitated before replying. His shoulders tensing.

"Yes," he said to the mortal queen's surprise. She hadn't expected the Fae King to say such a thing, something uniquely vulnerable. The mortal queen craned her neck to catch a glimpse of Lir's expression, his polished emeralds shadowed by memory.

Sympathy bloomed within the mortal queen before she bore the opportunity to trample it. But by the time Aisling blinked, the Fae King had already recovered, rather enchanted himself by the forest beyond.

Saoirse stomped her hooves restlessly. Aisling stroked her neck. The stag stood at the head of the procession now, eager to get this quest over and done with. The quicker they entered, the quicker they would leave.

"*Coirrigh an fhoirliú deo!*" Lir shouted to his men, turning Saoirse a step so he faced his knights. Each one nodded in response, slipping on their gloves, lifting their hoods, and clicking their tongues. Their mounts obeyed, propelling their riders into a steady trot behind their Fae King.

Falling effortlessly into formation, each knight rode in silence. Rian and Galad journeyed side-by-side behind their king and queen. Filverel rode next. Then came Gilrel and Liam, followed by the rest of the fae knights: Cathan, Aedh, Einri, Hagre, Tyr, Yevhen, and several others Aisling didn't yet know the names of.

Aisling held her breath as they neared the brim of the woods. That first step from glade to forest was the crossing of a threshold from one world to the next. To believe Lir was the sole sovereign to this wooded, arcane empire, the one whose breath now warmed her skin, sent a flock of crimson-eyed ravens through her belly.

Saoirse whinnied nervously, stepping one hoof and then another into the forest. One by one the fae knights sunk into the greenwood, peeling back curtains of firs and pines, nothing to indicate they once stood at the forest's edge other than the branches snapping back into place behind them, waving at the outside world. And just like that, they were devoured by the feywilds with nowhere to travel but onward.

The forest grew dense, dark, and deep. The arms and legs of the woods stretched their limbs to touch their visitors as the fae knights cut through the twisted roots, the fallen trees, and the carpet of fog slithering around the stags' hooves. Guardians leaning in close to whisper about their company in a language Aisling couldn't understand.

Together, ten Aos Sí couldn't wrap their arms around the trunks of the eldest trees nor climb their highest branch. Only the strongest of the moon's rays managed to break through the canopies in slender showers of white light.

They journeyed for several hours, parting the evening winds like rapids in a running river, never once stopping to rest. Aisling imagined that should this voyage be under any other circumstance, she might find herself dozing off while riding, lulled to sleep by the steady crunch of Saoirse's hooves on the pine needles below. But adrenaline fueled her. Not to mention, little could make her forget about the savage that rode behind her, plunging them further and further into the Northern wilderness. And with every snap of a branch, every hoot of an owl, every bristle of a nearby bush, Aisling's entire body seized, hand racing to the dagger on her thigh. A reaction met with amused laughter from the group when nothing more than a hare leapt from the surrounding foliage.

"You can rest if you need to," Lir whispered into her ear from behind. "I'll keep you steady."

"And wake to an ambush of some bestial horde?"

"As good a time as any to wake," Lir said. Aisling didn't need to turn to witness his smirk, his words steeped with amusement. "Very well, if you won't rest, tell me a story then, to keep myself from dozing."

"Surely the great King of the Sidhe does not tire?" Aisling said sardonically, fluctuating her voice dramatically.

Lir exhaled a laugh. "Rarely but he does grow bored."

"I know of no tales other than those smuggled by Castle Neimedh's staff, all stories revolving around your kind."

"And do these tales live up to the reality you've now faced?"

Aisling frowned. "Some, yes. Others, no. And still some, I'm not yet certain."

"Indulge me," he said, his voice vibrating against her back.

"There are those who claim the Aos Sí can shapeshift, take the form of a horse to steal children away into the forests. Is that true?"

Lir laughed, this time louder. "Unfortunately, no. It appears, in this story's case, the mortals have mistaken the Phuka for the Sidhe." Aisling had assumed as much after learning of the Unseelie. It was appearing more and more as though the Unseelie were often mistaken for the Aos Sí in the eyes of mankind. Many mortal civilians were too sheltered from either the fair folk or the Unseelie to understand the difference between them. Including Aisling herself. So why hadn't Nemed made this difference clear? He was among the few who might know of it. Instead, he perpetuated these stories.

"Tell me another," Lir demanded, leaning forward, his chest pressed against her back.

"There are tales claiming the Aos Sí reside in caves, tunneling through the highlands. There, the Aos Sí devour lost mortals and collect their bones. Bones and hair alike."

"Goblins," Lir said, "another."

Goblins. Aisling toyed with the word in her mouth. Perhaps one day she'd meet one.

"Someone once told me the Aos Sí inhabit even the oceans,

singing sailors to their deaths and collecting shipwrecks."

"There are Sidhe who occupy the seas," he said, adjusting the reins wrapped around his left hand, "but the creatures you speak of are sirens. Tell me something else."

"I have no other stories. Only those experiences shared with my brothers."

"You must miss them," he said.

Aisling considered changing the subject. She'd already shared her own name, but to share those of her family, to exchange memories of them with the Fae King, felt like a betrayal. Like a jewel she hoarded lest it fall and break, shattering whatever recollection she still bore.

On the other hand, she wished to speak life to the memories, to keep them alive and well. For each day, her upbringing in Castle Neimedh felt more and more like a passing dream.

"Aye, I do. I often wonder what they'd think of all of this. Of the Aos Sí, of Annwyn. Of everything."

"What are they like?" Lir continued, his voice so low only Aisling could hear. Another whisper among the forest's lazy drawl of groaning trees, ruffling canopies, and the skittering of those nocturnal creatures on the woodland floor.

The mortal queen's heart panged with an ache-like longing. She hadn't allowed herself to think of her family for longer than a moment. For longer than a passing thought. Not since she'd wept every last tear she thought her body capable of producing those first few weeks. And now that she let down those barriers, the dam began washing through, flooding the mortal queen with the days of her childhood past.

"Iarbonel is the kindest. He taught me how to hold my dagger." Aisling smiled to herself. "Annind is the most intelligent, knows every morsel of history on this continent and beyond. Fergus, on the other hand, is as thin as a rail yet perpetually insatiable. He'd struggle with the food here." Aisling swallowed the stone in her throat. "And Starn, the eldest, is the fiercest. The only one my father allows to accompany him, work with him. The direct heir to his throne." Aisling gnawed on the inside of her cheek.

"And yourself?" Lir continued. "Where does the princess find her place?"

Aisling frowned. "I'd often hoped to be the strongest, besting my brothers with a blade. Hoped to be the wisest, a well of guidance for the North when I came of age. Hoped to be the most disciplined, reaping the fruits of such self-mastery. But alas, I coveted that which wasn't meant for me; often weak, often foolish, often impulsive and disobedient, I was rather creative with my lies, stealthy when I cheated at our games, unteachable when it came to the law, my clann's savage daughter."

"You say it as though it's shameful."

Aisling considered. "I was a misfit. My only salvation, the love of my tuath and the Neimedh legacy."

For several moments, Lir was silent. Aisling's own voice echoed inside her mind until at last he spoke.

"The skin of a lamb will never flatter a wolf."

Aisling glowered, shaking her head. "You misread me. I am no wolf. My blood is rich in iron, my heart pledged to mortality, my will loyal to the North."

"Are those the qualities that enchanted the princeling?" Amidst the darkness, Aisling couldn't see Lir's grin but she could hear it, the self-satisfied inflection he awarded his words.

The mortal queen hesitated. What could she say about Dagfin? The mere mention of the Roktan prince brought fire to her lungs.

"Why don't *you* humor me with a fanciful tale? I myself am growing quite bored of these questions."

"Because your blatant refusal to answer a simple question now has me interested," he said, growing more amused. How strong were fae senses? Could they hear better? See better than mortals? For the forest was now stained in ink and Aisling was certain he couldn't witness her flush nor measure the pace of her heart.

"The King of the Greenwood is interested in the mortal Prince of Roktling? Dagfin will be quite flattered when I have a chance to te—"

"So, the princeling's name is Dagfin," Lir surmised, and Aisling clamped her mouth shut. "Let me guess, he proposed then chronicled his undying love in a poorly written mortal ballad."

"You're wrong," Aisling scoffed, toying with Saoirse's mane between her fingers. "He never proposed but we were to be married."

Lir jerked his head back then recovered. "That explains his indignation last we met."

"I can assure you that had nothing to do with myself."

"And everything to do with my race?"

"Aye, as does your loathing of our kind."

"I can assure you, princess, my loathing cannot be fully blamed on race alone."

"Neither can mine," Aisling simmered, her posture stiffening.

"And what do you loathe about me?" he asked, pulling her back towards him with a gentle press of her waist as they ambled down a steep slope.

"To begin, your bloodthirst."

He laughed. "Ah, yes, we often despise our own vices reflected in others."

Images of the trow's head rolling to the side, flashed across her mind's eye.

Aisling wished it were daylight, for if it was, Lir could witness her furious grimace. A scowl that reddened her mortal features.

Lir brought their stag to a sudden stop. It was only then that Aisling glanced over her shoulder and found the rest of

Lir's knights several paces behind. Steadily, they made their way towards herself and Lir, murmuring to one another in Fae. A far cry from their usual boisterous nonsense.

Lir tugged Saoirse towards a nearby tree. An ash tree, Aisling assumed by the looks of it, its darkly painted bark was riddled with deep grooves, like rivers painted on a map. It was also both wide and tall, roots bursting from the undergrowth, forming arcs and bridges in the surrounding land where moss clung, and arachnids scurried. This bestial tree was primeval. Exhaling and inhaling to the rhythm of the wind.

The Fae King positioned Saoirse directly at the tree's base. Lir removed one of his gloves and pressed his bare palm against the trunk of the ash. Aisling blinked, encouraging her eyes to dilate. She wanted to witness what it was the Fae King did. But the darkness didn't impede her understanding for Aisling first *felt* and then *heard*.

The ash moaned, leaning forward and pressing its bark more firmly against Lir's hand. The sound of the tree's voice haunting, travelling through its skin and into the earth beneath. Then, Aisling felt Lir's chest rising and falling against her own back. Both the Fae King and the tree were ... they were speaking to one another. Aisling could feel it.

Aisling dared not utter a word. Dared not interrupt whatever it was the Fae King and the tree whispered to one another. The words they passed from one charmed breath to another.

So, it was Lir who spoke first, releasing his hand from the bark of the tree.

"Now I'll tell you something," he whispered, nudging Saoirse even closer to the ash. "Her name is Yddra."

"The tree bears a name?" Aisling asked, remembering that Galad had once mentioned something similar. That Gilrel had described Leshy, the oldest spirit of the woodland to her.

"Aye, written in the rings of their trunks, unknown to all who are not of their kind unless they're split open." The mention of such violence incited the trees around them as if offended, moaning as they leaned closer to the Fae King and his queen.

"All, except you," Aisling gathered. "You speak to the trees," She was breathless and too stunned to do anything about it.

"The trees, the animals, all creatures who cannot use their voice as we do."

"Magic," Aisling exhaled, suddenly more aware of the clicking branches overhead, snapping their twigs.

"Whatever abilities they wield are aberrations. Perversities of nature. As they are themselves. Do not let them convince you otherwise."

"What the mortals call magic we call *draiocht*. In your tongue, it means breath. This, the ability to speak with the trees, is a form of *draiocht* reserved for the current sovereign of the greenwood to communicate with the entirety of their kingdom."

"And what do the trees tell you?" Aisling asked.

Lir considered for a moment, studying the canopies now alive with interest.

"They tell me of all who call these feywilds home, the names of those who enter, their age-old stories that would bleed days to retell, and"—Lir hesitated, turning back to Aisling—"they tell me of you."

Aisling whipped her attention to the Fae King, lifting her chin to meet his eyes.

"What do they say?"

"They tell me you're strange."

"Because I'm mortal?" For Aisling believed few if any mortals had ventured into these forests and if they had, they certainly hadn't journeyed this far.

"Because you're different. Not quite mortal. Not quite Sidhe," he said, piercing directly through Aisling with the intensity of his glare. The scrutiny of a bird of prey eyeing a mouse down below.

The mortal queen averted her eyes. Whatever the trees had told him, Aisling knew they were wrong. Nevertheless, she'd felt their keen gaze, examining her every breath. The way the hazels, alders, birches, and yews rustled outside her terrace when she woke and settled into stillness when she slept.

Before Aisling could respond, Lir grabbed Aisling's hand. The Fae King pressed her palm against Yddra's body, curling himself around Aisling so she couldn't move. Aisling squirmed, startled by his quickness.

"Let go of me!" she hissed.

Initially, Aisling felt no more than what she already had during Lir's conversation with Yddra. But the Fae King held her firmly against the ash, his grip impenetrable. And just when she made to curse his name, assail him with a verbal lashing, she felt not a heat but a pressure leaning against her palm. A swelling, invisible force that reached for her as though it had limbs of its own, running its smooth fingers along her arms, her back, her cheeks, her hair, caressing her lips as if it wished to slip inside and possess her fully. Crush her beneath its oppressive weight.

This force was sentient, alive with desire. But Lir persisted, holding her captive against the ash. And as the sensation grew more potent, till Aisling's ears flushed with white noise, it spread, and Aisling knew its name: magic, *draiocht* ringing throughout the forest in eager vibrations.

Aisling inhaled sharply, rendered mute by shock, afraid the *draiocht* would drown her. For now, the *draiocht* didn't limit itself to Aisling's exterior but dove inside, filling her lungs as it did the pines and oaks, the flowers and the weeds, the stones and the river. It spoke to her but she couldn't understand. Couldn't translate this lullaby Yddra spilled into her ears.

Aisling reached for Iarbonel's dagger with her free hand.

She hesitated briefly before swinging for Lir. The iron blade licked the back of his palm, singing a bloody red streak. With a curse, Lir released her from his grapple.

And at the loss of Lir's concentration, the *draiocht* dissipated as quickly as a passing wind, deflating the world of its impatient energy. Aisling's ears popped as she tucked her hand against her chest.

"The trees, the animals, they've been warning me for quite some time, and I ignored them. It was time I saw for myself," Lir said, glancing back at his fae procession, waiting on him a distance away. Had they felt what Aisling had felt? Been alarmed by the dancing of the trees on a windless night?

"And what is it that you think you saw?" Aisling seethed, too furious to mind who or what may hear her shouts.

"I don't know," he confessed, his voice ragged. "But know, princess, that like the Sidhe, trees cannot tell a lie."

Chapter XVIII

AS THE DAWN CAST RAPIDS OF LAVENDER ACROSS the horizon, each member of the fae party unpacked their bags and squabbled over the most comfortable place to rest their head. The grass here was soft, long, and interrupted by tufted beds of wildflowers. It was in this glade, pressed against a mound of boulders, that they would rest, feed their stags and themselves, until the early evening.

Three nights had passed and still there had been no sign of the Unseelie. Even the trees were evasive, reluctant to share more information with their Fae King than was necessary.

"Tonight, tonight they will show themselves," Rian encouraged, flopping onto a particularly fluffy mound of greenery.

"*We're near Fomorian land. I can smell them,*" Aedh added in Rún, observing both Gilrel and Liam brewing a fire at the center of their camp.

"So long as the mortal queen rides with Lir, they'll remain elusive. As will all the Unseelie. They aren't so stupid as to leap from their dwellings before Lir and his men," Filverel argued. The court advisor stood at the brim of the glade, squinting between the surrounding columns of pines.

"And a fire shan't help either," Hagre whined, "*they'll smell that smoke for miles."*

The lady's maid and squire hesitated, looking to Lir for direction.

"Would you prefer your queen freeze?" Lir said in Aisling's tongue.

"She may be mortal but surely the daylight will warm her enough," Cathan said, sneering at Aisling over his shoulder. Aisling stood by Saoirse, feeding her the blend of hay and molasses Liam had prepared for the trip. The beasts ate ravenously, already collapsing to their knees to feel the cool edge of the pasture beneath their round bellies.

"The night is cold, Cathan. Mortals need warmth and comfort for optimal survival," Gilrel chided.

Hagre staked his sword into the earth beneath him. *"I thought we were bringing her along as bait. Not a liability."*

"Come nightfall, we'll take a different approach to ensnaring any Unseelie," Lir said, leaning against a tree with his arms crossed. "For now, rest and think no more of it."

And as though prompted, Galad emerged from the surrounding woodland, five rabbits hanging limply by their ears in his right fist. Aisling glared at their bloodied hides as Galad skinned and prepped the hares to be cooked over the flame. The mortal queen had enjoyed rabbit before, but Aisling knew these rabbits would taste nothing like what she'd experienced in the mortal world. For fae spices, their manner of baking, their treatment of the creature was unlike anything mankind did to similar dishes. Aisling began to wonder: if she weren't here, would these fae knights have eaten the rabbits raw, considering how they griped about the fire? But Aisling realized to her own horror, she was just ravenous enough to eat the creature raw if she must.

As best she could, the mortal queen ignored the Fae King, deigning to glance in his direction. But she felt his eyes on her, watching her from across the glade. Those feline jades stalking her every step.

"Not quite mortal. Not quite Sidhe."
"The trees never lie."

Aisling wrenched her eyes shut. The smoke burned her eyes. It billowed in great clouds of grey, carrying with it the scent of cooking hare and whatever fae herbs Galad had spread across its back.

Gilrel sat beside Aisling now, fiddling with a bowl of mashed leaves.

"The sun has burned your face," Gilrel said when all the fae knights were too distracted to eavesdrop. Now, each of them sat around the crackling flames, their faces lit with orange firelight and cheeks pink with warmth. Everyone except for Tyr and Hagre; they stood at opposing ends of the glade, hands wrapped around the hilts of their weapons. These were the first of the knights to stand guard. And in a few hours, Einri and Aedh would take their shift. The males would continue to rotate this way until nightfall when it was once more time to pack up and venture onward.

"This is perhaps the most time I've spent beneath the open sky since I was a small child," Aisling replied. "The majority of life in Tilren takes place beneath the shadow of our walls, unless you manage to sneak away with evening's help"— Aisling considered for a moment—"and a brew just strong enough to put the guards to sleep."

Gilrel dabbed the balm onto Aisling's cheeks; albeit the slimy texture, the mashed leaves indeed soothed her skin, cooling and seeping into her pores. But Aisling hardly enjoyed the respite for the look on Gilrel's face told the mortal queen the marten pitied her. Aisling nearly scoffed aloud. When had Gilrel turned the corner from pure resentment to sympathy? Especially when it was she who'd lost her sister so tragically.

"Regardless, I was never a fan of the sun, always having preferred the moonlight," Aisling said, watching the fae knights pass around a large flask, adorned now with a sticky rabbit's foot.

"And yourself? What do you make of your own childhood?" Aisling asked as Gilrel set aside the bowl of mashed leaves.

"Marten kits born during the age of the Forge maintain their youth far longer than humans. The same applies to the Sidhe. Our childhoods are decades of whimsy and bliss. I was blessed enough to grow old with a member of my litter. As rare as it is for either Sidhe or Forge beasts to bear children, it is even rarer for them to raise two children near the same age. So long as Nuala was there, loneliness was as distant as Fiacha's Southern star. By the time she was gone, I was well into my first century," Gilrel swallowed. "Nevertheless, I'll never truly regrow the wilted roots she left behind."

Aisling knew not what to say. Only that Gilrel's own sorrow seemed to pool within the mortal queen. Bottomless, cold, and silent. To carry such misery for an eternity was a burden Aisling couldn't begin to imagine.

Against her own volition, Aisling reached out and took hold of Gilrel's paw. In the first breath, Gilrel tensed, straightening as stiff as a rod. In the second, Gilrel slowly exhaled whatever tension had taken hold, slackening her muscles. And in the third, she smiled at the mortal queen.

"She is in the Otherworld now," Gilrel said, more for herself than Aisling. The mortal queen knew not what the Otherworld was. She'd heard tales. Used the expressions. But didn't know what it *truly* meant. An afterlife of some kind, she gathered. And although the mortals believed death was final, it only made sense that the Aos Sí, with their religion and Gods, would have faith in another place. Another time. Another world where the long passed could rest.

"There are no Gods, do not let the religion of the Aos Sí deceive you, plague your mind. This world is an earthly one, designed by mortals and for mortals." Nemed's words found her when she least expected them, warring with the Aos Sí even in his absence.

"Nuala was a beloved member of our society," Filverel interjected.

Had he been eavesdropping this entire time? Of course, he had. How had Aisling expected anything less from the advisor?

"One of countless of our kin lost at the hands of mankind. A sister of the Forge. In fact, just around this very fire, there are stories of similar loss to be told." Filverel raised his voice, gathering the attention of the rest of the group. One by one, the knights hushed their conversations and dragged their gaze towards Filverel.

"Hagre," Filverel addressed the knight in specific, "I'm certain our mortal queen has yet to hear of yours."

Hagre tore a large chunk of meat from the bone he gnawed, flashing his pale eyes at Aisling.

"I'm sure the mortal wench is fully aware of how the Fire Hand spends his days," Hagre growled, "but I'll tell it in case you've forgotten." His lips peeled back in a cruel smile, boasting wickedly sharp fangs painted pink with blood. Aisling clenched her jaw, willing herself to meet his glare. The knight wished to intimidate her. To give him the satisfaction was to surrender what pride she hoarded.

Lir lounged on the other side of the fire, eyes wrought with something dark as he glared at his knight.

"Your father had just set fire to the Southern edge of the forests. The sky was black for the days following, as myself and various of our kind searched those scorched forests. We turned over the burnt remains of centuries-old trees, sifted through the ash that lay like blankets of brittle, grey-clad snow. Nearly drowned ourselves in soot, smoke, and leaping embers in search of the Sidhe who weren't able to escape in time. Among them Sidhe children."

The group held their breath, glaring into the licks of flame flaring at the center of their circle. Aisling bit her tongue, clenching her fists at her sides. He was lying. And if he wasn't, Nemed would've never burnt down forests had he known innocents remained within their keep. To kill an enemy soldier was one thing. But to kill a child? No. That was the sort of evil the Aos Sí participated in. Not the mortals. Not her father.

Aisling flicked her eyes away from Hagre, meeting Lir's own glaring back. He sat across the circle from her, elbows resting on his knees.

"I went after him. Forge be damned the consequences; I went after the Fire Hand myself. To make him regret lighting that torch until his dying breath."

Aisling tried to swallow but couldn't.

"I found him soon enough, fleeing towards your precious mortal walls, afraid of the vengeance snapping at his heels. So, I attacked. Striking at that bastard with every morsel of my Sidhe strength. But it wasn't enough. There were too many of them. Too many mortals defending the Fire Hand till they were able to shackle me down with your iron chains." Hagre lifted his wrists, revealing scarlet scars, bubbling like fossilized blisters. "And if that weren't enough, they tied me to their horses, dragging me for miles. Hooves embellished with iron horseshoes, nicking at my skull for—I don't know how long."

Aisling's eyes betrayed her, wandering towards the scars she'd noticed when she'd first laid eyes on this member of the fair folk, hundreds of red scrapes around Hagre's shaved head.

"If it weren't for Lir's intervention, I'd be dead," Hagre spat, turning from the mortal queen as though she were scum beneath his boot.

Aisling's hands trembled so she hid them at her sides, clutching the rock on which she sat till her knuckles grew white. But her attempts were thwarted by the Fae King who'd already witnessed it.

"Rian?" Filverel turned to the red-haired knight, gesturing for him to go next.

Rian sighed, passing his flask to Einri. "Before Lir's reign, Sidhe villages were spread throughout the Isles of Rinn Dúin. Only the capital, Annwyn, stood where it does now, surrounded by a humble kingdom. Your great-grandfather took advantage of this. The Sidhe overpower the mortals but against your endless iron fleets ... they could overtake our small, divided villages. So, they did. Your grandfather ransacked my village, taking and destroying all they could before Sidhe retaliation. In a single morning, everything I had was gone."

Aisling's ears rung. Her skin was uncomfortably hot. Aisling felt like an insect trapped beneath a glass, the sun glaring through the center, threatening to scorch her alive. There was little she could say. Little she could do. And even if she attempted to speak, she didn't trust herself enough to withhold the flood of tears glazing her eyes. No, she'd transform herself into stone. Strong and resolute. Immovable. But within, Aisling was cold fury and insatiable sorrow, cannibalizing from within.

"After that, Lir brought all of the villages under his immediate protection. Brought them all into Annwyn, where we cannot be outnumbered." Rian snatched the flask back from his comrade, speaking those last words as threats. As though Aisling herself planned to lay siege on their fae home. Didn't they understand she was a harbinger of peace? That her very presence in Annwyn and amongst the Aos Sí was not a declaration of war but of peace between their kinds? But of course, they would not trust her. How could they after centuries of rivalry?

"Galad?" Filverel tipped his head to the knight beside Aisling. The mortal queen bit the inside of her cheek. She couldn't handle, couldn't take, another tale especially if it left Galad's lips.

"She's heard enough, Fil," mercifully Galad scolded.

But Filverel had not. The advisor flared before speaking, "Allow me then."

For a moment, Aisling wondered why he bothered torturing her so. There was little purpose in re-hashing the crimes of mortals after Aisling had sacrificed everything for peace between the races. But then Aisling realized this was Filverel's small form of vengeance. To humiliate her, to hold the mortal queen accountable for her race. Even if it meant nothing. Did nothing, it was enough to witness Aisling squirm.

"Galad's *caera* was a knight, Morrin. Could best any one of us in hand-to-hand combat," Filverel said, moving closer to where Galad and Aisling sat side by side. "And in any conflict with the mortals, she fought valiantly, sweeping through more of your kind than any soldier I've yet to meet," Filverel grinned.

"She was the reason for our victory on the Hills of Hidris. She fought for the Sidhe on this continent and beyond for the Sidhe's continued survival in this realm. Without her, the Sidhe may've met a different end. Without her, none so many knights would be sitting around this very circle."

The Aos Sí exchanged glances, speaking without uttering a word. All except Lir, whose attention remained latched to the mortal queen. What loathing he must feel for her, Aisling realized. She knew of the horrors centuries of war had rendered on both races, but to hear the individual stories aloud ... Aisling felt ill.

"And after this fateful battle, along with a handful of others, Morrin stayed behind to tend to the injured, aiding the healers in all they required. But of course, the mortals felt nothing of honor. They spit at the foot of integrity when their surviving battalions captured the Sidhe who remained, outnumbering and binding them with iron. Morrin among them. For decades, Galad searched for a way inside the walls of Tilren. Into Castle Neimedh. To find Morrin and lay waste to that mortal pot of filth," Filverel was behind Galad now, hovering above him like a vulture. "And in the depths of one night, Galad managed it. Snuck his way into Tilren, through your city streets and towards Castle Neimedh, only to be caught and held prisoner for years. And Morrin—poor, brave

Morrin—was never found."

This was not true. Had a Sidhe been harbored in her own castle for years, Aisling would've known of it. Would've been aware that Galad, one of the few Sidhe who'd shown her some fleck of kindness, was held captive in the dungeons. These were lies, Aisling repeated in her mind.

"Show us what marks those years left," Filverel commanded the knight.

Galad glared straight ahead, a cord snaking down his forehead.

"What matters is that Lir sacrificed greatly in return for Galad's life," Gilrel piped, "and we're grateful he sits amongst us now."

Filverel ignored the marten, eyes burning a hole through the back of Galad's head.

"Show us," Filverel repeated, his tone growing impatient. Still, Galad didn't flinch, only clenched his teeth.

"Enough, Filverel," Gilrel growled.

"Very well." And with that, Filverel bent down and raised Galad's shirt, so quickly, Aisling had scarcely seen the advisor lunge. But it mattered not, for what Aisling glared at, took her breath away: across the knight's rib cage was an enormous branding. The symbol of mankind. The fist gripping the flame. The same shape that was carved into the pommel of Iarbonel's dagger. The image etched into his skin, bubbling the flesh with nasty red lesions that interrupted his slick, fae markings. As fierce as though it had been burnt into his flesh yesterday.

Aisling gasped, clasping a hand over her mouth. And now, there was little Aisling could do to prevent the tears from spilling down her cheeks till they dripped from her chin.

"A token but not from your father as you might've guessed," Filverel continued, his dark eyes burning like coals, "One of the King of the Greenwood's first Sidhe knights branded by the heir to the Tilrish throne. Starn of Clann Neimedh."

Aisling was grateful for the crackling of the fire, the woodland gale, the whistling of songbirds perched in the canopies. For these sounds masked the grinding of her jaw as she lay at the center of the glade. The rest of the fae knights already dreamed or drank by the stags. All except for Einri, Aedh, Filverel, and Lir. Einri and Aedh paced the clearing's edge, eyes locked on the realm of greenwood. The Fae King and his advisor, on the other hand, whispered for hours, plotting their revised approach to ensnaring the Unseelie, Aisling assumed.

But Aisling couldn't sleep. Rage kept her an arm's length from rest, her blood boiling.

To hear her eldest brother's name on Filverel's lips struck Aisling like a blow to the gut. Starn had always been Nemed's favorite: the only one of all five siblings allowed to escort the mortal king on his weeks-long missions. Favored to fight beside Nemed, to take his place at court when Nemed was too preoccupied. Because Starn was the heir to the kingdom. Starn had always been fierce and cruel and cold, but a king needed to be if they wished to rule. And a king, Starn would one day be.

These fair folk knew nothing of her brother, her father, or the struggles that mankind endured, Nemed's reasons for burning the forests: Tilren and all of the mortal nations were overpopulating, bursting at their kingdom's seams and because of the Aos Sí's monopoly over the wilderness, mankind couldn't hunt or gather sufficiently to provide for the growing demand. So Nemed burned the feywilds to spread Tilren's walls. To make room for his multiplying realm.

On the other hand, the Aos Sí carried the opposite dilemmas: their primordial race was dwindling, dancing on the cusp of extinction, Aisling was realizing. A result of the fair folk's inability to birth enough children to compensate for the casualties of war. They were far outnumbered and crippled by their susceptibility to iron. How much longer could the Aos Sí survive in a world where man demolished the wilderness to carve out their bastions, their roads, their cities, their overeager goals of conquest?

And if rage were not enough to keep the mortal queen from resting, her pity overwhelmed her. Swelling from within like a cold shadow, both sadness and guilt extinguished the irate flames she tried desperately to stoke. She wouldn't allow herself to feel sympathy for them, Hagre and Rian's accounts, all the knights' stories that had yet to be spoken. Not even Galad whose branding was etched into her memory forever. She couldn't. Wouldn't. And yet she did.

Without an approaching sound, a figure stretched themselves down beside the mortal queen. Aisling rolled from her position as quickly as she was capable, Iarbonel's dagger in hand. But her attempts at self-preservation and privacy were futile for Lir caught her wrist easily.

He lay on his side, considering her and she him, the perfume of the wildflowers swirling around them like pink clouds of cologne.

"You've been crying," he said, eyes tracing the saltwater stains around her swollen cheeks. Aisling wiped her face with her sleeve, scrubbing away the tears. Still, he regarded her like a riddle, taking Aisling apart before reassembling her in his mind.

"Wasn't that your intention? To torture me?" Aisling bit, jerking her hand back.

"Filverel's intention. Not mine."

"Yet you did nothing. And because you did nothing you are just as much to blame," Aisling simmered, speaking in angry whispers lest she wake the rest of the Aos Sí. Normally she wouldn't care but as it currently stood, she bore no desire to interact with any of them quite so soon. Regardless, it didn't matter if Lir involved himself or not. He didn't owe her anything more than preserving her life for the sanctity of the union. A union Aisling felt more and more was made of brittle glass.

"You needed it," Lir said.

"Needed to be humiliated?"

"Needed to hear from the mouths of the Sidhe their stories. Their perspective," he said, rolling onto his back. His hair fell away from his face, his striking features bathed in the shadows of the yews hanging over.

"You didn't know of any of it, did you?" He asked, turning his head to the side, sage eyes flashing brilliantly, "You didn't know what your father did—*does*, do you?"

Aisling thought for a moment. The mortal queen wasn't certain how to articulate the truth nor if she should speak of such things with the sovereign enemy of her father.

"I know some. I know he tortured your kind. I know he destroyed forests for the sake and protection of mankind. He described himself as a guardian from the savages who stole our land. All his crimes were fulfilled in the name of goodness and thus, in Nemed's eyes, not crimes at all. But no. I wasn't aware of the extent of his"—Aisling hesitated—"I didn't know the details. Political discussions were forbidden to me at my age as well as the majority of Tilren. As was, as you know, the Lore."

"You only know what your father told you," Lir gathered.

"And my tuath, my tutors. What reason would I have to doubt them? They're my kind, my family, my clann."

"And now?" he asked. "Do you doubt them now?"

Aisling opened her mouth to speak but the words eluded her. Much of what Nemed had told her was wrong, inaccurate, or a misunderstanding of the truth. But surely such misinterpretations were common in feuds and wars. The embers of rivalries. Aisling couldn't believe Nemed had lied to her. Her clann was all she knew. All she had.

"*None are innocent in war. But, if a centuries-old Aos Sí*

may impart some wisdom, I suggest you find the truth for yourself instead of parroting the words of your kind. Of your father. All of us claim to know the truth, only some of us do. Find it for yourself before you stake your life and your loyalties on unchallenged lies."

Filverel's words were salt in a wound. They spun in her mind, swirling alongside the image of Hagre's scars and Galad's branding. Painful and terrifying yet perhaps, Lir was right. Perhaps despite the torment they brought her, it was necessary that she look, to refrain from averting her eyes.

Aisling wished she could assume every word that parted from fae lips were lies and manipulations. Exactly as Nemed had taught her. But the mortal queen had heard the sharp edge of trauma in their voices, seen the scars, the physical remains and proof of their accounts, herself. How could she deny that? What reason did the fair folk have to lie to the mortal queen? Her opinion of them meant little. If only Aisling could receive word from her father. One conversation could clarify everything. He'd have a reason for all of this.

When Aisling didn't respond, Lir continued, "You're perhaps the only creature on the earth that has been given the opportunity to view this war from two pairs of eyes. Don't blind yourself to one to uphold the lies of the other."

Chapter XIX

WHEN AISLING WOKE, THE SKY WAS BLACK ONCE more. The moon sailed on a current of stars, glittering with mischief. But the mortal queen felt the night before she saw it: the crisp hues of midnight blue, dew beading the grass with crystals, the lullaby of mating insects humming the world to sleep, the burnt, ashen wood still smoking from a dying fire.

Aisling, lazily rolled over, bumping into the Fae King. Lir lay dangerously near to her. Had she fallen asleep beside him? The mortal queen couldn't remember. One moment she'd been awake, watching Lir's breaths rise and fall, careful not to wake him lest he snap at her like a wolf, and the next, she was rousing.

Aisling sprung from her place on the ground, her wrist snatching and the resistance slamming the mortal queen to the grass once more. Aisling looked in horror at the silver, threaded chain wrapped around her wrist. Starlight threads, Aisling realized.

The tether wrapped around her joint, spiraling down in a long, wispy chain, tangled between herself and the Fae King. At last, the mortal queen managed to follow the string to its end, tied around Lir's wrist. He'd bound them together. Strung them with an impenetrable thread.

With all of Aisling's commotion, Lir woke, or perhaps he'd been awake this entire time. Aisling couldn't tell in the darkness.

"Good, you're up," he said, sitting upright, his voice ragged. "You should eat something before we leave."

"Why have you bound me?" Aisling asked, uselessly fiddling with the knot around her wrist.

"It's for your benefit, lest you're eager to be stolen away or bewitched into the Unseelie's waiting hands while we sleep."

Aisling swallowed.

"Bewitched?"

"Aye, led happily to your death," Lir clarified, standing himself. The Fae King took hold of the string between them, tugging Aisling closer. "This way, I can keep you close," he grinned.

"And how will this shackle allow for the Unseelie to be lured if you're always near?"

The Fae King brought them face to face, Aisling glaring up at his devious expression just visible beyond the midnight veil.

"You needn't worry yourself with that," he said, smiling devilishly, "it's all sorted." A statement that made Aisling more concerned for her own longevity amongst the Aos Sí.

"Is it already time?" Galad interrupted. Aisling whipped her attention to the knight, wearily uncurling himself from the ground. One by one, the rest of the knights woke as well. The glade stirred with Aos Sí dressing themselves, readying the stags, and sheathing their weapons.

"As the cock crows," Gilrel replied, stretching her arms, two daggers in either hand, "or, in this case, as the owl hoots."

The fair folk munched on cheeses, dried breads, fruits, and honeycombs, braiding back their hair and slipping on their boots. It wasn't long before they'd thoroughly dusted out the fire, gathered their belongings, and saddled the stags, leaving the glade as though they'd never been. All save for the blackened hole at the center of their camp where the fire burned throughout their sleep.

The party mounted their stags save for Aisling and Lir, still standing on the grass. The mortal queen looked between the group and the Fae King, wondering why they weren't joining the others. For now, where Lir went, Aisling also went, bound to him by threads of starlight.

But the Fae King said not a word, deigning to explain himself as he approached the scorched circle. Lir knelt beside the ash in a shower of moonlight. A snow-white luster illuminated him against the pitch black of night. For a moment, Aisling believed his wings would unfurl from his back, catching the misty glow of evening. As they had in her dream. But to the mortal queen's disappointment, he kept them hidden away.

With the hand untethered to Aisling, the Fae King placed his palm onto the earth and stilled. His long, elegant fingers curled into the powder of cinders. His other elbow rested on his knee, his hand lazily hanging from the joint. None of the others questioned their king, watching from the edge of the clearing where they sat on their stags.

So, the mortal queen waited patiently, studying the Fae King bent over the ash. His back swelled with breath. The sound was indistinguishable from the brush of forest leaves against the mountain's spires. Lir steadily inhaled and exhaled as he, Aisling realized, summoned the *draiocht*. Magic.

It didn't take long for the ground to pulse beneath their feet. As though Lir and Aisling stood on the lungs of the earth, its ragged breath billowing into Lir's chest and filling him with the wind of the wild. A gale that seeped through his fingertips till the ashen ground beneath him sighed with green. Aisling felt the *draiocht's* touch. Felt it watching her, studying her as it swept the glade in its magic. Was it sentient? Conjured like a curse or a blessing?

Yellow and cerulean flowers bubbled over freshly grown verdant sod. A layer of pasture blooming in a fleeting, passing moment beneath the moonlight. The greenery slipped between Lir's fingers, once caked in soot, curling around his fae markings, his king's rings with sweet fondness until the black mark was gone. Vanished. As though it never was.

And so, the Fae King undid the fire. Gave back the life the flames had stolen.

"How did you do that?" Aisling asked Lir. The Fae King rode behind her as the procession continued their quest through the forest. And the further they travelled, the thicker the forest became: a labyrinth of ancient, wooded sentinels, inky rivers, caves, and the edges of snow-peaked summits. Long gone was the world of man; out here, the age of iron was a distant dream. Untouched by mortal sovereigns, they trekked through the dominion of yews, apples, and Wych elms.

"How did you regrow the earth?" Aisling clarified, idly stroking Saoirse's mane.

"It's a simple spell. One the *draiocht* longs to be used for," he replied, his muscles strung tight against Aisling's back. Poised to fight at a moment's notice. Aisling felt it too, the growing thickness of the air they breathed, the pressure descending from the midnight skies like a thick quilt.

"Can you regrow the forests?" Aisling whispered, "After what Nemed has done?"

"Perhaps in another few centuries I'll find a way but now ... no," he said, "the trees are too old. Too ancient. Centuries of memory and thought. To breathe so much life into the thousands that have been destroyed, it's not possible. Only the Forge itself has such power. Has enough will to feed the *draiocht*."

Of course, Aisling thought to herself. Otherwise, Lir would've already done so.

"Did Nemed or your mother ever speak of the *draiocht* with you? A tutor?" He asked, leaning his head so he whispered in her ear.

"No, my father claimed magic was a perversity of nature."

Lir laughed coolly, unsurprised. "But no one—even in passing—mentioned the *draiocht*? Not in your family's history?"

"In Tilren, to speak of such things is forbidden," Aisling said, "so if there were mention, I wouldn't know of it. But in Annwyn, they teach the children of the *draiocht?*"

"Aye, but it's not so much taught as it is experienced. From the time we're born we begin to speak with the *draiocht*, living with and through it. It's inseparable from our very nature and all the while an entity in and of itself."

Saoirse stumbled over a loose stone, so Lir clutched Aisling's waist, bringing her against him. The mortal queen heated. The sensation of him against her, behind her, overwhelming. Prickling every inch of her skin till she managed to squirm free once more lest she dissolve in his arms.

"My mother did, however, teach me to fly," Lir said. Aisling tilted her head to study his expression. It was strange to think that such a powerful creature as Lir had once been a child with a mother and father. Parents who were likely once as powerful as the Fae King is now. Were they dead? Alive? Lir never spoke of them. Surely, if his mother were alive, Aisling would've already met the former Queen of the Greenwood. For she'd married Lir's father after all. Aisling bit her tongue. Or had she? Why had Aisling assumed Lir's parents to be husband and wife simply because they bore a child? That his parents had been *caeras*? In the mortal world, such customs were expected, but that certainly didn't imply fae culture followed similar rules. Perhaps they'd simply been fortunate enough to bear a child, not yet wed or proclaimed *caeras*.

"Flying is an inevitability, taught or not, but with

guidance, a Sidhe child can learn to perfect such an ability for themselves and, do so more efficiently, lessening the likelihood of ill-fated falls and recklessness."

"And how does one learn to fly?" Aisling asked.

"When I wouldn't sleep as a bairn, my mother would cradle me as she flew, praying to the Forge I'd drift to sleep so she could dream herself. From the time we're born we memorize the rhythm of our mother's flutter. Then when I was old enough, she'd let me graze the canopies on my own, demonstrated how to propel through a storm, manage turbulent winds, mend a tear."

The Fae King's voice was ragged with grief, implying his mother was gone. What must it be like to carry such grief for an eternity? Especially when natural death was few and far between amongst the Aos Sí. Which begged the question: how had Lir's mother died?

Abruptly, Lir brought Saoirse to a stop. Their fae procession mirrored their monarch. Did they hear something Aisling couldn't? See something? The mortal queen paled, dreading what was to come next.

"What is it?" Aisling whispered.

"Sshh," Lir hushed softly, leaping off Saoirse's back. "I'd encourage you not to be afraid, but I'm almost certain you'll enjoy this."

"Enjoy what?" Aisling continued. The Fae King didn't respond. Merely lifted Aisling from the stag, setting her on the ground beside him. Quickly, he slung a bandolier over his head and across his chest, lifting his hood so the top of his face was veiled with shadow.

"Have you heard something?" Aisling continued.

"Do you trust me?" he asked.

The Fae King gestured for Aisling to follow him, their wrists still tethered by the rope of starlight.

"Where are we going?" Aisling answered with a question, glaring back at the group of fae knights, dismounting and disappearing into the surrounding trees. They were ghosts, silently floating through the woods, every breath shared with the wilderness around them.

"Are all mortals as incapable of being silent?"

"Only the ones who know when to fear for their lives."

"That's the fun of all of it, isn't it, princess?" Lir grinned wickedly. Aisling couldn't argue, stumbling along after him as he led her to the edge of the forest.

Beyond the thinning woodland, in a wide and rocky clearing, rested three colossal mountains. But it wasn't a clearing at all. In fact, this grey, gravelly expanse of mountain and stone was once a part of the forest, now caked with black dust. Dust that smothered the great crater, wilting all the greenery beneath it. And carved into the mountains were three large caves. They tunneled into the summits like gaping mouths waiting to snap shut. Dark and deep. Silent and eager. What Aisling imagined were bats, hanging from the cave's gums and blinking back.

Lir shielded Aisling against a tree. The mortal queen opened her mouth to speak but Lir lifted his finger against his lips, silencing her. Were they near the Unseelie?

Lir reached for the mortal queen's hand. His fingers holding her by the wrist, palm up. Aisling paled as the Fae King then drew one of his throwing knives, the edge glinting yellow-gold and boasting its sharp edge.

"Remember, this is for your kind too," he whispered, "negotiations with the Unseelie could save us all the bloodshed of mortals and Sidhe alike."

"Aren't we waiting for them to find us?"

"They won't approach if they know I'm with you," Lir said, "so we've come to them."

So, the Fae King hadn't planned to tether Aisling to a sacrificial rod, like she'd anticipated. A way to lure the Unseelie without Lir being near her, a fear Aisling hadn't realized she harbored until now.

"And what of me as bait?"

Lir's eyes flickered with something Aisling couldn't place. "You're still going to help."

"How?"

"You're going to lure them from their caves."

Aisling's legs grew numb as her gaze darted between the hollows: black, bottomless, and glaring back. Thresholds to the inner workings of the mountains, where some hideous, bestial aberration no doubt lurked.

"Why don't you simply get them to come out yourself?" Aisling demanded, more curious than anything else.

"It wouldn't be tactful to enter their lair with only a handful of Sidhe. Besides, the Fomorians will interpret any such liberties as a direct insult and threat to their municipality. Territorial fiends." Lir said, "I'm trying to avoid further bloodshed."

The Fomorians. That was who called this dreadful, stony expanse their lair.

The Fae King slipped the dagger beneath the starlight tether, wrapped it around Aisling's wrist, and pulled, severing the thread that bound the mortal queen and Fae King together.

Aisling watched the thread uncoil and slither from her wrist, tangling about the floor: a silver snake.

"Aren't you afraid I'll run?"

"No," Lir said. "I believe you'll do anything for your kind."

"And what if you're wrong?"

"I'm not," he said, meeting her eyes. "I know what it is to want to protect those you love. It's not always possible but when it is, there's little to prevent either you or I from doing so."

"How do you know that?"

"Because you've already done it. By tethering your fate to mine," he said.

Aisling's heart panged; with what, she did not know. Only that it hurt. For her union to Lir felt like an eternity ago and all that occurred before their marriage was another life.

"*Do not be weak,*" Nemed had always told her. This was her opportunity to be as strong and as brave as her brothers. To participate in the danger of it all as she'd always craved. She couldn't wither now. Not when she could play a hand in protecting her people from these beasts.

Aisling tried to swallow but her tongue turned dry and brittle, an immovable stone in her mouth.

"This is for cutting me beside Yddra," the Fae King said, lowering the knife to poke her fingertip. A ball of blood bloomed from the puncture, dripping onto the forest floor between them. Aisling winced, startled by the prick.

"The quicker they smell you, the quicker we can leave," Lir explained.

"So, what happens now?" Aisling asked, holding her finger as she warily searched the expanse beyond, a land of grey and ash and rock.

"Now we introduce you."

"We?" Aisling asked.

Lir winked, sage eyes dancing. But the longer Aisling looked, the dimmer they grew, nearly translucent. Aisling blinked and rubbed her eyes and by the time she lifted her head once more the Fae King had vanished. Like the fog on a windy sea, Lir dissolved into nothing. Suddenly gone.

Aisling's heart hammered, swiveling on her heel.

"I'm right here," he said, his voice an incorporeal purr amidst the darkness. Lir reached out and grabbed her hand, knotting his fingers between hers. Aisling gasped, stifling the urge to scream at the contact.

He'd glamoured himself.

From nothing, Lir exhaled a laugh, his breath white clouds in the cool evening air, the only evidence that he still stood beside her. That and the sensation of his calloused hand knotted in her own.

"Follow me," he said, pulling Aisling from the forest's edge and into the ashen clearing. And as they neared, Aisling realized to her own horror that the black, swampy mounds littering the center of the clearing were not rocks or foliage or some other natural substance. No. These were bodies. Rotting corpses whose bones stuck out at odd angles as the mice scuttled across them, painting their paws red and brown. The stench was unbearable, summoning bile to her throat.

They walked until they reached where the three summits stood. The gravel's dust plastered their boots, clouding around them till it took the form of fog.

The three summits stood facing the center of the clearing like a council, prepared to both judge and measure the mortal queen. A mortal queen who appeared to stand alone, unaccompanied. A glittering speck of raven black in the shadows of the mountain, her plaits reflecting the light of the moon.

And where Aisling believed she'd find fear, Aisling was far more excited, thrilled, exhilarated than afraid. A sensation she couldn't explain or rationalize even if she wanted to. A sensation that had plagued her since the loss of her innocence when she'd beheaded the trow.

And standing there, before the scrutiny of the peaks, Aisling weighed the silence. The hum of the gale winding through their bodies. Studied the smell of rot and bilge vegetating in the air. The taste of the citrusy forest combined with rot surrounding them. The touch of the moonlight on her pale complexion. The drip of her fingertip onto the stones beneath. Until the steady thump sounded from within the center cave. The step of a foot followed by the limp hauling of both one metal object and another fleshier belonging.

Step, drag.
Step, drag.
Step, drag.
Step, drag.

The sound grew louder, crunching some brittle substance beneath.

Lir squeezed Aisling's hand. "Don't move until I say."

They were coming.

Chapter XX

AISLING FROZE.

From the pits of black, they emerged: formidably large, waxen figures cautiously lumbering into the light. Her eyes were nailed to their moonlit faces, the wrinkled, scaly, balding heads of great bipedal beasts, who hunched their shoulders and walked like men, giant men. Their expressions were twisted with fury, blistered mouths stained with crusting blood. And on their bodies, they wore rusted armor, steel that appeared a millennium old, hanging from their brutish forms.

From the center cave emerged the largest ogre of them all, limping and dragging a mighty battleax across the expanse. His fangs bruised his bottom lip. And sliced diagonally across his face was an iron wound.

Aisling's expression twisted at the sight of him. Her excitement quickly bled into horror.

The creature growled in Aisling's direction, lifting his flared nostrils to smell her more clearly. To inspect what the midnight wind delivered from across the clearing.

Had Aisling believed in the Gods, she would've prayed to them now. For this was how she'd always imagined the fair folk before she'd laid eyes on them for herself. Not even the trow held a flame to the bestial monstrosity that approached her now. These primordial, grim titans. The antithesis to the beauty of the Aos Sí. For while the Aos Sí inhaled from the life-breath of the forest, the Fomorians exhaled its death.

"What is it?" A thin one asked, prudently cocking its head as it approached. Its voice was mangled and rough, pricking Aisling's flesh till her shoulders shuddered.

"A mortal," another replied. The creature hissed, boasting an inky tongue and a collection of razor-sharp canines.

In sight, there were perhaps fifteen Fomorians emerging from each cave and crawling into the light. But Aisling knew there were more hidden away, watching. Waiting.

"How can you be sure?" The first said, blinking its saucer-like eyes bulging from its head. Eyes whose pupils were slit down the center like a wild cat's.

"She looks like one," the second said, inhaling deeply, ravenously, "small and pathetic. Delicious."

Lir moved closer to the mortal queen, brushing her shoulder. Aisling willed herself not to respond. Not to reveal that the Fae King stood beside her, invisible. For she knew not what wrath the Fomorians would unleash should they know they were being herded into the Fae King's presence.

"But is it a trick?" The first Fomori was now a measly pace from the mortal queen.

This close, Aisling could smell them. Beasts who reeked of manure and rot.

"She doesn't smell like a mortal." The horde of Fomorians inched closer, surrounding her from every direction. Aisling held her breath. Could they smell Lir?

"Does it matter?" The second replied, joining the first's side. "Just a lick won't hurt. Or a bite."

"Don't be an idiot, Gnoll," the first growled, leaning closer to smell Aisling more thoroughly. "She doesn't smell of Sidhe either." That ruled out Lir's scent. Did his glamor mask even his smell?

"Look at her ears, round as a rat," hissed another from the

mouth of a cave.

"Perhaps she's a banshee," chimed a Fomori crawling on all fours.

But it was the mighty shadow cast over her head that focused her attention, the largest Fomori a pace away.

"What is your name, fleshling?" The Fomori asked. His voice was guttural, deep, as though the surrounding mountains themselves addressed her.

Aisling cringed, opening her mouth to speak but her words ran dry.

"Can it not speak?" a gangly one said.

The largest Fomori blinked at Aisling, lifting its skeletal, spidery fingers to touch the mortal queen's hair. Aisling flinched, her stomach knotting. She could feel Lir's body tense beside her own, his arm turning to solid stone.

"Aisling," the mortal queen blurted, "my name is Aisling."

The Fomorians reeled. Exploding into whispers slithering between one another's ears. Why Aisling's name meant anything to these creatures, the mortal queen knew not. They reacted strangely, their bulging eyes lit with curiosity as they examined her more fully.

The great Fomori before her, on the other hand, glowered at the mortal queen instead. Eyeing Aisling from head to toe until his scrutiny landed on Iarbonel's dagger sheathed on her thigh.

"You speak my tongue," Aisling said, unintentionally speaking her thoughts aloud.

"No," the second Fomori, Gnoll, said, "but it's understood by mortals and varying species regardless, translated in the breath between us."

"The trees said you came from the land of iron," the largest said.

"Now, now, Balor. You're in the presence of royalty," Gnoll crooned, peeling back his lips in a gross, crooked smile, a broad smirk of dull, yellowed teeth.

"I expected as much. Could smell her in the winds," Balor, the largest, said, "and what brings the mortal Queen of the Greenwood to Fomorian land?" Balor moved closer.

"Do you come alone?" Another Fomori asked.

"Don't be stupid, Kikkul. Where there is a queen, a king is never far behind," Balor boomed and Kikkul shrank at the insult, sinking back into the caves as the others snickered around him. "I've smelled him too." Balor stabbed the earth with his axe, dropping to one knee. The earth rumbled beneath his great weight. And despite his kneeling position, he still towered over the mortal queen.

Closing his eyes, Balor leaned closer to sniff Aisling. The crater held its breath, listening to the Fomori's lazy, indulgent inhale, pulling his head back.

"You're soaked in his scent, *mo Lúra*."

Balor reached out to caress Aisling's arm, and in response Aisling bit her tongue. It was all she could do to not recoil at the sight of the dried gunk buried beneath Balor's jagged fingernails.

There was nowhere to run. Nowhere to hide. And even if there were, this is where she was to remain. She could do this. She could be brave. The mortal queen held her breath as Balor's fingers hovered above her shoulder.

"Just a quick taste then, Balor," another nameless Fomori said from afar, "before *he* comes to fetch her. This is too perfect."

"Yes, yes," said another, "I thought we'd have to hunt her down. Steal her from *his* castle to undo this union. But now that she's here, we can do it quickly. Nobody will know. Just a taste."

"What makes you think you get a taste, Mul?" Two Fomori shoved Mul to the side.

"Just a finger," Mul whined.

"Let him have the fingers. Meatless and useless," one said, "but I claim the thighs."

"I'll skin you alive before you claim all that flesh, Bashuk," A female growled from atop one of the caves.

Balor whipped his head and roared at the horde. He silenced their griping and sprayed both saliva and slimy, unidentifiable chunks across the rocky meadow. They flinched at the reprimand, knocking their knees as they withdrew, cowering.

"Just one b-bite, Balor," another Fomori pleaded, madly fiddling with his own fingers. "It'll be even more delicious knowing it's his bride. Knowing it won us our rights once more. The fury in the Sidhe king's eyes—" the Fomori stopped, unable to finish the sentence for the squeals of delight that possessed him.

Balor growled, "don't speak his name nor his title here." And so, the Fomorians shrank away, hiding behind one another once more.

Balor eyed the mortal queen from head to toe, bringing his icy fingers to her chin and examining Aisling's face. Aisling jolted at the contact, willing herself to stay put. How long was Aisling to stand there before Lir intervened? How long must she endure this? It occurred to Aisling then, she should've, at the very least, inquired of Lir's plan more fully.

And once Balor was satisfied with whatever he'd studied in Aisling's mortal features, Balor's pupils flared at the blood still dripping from Lir's prick. Red and warm and wet.

Balor licked his lips with a thick, textured tongue.

"Why are you here, fleshling?"

"To speak with you," Aisling said dumbly, biting her bottom lip.

"Perhaps *he* has given her to us as an offering," a small Fomori said. "To remedy the damage this marriage has done to us."

"Yes, yes, after all, *he* wouldn't leave his queen all alone should *he* care for her wellbeing."

"It could be a trick," one shouted from within the caves.

"Or she ran from him; you know how these mortals are."

"Just one taste, Balor, then we can sort it out."

Balor inhaled again. His eyes rolled to the back of his head, lost in ecstasy.

"Alright," he relented, his raspy voice cracking mid-word, "one nibble. But do it quickly. Before and if *he* comes for her." Balor grinned, yellow eyes glittering. "On the other hand, take your time. I'd indeed enjoy the look on his face if he found her mid-meal."

The horde of Fomorians scurried towards Aisling, descending from their caves like a colony of ants.

Aisling gasped and before she could move, Lir wrapped his hand around Aisling, reaching for Iarbonel's dagger and puncturing the nearest Fomori in the neck. And at the touch of iron, the ogre's skin sizzled, boiling and dissolving the nearest flesh. Nothing like the clean cut she'd given to the trow with Lir's axe. No. This iron was ruthless, blistering the Fomori's flesh like acid.

The impaled Fomori collapsed on its back, writhing viciously as the others paused and looked on in shock.

"Iron! She carries iron!" They shouted. But soon their attention was not on her but on the Fae King who materialized beside her. Glamour gone, he stood with one hand around Aisling's, the other twisting the dagger into the Fomori still gurgling on his own inky blood.

Balor's jaw fell open as he stumbled back, wincing at the weight misplaced on his lame leg. The rest of the Fomorians recoiled and clamored behind their leader as though death itself had been named. And perhaps it had.

"You filthy fleshling," Balor growled, flicking his bulbous eyes between the mortal queen and the Fae King at her side.

Aisling's heart leapt as she beheld him: the Fae King glimmering in the moonlight, crowned by the whispers of the bygone pines as he straightened, dagger dripping with Fomori blood between them. Beheld him as if for the first time. A warrior and guardian to the arcane spirit of the forest.

The Fomorians' knees rattled, their fangs chattered, cold sweat caked their sickly chests and backs. They feared him. Observed him in both horror and fury. And Aisling found a strange, sadistic sort of joy bloom within her. That the creatures who'd delighted in her own torment were now the tormented.

Lir's eyes lit with verdant storms, every muscle in his body taught with cold, calculated rage.

"How quick you are to break Sidhe law," Lir growled, his voice the groaning of the oak in a storm.

Balor cackled nervously. "It is you who breaks Sidhe law, *mo Damh Bán*. No mortal, no Unseelie, and no Sidhe are to enter Fomorian territory and if they break such law, it is within Fomorian right to do with their intruders as they please."

"You appear well acquainted with the law when it suits you, Balor. And, once said law has changed against your favor, you turn a blind eye."

"And should we disagree with such change?" Balor took a step closer. "Tell me, *mo Damh Bán*, why jeopardize your allegiance with the Unseelie for humans? Those who burn our land, light fire to the Isles?"

"To prevent the continuation of such crimes from harming either Unseelie or Sidhe," Lir growled.

"You're naive, *mo Damh Bán*. There is no such thing as peace between mankind and the Sidhe. Maybe you should've spoken with Danu before seeking an audience with the Fomorians. She would've told you all there is to know. Or do you fear what the Empress has *seen*?"

Danu. The Empress. Aisling turned her attention to Lir, in time to witness a muscle flicker across his jaw.

"You will obey me, Balor," the Fae King commanded, his voice startling the nearest Unseelie.

"And what if the Fomorians reject your leadership?" Balor

challenged and the surrounding hordes of Unseelie inched nearer, drawing their weapons. "We've heard rumors of what you did to the Cú Scáth. Only what the trees have whispered. How quick your loyalties change when the possibility of an heir is dangled before you," Balor spat, pointing his axe at Aisling.

Lir stepped before her, shielding Aisling with his shoulder.

"Especially after what happened with the last. What was her name? Narisea?"

Aisling's heart skipped a beat. The name of his first *caera* and mother of his passed child.

Lir grinned but it was humorless. Unholy. The boasting of fangs in the mouth of a hungry wolf. Aisling shivered, beholding the Fae King as he curled his hands into fists at his sides. The knuckles turned bone-white around the hilt of her dagger.

"I'll tell you what, *mo Damh Bán*," Balor spat, "the Fomorians will give you your peace. Obey your Sidhe law. Vow to you their continued allegiance"—Balor licked his teeth—"in exchange for the mortal queen."

Dread was a snake coiling around Aisling to release whatever breath remained within the mortal queen's lungs. Aisling couldn't see Lir's face but every muscle in his back tightened, forcing him to roll his neck from side to side.

The Fomorians shrieked with delight, whispering to one another wildly. Their hunger a bitter taste in the midnight air.

Lir licked his lips, glancing at Aisling over his shoulder.

"Never let your guard down around him, Aisling. Never give him an opportunity to choose between you and what he covets."

Aisling's stomach twisted. It would be so simple for him to hand her over to the Fomorians. Hide the truth of her violent death from the mortals for another handful of decades to ensure the treaty didn't lose its value. Would Nemed demand to see proof of her? Or could the Fae King trade her to the

Fomorians with no negative consequences?

"And should I refuse?" Lir asked, returning his attention to the giant before them.

"As Danu foresees, the Sidhe have already lost the war against the mortals. You are no longer my king," Balor said. "In fact, after you failed to prevent the Fire Hand from destroying the feywilds you haven't stood as my sovereign. Should you refuse to hand over the mortal queen, we will denounce your kingship once and for all. And, with no Sidhe king, there's no Sidhe law; all those who find themselves unfortunate enough to stand in Fomorian territory or elsewhere will be ours to do with as we like."

The hordes of Fomorians leapt up and down, slamming their weapons against the earth and pounding their chests. The expanse lit like the audience at a tournament, stretching their ugly faces and stripping their vocal cords to shriek.

Lir rotated the iron blade in his palm, toying with the haft.

"I won't let any harm befall you." He'd promised the mortal queen, but Aisling didn't know the worth of a fair folk's word. To her father it meant nothing. But what did it mean to her?

And even as she repeated Lir's words in her head, she doubted them. Vows, if Aisling were being honest, hadn't taken seriously herself. Hadn't taken any of the fae superstitions seriously. For they were all nothing more than empty religion and poison from the Forbidden Lore.

"Never let your guard down around him, Aisling. Never give him an opportunity to choose between you and what he covets."

"I won't let any harm befall you."

And just as the words began to lose their meaning, Lir flicked his wrist, releasing Iarbonel's dagger. The knife spun four, five, six times, pegging Balor between the eyes. The mighty ogre gaped, eyes flooding from within. He swayed to the left, then the right, glazed orbs unblinking.

The hordes of Fomorian held their breath. Balor was a giant. Surely such a small weapon was ill-equipped to slay the great Fomori where he stood. Unless Lir had nailed him in the brain. Shot the target on a whim.

At last, Balor sagged backward, colliding against the gravel, a great thud that rattled the ground in which they stood. The image of a tree chopped down in the forest with a needle-like blade lodged in his creased, pale brow.

The next few seconds were a blur of fangs, armor, arrows, and blades as the rest of Lir's knights swarmed the crater. They descended like the mighty warriors and the legendary heroes the Forbidden Lore described them as—a secret Annind had whispered when he'd drunk himself silly, and Aisling was forced to help him up the stairs to his chambers.

Swathed in tribal markings, these glorious fae warriors seized the Fomorians, slaying all those who dared to fight against them or their Fae King. With lethal speed, Galad beheaded the Fomori who charged him, sliding beneath the beast and swiping his whetted blade through Unseelie bone. Six Fomorians surrounded Yevhen. He was outnumbered but thrived nonetheless. The knight thrust at one and kicked at another. But still they swung their kris blades and scratched with their blood-soaked nails. So, Tyr shot these Unseelie down till Yevhen could unsheathe his bloodied blade from the heart of the largest. One by one, Tyr's reeds nailed the Fomorians to the ground like flightless birds.

A hunched, crooked Fomori leapt from the top of the cave to catch Gilrel unaware. Silently, it lifted its spear above its head. Poised to sink into the lady's maid. Aedh, having spotted it the same moment Aisling did, shouted in warning. Gilrel spun on her heel, raising her throwing axe and swiping left. The blade made contact, digging across the chest of the Fomori. The creature screamed an unearthly bellow, tumbling across the dirt and down into the crater. But it wasn't finished, it turned furiously, charging the marten. Gilrel adjusted the axe in her paw, positioning her feet and hurtling the axe towards the approaching Unseelie. The blade flew, lodging in the fiend's neck. Fountains of scarlet oozed down its thick crane and before the creature could snort its last breath, Gilrel was already racing to unpluck her axe to wield at another.

And a mere pace before the mortal queen, Lir slit the throat of one Unseelie, spinning with impossible speed to drive his dagger into the belly of another. One of the larger Fomori swung his spiked mace at Lir. The Fae King ducked, sprung to his feet, and kicked the Fomori in the jaw. The ogre flew, landing face down on the gravel. But Lir wasn't finished. The Fae King pounced atop the beast, lifted its head to slice open its neck in a movement so quick, Aisling scarcely saw it occur.

His expression was feral, devoid of the kingly fair folk who breathed life into death. Turned black to green. Now he was the wild savage, all bloodthirst and fury, rippling with corded muscles visible even beneath his leathers. His slim figure cut through the Fomorians as a deathly shadow. The same animal that had slain the Cú Scáth the night of the *Snaidhm*.

The mortal queen scoured the battleground for her dagger. No longer was it lodged in Balor's skull. Somehow amidst the chaos, it had disappeared. It could be anywhere, buried beneath the bodies of Fomori steeping in their own sticky blood.

Lir grabbed Aisling's wrist and spun her towards him. Hiding the mortal queen in the curve of his chest, Lir raised one of his twin axes above his head and hurtled it towards a Fomori who—had Lir not pulled Aisling away—was an inch from beheading the mortal queen. The blade flipped, at last impaling the Fomori in the stomach. But there was no time to rejoice. Another ogre, standing atop the center cave launched a shower of arrows at Lir and Aisling. The Fae King reached for the shield from one of the freshly deceased, falling to his knees and raising the rusted contraption above both their heads. Seven hollow pangs struck the center of the shield and when Lir tossed it to the side, Tyr had already shot the Fomori down, the bestial thing strewn across the arch of the cave with a reed pulled through his left eye.

Aisling couldn't tell how long this chaos continued. Red seeping into the crater till the mortal queen believed it would surely transform into a shallow lake before the Aos Sí had finished. Mightily, they slayed all who threatened themselves or their comrades, deigning to approach all those Fomorians who hid in the caves or cowered behind the mountains. Even those who wept over the recently dead. No, those were left untouched.

"Go," Lir shouted at her during a feint, "take Galad and hide in the forest. I'll come find you."

Aisling hesitated. Her dagger was still here. Still lost somewhere on the ground, perhaps lodged in the gut of the dead.

At last, Aisling nodded her head and turned to search for Galad, unaware that Gnoll approached her from behind. She scrambled, stumbling through the chaos, tripping over bodies and primeval armor. Aisling's head swiveled on her shoulders, searching for the sapphire-eyed knight. He'd be looking for her too if Lir had requested it. But all Aisling could see, could determine from the bedlam, were weapons flying, limbs kicking, screams of pain, the crunch of broken bones, and then Galad pinned beneath a large Fomori, struggling to free himself. Aisling paused, searching for something, anything, to help. To make use of her increasingly useless self. But there was no time.

Gnoll tackled the mortal queen from behind, sticking her to the rocks. Aisling screamed but the sound was lost amidst the discord.

Ice seeped beneath Aisling's flesh as Gnoll held her against the earth. The Fomori rubbed his corrugated tongue atop her clavicle, inhaling and savoring the scent of her mortal flesh, eager to sink his teeth into her skin and munch on her bones.

"You do smell strange, fleshling," Gnoll drawled. "I'll eat half of you today and half tomorrow."

Aisling screamed, thrashing wildly to no avail. A mortal man could pin Aisling to the ground easily, and so she stood no chance against an Unseelie thrice her size. Fae and mortal warriors alike feared for their lives before the Unseelie, fighters trained and bred for bloodshed. So, the prospect of Aisling, nailed to the earth before this ravenous, insatiable aberration was as certain as death itself.

None appeared to hear her screams as she writhed beneath Gnoll, too distracted by their own brawling to behold the Fomori widening its gaping maw to peel apart her skin. Six Fomorians surrounded Lir with more on their way, his vision obscured by their massive bodies.

"Please," Aisling begged, for pride seemed useless now. Tears streamed down her cheeks. A wave of hysteria washed over the mortal queen, tossing her like a violent sea till she knew not which way was up and which was down. She grew numb to his touch. Deaf to the bedlam surrounding her. Blind to the night.

Was she dead? Killed by the Fomori so quickly? Without as much pain as she'd anticipated? Or perhaps horror consumed her? Fury? She couldn't tell, both blended seamlessly, slapping at her inner walls to be let loose. A sentient, eager, tempest pleading to be set free. Aisling fought the urge, the desire to allow such a thunderous rage to spill forth from every pore in her body. Like the impulse to drink when one is thirsty. To eat when one is hungry. To sleep when one is tired. To run when one is afraid. To scream when one is angry. To tear away the bridles of civilized society.

The lust for such release scared Aisling. For now, it was

not only she who occupied the sentiency within her but another whose name she knew not. Someone else asked to take control. To stoke the embers that hungered for a kill, embers looming in her periphery since the trow. Even the Cú Scáth. And what's more, she *wanted* to hand over control to this sentient, persuasive creature within. *Needed* that vengeance so clearly, it brought more tears to Aisling's eyes.

So, Aisling complied to this voice within her, inhaling as deeply as she was capable and when she exhaled, the world spun back into motion.

It was painful. Alarming, like the sudden bang of a loud, unexpected crash. But a crash that whirled around her in not only sound but also sight and feeling. For when Aisling opened her eyes, she beheld Gnoll leaping off her, swaddled in amethyst flames.

The Fomori danced. He swatted at the fires enveloping him, but it was useless. The more he struggled, the greater and more brightly the fire burned. And, once Gnoll realized this, he turned towards Aisling, horror swimming in those yellow pits for eyes.

The mortal queen crawled backwards, clawing at the earth beneath her. Gnoll knew he was dying, eager to take Aisling with him. The Fomori stumbled towards her, the scent of his burning flesh rancid. Aisling floundered to her feet in search of a weapon. There was no time. Gnoll lunged, flying towards her like a pale, violet breath of flame.

The mortal queen squeezed her eyes shut, bracing herself for the impact.

It never came.

When Aisling opened her eyes, Filverel stood behind the Fomori, a sword staking the creature through the center of its chest. Gnoll glared blankly at Aisling, eyes vacant. And as if they knew, as if the fire listened for the beating of the Fomori's heart, the flames stilled, dimming until only smoke swathed the Unseelie's charred corpse.

Filverel slipped his blade from Gnoll's chest. Aisling soured at the slushy sound of it. The Fomori slumped to the ground, a blackened pile lying amongst countless of his dead comrades. For now, the mountain clearing was a graveyard of Balor's horde; only a handful, those who'd chosen not to attack, maintained their lives, scurrying into the caves from which they'd emerged.

Filverel wiped his sword on the body of one of the deceased before sheathing it on his back. The fight had loosened his braid, strands of white-blonde hair falling across his blood-splattered face.

And once his eyes found Aisling's, he considered her, circling like a vulture. But there was something more in the glint of his opal glare. Something Aisling hadn't seen before.

"What are you?" he asked.

Chapter XXI

BY THE TIME THE FAE KNIGHTS HAD MOUNTED their stags and continued their travels, the dawn had yet to arrive. Nevertheless, their fae procession would continue to travel through the night, eager to burn these dark hours before they found another place to rest, deep within the forest. And find it they did, far in the highlands of the North, where the trees grew tall and thin and the snow melted off the mountains in great, frothing rapids.

"Are they all dead?" Aisling asked the Fae King riding behind her. The image of his wide eyes, glaring at Aisling from across the rocky glade, flashed repeatedly in her mind, crimson speckling his Otherworldly face as he rushed towards her, a circle of dead surrounding him. For although each of the fair folk had been outnumbered during battle, none had faced the brunt as greatly as had Lir. Aisling couldn't count the bodies that lay tangled at his feet.

The Fae King hadn't bothered to wipe his weapons, blades dripping as he inspected the mortal queen for injury. His sage eyes darted between herself and the Fomori blackened by the violet fire.

"No, some, those who didn't attack, are alive."

"And what of them now?"

"They will continue as they always have over the past millennia," Lir said, tugging Saoirse's reins so she turned on a steep bend. "But if one breaks Sidhe law, they'll meet similar ends as their brethren did tonight."

There was a part of Aisling that found herself hoping the Fae King cared for mortal well-being. An irrational part of her. But Aisling knew his enforcement of Sidhe law was exclusively for the sake of his own kind; in order to prevent further conflict with Nemed and the rest of the mortal sovereigns, the Unseelie needed to comply with the laws of the Sidhe.

"Many Unseelie establish dominance and leadership through brute force. The strongest among them, he or she who fights for ascendancy and wins, is to be crowned the rightful sovereign of their group," Lir explained, his voice a whisper.

"So, the Fomorians, they view you as their leader once more?" Because Lir had killed Balor effortlessly. With the flick of his wrist and an iron dagger.

"For now, I've gained their obedience. Demonstrated dominance."

"That's barbaric," Aisling said.

"It's their order. How they establish social hierarchy, an understanding that the mortals enjoy pretending they're above but partake in all the same. In their own way."

Aisling knew the Fae King was partially correct. Man, Aos Sí, Unseelie sought out powerful leaders. Sovereigns, masters, kings, and queens who could protect and provide for them. And while the mortals followed strict bloodlines to name the rightful heir, strength, power, and control were nevertheless required to deter usurpers, coups, or revolutions. Such uprisings had occurred in other mortal states, Aisling knew.

So, the queen bit her bottom lip, ignoring the pressing of new, violent memories on her mind. She could feel such experiences—the death, the destruction, the pain—tweaking with her thoughts. How she thought. What she thought.

Brutality is easier and easier to cope with. To behold, unlike when she'd slain the trow. The exposure to such horrors desensitizing her slowly. She tasted it, the numbness. The disregard for the death of those she believed deserved slow and painful ends.

"I'm sorry," he said, his voice soft and new. Aisling didn't need to crane her neck to read his expression; even in the dark, she could feel the tension hiked in his shoulders and arms. Could see the flexing of his hands, veins coiling around the backs of his runed palms. "I didn't intend to leave you out there so long. For them to"—he hesitated—"touch you."

Aisling cringed at the memory. The filthy stench their proximity had smoked her leathers with. How Gnoll had indeed touched her.

"We needed to see if they'd comply with the new laws. Refrain from assaulting a mortal," Lir continued.

"An infraction punishable by death," Aisling surmised.

"An infraction alone, a breaking of Sidhe law, is rarely ever punishable by death," Lir said.

"But to disrespect their king is—" Aisling conjectured, for Nemed would've done the same to such treasonous slurs, if not much, much worse.

"The Sidhe have already lost this war. You are no longer my king." Balor's voice would haunt Aisling—the mortal queen knew this—for long after this night. Aisling was quickly realizing that not only were the Aos Sí outnumbered by the mortals, suffering by their susceptibility to iron and their inability to produce offspring, but their alliance with their sister race, the Unseelie, was falling apart as a result of Lir's attempts to preserve the Sidhe. To protect the Sidhe he'd risked everything. And now the consequences were raising their vengeful heads.

"No," Lir said, his voice darkening, "to threaten your life."

Every muscle in Aisling's body tightened at the words. She felt—she didn't know how she felt. Strange and perhaps grateful he'd indeed lived up to the promise she'd doubted he would. For Filverel, despite his palpable disdain for Aisling, had protected her in the name of his king.

Aisling searched for something to say but no words came to mind. So thankfully, Lir spoke for her.

"You should sleep," he said as they began their ascent up a rocky path. With one hand, he released Saoirse's reins, reaching around the mortal queen to hold her waist. The other hand remained on the stirrups, directing the stag onward. "I'll steady you," he whispered in her ear.

Aisling opened her mouth to protest. But the warmth of his body wrapped around her own, the heat that such contact conjured within herself, and Saoirse's steady gait, lulled Aisling to sleep.

The mortal queen plunged into a deep slumber, a flailing body driven by a current of nightmares. Time after time, she relived the images of the Fomorians racing from their caves and swarming the crater. Gnoll's hungry embrace. Their putrid smell. The scratch of their nails against her skin. Gnoll wrapped in flames of violet. But in her dreams the Fomorians bore burning coals for eyes, their horns wrapped in those strange flames, devouring her fingers, her legs as she watched, immovable. Unable to stop them, for she was too weak.

Aisling woke furious, cooled by the world around her. Lir was guiding Saoirse deep into the forested mountains of Rinn Dúin. The Fae King weaved Saoirse between the pines and ducked beneath the frosted needles that mirrored the sparkling skies above. Skies whose luminous blue was gradually fading into spring rose with the arrival of dawn.

Here in the highlands, the wilderness morphed into something new. One moment, the fae procession had been swept in the cool, evening winds of the verdant Northern forests, delighted come morning when the sun warmed the earth once more. And the next moment, the fae parade had seemingly stepped into a realm of rock, crystal, and cold where the highlands rolled in their sleep to the lullaby of trees dressed in ice, clicking their frozen branches in the wind like the cylindrical chimes hanging in Annwyn.

At last, they stopped to set up camp beside a cliff's edge. Gradually, they unpacked their belongings, tethering the stags to the surrounding pines. Not because the stags would run. No, Lir spoke with them and knew they were loyal, obedient creatures. But because the Unseelie were deceitful fiends, the fair folk explained, capable of luring even the animals into their depths when none were awake to witness their mischief.

Gilrel brushed through Aisling's hair, locks knotted with dried blood, dirt, and Fomorian death dust. Already the chambermaid had prepared Aisling a fresh pair of clothes and a bathing rag, the best means of cleanliness given the circumstances. Not too long ago, Aisling would've been horrified at the prospect of not being able to bathe in a proper tub, to eat her mortal meals, to spend the days travelling and walking and hiking through the wilderness. Excited, curious, intrigued but horrified nonetheless. She'd never not been spoiled with every luxury man had to offer. And now that she lived this way, trekked alongside the Aos Sí, she found she enjoyed it. Of course, her face was burnt, her muscles ached, her thighs were chafed, her feet blistered by the leather of the boots, and her stomach growled for something other than wild rabbit, or deer, or boar, or berries, or leaves. Craved a proper bath more than anything. But she could grow accustomed to not having those things. The mortal queen's muscles would eventually grow stronger, her skin more resilient, her stomach content with the diet of such questing. Aisling, however, became increasingly concerned she could never return to her life before, a life locked away in an iron keep. Forced to walk, talk, eat, read, sleep like a lady. Not the barefoot savage she claimed to be in the make-believe games she played with Dagfin.

"No matter what, Aisling, do not forget who you are," Nemed had said. "Don't forget the world that made you. No matter what or how much they take from you, do not let them take who you are. Where you come from."

"Are you well, *mo Lúra?*" Gilrel asked.

"There's no need to call me that, Gilrel," Aisling replied. "You can call me Ash."

Gilrel hesitated as she pinned back Aisling's hair.

"Very well ... Ash," the chambermaid said, her voice softening, "are you faring alright? Nuala always hated encountering the Unseelie. Even if she'd done so despite my guidance, it was always out of a responsibility she felt burdened to carry. I can't imagine what a mortal might feel ..." Gilrel trailed off, sitting beside Aisling. The firelight danced across her stained fur.

"Yes, thank you, Gilrel," and it wasn't a lie. Aisling felt surprisingly alright. Of course, the Unseelie would haunt her dreams till the day she died but the mortal queen was content. Fine. Eager to continue travelling through the forest. What sort of monster did that make Aisling? That she could behold violence, bloodshed, primordial beasts, and feel ... hungry for more?

Gnoll's burning body flashed in her mind's eye. What she'd felt in that moment was frightening, to say the least. A power she'd never held before. Not as a sheltered princess. Not as a sacrificial lamb. An unbridled barbarity within her mortal bones. Another voice coaxing her to unleash it. Nemed had warned her of the beasts outside their iron walls but never of the beast that lurked within.

The rest of the fae knights sat around the fire, stealing glances at the mortal queen as they chewed their strips of freshly broiled meat. Lir, Filverel, Galad, and Rian whispered wildly by the stags, spitting back and forth so quickly it was evident enough they were arguing. Even if Aisling couldn't understand their fae tongue.

"Can you hear what they're saying?" Aisling whispered to Gilrel, popping several berries onto her tongue. Between bites, the chambermaid cautiously snuck a glance in the Fae King's direction.

"They're arguing about you."

"And what do they say?"

But before Gilrel could respond, the Fae King, Filverel, Galad, and Rian were approaching the fire. The mortal queen avoided Lir's gaze, those feline eyes studying her till she felt bare before him. The knights, on the other hand, steered clear of meeting her expression entirely, taking their seats around the fire.

The next several days passed similarly. The fair folk eyed her suspiciously, lengthening the distance between themselves and the mortal queen while Filverel and Lir argued for hours on end in Rún. And no more Unseelie crawled out of their holes nor did the Aos Sí approach any.

So, what were they waiting for?

After the first few weeks, Aisling stopped counting the days. It didn't seem to matter out in the wilderness. In fact, time moved differently out here. A day was a week and a week a month. And as far as Aisling was concerned, they'd spent years blazing through the feywilds during the evenings and sleeping during the day. Everyone, except Aisling.

The mortal queen struggled to sleep so Lir lied awake with her most days, recounting tales of the Forbidden Lore. All stories that were incongruent with the versions her father had taught. A father who, for all Aisling knew, had been swept off the face of the earth for he still hadn't responded to her letter. Did he not believe her any longer? Trust her? Care for her opinion? Aisling's greatest fear was swiftly becoming realized: in the eyes of the mortals, Aisling had died the night of her union. Contaminated by her marriage to the Aos Sí.

But out here in the wilderness, where she ran and hid and faced Otherworldly danger, none of that bothered her. Not the opinion of her mother, the approval of her father, or the validation of her brothers. It was just the fair folk, she and the trees who leaned closer as she passed. The wildflowers she collected in her pockets. The newly made scars she counted. The number of woodland creatures that visited Lir when they believed none to be watching.

Nevertheless, although softening each day to the mortal queen, the Aos Sí still distrusted Aisling. Kept her an arm's length away, wary of her mortal blood.

In the last hours of this night, the fae procession stopped to rest beside a frozen lake. The stags drank their fill, tethered to nearby trees. The fae knights drank and sang and played, less anxious than they'd been since their journey had begun.

"Place your feet here and grip the sword with two hands," Galad said, demonstrating himself. Aisling mirrored his position, struggling to hold the blade's haft steady by the brim of the lake.

"You're shaking like you've just seen a sluagh," Rian said, steadying her hands.

"It's too heavy." Aisling's arms shook despite Galad's sword being among the thinner longswords, one the mortal queen recognized from the night of her union to the Fae King.

"Perhaps we should stick to daggers," Rian said.

"She can hardly throw one more than a few feet." Galad steadied the tip of the blade, releasing Aisling from the entirety of its weight.

"Then maybe our time is better spent teaching her to run," Rian laughed before he too assisted Aisling in lowering the blade's tip to the pebbles carpeting the lake's shore.

Aisling exhaled, blowing the loose strands out of her freckled face.

"I can run fine," Aisling huffed.

"But faster than the White Lady? The Phuka?" Rian challenged, an amused grin sweeping his features.

Aisling scowled, "teach me to fight and I won't need to."

"Don't bother," a voice called from a few paces away. Aisling dragged her gaze to Filverel. The advisor approached silently, circling the three of them till he stood directly behind the mortal queen. "She doesn't need it."

"*Go skeor keis veo*, Fil," Galad snapped but Filverel brushed him off.

"Show us what you can do," Filverel ordered the mortal queen.

"I don't know what you speak of—"

"You do. You can end this tedious pretense," the advisor growled, sending chills down Aisling's spine. "What are you? One of the Leanan Sidhe? A Changeling enslaved by Nemed and sent into the heart of Annwyn?"

"I'm a mortal, Filverel, something you remind me of often."

Filverel ignored her. "Whatever you did to that Fomori, repeat it. Show me."

Aisling stilled, grimacing at the weight of his proximity as he stood behind her.

"Enough, Fil. You don't know if any of your suspicions are true," Rian said, placing a hand on the advisor's shoulder. And at the sound of the commotion, Aisling felt Lir's attention cock towards them, lifting his head from the conversation he was currently immersed in by the fire, to inspect their group by the lake.

"Then why don't we ask?" Filverel said, shrugging off the knight's hand. "Why does the *draiocht* favor you?"

Aisling's brows raised, resisting the urge to sputter.

"You believe I can wield magic? That I'm some Unseelie instructed to terrorize Annwyn and its people?"

"Aye, that's exactly what I think," Filverel narrowed his eyes.

"What Sidhe or Unseelie do you know that can summon fire, Fil?" Rian asked, "this is unprecedented and surely nothing Nemed is aware of."

"She would've already killed us all and returned to her mortal kingdom by now if she were being instructed by Nemed," Galad chimed. "The Forge knows she's had plenty of opportunities."

"So, you suggest we simply trust this"—Filverel considered—"this *weapon*?"

Weapon. Aisling's eyes darted between the Aos Sí around her.

"I can hardly lift a sword much less be considered a weapon," Aisling said, turning to face Filverel. "And as far as whatever it is you believe I can do, I assure you, I know nothing."

"We should keep it that way," Rian said, crossing his arms. "The more she knows, the more dangerous she becomes."

"You're all mad," Aisling said.

"They're not mad and neither are you pretending," Lir interjected.

"How can you be sure?" Filverel asked, snapping his attention to the Fae Lord approaching.

"I could feel the *draiocht* as it reached for her. I thought it was myself at first. But it was pleading to be used. To be inhaled, encouraging her to trust the impulse. And once she did it was overzealous and young. An emotional burst through the breath of the *draiocht*," Lir stood near to her now, glaring down and searching her expression. "The trees have told me the same."

"And you trust their council?" Filverel asked.

"Aye, I do."

"If she's neither Sidhe nor Unseelie, what is she?" Galad asked, cocking his head to the side to inspect Aisling as though for the first time.

"I don't know," Lir confessed, "and neither do the woods."

The fair folk exchanged glances.

"Can you do it again?" Lir asked Aisling, "whatever it is you did to that Fomori, can you replicate it?"

"How can you be so sure it was me and not another nearby?"

Filverel shot daggers at the rest of the Aos Sí, threatening them to say no more. So, it was Lir who spoke, "as far as the Lore has described and as far as any of us have experienced or known, there is none who can summon fire. No Seelie. No Unseelie. No beast or creature or fiend known throughout the continents and beyond. It is a mortal tool that destroys what the Sidhe seek to build. We can use it, yes. Manipulate it, perhaps. But never summon it. Not through the *draiocht* and not at all. Nor can the Unseelie."

"And the mortals? Can they breathe through the *draiocht*?" Aisling asked.

"As far as anyone has ever been concerned, no. It's against one of the original laws," Lir said, the evening wind running its cool fingers through his dark hair.

"Do you recall the story I once told you?" Rian said. "The tale in Cathan's song?"

Aisling remembered the night, one of the evenings following her union. Before she'd ever set foot in Annwyn.

"After Ina attempted to save her love, Bres, from the Kingdom of the Greenwood, she was cursed. One of the more unfortunate consequences of such a curse was forbidding the mortals from ever being able to wield the *draiocht*."

Aisling shook her head. "What does Ina's curse have to do with the mortals?"

The Aos Sí exchanged glances again. They were keeping things from her.

"No one else could've summoned the fire," Lir continued, "it was yours. I could feel it."

Aisling held her hands before her, turning them over in dawn's first light.

"Wield the flames again," Filverel demanded.

"*Easca*," Lir hissed. To which each of the fair folk shuffled uneasily.

Galad stepped before the mortal queen. "Can you try?" he asked more gently.

Aisling considered him. Of course, she could attempt it, but Aisling knew nothing would occur. They were all mistaken. Misunderstanding whatever had happened to Gnoll. She was a mortal through and through. The only mortal princess in all the Isles. She'd never heard of the *draiocht* until a few weeks prior to this day. Still, there was a part of Aisling that hoped it was true. Prayed to the Gods she'd never believed in that perhaps, just maybe, she did possess some magic. Was capable of wielding something of such power.

Aisling pushed past each of the Aos Sí surrounding her to face the lake's expanse. It shimmered in glassy sheets of ice. Still. Silent. Frozen. Pines bowed around it, weighed down by the piles of snow sitting on their backs.

Lir moved behind her, the smell of him clouding around her in dreamy wisps. As always, the nearness of him warmed her lower abdomen, setting loose flocks within her stomach.

"Hold your hands out before you," he said, tilting his head to whisper by her ear. Aisling batted away the heat creeping beneath her cheeks. She willed herself to focus.

"Close your eyes," Lir commanded. And Aisling obeyed. "Inhale and exhale slowly."

Aisling steadied her breath. So far, she felt nothing.

"Now what?" She asked in return, keeping her eyes closed.

"I like to imagine what I intend to summon," Lir said.

"And then?"

"And then I invite the *draiocht*. It will try to rule you but you mustn't let it. Like any wild animal, it seeks to be dominated lest it need to dominate. To be used and be useful."

Aisling did as the Fae King described, calling out to the *draiocht*.

I wish to summon the fire. Aisling said in the hollows of her mind.

No one replied.

Are you there?

Silence.

I wish to summon the fire.

Aisling tried again and again to no avail. The silence and darkness mocked her, her words echoing off the walls of her consciousness. There was nothing and no one to answer her calls. Not that sentient little creature the Aos Sí had dubbed by the name of magic. The personification and origin of spells, charms, and enchantments, Aisling was quickly realizing.

Aisling held back the urge to cry. She wasn't the weapon they believed her to be. Not the dangerous magic wielder she'd hoped herself to be. She was mortal. A poor princess. A necessary sacrifice. Fae bait. Nothing more.

"No matter what, Aisling, do not forget who you are. Don't forget the world that made you. No matter what or how much they take from you, do not let them take who you are. Where you come from."

Chapter XXII

AS THE REST OF THE FAIR FOLK SLEPT, AISLING lay awake, studying the silver thread Lir had tied around her wrist each morning. A few paces away, Lir slumbered as well, his twin axes tucked neatly beside him.

Another week had passed since the incident at the lake. At the very least, Aisling's failure had silenced Filverel for the meantime. No longer did he bicker with the Fae King, nor glare at the mortal queen suspiciously each time she needed to relieve herself in privacy.

Rian, Galad, and Gilrel, on the other hand, had continued to teach Aisling the basics of blade-wielding. The mortal queen now knew how to find her opponent's heart with the tip of her sword or dagger, where to cut if she wished for her enemy to bleed out, and how to throw a blade so it met its target. Aisling was rather bad at each of the former lessons but nevertheless, she persisted. In time she would learn to defend herself. These Aos Sí had centuries to learn, Aisling needed to remind herself lest she be discouraged.

Aisling turned on her side, finding Lir lying on his back. The sun's softest rays percolated through the canopies above, dappling the Fae King's face with shadows and light alike. There was something about watching Lir sleep that Aisling enjoyed, as strange as that may sound. He was a wolf curled to sleep. Not to mention, Aisling could watch him without fearing he'd catch her glaring.

The mortal queen couldn't count how often their eyes accidentally met throughout the day. As though each had an intangible sense for the other, a knowing for when one's eyes grazed the other, pulling their attention with an irresistible tug. For indeed, Aisling often felt as though she could feel his glances. The kiss of his eyes as he watched her ride Saoirse on her own, train with Rian or Galad, talk for endless hours with Gilrel or await a raven that never arrived with correspondence in its beak. So, did the Fae King also feel her watchful eyes, studying him through the night and as he slept?

The mortal queen closed her eyes for perhaps five or ten minutes, oscillating on the brink of sleep, when she was startled awake by a woman's song.

It began slowly. A sweet melody was being sung, perhaps by a woman Aisling's age. Her voice was haunting, dancing through the forest and into the fae party's camp like the flowery clouds of her mother's perfume.

Aisling bolted upright, searching through the trees. There was no one and nothing in sight. The voice grew in volume, becoming quicker, livelier. It was intoxicating. A taste of some sweet pastry that begged to be devoured bite after bite. To feel its texture on her tongue and savor the taste. Aisling's mind became fuzzy, her thoughts muffled. All that mattered was the woman's song. The poetry that the mortal queen couldn't understand.

Aisling knew she shouldn't follow it. What had Lir said? The Unseelie lure their victims into the forest with various tricks and traps, among them, song. But somehow, none of that seemed consequential. Even the mortal queen's memory became a distant thought, lost somewhere in the subconscious.

Surely the wielder of such a voice was a benevolent creature. For how could such beauty be anything but goodness itself?

So, Aisling stood from the ground and followed the sound. She tiptoed past the sleeping Aos Sí, careful not to startle them. And Aos Sí were easily alerted, even in their sleep.

Aisling hesitated at the edge of the fae camp. She shouldn't go forward. Not alone. It wasn't right. Something somewhere was hammering at her mind for her to return to camp. To wake Lir or Galad or Rian and tell them what was happening. But another part of her, the part that was in control, was eager to go forward. So, she did.

Aisling moved into the trees, allowing the voice to guide her. The first step was the most difficult. All the rest came effortlessly. The mortal queen spilled through the forest, lost to the potion steeping her human ears. And that internal voice that told her to return faded until only the song remained, enchanting her forth. That was until her wrist caught.

The mortal queen flew back, tumbling into the arms of another.

Immediately, the spell broke and Aisling bristled at the contact.

"Sshh," Lir said softly, folding her into his arms and hiding her behind a rather thick pine. One whose branches grew low to the ground, expanding like arms. The Fae King peered into the forest, eyes narrowing in the distance. "In the future, remind me to shorten this thing."

Aisling's eyes darted towards the starlight thread, binding her to Lir. That was how he'd known. She must have tugged him awake. The mortal queen had never been so grateful for that silver, braided snake.

"What is it?" Aisling asked, following the Fae Lord's gaze.

"Merrow," he said, hands still holding onto Aisling. And once she realized this, she stepped away, increasing the distance. A gesture met by the sharp glint in Lir's eyes.

"Another species of Unseelie?" Aisling asked.

"Not quite," Lir said, his voice barely a whisper, "these are the Sidhe the Gods sanctioned to the seas."

"But there are no bodies of water near here," Aisling replied, "are there?"

"There are areas in the Isles where the water runs beneath the earth. In caves, tunnels, currents that lead towards the Ashild." The sea that surrounded the Isles of Rinn Dúin. Waters of spice trades and shipwrecks.

"Are they your subjects then?" Aisling asked.

"All Sidhe are subject to the original or descendant Sidhe kings and queens whether they reside in one kingdom or another."

Lir stood silent for a moment, listening to the surrounding forest. He closed his eyes, brow pinching as he concentrated. Whatever it was he communicated to the trees, they responded, groaning on a phantom wind. A wind that tunneled through the forest, Aisling's braid catching the leaves that flew like sparrows. By now, the strange hum that'd called Aisling into the forest had lowered, buzzing in the distance.

"This way," Lir said, gesturing for Aisling to follow him.

The mortal queen glanced over her shoulder, searching for the fae camp they were leaving behind.

"What about the others?"

"What about them?"

"Won't we need their help?"

Lir stopped in his tracks, turning to face the mortal queen.

"You doubt me?" He asked, a roguish grin baring his fangs.

"I doubt myself. I can't be of much help should anything happen," Aisling said, thinking of the countless Fomorians that descended upon both her and Lir a few weeks prior.

"You shouldn't," Lir said, "you may be more capable than I."

Lir turned his back to Aisling, continuing further into the icy woodland.

"You still believe I can wield the *draiocht?*" Aisling hurried after him.

"Why wouldn't I?"

Aisling wrinkled her brow. "Because I couldn't summon the fire the night at the lake."

"I'd have been surprised if you had," he said, "your use of the *draiocht* is still young. Undisciplined. I can sense it. And so can the forest. We feel it in your blood whenever you're near." His eyes flickered towards her, their regard as frightening as any great predator but equally as lovely.

Aisling tore her eyes from the Fae King. Is that what Yddra had told him? What the trees whispered to Lir throughout the day and night alike?

"Initially, I thought it your will. That wildness within you, you seek so persistently to stifle. That heathenous heart that allows you to live amongst us," Lir gestured towards the surrounding woodland. Aisling paused. For indeed she craved the grass beneath her bare feet, the smell of wet leaves, the wind purling through the forest.

"Within you lives a wild spirit." The forest stirred then, swaying their great bodies to the sound of their lord's voice. "There's magic in your blood."

Aisling clenched her fists at her sides.

"Then do you fear such magic in me?" Aisling searched his expression, an expression that rarely gave anything away it wished not to.

Lir met her gaze. "It interests me."

"Then why does Filverel—"

"Fil fears your father will use you as a weapon if he discovers your abilities."

"Filverel believes I'd burn the forests for my father?" Aisling asked.

Lir stopped in his tracks, glaring at the ground. Aisling followed his gaze. A stone staircase travelled deep into the earth below. Steps that faded into blackness.

Moss, flowers, and vines snaked around the staircase, stretching their fingers and plunging into the earth until they too, disappeared into the abyss. But that wasn't all. As the staircase crossed the surface of the earth and into the underground, there stood an open doorway made of stone carved into the likeness of a woman's head frozen for eternity with a gaping maw. A cavernous mouth where the staircase unfurled like a rock-ridden tongue.

"Aye. He thinks that if you're reunited with your father, you'll let him use you," Lir continued, "to destroy the woodlands and burn the Sidhe."

Aisling blanched, lips parting as she considered the Fae King.

"You don't know do you?" he asked. "Surely your father has told you this."

Aisling shook her head.

"The only other weakness the Sidhe bear from which they cannot heal—other than iron—is fire."

Aisling's heart panged.

"Nemed doesn't just burn the forests to spread his walls. With fire, he purges the Sidhe without having to risk his men in battle."

Lir was wrong. He had to be. Nemed wouldn't, couldn't, know that by burning the woods he was not only slaying centuries-old, sentient trees but also the Sidhe. It was an accident. A misunderstanding for her father couldn't be so cruel. His methods were harsh, cold, ruthless at times but always to defend mankind. Never to be the aggressor unprovoked. Aisling knew her father was a man of great fury, of hatred at times. Capable of doing what the average man could not. But that was what was required of a king: to do what others couldn't for the sake of his people. Even if it meant sacrificing his own morality and goodness. Hadn't Lir done the same with the Fomorians?

Lir descended the staircase first, gesturing for Aisling to follow. The walls and steps were caked with slick, defrosting moss, stone wet and marbled away by the millennia before it.

Aisling could both hear and smell the water sloshing around down below. Salt and mildew lurked beneath this cavern where the light from above faded until both she and Lir were shrouded in shadow, nothing but the walls on either side of the narrow passage to guide their way.

"Hold onto me," Lir said, his voice an unembodied spirit amidst the darkness. Aisling swallowed, reaching for the back of his leathers and pulling herself closer to him. He was warm, a beacon guiding her further into the abyss. Every step was a blind one, trusting the rhythm and pace of the ones before it.

At last, they reached the bottom of the staircase. The floor levelled and Lir walked onward, one stealthy step after another. Aisling fisted her hands in his shirt, avoiding the twin axes crossed at his back and resisting the urge to squeal at the frigid touch of the water splashing her boots. Shallow waves, lapping onto the jagged rocks upon which they walked, reaching for their ankles, hungry to pull them under.

But still there was no light. Only darkness and the sound of water in an endless underground cavern, slapping at the walls around them.

Lir reached for Aisling's hand. The mortal queen wrenched her eyes shut. She knew what was coming. And, sure enough, the scrape of the Fae King's dagger sliding from his scabbard echoed in the cavern.

"I'll try to make it painless," he said, pricking the mortal queen's fingertip. Aisling flinched at the sting of it. Her blood warmly oozed down her finger, so Lir extended her hand and allowed every scarlet drop to drip into the waters below them. Her blood burst into inky, crimson clouds just below the surface of the water.

But there was little time to focus on her own blood. The waters below them bubbled like a boiling cauldron, birthing a strange, green light from the heart of these inky depths. The light grew, casting a pale, sickly glow into the cavern.

Aisling's eyes widened, her chest tightening at the sight of what emerged from below. Several of them. Perhaps twenty, writhing beneath the surface of the water.

Lir reached for the tether of starlight between them, wrapping the excess thread around his wrist till they were separated by only a handful of breaths.

"Stay close to me." Lir stepped forward, placing himself before Aisling on the stone platform.

And from the frothing waters, the figures emerged. Creatures who bore the upper bodies of darkly beautiful women but where legs should sprout there were none. Only the lengthy, thick, scaly tails of shimmering ivory, glittering in the waters beneath them like eels, eels tangling their slippery bodies. Knotting and unknotting.

They glared up at Aisling and Lir with round, pearly eyes, their alabaster hair plastered against their scalps, a wicked contrast to the soft green of their fair complexions. And as the water washed over their slick and Otherworldly forms, they swam nearer to the small peninsula in which Lir and Aisling stood. Shimmering, sharp, onyx rock stroked by the spidery fingers of the creatures below them.

"*Mo Damh Bán*," the first said in Rún, her voice as lovely as her song, "*it's been too long. I've thought of you every day since we last met.*" The merrow swam closer, seductively eyeing the Fae King. But before Lir could speak, her eyes landed on Aisling.

"*Is this she? The mortal Queen of Annwyn?*" Each of their bobbing heads turned towards Aisling, eyeing her skeptically. "I smelled her in the forest but never have I tasted anything quite like her blood." The merrow shifted into Aisling's tongue effortlessly. She licked her lips, exposing a collection of razor white teeth punctuated by fangs longer than Lir's own. Aisling shivered, instinctively stepping nearer to the Fae King.

"Although," the merrow continued, "she certainly isn't Peitho or Narisea."

Aisling bristled, folding her hands into fists at her sides.

The mortal queen wasn't certain why the mention of Lir's first *caera* aroused anything in her other than pity, sympathy for the Fae King's loss. But it did. Like a knife twisting at the center of her chest.

"I have a question for you, Sakaala," Lir said, kneeling and peering into the variant Aos Sí's luminous orbs.

"Anything for you, *mo Damh Bán.*" Sakaala grinned, batting her jeweled eyelashes and moving closer still. "Lest we meet the same fate as the Fomorians."

"Their blood seeped through the earth, into our caverns and drove us mad." Another creature grinned, slithering in place

"Let it be a lesson on the consequences of threatening their queen," Lir said, and all could discern the threat lurking within. That promise of violence in every drip of his fae accent.

Sakaala's eyes met Aisling's: eyes whose depths held the secrets of the sea and its pearl-tipped storms.

Aisling willed herself not to flinch. Not to stutter before such a frighteningly beautiful monster as this. One whose skin detailed years, potentially centuries in the darkest depths of the Ashild Sea.

"Always so territorial, Lir. I can't say I'm not jealous," Sakaala purred.

Aisling glanced at the Fae King, but Lir's expression only darkened as he pulled back his hood. A severity in his eyes Aisling had beheld once or twice before.

Sakaala pulled her torso above the water, her thin fingers gripping the stones beneath. Now, Aisling could see the merrow's fae markings, the tribal tattoos that spun around her sculpted abdomen and arms. A warrior, like the fair folk she'd come to know in Annwyn.

Sakaala leaned forward until her pointed nose was but a mere breadth's width from Lir's own. She licked her lips again. Full, ruby lips sensually shimmering in the cave's light. Against her own volition, Aisling's eyes trailed towards the exaggerated arch of the merrow's back, her lean torso, the supple curve of her bare breasts.

The mortal queen's ears burned at the sight. The potent fragrance of *lust* was thickening the air of the cave as Sakaala's eyes explored Lir's own with unrelenting focus. Aisling had never beheld a nude woman before, save for the statues and paintings she'd witnessed in passing, much less a nude man. For, this form of seduction and enticement was a sort of magic in and of itself. A lawless sort of magic. One that made Aisling's toes curl. Went against everything she'd been taught of the wetting of fires and stilling of storms. And to witness this fae female so boldly covet another male, attempt to lure him into the waters around her, it stunned Aisling. Made her flush. Made her confused. Made her angry. Made her envy that power. That influence she harbored so effortlessly.

"Balor mentioned Danu. I need to know where I can find her." Lir's voice was deep, challenging the bubbling of waters beneath them.

"Always straight to the point, Lir," Sakaala pouted.

Lir's lips curled. "Is there anything else more pertinent?"

"As pertinent as slaughtering your own Unseelie?"

"Only when they break Sidhe law."

"How boring," Sakaala replied, "the humans deserve this, Lir. The Gods will smite them for what they've done and if it's the Unseelie they wield as harbingers of justice then so be it." Sakaala tore her eyes from the Fae King, shooting daggers at Aisling. The rest of the merrow followed her lead. Their glares dug into Aisling's skin.

"The Aos Sí's survival depends on this peace. Reject it, and we'll be smote alongside them."

"So be it. I'd rather drown in the Ashild than align myself with them," Sakaala spat, wrinkling her nose in Aisling's direction.

"Danu," Lir pushed, "tell me where she is."

"The elusive Empress of the Dryads," Sakaala hissed, "are

you certain you wish to find her?"

Dryads. The same dryads they'd encountered upon entering Annwyn? Aisling wondered to herself.

"Balor implied she's foreseen the end of this feud," Lir said, his voice growing cold and hard. "So naturally, I need to speak with Danu myself."

Indeed, if one knew the outcome of centuries of war, could foresee the future as Balor had intimated, Aisling knew Lir wouldn't let such knowledge slip through his fingers so easily. He'd need that knowledge. That insight. For it would grant him power, leverage, and advantage over the mortal race should tensions continue.

Had Aisling been so naive as to believe her marriage was an end to the feud between mortals and Sidhe?

"And what will you give me in return?" Sakaala challenged, lifting a hand to touch the Fae King's hair. Her nails were as long and sharp as claws, flirtatiously fluttering towards Lir. Cupping his sharp jaw as lightly as foam embroidered itself at the edge of a wave.

Lir snatched her wrist, his knuckles growing white around her slim bones.

"Don't bargain with me," he said, the ice in his voice sending chills down Aisling's spine.

"How about a kiss, Lir," she whispered, undeterred by his violence. The corners of her lips curled amorously. Her eyes darted towards Lir's mouth, watching him with unveiled desire. She was afraid. Scared yet lured by the Fae King's deadly grace. As all the world appeared to be in his presence.

"Just one kiss," she pleaded.

Lir stilled, the image of the forest at the heart of the tempest stirring behind his thick lashes.

The merrow's lips parted, her large eyes fluttering shut as she began closing the distance between them. She moved slowly, seductively, body tightening the nearer the Fae King became and her long slippery hair veiling her breasts as she lifted herself higher.

Aisling ground her teeth. Squeezed her fists as tightly as they'd shut. Her heart quickened with each passing second.

Just a thread's width from the Fae King's lips, Lir reached for her throat and squeezed. Sakaala shrieked in harmony with the rest of the merrow. Their wails bounced off the walls of the cavern. Aisling covered her ears.

"You'll obey me," Lir growled, every word punctuated by the flash of his canines, "tell me where I can find Danu."

Relief swept through Aisling. Relief coupled with terror. Her knees locking. Icy sweat beading across her forehead, lower back, and hands. For she could nearly taste his strength, his *power* rippling off him in waves of potent heat. He was no longer the *Damh Bán* now. Now he was the wolf. Savage, ruthless, determined to spread his dominion.

The merrow each treaded madly in the surrounding waters, witnessing their Sakaala desperately clawing for breath. Aisling could smell the fear, the terror the Fae King instilled, cold in the breath between herself and these aquatic Aos Sí.

"She resides west of here," Sakaala spat, "that's the last anyone has heard or seen of her."

"Where west?"

"I don't—"

"Where?" Lir squeezed her throat harder, purpling the merrow's complexion.

"Please!" Another creature screeched from the edge of the cave. Lir ignored her.

"The Isle of Mirrors," Sakaala coughed, scratching Lir's fingers with her claw-like nails. The Fae Lord's jaw clenched in response, his hands flexing, considering the female within an inch of her last breath.

At last, Lir released the merrow and Sakaala collapsed against the rock. She heaved for breath and pawed at her own throat. The Fae King considered her, uncurling and standing once more beside Aisling.

"I have one more question," Lir said, watching as Sakaala gathered herself.

"Anything, *mo Damh Bán*," the merrow said venomously, pulling her upper body up with her arms. At the sight, Lir smiled. A flicker of wicked triumph flashed across his expression.

"He is the worst of them: ruthless, merciless, no more than a beast driven by hunger, need, and power. But, unlike the wolf, he is insatiable."

"What do you sense when you smell her blood," Lir said, gesturing towards Aisling. The mortal queen froze, eyes darting towards the merrow eyeing her like a fish within reach.

"Give me her hand," Sakaala demanded. The creature extended her own hand. Lir eyed the merrow's outstretched fingers, his eyes narrowing.

"I cannot distinguish her from another by only a few drops of blood. I need to touch. To let the waters feel her." Sakaala's face twisted with both fear and frustration, more the hungry beast Aisling knew she was behind her cruel beauty. Her sensuous magic. Behind her lust.

Lir considered, his wicked temper brewing behind the tension in his shoulders. What ran through his mind, Aisling wondered. What variables did he consider and weigh when it came to her life? To the treaty he'd bound himself to with the mortals? Humans Aisling had once believed cowered in the fair folk's shadow. Not burned their villages and dwindled their numbers.

"No," Lir declined, his voice resolute.

Aisling, without thinking, grabbed his arm.

"It's all right," she said.

Sakaala grinned, curling her fingers impatiently.

Lir's eyes flashed, searching her expression. The mortal queen could sense his apprehension. The conflict he battled internally, a taut cord snaking around his neck. Lir's jaw clenched more tightly, silently watching as Aisling stepped around his shoulder and towards Sakaala.

The mortal queen placed her hand in the merrow's.

Her skin was as cold as ice, near biting at the touch. But what's worse was its texture, slimy and slick, the oily belly of a fish.

Cautiously, Sakaala pulled Aisling towards the waters. The mortal queen rested on her knees at the edge of the peninsula. Lir stood behind her, holding the thread of starlight so it bore no slack.

Sakaala paused, the water licking the tip of her chin. The merrow raised a brow in silent question: *Are you ready?*

Aisling nodded in response.

Sakaala sunk into the water, pulling Aisling's hand till the waters clasped her forearm. The choppy waves sent shivers beneath Aisling's skin, numbing her knees pressing against the sharp rocks. But the cold was temporary, for what followed was heat. Heat and the unveiling of the *draiocht*. A whisper that called that strange creature from whatever depths it resided till the *draiocht* crawled into the light to inspect its summoner.

The sensation was familiar. For it wasn't only Sakaala breathing through the *draiocht* but also the sea itself. Just as Lir spoke with the trees, so too was Sakaala speaking with the cold currents spinning around the mortal queen's hand, inspecting her. The ocean harbored a millennium of knowledge, of memory, ancient waters of salt and foam. Of shipwrecks and lost sailors. Of creatures of both the shallows and the deep. Whispers from the beginning of time till the heartbeat of the present. Fingers that stretched to one continent and the next. Of anger and fury and calm and peace. Ruthless. Immeasurably powerful.

Lir bent down beside the mortal queen and pressed a hand against her lower back. A touch that would otherwise burn through Aisling's very flesh but now all she felt was the pressure building around her hand. The waters rose to kiss her mortal skin and taste whatever strange power the Aos Sí believed her to possess.

The merrow whispered amongst one another, heads bobbing wildly at the spectacle. What did they understand that Aisling couldn't? What did the ocean hiss as it stirred and frothed?

Sakaala released the mortal queen. All at once, the heat, the *draiocht*, the voice of the ocean quieted until only the churning of the cauldron waters surrounded their black island. Aisling stumbled back into Lir, the Fae King catching her shoulders and steadying her once more.

"What did you sense?" Lir asked.

Sakaala slicked her mane away from her face, glaring at Aisling as though she were a talking fish. Eyes wide and bewildered. Possibly even frightened.

"Sakaala—"

"She's strange, Lir," the merrow hissed, eyes darting between the Fae King and his mortal queen. "Strange and powerful. The Ashild doesn't recognize her blood."

"Neither did the trees," Lir confessed, turning towards Aisling. The mortal queen shifted awkwardly. She glanced at her pale, wet hand. So small in comparison to the Aos Sí that surrounded her.

"The daughter of the Northern Fire Hand is not the lamb she was presumed to be," Sakaala said, seemingly speaking her thoughts aloud.

"How did you do it?" The merrow's lips peeled back as she bore her fangs.

Aisling paled, speaking through her dried throat.

"What?"

"How did you steal the *draiocht?*"

"I didn't steal anything," Aisling said as Lir helped her to her feet.

"No mortal can wield the *draiocht*. It's part of the curse. You've done something, you fleshling. What have you done?!"

The Fae King took a step forward, protectively curling an arm around Aisling.

"*Féachail art dol thring*," Lir warned, his words sharp as shards of ice. Sakaala recoiled further into the cavern, the rest of the merrow, following her movement or spiraling down into the depths of the pool.

"Once the rest of the Sidhe find out what she is, what she's taken, they'll want her dead. Treaty or not." Sakaala's delicate face twisted with loathing. "They'll ask for her head on a pike."

"Speak that way again about your queen, a Queen of the Sidhe—"

"She is no Sidhe queen, Lir. She's a thief. The Fire Hand's thief. This is thieves' sorcery. Nothing good can come of it. He will use her. He will take her and use her to end this war. Just as Danu has foreseen."

"No longer is she the Fire Hand's," Lir growled. A sound so menacing Aisling wrenched her eyes shut. It was true. Up until Aisling's marriage to the Fae King, she'd been her father's. Under his veil of protection, of care. But once she was bound, tethered to the fair folk, she was released from Nemed's hand. Nevertheless, to hear the words on Lir's lips was strange. Liberating, yet terrifying as all freedom was. Even if she wasn't free entirely. No. She'd gone from one prisoner to the next, she needed to remind herself.

"You may wish to erase the pain of Narisea and your unborn child's death with love from another. A second *caera*. But those desires will only prove you are your mother's son. Don't make the same mistakes as she."

Lir bared his teeth, vines growing from his fingertips in rage. But Sakaala continued.

"A word of advice, *mo Damh Bán*. Once they uncover her *draiocht*, Aisling's death will be demanded by the Sidhe. Better it be at the hand of her *caera* than another's."

Chapter XXIII

THE FAE PROCESSION RODE WHEN THE MOON sailed currents of midnight blue and slept when the sun blanketed them with rays of gold. But now, Lir challenged their harts, exhausting each stag until they collapsed against the clearings, mounds, valleys, and cliffsides where they rested. Aisling could feel Saoirse's stress, the longing for water throughout the night, and the relief of sleep when the sun shattered the shadows and ascended come dawn.

"How much farther?" Aisling asked her handmaid, both kneeling beside Saoirse resting on her side at the center of a frosted valley. The rest of the Aos Sí spoke amongst themselves, built a fire, and argued over the coming weather. Lir, however, had disappeared into the surrounding forest.

"I'm not certain. I've never been to the Isle of Mirrors before," Gilrel said, lovingly stroking Saoirse's belly.

The Isle of Mirrors, where Danu had foreseen the outcome of centuries of blood rivalry between man and fair folk. Answers Lir needed. Wanted with a manic sort of thirst that frightened the mortal queen more than she'd admit.

"Have any Aos Sí gone there before?"

"None that I know of. It's nearly a place of both myth and legend."

"I didn't think the Aos Sí had those. To the mortals, the Aos Sí are myth and legend."

Gilrel laughed. "Aye, we have many. Stories that aren't recorded in the Lore but passed down generations with seemingly no beginning nor end."

"Tales of Gods and monsters and mystical lands," Aisling says, hushing Saoirse's restless snorts as the beast struggled to rid her muscles of the adrenaline purling within. "My father says there are no Gods. That the Lore is forbidden to mortals because it is a deception of the true history."

"And what is the true history according to the Fire Hand?" Gilrel asked, meeting the mortal queen's eyes.

"Man was born of nothing, but nevertheless born first. Burned his way into the earth and thus, became its master. Taking the earth's stone to build his castles, the earth's wood to burn his fires, the earth's water to propel his mills."

"And yet, the mortals cower at the coming storm. Fear the beasts of the wood. Shut out the winter lest they die of sickness and frailty," Gilrel huffed, averting her eyes to watch Rian and Cathan playfully wrestling on the ground. Snow dusted their leathers as they rolled around the meadow.

"And what of this Danu? The Empress of the Dryads Lir pursues?" Aisling asked.

Gilrel's brow furrowed, turning towards the surrounding forests eavesdropping on their conversation.

"What of her?"

"Who is she? Lir seems to believe she holds the answers to his questions, the outcome of the feuds between our kinds."

"If anyone does, it would be her. She's one of the few to bear the *sight*."

"So, she can foresee the future like Ina?" Aisling remembered Cathan's story that night by the fire: a tale of one of the original fair folk sovereigns, one who fell in love and was cursed for it along with her kingdom of the mountains. Iod.

"Aye, like Ina," Gilrel said, seemingly surprised Aisling knew that bit of their history at all. "An axis between the then, the now, and the will-be. One of the most powerful, chaotic Unseelie on this continent and beyond."

"And the Gods forged such a creature?" Aisling asked.

"The Gods have created many monsters," Gilrel said, eyeing the mortal queen knowingly.

"If what the others are saying is true, you cannot deny the Gods or the gifts they've given you."

"What are the others saying?" Aisling shifted her attention to the fae knights wrestling or jeering on the side.

"Filverel tells them your blood is steeped in the *draiocht*. Many believed him mad at first. But he wasn't the only one to witness that Fomori light up in flames."

"He believes me to be a weapon."

"Aye. Fire is powerful, Ash. No Seelie nor Unseelie can wield it. A mere spark can extinguish our kind. It steals what we create, what the Forge has cast in our bones, flesh, and veins. Devours what we breathe."

"I cannot use it. I don't know how ..."

"But you will," Gilrel said, her voice becoming hoarse. "And when you do ..." Gilrel trailed off, her eyes growing distant.

"I would never hurt you," Aisling said, the words as much a surprise to herself as they were to the chambermaid. Aisling couldn't ... The thought trailed off.

Before her marriage to Lir, there were many things Aisling didn't believe herself capable of that now haunted her consciousness. With every passing day, she felt something waking within her. Something the mortal queen had kept catatonic.

"Forge be willing, you keep your word," Gilrel said, averting her gaze. The marten feared her. And while the mortal queen would've thought such fear to be isolating, she found pleasure instead.

Before Aisling could respond, she followed Gilrel's line of sight: Lir emerged from the forest, through the prickly curtains of pine, catching Aisling's eyes across the meadow.

Aisling's heart quickened, standing to her feet as he approached her. The northern wind tossed his dark hair, wrapping around his lean legs with every lithe step forward.

"I want to show you something," Lir said, extending his gloved hand once he was a mere pace away. The mortal queen glared at its long, elegant fingers.

"What is it?" She asked, internally cursing herself for stepping closer to him.

"A surprise."

Aisling hesitated, tilting her head to look past the Fae Lord and into the woods.

"Her death will be requested by the Sidhe. Demanded. Better it be at the hand of her caera *than another's"*.

Sakaala's words accompanied Aisling's every waking thought since. There wasn't a moment the mortal queen didn't anticipate would be her last. For there was little if not nothing that Lir wouldn't do for his people. Willing to make as great of sacrifices as Aisling was herself. And Aisling knew the potent weight of duty all too well.

How long could Lir protect Aisling, she a symbol of this unity between the mortals, from the Sidhe and Unseelie alike? How long could he temper their rage, their hunger, before it came at the cost of both Aisling's head and the treaty itself? Lest his alliance with the Unseelie and his dominion over his own kingdom implode.

"You aren't afraid of surprises, are you?" Lir taunted, the ghost of a smile brightening his fae features.

Aisling straightened. The mortal queen wasn't afraid. But she was cautious. Afraid to let herself believe, to trust in Lir and the promise he made her. The vows he claimed bound him to protect her. For up until recently, Aisling believed the Aos Sí to be liars. Manipulators. Now? She wasn't certain what she thought. The fair folk were strange, different than anything she'd anticipated or been taught. And somehow, she found herself *wanting* to trust the Fae King. When had that changed?

Wordlessly, Aisling placed her hand in Lir's.

The Fae Lord grinned, dimples framing his broad beam. "Follow me."

"Are we close?" Aisling's boots crunched the quilts of snow, stumbling to keep Lir's pace.

"Almost."

"And what of everyone else?" Aisling asked.

Lir glanced at her over his shoulder, the corner of his lips curling in the slightest. "They'll continue setting up camp."

Aisling steeled herself against both her nerves and the cold. Perhaps he was leading her to her own execution. Where the alder roots could taste her blood once the puddles had seeped into the frozen earth.

"Where are we going?"

Lir's lips spread into a smile that stole the mortal queen's breath.

"Here," he said, guiding Aisling towards a row of trees. A wall of needles and chocolate bark. So, Lir peeled back the curtains of frosted pine and nudged Aisling forward till they emerged on the other side.

Nestled between the slick bellies of two neighboring mountains, were hot springs, countless individual cerulean pools spilling over until all gargled the same steaming waters. Snow clung to the steep walls of rock, ice beaded the forest's limbs, branches that hung loomed over the springs in chandeliers of needles and icicles and snow.

Breathless, Aisling's eyes grew wide with wonder. This was a palace. A fortress sculpted by the wild, every morsel of verglas carved by nature's immaculate hands.

"Can you swim?" Lir brushed past her, boots stirring up clouds of snow

"Yes," Aisling replied, glaring at the milky waters by the brim of the springs. Waters that rippled with the drops of melting ice, showering from the alders above. "There's a lake beside Castle Neimedh. Where my brothers and I were taught to swim." And Dagfin, but Aisling refused herself the permission to speak his name aloud.

"Good," Lir said, shucking off his boots, "you reek."

Aisling scowled, eyes darting between the waters and the fae warrior on her left. Her pulse pounding through the rivers in her ears, unsure whether she should be angry or terrified at the prospect of Lir intimating they enter these springs together. Regardless, the thought of bathing herself was too tempting to withhold from her consideration entirely.

"Are there … Is it safe?" Aisling asked, inching nearer.

"There are no Unseelie in these waters if that's what concerns you," Lir said, already pulling off his bandolier, his axes, and his outer jacket. And before the mortal queen could avert her eyes, she glimpsed the cut image that'd graced her at both the *Snaidhm* and in her dream, all save the wings she was more than curious to witness for herself.

Aisling stilled, her expression reddening till she lit like an ember amidst the landscape of white and hunter green. And in response, Lir bore his fangs wickedly, the corners of his lips twitching up.

"Relax, princess," Lir said, unbuckling his belt. "I anticipated your mortal prudishness."

"Modesty," Aisling choked.

Lir gestured towards her leathers. "Enter with your clothes on, if you wish. The camp is near enough."

"And yourself?" Aisling asked, deigning to meet his eyes. For now, all he wore were his trousers, lowly, indecently hanging from his narrow hips. Enough to summon her stomach up her throat.

"I'll keep my trousers on," Lir said, climbing down the rocks and into the pool. The waters seeped into the fabric of his pants and the steam danced around his perfectly muscled abdomen, near veiling him from Aisling's vantage point. A small mercy.

"Unless you prefer otherwise," the Fae King flashed another wolfish grin, gleaming despite the mist. Aisling glowered in return, clenching her fists at her sides. Unfortunately, Lir was right. Aisling did reek, smelled of the Fomorians and blood and dirt and stag and sweat. Even her long, dark hair was knotted and matted in its braid, loosely falling around her face.

The mortal queen swallowed, shaking her head. She couldn't enter fully clothed. Not only would they weigh her down, but it was an admission that she bore any nerves, embarrassment, hesitancy around a creature she deigned to reveal any weaknesses to.

So, Aisling stubbornly slipped off her outer jacket and draped it over a nearby boulder. She removed her belt, her leather corset, then her boots, unraveling her hair from its plait. Lir watched as she undressed until only her trousers and blouse remained, eyes darkening. His regard warmed every inch of her flesh.

And there was a moment, a passing temptation, to remove everything. All her clothing till she stood bare before him. To see if she could wield the same sultry power as the merrow. An unprecedented urge that went against the world she'd been raised in. An impulse that became difficult to stifle.

The mortal queen lowered herself down the slick edge. After a few missteps, Aisling submerged herself in the pool. She gasped at the heat of the waters, near scalding against her frozen, dirty skin. But after a moment, the sensation was pure bliss, waters soaking and untangling her nest of hair.

She scrubbed her skin, clawing beneath her sleeves and

the legs of her pants to reach every inch of herself. Nevertheless, it would take days, weeks, months before the stench of their travels fully left her. Was this how Lir always smelled of the woods? Of the hours after a storm, of wet leaves, of pine needles?

Aisling could grow accustomed to a life like this. Riding endlessly, venturing the wilderness, bathing in springs and rivers. It was a dream, a life she'd longed for. A wild fantasy her body craved, needed more than breath itself. Yet such a life, Aisling hadn't realized, belonged to her enemy.

At the thought, the mortal queen met Lir's eyes. His lashes beaded with moisture.

"Are you ready?" Lir said, his voice more rough than usual.

"For what?" Aisling eyed Lir as he washed the blood from his hands, his neck, his face, and the length of his arms. Aisling looked away, forcing herself to concentrate. Perhaps he really would kill her out here.

"Whatever it is you did to that Fomori, I want you to repeat it." Fomorian blood and dirt clouded in the waters around him.

Aisling flinched at the memory of Gnoll igniting like a torch.

"The water will keep you from burning any trees should you make a mistake," he said.

So that's why he'd brought her here. For a moment, Aisling believed it to be a kindness, a moment for the mortal queen to bathe away the past several weeks, or however long it'd been. Instead, this was a plot, the Aos Sí's premeditated attempt to control whatever abilities they believed Aisling could perform.

Lir stepped towards her, encouraging the wild thrashing of her heart.

"You're going to show me how you summoned that fire," he continued, his voice low.

Aisling straightened lest she expose the flock taking flight within her stomach.

"I don't know how."

But Lir already knew this. Had already witnessed her failed attempts to light a fire by the lake.

Lir moved closer still, a wolf padding towards its prey.

"I'll teach you," he said.

"Hold out your hands," the Fae King ordered. Reluctantly, Aisling obeyed, cupping her palms above the surface of the water. Lir craned his neck to the forest, as though waiting for someone or something to emerge. And emerge it did.

A familiar snake slithered through the branches of glass littering the forest floor, hissing excitedly as it dragged its sinuous form down the rocks and into the waters. Nervously, Aisling eyed it but the Fae King was unbothered. So, Aisling allowed the creature to approach her.

The snake coiled between her hands, tickling her fingertips with its forked tongue.

"You spoke to it?" Aisling asked, resisting the urge to smile.

"Aye," he said, studying her, "and so can you, can't you?"

Aisling met his glare. Emerald pools brimming with the life-breath of the forest, the rage of the wolf, and the serenity of the stag. Filled with winds and shadows and hollows, tempered by the sunlit canopies, budding flowers, and sweet frosted earth. Aisling tore her eyes from the Fae King, cursing the ache in her chest.

"I can, at times, sense something, a feeling that is not my own," Aisling confessed, "a sensation separate from myself: the pangs of hunger from a fox hunting nearby, the anxiety of the doe caught mid-stride, but I cannot speak to them as I would with my voice."

"That's how it begins," Lir said, stroking the snake with his knuckle. And with every supple glide of his fingers against its scales, Aisling could nearly feel the warmth of his skin on her own.

"Once the ability matures, they'll communicate with you and you them. Unknowingly. Effortlessly," he said. "In time, you'll be capable of many things."

"How do you know?"

"When I was a child, my abilities were the same. I could only feel their most base urges as they brushed past. But as the *draiocht* matured, I learned to communicate with the wilderness. To summon the earth. To call upon the wind."

Is that what Yddra had told him? What the trees whispered and sang to the Fae King throughout the day and night alike?

"You remind me of this serpent," he continued, allowing the snake to knot their hands together. "Scales as black as the crow, bedizened with rare shades of violet." His eyes grazed her undone hair. Sable tresses that rivered down her back, glossy with spring water. "The most venomous creature in all the Isles of Rinn Dúin despite its size." As if boasting, the serpent widened its maw and flashed two ivory, needle-like fangs.

Aisling held her breath, turning to the Fae King. And once their eyes met, she wondered when he'd come so close, his breath brushing her lips.

Aisling didn't know how long they glared at one another before the snake hissed, severing their line of sight.

"The snake agrees," he said, toying with its bobbing head. "In time you'll learn to use the *draiocht* like the Aos Sí and the forest." The woods stirred then, swaying their great bodies to the melody of their king's voice. So, the snake untangled itself from their hands and swam through the waters, crawled up the rocks and into the woods, lost to the glare of the rising sun.

Aisling faced Lir.

"Filverel calls me a weapon. Aren't you afraid of what you claim I'm capable of?" Aisling asked.

Lir considered for a moment.

"My curiosity far outweighs my fear," he confessed. "Besides, it's unnatural to deny oneself power. There are few happy endings when it comes to those who refuse to wield their magic."

"What do you mean?"

"For the Sidhe, not using the *draiocht* is suffocating. An essential need to survive and grow."

"And for me?"

Lir considered her. "I don't know what it'll be like for you. But I do know the *draiocht* is a greedy creature. One that must be fed."

"You speak of it as though it's sentient."

"That's because it is a spirit with great agency. One the Gods Forged into the lungs of the Sidhe, the Unseelie, the forest, and the wilds, the *draiocht* lives within us all. Through us. With us. You, however ... I don't know how it found you."

Aisling released a breath she hadn't realized she'd been holding. If it were true—if Aisling did possess the ability to wield the *draiocht*—she couldn't waste it. Couldn't let such power slip through her fingers.

"Teach me," she said, her voice more settled than she felt herself, "if it was indeed I who wielded those flames, teach me to do it again."

Lir licked his lips, resisting the urge to smile ear to ear.

"Very well. Follow me."

The Fae King swam towards the other side of the spring. Where the waters sank deep, plummeting into the earth till only the black eye of the abyss glared back.

"We're to swim down there?" Aisling asked, careful not to slip over the lip of stone beneath her bare feet.

"You won't need to," he said, taking her hand and pulling her under. Aisling inhaled as deeply as her lungs would allow, holding her breath as she sank deeper into the spring. They descended, ears popping from the pressure, until both floated at the center of an enormous cylinder of jagged, black rock. The surface rippled a few meters above while the bottom was lost in the clouded distance below.

Bubbles beaded around them, dancing through her ebony hair as the Fae Lord held her under.

Panic swelled within her chest. So, Lir tugged Aisling nearer to himself, releasing her hand and bringing her body against his own. If Aisling were capable, she might've pushed him away, but within this sub-aquatic realm she could only trust the Fae Lord lest she drown, held beneath the world by a strength far more potent than her own. So, she did, allowing him to hold her. His flesh to touch her own and coil her lower abdomen. The rapid pace of his heart against her breast.

Lir closed his eyes.

Pressed against him, Aisling could feel his body still. His legs stopped moving and his arms loosened around her. Aisling's heart stuttered, fear gripping her from the inside out. They floated, tangled in one another.

At last, Aisling felt the rhythm of his chest rise and fall. The great sweep and brush of his breath against her own chest. Aisling hesitated. His breath?

Lir opened his eyes, reaching out to cup her cheek. And from his palm bloomed rare violets, weaving through Aisling's hair and tickling her ears. Aisling's eyes grew wide. And the flowers floated towards the surface like maidens twirling their ball gowns, their skirts ballooning around their green and slender legs.

An explosion of breathy bubbles escaped her lips. She'd witnessed this *draiocht* before but still, it impressed her. The ability to grow and create green life from the palms of his hand. Aisling didn't think she'd ever grow accustomed to it. But to *breathe* under water—Aisling was left stunned by such an enchantment.

Lir wrapped his arms around her once more, tipping his head towards her.

Your turn, he said wordlessly.

So, Aisling closed her eyes. Her lungs burned and her vision blurred, dark shadows dancing at her sight's edge. She was running out of breath.

Aisling concentrated, searching for that sentient push she'd felt in the Fomorian crater. All she felt, however, was as she always had: mortal. No other foreign will to accompany her own.

Aisling opened her eyes to find Lir watching her, his grip tightening around her torso. Still, his chest rose and fell against her own. Perhaps the fair folk were wrong. Perhaps she knew no magic and now she'd drown, attempting to do the impossible. Mortals and magic were unsuitable.

"*The Aos Sí say their magic comes from the Gods. There are no Gods. Whatever abilities they wield are aberrations. Perversities of nature. As they are themselves. Do not let them convince you otherwise.*"

Wordlessly, Lir encouraged her to try again. The world around Aisling spun as she closed her eyes, clawing through the caverns of her mind for that creature, that incorporeal will that pleaded to be let loose. The panic, the anger, the frustration sparked as she felt herself losing consciousness, slipping away. Aisling clawed at Lir's arms till she believed she'd tear through his skin.

Where are you? She called the *draiocht*.

No answer.

She had but a breath left.

Where are you? She said again, grinding her teeth.

Silence. Ruthless silence. A stillness that struck fear in her, her body instinctively resorting to panic or fight till she reached the surface of the water. Until at last, Aisling felt that spark, crawling from some ancient depth. Its fingers latching onto the corner of whatever cavern it occupied.

Here, it replied.

It burst forth like a broken dam.

On the brink of exploding, her chest heaved, forcing Aisling to inhale. A sharp pain was stripping her lungs. But such pain was brief, for then she breathed underwater. Not as the fish do with their gills. Not as the mortals do with their lungs. Not by inhaling the steaming currents of the springs. But through magic.

"What the mortals call magic we call draiocht. *In your tongue, it means breath.*"

And despite her newfound ability to respire alongside the Fae King, her hands lit with fire, flames of plum and lilac, flowering from the palms that clung to Lir's arms and illuminated the Fae King in its heated luster.

Aisling released him, shock muddling every coherent thought. The mortal queen held her hands between herself and Lir, floating in the throat of the abyss. She wiggled her fingers, cupped her hands, capturing and releasing the flames, allowing them to dance across her fingertips like amethysts.

Both she and Lir watched, transfixed. Bewitched. Enchanted by the fire that bubbled deep below the surface of the water. A rare gem, alive and glittering between the mortal queen's hands.

Chapter XXIV

THIS FAR INTO THE WILDERNESS, GIANTS WERE born. They sat on their haunches, stony faces glaring down at their own sleek, snowy ridges dappled in evergreens and persistent field flowers, in the Oxheim Highlands, Aisling was told.

The Isle of Mirrors was close. Out here, magic seeped through the forest, the mountains, the fog that clouded around the fair folk's weary, horned creatures. The nearer they approached, the thicker it became. Like a potent perfume rippling from the source.

Aisling rode ahead, enjoying Saoirse's burst of energy after a lengthy day of rest. By now, the strict precautions Filverel had instilled initially for the mortal queen had slackened greatly. And although Aisling knew it was wise to save Saoirse's strength should they need to outrace a horde of Unseelie, she couldn't help herself. Riding as swiftly as Saoirse was capable was an opiate: the cool caress of the mountain breeze, the fragrance of wildflowers, the steady thump of Saoirse's hooves on the grass, and the beast's own excitement charged her. That and the mortal queen's need to escape Lir's advisor.

Filverel hadn't missed an opportunity to scold his Fae Lord

for teaching the mortal queen to use her abilities. Small lessons every day, concentrating on summoning the *draiocht*. An hour or so each night that Aisling savored, looked forward to more than anything else. And with each passing lesson, the mortal queen was improving. Slowly. Gradually. But improving, nonetheless. She could now summon a flicker of flame without risking her life, enough to light a candle. Enough to stoke and begin their campfires come daylight.

The fae knights watched her warily as she practiced, eyeing her with increased suspicion. There were days Aisling believed them to be friends. Days that were quickly replaced by the fury in their eyes each time her fingers lit with claws of violet fire. So, Aisling lay awake most days, when everyone else was asleep, toying with the *draiocht* that rose from her palms.

She spoke with the *draiocht* too, learning to summon it, to listen to it, to scold it when necessary, to praise it, to foster its growth within her lungs.

This magic was addictive. A surety of power the mortal queen never believed she'd possess. One she longed to grow, to cultivate, to understand. And she wanted more.

Aisling brought Saoirse to a halt, pulling back her reins. One glance over the mortal queen's shoulder told her the procession was still a ways behind her, slowly following her tracks. Aisling glanced around the mountains as Saoirse pranced eagerly beneath her. The mortal queen was suddenly struck by the sensation of wind—a strong, whipping gale slipping and ruffling through obsidian feathers. Then came the determination, the need to pursue and to find. To deliver.

Aisling looked up into the skies. Above her a speck approached, gliding through the stars like a ship on a stormy sea.

Aisling considered turning around. Seeking the security of the fae procession behind her, gradually closing the distance between themselves and the mortal queen. But instead,

Aisling kept Saoirse in place, watching as the creature soared over the summits and dove into the valley in which Aisling rode. A raven.

The bird flapped its wings, driving it quicker, more swiftly towards Aisling until it hovered before her. Clutched within its talons, was a scroll, wrapped in a royal blue, braided tassel. Someone had written to the mortal queen and this wondrous winged creature had found her, delivered it to her. Just as Lir claimed it would.

The rook dropped the parchment before perching atop a sickly-looking pine. Aisling lunged for the scroll and caught it before it fell to the ground.

The mortal queen's heart pounded within her chest. She knew this seal. These colors. Remembered the braided tassel. A part of her was disappointed and another, bubbling over with enthusiasm. For this wasn't her father's long-awaited response. No. This was a message from Roktling, the northernmost country amongst the Isles.

Aisling quickly broke the seal, unravelling the rolled parchment.

Dear Ash,

I've written and re-written this letter countless times and none seem to bear the news any lighter. Your letter to your father was received with great uproar. The Mortal Sovereigns have discussed its contents at length and are eager to request further council with the fae crown. A conclave they hope to celebrate with another interracial union to solidify the treaty your union has already established, a marriage between myself and a fae princess of the Aos Sí's choosing.

There was a pause in Dagfin's writing. A scribbling and a crossing out before he continued.

I wanted the news to come from me before you heard it from another. Hopefully, if you attend, we'll see one another again. I hope to speak with you.

I've missed you.
Dagfin

Signed by the seal of the Prince of Roktling.

Aisling read the letter more than once. Nemed had indeed received her letter regarding the Unseelie. In fact, the mortal sovereigns were discussing her correspondence. Her father had listened to her.

Relief swept over the mortal queen. There were moments, quiet moments, Aisling believed her letter had been lost before it arrived at Tilren or worse, burned once it'd arrived, ignored by her father as the machinations of a silly woman. But the mortal sovereigns had headed her word and were actively organizing a response to such threats. Even the mortal walls still stood. Protection against a new and ruthless foe: the Unseelie. And it was because of Aisling. So, she allowed herself a moment to glow with pride.

But such a moment was short-lived, for dread too gripped the mortal queen—Dagfin was to be wed to a member of the fair folk.

The last she saw of her kind, their loathing for the Aos Sí was matched only by the Aos Sí's loathing for the mortals in turn. A hatred she believed could only *begin* to dissipate after centuries of necessary peace. So why had her father and the mortal court agreed to more unions so swiftly? Were the benefits truly so wonderful? And the risks it posed to Dagfin's life should he not be the fae princesses' *caera*.

The last lines of the letter were perhaps the most difficult to read. Yet they were the ones Aisling read the most.

"Tsk, tsk, tsk," a voice erupted from behind. Aisling jumped, turning Saoirse to face the fae procession swiftly approaching. "You know better than to open a letter before the court advisor has had an opportunity to oversee it." Filverel moved his stag beside Aisling's, snatching the letter from her hands.

"It's addressed to me and therefore mine to do as I please," Aisling growled, reaching for the letter. But it was too late. Filverel was already scouring the page with his moonstone eyes. Studying every one of Dagfin's strokes as though they might leap from the page at any moment and attack.

"Another union?" Fil said, at last, his eyes flicking towards Aisling hesitantly.

"What's this?" Galad said, approaching within ear shot.

"It appears the Prince of Roktling has corresponded with our queen," Filverel said. And at the mention of Dagfin's title, Lir's head cocked to attention, eyes flicking towards Aisling.

"What does it say?" Galad asked.

The advisor didn't respond. Merely handed the parchment to Galad so the knight could read it for himself. Aisling ground her teeth, near simmering despite the highland chill.

"Hand it back," she ordered. Heat flushed her cheeks, her hands, her ears. Galad, reluctantly, offered her the letter, eyeing Filverel as he did so. Aisling snatched the page back and tucked it into her jacket.

"'Fae princess?'" Galad repeated Dagfin's words.

"Aye, he must be referring to Peitho." Filverel ran his fingers through his hair. "She's the only trooping female of such rank in Rinn Dúin."

Aisling swallowed. She despised Peitho uniquely and to imagine Dagfin, her childhood friend—her only friend—either destined to duel or be *bound* to her? Aisling grimaced.

"She'll never agree," Cathan said, joining their conversation.

"She might not have a choice," Filverel said, "peace is

fragile. A rejection, one so early on, could jeopardize all our previous efforts."

"So, we do whatever the mortals bid?" Rian chimed.

"We satiate them where we can," Filverel replied. "Peitho was raised for the potential of one day marrying for her court."

"Not to the mortals," Aedh said, spitting on the ground.

Hagre, unbuckling his flask from his hart's saddle, lifted the canteen to his lips before piping in as well: "Lir will never allow it."

After all, Peitho and Lir had once been ... what had they been? Lovers? Friends? Something in between? It was never clear. If it was up to Peitho, the fae princess would have Aisling believe the former.

"Peitho will do what the Sidhe require of her," Lir said at last. Aisling whipped her attention towards the Fae King. "If what the Sidhe need is another union, she'll give it."

"But if this prince isn't her *caera* ..."

"Peitho is aware of her duty to all Seelie and Unseelie alike." After all, Lir had taken the same risk. Was he so willing to risk it once more? Were the mortal sovereigns willing to risk it once more? The odds that, according to fae superstition, two of the fair folk were matched with two mortals were unlikely. Like a surefire way to renew tensions and throw Aisling's own union out the window. Should this marriage end in bloodshed, not only would Aisling's life be in jeopardy but Dagfin's as well; no, she couldn't dwell on such possibilities, so she ripped it from her mind. When it came to Aisling's own throat, had Nemed done similarly in the name of mankind?

"I'd quite enjoy watching Peitho behead a mortal nobleman," Rian piped.

"Nothing has been cast in the Forge as of yet," Filverel said. "It'll need to be discussed. Weighed. Planned—"

"*How do we know we can trust this prince? Who's to say any of this is any more than rumor?*" Hagre growled in Fae, nodding his head towards the letter Aisling had tucked away in her doublet.

"We don't." Rian ran his fingers through his flame of hair. "We'll need to discover the surety of his letter for ourselves."

There was silence for a moment. Each of the knights silently mulling over the possibilities. Another wedding would be a grand request indeed and for what measure? Aisling couldn't imagine Peitho sworn to a mortal. He'd be dead within the year even if they were by some miracle *caera*.

"*You need to return to Annwyn,*" Lir said in Fae, locking eyes with his advisor.

"I can't turn around now, not when we're so close," Filverel protested, his mount stomping under the stress of the advisor's grip on his reins. "The Empress is nearby. I can taste it."

"Aisling and I will fare the remainder of the way on our own. The rest of you are needed back home," Lir said, his voice bored, unamused. But Aisling knew beneath that layer of calm, collected arrogance, uncertainty lied. "There's too much afoot for the majority of my court to be away from Annwyn."

The knights exchanged dubious glances. "*But* mo Damh Bán—"

"Return now. Aisling and I will continue to the Isle of Mirrors and return within a fortnight," Lir insisted, eyes flicking towards the mortal queen.

"*Let me stay—*" Filverel pushed.

"*You're needed most in Annwyn, Fil. Myself and Rian will journey alongside them,*" Galad interjected. "*Danu would consider this many of us a threat and a challenge to her dominion regardless. Whatever Lir intends with the Empress, it's wiser to approach in fewer numbers.*"

"He's right," Rian said, "if what the prince says is true, you're needed in Annwyn."

"Of all of us, Galad, it should be you returning as well. Your input is needed alongside Filverel's in the king's absence. Let me go on with Lir," Hagre offered.

Galad shook his head. "I'll not leave Lir's side. My responsibilities at court come secondary to my oath. I'm confident the rest of you will manage exceptionally without me." Hagre's lips pressed into a thin, white line as he considered.

"I'll be accompanying them as well," Gilrel chimed, lifting her muzzle high.

"That won't be necessary—" Galad began but was swiftly interrupted.

"Need I remind you, I took a similar oath, Galad. To service the queen and her every whim until her dying breath. How am I to do that if I'm forests away?"

"If the marten is going, then I'm going," Cathan said, hushing his restless stag beneath him.

"Neither of you are coming," Lir said, his voice resolute. "Annwyn needs each of you. Myself, Aisling, Galad, and Rian will return as soon as we've held an audience with the empress. It won't be long."

"But—" Gilrel began before Aisling reached out and took her paw.

"It's alright," the mortal queen said, squeezing the creature's paw. "Our return will be swift." Aisling's violet eyes searched Gilrel's own. The handmaid parted her muzzle to speak but no words emerged. Instead, she nodded her head, ears lowering. An expression that both warmed the mortal queen and weighed heavy on her heart.

Filverel darkened but Lir said nothing. The fae sovereign had already made up his mind and his word was final. He wouldn't repeat himself nor take kindly to further arguing. Brethren, comrades, council or not. Even if each of them struggled to conceal their palpable frustration and concern for abandoning their king just before he was to meet the Empress of the Dryads.

Furious, Filverel, cast one last glance Aisling before darting down the valley from where they'd come, a threat to the mortal queen should she harbor any intentions of harnessing her young fire against the Fae King.

Gilrel turned to Aisling.

"Be safe, *mo Lúra*," the lady's maid whispered, kissing the mortal queen on the cheek. A peck as cold and soft as a dew drop in spring. "I'll eagerly await your return."

Gilrel and the rest of the knights hesitated for a moment before following after Filverel, encouraging their harts back through the highlands. Every step a step further from the king they'd sworn to protect and fight beside.

Lir, Aisling, Galad, and Rian stood in silence for several moments, watching the rest of their procession disappear amidst the landscape of rock and pine and snow. Listening to nothing but the howl of the wind, barreling through these stony corridors, and the fading chorus of hooves upon grass and gravel.

They were alone now. The four of them. A day's worth of travel from the Isle of Mirrors.

Chapter XXV

AN HOUR BEFORE DAWN, AISLING SAT ON A cliff's edge. Lir, Galad, and Rian were already dozing beside the fire Aisling had lit earlier, dreaming deeply. But sleep, ever since Aisling's union, had eluded the mortal queen. Dreams came at a steep cost: hours of thinking, of worrying, of anxiously waiting for the sun to set so she could trail onwards. Nightmares that embellished her most wicked memories with greater horrors. The Cú Scáth devouring her belly as she watched, the Fomorians forcing her to dance upon the fae knights' bones. Losing control of her violet flames till they devoured her in licks of an all-consuming wildfire. At times, she even found herself running through Tilren, banging on Castle Neimedh only for her tuath to have forgotten her. To her clansmen, her name, her face, her voice was but a foreign word in their ears. Meaningless. A series of vowels strung together. To her family, she'd vanished like a ghost come morning light.

So, Aisling sat on the cliff's ledge, dangling her legs over the steep drop. A wall of bark-like stone descended into a mess of clouds beneath her. And further beyond, on the horizon, was the endless feywilds preparing for the coronation of the rising sun. But even from this vantage point, Aisling could see blotches of black. Areas where Nemed's fires had burned through the wilderness. A thief of fire and ash—fire that Aisling recklessly toyed with on her fingertips, jewels of deepest plum fluttering from the tips of her nails.

"You should be resting or are you unable to resist certain peril," a familiar voice purred from behind. Aisling turned to find Lir approaching, brushing sleep disheveled hair from his eyes.

"You've said that to me before," the mortal queen replied, doing her best to steady the rapid pace of her heart the Fae King's presence inspired.

"You need to be reminded of your more destructive tendencies," he said, sitting beside her on the cliff's edge. His legs were much, much longer than her own. His boots dangling farther down the wall than Aisling's. The mortal queen swallowed as his thigh brushed her own.

"Perhaps you should focus on your own destructive tendencies instead of mine," Aisling quipped, forcing herself to concentrate on the flames at her fingertips.

"I have many."

"Tell me one," she said, daring a glance in his direction. Lir's sage eyes shimmered with lilac, reflecting the light of Aisling's fire. He sat transfixed by her fingers, toying with the flames. Aisling had never seen him look at anything like that, with such fascination. An expression that softened his features. Made him nearly real and not the Otherworldly king that the mortal queen knew he was. But moments like these, looks like those, made her forget. Just for a moment.

"You," he said, eyes flitting towards Aisling. Capturing her glare before she had a chance to look away. Aisling blinked at the Fae Lord, her breath hitching in her chest.

"Do you fear me?" She asked against her own volition. But the words didn't feel like her own. As though she were listening to another woman speak to the mythic warrior beside her.

The corners of Lir's lips curled slightly. A mischievous smile, steeped in the promise of something forbidden. Something dangerous. Something she shouldn't explore yet wanted to all the more.

"Aye I do," he said, returning his attention back to Aisling's hand. Emerald vines grew from nothing, twirling around her arm, tickling the bare skin of her wrist. Aisling shivered at the touch. A caress as light, as gentle as the kiss of a taunting breeze.

The vines curved towards her fingertips, bedizened by her flames. And once the lianas touched her fires, they sizzled, blackened, then wilted until they were nothing more than ash, floating off the cliff and into the sea of clouds below. All the life he breathed, she destroyed.

"You once told me you live in fear," Aisling said, remembering his words. "What else do you fear?" As soon as the words left her lips, she regretted them. It wasn't her place to ask such intimate questions of the Fae King. One whose armor ran deeper than the steel plating he sported. One who bore his fangs and snarled at the slightest provocation or threat. He wasn't simply the stag, the winged Aos Sí in her moonlit dreams, she needed to remind herself. He was also the wolf—insatiable, predatory, lethal. Gloriously fierce. A fact that had been all-encompassing at one point.

Lir averted his gaze, turning instead towards the forested expanse before them.

"I fear my people's suffering," he confessed, his voice deeper than it had been before. "I fear making an unforgivable mistake, a lapse of judgement that would put my people in jeopardy"—he paused—"like my mother did." His eyes flicked back to Aisling,

Like his mother did? Lir had only ever mentioned his mother once before. Before they'd come across the Fomorians. But what crime could his mother have committed to harm the people of Annwyn? The Kingdom of Greenwood? Aisling stilled, afraid to move lest the Fae King build up those walls of ice, stone by stone, once more.

"I fear losing what's mine."

"Like you lost Narisea and Peitho," Aisling surmised, deigning to mention the child he'd lost alongside his first *caera*. It was too great a risk but she couldn't help herself. Despite her better judgement, she needed to know. Wanted to know.

Lir bristled. But whatever he found in her amethyst eyes dispelled the tension her query aroused, his shoulders softening.

"Like I lost Narisea," he confirmed, seemingly surprised Aisling knew of her at all. But of course, she did. Not only had Peitho mentioned his first *caera*, but others had spoken her name as well. Balor. Sakaala. And his neglect of Peitho didn't escape Aisling's notice.

"What was she like?" Aisling asked, torn between wanting to know the answer and running before she heard a genuine response.

Lir's expression fell as he studied his hands in his lap.

"She was born with a spear in her hand and the forest in her heart. A wicked temper." The Fae King smiled, fangs flashing in the firelight. "She was wild," he said, considering for a moment, "like you."

Aisling's heart skipped a beat. But Aisling was no warrior. She was a princess, hardly capable of throwing a dagger, much less a spear.

"And you?" the Fae King asked. "Have you ever given your heart to another?"

As if the question had summoned his face, Dagfin appeared in the mortal queen's mind. Aisling shuffled away the image, her heart twisting at the thought of him. The way he smelled of smoke and Roktish incense. His voice, a song of home. A place that now felt more like a dream than reality.

"I've missed you."

"Don't tell me it's the princeling," Lir said, as if reading her thoughts.

"No, I've never given my heart to another," Aisling bit quickly, wrinkling her nose.

"But the princeling gave you his?" Lir watched her closely.

"No, never. We grew up together. We were friends—"

"To you perhaps," the Fae King smirked, unable to mask his amusement. But there was something dark behind his thick lashes. Violent. Something sharp he was hiding.

Aisling opened her mouth to speak but knew not what to say. Dagfin was her friend. Her companion when she was loneliest. The only one who had ever paid her mind or valued her thoughts. Encouraged her to pursue the adventures she craved. Was complicit in her mischief as a child. Just a friend. Nothing more.

"I've missed you."

"Galad told me what he wrote in his letter to you," Lir continued. "Are you truly so blind to his affections?" Lir shook his head. "That must drive him mad."

Aisling flushed, clenching her hand into a fist and wrapping it in fire.

"It doesn't concern you," she snarled even though she knew of its inherent hypocrisy. Lir had no obligation to have told her anything of what he'd already confessed. Yet he'd done so regardless. Done so at her request.

"You're my *caera*. Of course, it's my business," he said, his voice ragged with recent sleep.

Aisling stiffened, aware that the Fae King had never mentioned that word to her before. Had never explained it to her. Had never called her so. The only reason she knew it at all was because of Gilrel. Aisling didn't believe in its meaning the way the fair folk did and she didn't think the Fae King took it seriously either. They were enemies. Their hatred for one another swam in their blood.

"Do you know what that means?" He asked, his eyes

flicking towards the mortal queen's mouth. A gaze that burned her lips.

"Gilrel explained it to me in passing."

"Did she tell you of its origins? The Lore's telling?"

Aisling shook her head. There was very little she knew of the Forbidden Lore. The history and conception of the world according to the fair folk. She'd never minded not knowing. Before her union, Nemed had ensured it was nothing more than deceit. Now, Aisling could no longer refuse how much her father had gotten wrong. Possibly lied about. But Aisling couldn't dwell on that possibility for long. Still, what else did the Forbidden Lore contain that would ring true for Aisling?

"Once the Gods were satisfied with the barren realms they'd created, this plane and the plane of the Other, they returned to the Great Forge of Creation to cast its inhabitants: the Sidhe came first and the Unseelie second."

"Man was born of nothing, but nevertheless born first."

Aisling bit her tongue. There was no point in contesting Lir's version against her father's own. Their disagreements were clear and her mind ached when she thought of their contradictions.

"From the primordial elements, they cast the first Sidhe, the original twelve Sidhe sovereigns: water, earth, wind, and the *draiocht* built the Sidhe bones, our blood, our flesh, our breath. But not fire. Fire was the essence of the Forge. Bubbling magma from which the Sidhe were built and could equally be destroyed." Lir glared at the lilac fires in Aisling's hand, his expression hardening as if bewitched by their light.

"The Gods continued by forging the twelve Sidhe kingdoms and all of their subjects, granting those belonging to a certain environment more of one element than another." Lir held out his hand once more until moss flowered from his palm, spreading like a contagion across his arm. "But there were other elements, elements even the Sidhe do not recognize. Minerals. Precious substances that only reside in the pits of the Forge."

"And you don't know their names?" Aisling asked.

"There are legends that claim such arcane elements are stardust or lightning or the tears of the Gods. Others say it's a nameless substance we would understand as fate. A substance that takes such an abstraction and makes it a physical entity, a string that binds two souls."

"Is that what you believe?" Aisling asked.

Lir's brow knotted, considering.

"I don't know," the Fae King confessed, watching as the moss around his arm faded away with the first breath of sunlight, peaking over the mountains.

"The Gods bound two of their original sovereigns with this invisible, elemental string, curious to know what would occur should they do so."

"Bres and Ina," Aisling realized. For, Cathan's song had described the original Sidhe king and queen as having been forbidden lovers. Besotted but unable to commit to their love lest they forsake their individual kingdoms. A crime the queen of the mountains eventually committed and was cursed eternally for it. Alongside every subject in her kingdom. The Kingdom of Iod.

Lir's eyes flickered with grief. A grief so potent, Aisling could feel its shadow darkening the world around him.

"Aye, Bres and Ina were the first *caera*. Both born of the Forge with a string that bound their heart to the other. Two souls destined to be pulled towards the other no matter how the string tangled, stretched, knotted, no matter the cost." And Ina had paid such a cost. A cost Aisling wondered about often for none had ever deigned to speak of the queen's curse. What had become of her people as a result of her love?

"But then, according to the Lore, only the twelve original Sidhe sovereigns and their subjects were cast directly from the Forge. Only they'd be capable of having this elemental string. What of all those who come after?" Aisling asked, searching the Fae King's expression, a shadowed glare that cut into her chest.

"Like the *draiocht,* as you now know"—Lir gestured towards Aisling's fire—"the element is sentient. It grows, spreads, seeks. Wishes to be felt and used and indulged. If such an elemental string is made of fate, fate is a hungry creature. But rare."

Aisling remembered the night of their union. The three blades staked before her, unaware that her choice was a decision between life and death. No, not a decision. A gamble. One whose loss meant her own severed neck and continued conflict between the fair folk and the mortals.

The mortal queen tore her eyes away from the Fae King, ignoring the burning behind her lids.

"And all of this. Your belief in this elemental tether. It's the only reason you didn't behead me at our union. A union you entered believing you'd paint the grass with my blood."

Lir was taken aback, wincing as though he'd been touched by iron.

"Why would I believe that?"

"Because you'd already promised yourself to another *caera*. And two *caera* ... it's unheard of, isn't it?" It was a rhetorical question. Aisling already knew it was a myth amongst the fair folk, a shock to all those who'd attended their wedding and heard of their union after. "That night, you had every intention of ending me."

Aisling didn't know why the words, the thought, the memory, made her so furious. Of course, he'd harbored those intentions. But the fury she'd grown over the last several months had burst past her defenses, leaking from between her teeth.

"You know not what you speak of," he said, a muscle flashing across his jaw. He was angry. And in this moment Aisling didn't believe the Aos Sí weren't made of fire. For fire is what brewed behind his lashes in wicked electric storms.

"Don't condescend," Aisling snapped. "I know enough. You never believed I'd choose your axe." Twin axes still crossed at his back as they spoke. Axes Lir never let out of his sight. Axes Aisling often wondered about.

"It's easier for you this way, isn't it? So be it; believe me your wicked fae legend, your nightmare come to life," he growled, the rage in his voice thrumming through Aisling's core.

The mortal queen stood from where she sat, blowing out her fist of fire as the sun peaked its golden eyes over the summit's edge.

"If I'd been in your position"—she forced herself to meet his eyes—"I would've killed you too." And she was cursed with knowing that deep down, she would've enjoyed doing it.

Chapter XXVI

"YOU'LL NEVER KILL A MAN LIKE THAT." RIAN spun on his heel, catching Aisling's wrist. The mortal queen attempted a strike with her left fist. She swung her knuckles towards the fae knight's jaw, but Rian blocked her blow easily.

"Too slow." Rian twisted her whole body, pulling her back towards his chest, captured and rendered prone, her arm shoved behind her back. "And much too loud. I've heard dragons breathe quieter than you."

"Dragons?" Aisling asked, struggling to wiggle out of his grasp.

"Careful, you'll break your arm," Rian softened his hold. Aisling took the opportunity and stomped his foot, loosening herself enough to twist and knee him between the legs. Rian swiftly stepped to the side and Aisling flew. The mortal queen collapsed into a nearby bush bubbling over with plump berries and crimson buds.

"Not so rough, Rian," Galad scolded. "I'd rather not be the one to inform Lir you've wounded his bride."

"She pounced on me," Rian lifted his hands up innocently. "Besides, she needs the practice."

Galad extended a hand to Aisling. Once the mortal queen had floundered out of the bush, she took the knight's offer and stumbled awkwardly to her feet.

"Dragon?" Aisling brushed the berries off her shoulders and the buds from her braided hair.

"You've never heard of a dragon?" Galad asked and Aisling shook her head in response.

"A peist? A wyvern? Any sort of drake?" Rian continued.

"No, what are they?" Aisling sheathed the dagger Galad had lent her after she'd lost Iarbonel's gift. A gift she longed for like a severed limb. Iarbonel would be furious if he ever knew she'd lost it.

"Monstrous, glorious beasts. Some have fur. Most have scales. You'll encounter them in oceans, mountains, forests. Greedy bastards, though. Always hoarding whatever they get their claws on."

"Are they rare? Will I lay eyes on one?" Aisling asked, following Galad back through the forest. Only she, Rian, and Galad travelled through these icy woods now. Lir had ventured on ahead, eager to scout the path ahead, commanding even the stags to stay behind and wait for their return. The Isle of Mirrors was close. Aisling could feel it. Taste it in the air. Hear it like drums, running into the earth and thrumming through her bones.

"Forge be willing, you never will," Rian said, plucking twigs from the mortal queen's curls.

"And why's that?"

"They're primordial, dangerous beasts, Ash," Galad said, her nickname on his lips strange yet ... welcome. Initially, Galad had begun calling her Ash to ridicule the mortal queen after reading the way Dagfin had addressed her in his letter. But now, it felt comfortable coming from him. It was a sweet sound amidst the animosity she'd received from the Aos Sí thus far. Rian, Galad, and Gilrel were her only *friends*, if she could indeed call them that. They were as close as she would come to such a word while amongst the fair folk. And Lir—Aisling wasn't certain what Lir was.

"And? The first ancient, dangerous beast I ever encountered I married."

Both Galad and Rian laughed. A sound that inexplicably warmed the mortal queen's heart, for none had laughed with her since she'd left her mortal world; the sound of her brothers' howls while they chased the feast pig down Castle Neimedh's corridors echoed in her heart.

"I agree with the mortal queen," Rian said, "she might even find herself right at home amongst the dragons."

"Some breathe fire," Galad's eyes shot towards her hands.

"I thought the Sidhe and Unseelie were unable to wield fire," Aisling asked, clumsily doing her best to match their lengthy strides.

"The Sidhe cannot. But the Unseelie don't follow the same rules as we do. They are a subspecies. A variation of the original race that is the Sidhe and so, the Gods created rare but few exceptions for a select few."

Aisling opened her mouth to respond but before she could, Lir made himself visible amongst the trees.

Immediately their eyes met, his emerald pools glittering even from a distance and piercing her, a spear straight to her chest.

Aisling's breath caught, unable to look away. The Fae King's face was just as forlorn as it'd been since their last conversation at the cliff's edge. Not even Galad nor Rian dared provoke their king in such a state. He was the image of a wounded wolf, burdened by the pain of his afflictions. Surely it hadn't been Aisling's words that had affected him so. No, there was something more. The way his expression had twisted at the mention of Ina and Bres ... there was something the Fae King wasn't fully prepared to divulge.

"We're here," Lir said once he was within earshot. "We've reached the Isle of Mirrors."

Aisling couldn't see the *draiocht*, but she could hear and feel it rising from the earth and evaporating into the woodland air. Such magic danced alongside the fog billowing playfully at their knees, tickled the trees, and skulked amongst the shadows. Watching, listening, clouding the world around them in a dreamy haze. As invisible yet forceful as a pungent fragrance, straight from the bottle of an empress.

Lir pulled the thread of starlight from his pocket, spreading it out and reaching for Aisling's wrist. The Fae King wrapped the tether around her joint. One, two knots this time. Their eyes met and Aisling held her breath unwittingly, eyes that mirrored the chartreuse, peppermint, and juniper of the forest around them.

The snowy land they'd trekked through thus far was swiftly melting away. The nearer they approached, the greenwood transformed into a world of eternal spring: mighty oaks and firs, ashes and cedars, bedizened with needles and leaves like verdant jewels. Blooming with pastel buds and ripe fruit.

"Don't leave my side," Lir said, his voice low and quiet enough that only she could hear.

"Lir," Rian interrupted, approaching alongside Galad. "They're here."

The Fae King nodded in response, tearing his gaze from Aisling. Unsheathing his great axes from his back, the sound of metal scraping against one another echoed in the hollows.

Aisling bit her bottom lip, following Lir onward. Galad and Rian walked shortly behind.

It began as a single whisper, a woman's voice slithering through the undergrowth. Then it became a chorus, a symphony of unintelligible sighs, a collective susurration of phantom breath. A sensation that reminded Aisling of her first journey into Annwyn and all she'd experienced while cloaked by Lir's glamour. Now, she wasn't glamoured. There was no magical barrier or bubble to muffle the dryad's spell. It was overwhelming. All consuming. Hauntingly divine. Sinister and seductive. Both a caustic clamor of mismatched ruckus and the supple glide of voices made of rich velvet. All reaching towards her, pulling at their disembodied joints to come closer. To see her, to hear her, to smell her.

Aisling willed her gaze straight. Despite fear's pleading for her to swivel madly on her heels, searching to the right and left, above and below. Instinct told her to swallow hard, to grind her teeth, and keep one foot in front of the other. Lir's stride beside her a steady beat beside the staccato of her own heart.

The trees ahead, at last, bent on their sides till their branches connected at the top. A steeple made of birch, groaning as the bark snapped and pulled beneath the bend. Impressive, fearsome if not for what came next. The skin of the trees peeled forward, as though duplicating themselves, stretching from the body of the birch until another entity stood before it: two females, one from each tree, whose skin gradually shed the layers of the woodland's sheathing like a snake strips its old flesh. And once every morsel of the birch was clawed away by an invisible hand, the strange women stood before them, mossy hair billowing in the sighs of the forest, embellished with berries and twigs. Their wood-like complexion was a canvas for their sharp features: onyx eyes, pale lips, and two pairs of finely tipped ears. Ears far longer than their Aos Sí counterparts.

"At last, *mo Damh Bán.*" The one on the left spoke first, her voice as ethereal as Aisling had anticipated. A sound so delicate, it could very well be an echo in her own mind.

"The wait has been excruciating," the second purred, both inching forward on bare feet. The vines coiled around each of their limbs, crawling like serpents whenever they moved.

"How long has she known?" Lir said, his expression bored. And if it weren't for the grip he held on the tether of starlight, wrapped around his wrist and bundled in his fist, Aisling would've believed him entirely unamused.

"A few weeks. Perhaps more. She saw you with the Fomorians first. The merrow. But before she saw you coming, she smelled you," the dryad said, eyes flicking towards Aisling.

"Take me to her," Lir commanded, stepping forward. Where Aisling believed the dryads would hiss with disapproval for their sovereign's boldness, instead they flinched, pacing back like cornered cats. Their gowns of greenwood scrap, swaying around their lithe forms.

The two dryads nodded their heads in response. And with their long thin limbs, they gestured for the Aos Sí and their mortal queen to follow.

With each of the dryad's steps, flora sprouted from the earth. The chorus of whispers continued but dampened in the slightest. A great, invisible council murmuring to one another as their guests passed. Aisling swallowed, glancing back at both Galad and Rian. Their hands rested on the hilt of their greatswords hooked to their belts.

Up ahead, the dryads guided them towards an audience of weeping willows. These trees swayed to the hums of the dryad's song, but Aisling knew they weren't normal trees. They were dryads themselves. Waiting, watching, leaning closer to behold their guests. Their giant bodies stretching to the heavens and canopies above, like the cross-vaulted ceilings of a cathedral, flowered branches hanging like chandeliers that dusted the floors beneath with sweetest pollen.

Across the fluffy, green field that stretched before them, countless pools glimmered in the afternoon smog. Aisling gaped at their still bodies, reflecting the dancing of the dryad willows. Sheets of finest, thinnest glass whose depths dove into the earth in blue, crystal-clear waters. Separated only by the thin paths of softest moss. The frothy breath of the forest, bridging a trail for the Fae King.

This was the Isle of Mirrors.

Leaning over the brink of a pool, the mortal queen peered down. Deep, bottomless ponds filled to the brim with sparkling waters. A looking glass that faded into endless black below. Somewhere far within them, Aisling could hear the *draiocht* murmuring to itself. Swimming and calling her under. Then it showed her an image. A strange, blurred vision of another place. Perhaps another time. A mountain valley filled to the brim with winged Sidhe.

Aisling craned her neck. She needed to see more. To understand. But it was a mistake. The mortal queen's boot slipped and she flew towards the pool, the waters rushing towards her face. Aisling wrenched her eyes shut, waiting for impact. Instead, two hands reached around her waist and pulled her up. Aisling spun, colliding against Lir's chest; his arms wrapped firmly around her.

"Watch your step," he said with the ghost of a grin, pulling her back onto her feet. Aisling tilted her head up to face him, shivering at the sensation of his arms around her.

"And don't look too closely," Rian added.

The dryads escorting them giggled beneath their breath.

"What's down there?" Aisling asked, carefully placing her boots from here on out.

"Some are nothing more than mirrors, glaring back at what glares in. Others are passages," Lir said, spinning his axes in his hands.

"Passages? Like doorways?"

"Aye, thresholds to another place. Sometimes another time."

"And what would've happened had I fallen in?" Aisling asked, following closely behind the Fae King and tiptoeing along the narrow paths of grass interspersed between the pools.

"Depending on the pool, you could've been soaked for the

rest of the evening. Or, you could've been lost to both time and space."

Aisling's violet eyes snapped towards the Fae King. But before she could reply, the rows of willows stirred around them. It didn't take long before the dryads, just as the two guiding them forward had done moments ago, peeled from the bark of their trees, leapt down from the canopies, crawled down the trunks like spiders, and perched atop the highest branches, all ogling the Fae King, his bride and his two knights approaching. There were hundreds of them. Creatures part flora and seemingly part fair folk. As though the two were once blended in some primordial soup and spat out with a vengeance. But most impressive of all was what awaited them.

A gargantuan ash stood at the end of the field of mirrors, a tree so large that a kingdom of Aos Sí couldn't wrap its arms around its grooved body. One whose branches exploded from the trunk in a great web of wooden limbs, hungry to expand as far as its branches would allow. Tangling amidst the willows surrounding it. And beneath it, unravelling like colossal snakes, its roots burst out before diving deep into the earth below them.

A groaning that nearly stripped Aisling's ears, erupted. The mortal queen pressed her palms against the sides of her head, wincing at the sheer volume of the noise, a roar as great as any fanged beast's. The skin of the tree then, as if dissolved into a liquid form, began to move. Creaking and growling, from the ash a giant female took form, pulling against the bark to release herself like the dryads before her. Hair of flowering vines and thorny branches braided down her shoulders, sweeping the pools and stirring their depths. A woman as colossal as the tree itself, she knelt on her knees, blinking open eyes of glorious grey. For she bore no pupils nor an iris. Bulbs of smoke, glaring down at her guests with wicked delight.

Aisling sucked in a breath and trapped it in her chest.

"Hush now," the giant cooed to the surrounding dryads,

who whispered furiously to one another. "We're in the presence of a king."

A king. Not 'our' king, Aisling noticed. The beast's voice boomed, a song of silk and velvet rattling through Aisling's core to the soles of her boots.

She bent her head and knelt before the Fae Lord.

"Danu," he said in greeting. "I'm assuming you know why we've come." Lir tilted his head in return, his expression unreadable.

The Empress grinned, her dark skin stretching. Vines of leafy hair, falling around her rounded features and cloaking her bare breasts as she cocked her head to the side.

"I do, *mo Damh Bán*. I know what each of your desires are. Those that were, those that are, and those that will be."

"Then you know I've come seeking what you've *seen*: the end of the war between the mortals and the Sidhe."

The empress laughed then, feirdhris, aiteann, and dris berries blooming across her arms, her chest, her hands, her hair, with every gleeful sound.

"I've seen the end of your petty feud. I've seen the end of everything. I've seen the beginning as well. But what's more interesting is everything in between. For that isn't the only thought that occupies your mind, is it *mo Damh Bán*?"

Lir considered for a moment, toying with the thread of starlight in his fist. But there was no fear in his posture. He was rather angry. Resolved to do what he must to get what he wanted.

Danu leaned closer, eyes wandering from Rian to Galad before landing on Aisling herself, standing on Lir's left-hand side. The hair on Aisling's arms stood to attention, her steely eyes like those of a spider studying her insect locked in the web.

"One of which being this beastly thing beside you," Danu purred, "don't be rude, Lir. Introduce us."

Lir hesitated, his body tightening as he considered. "This

is Aisling, Queen of the Greenwood and of Annwyn."

Aisling lowered her eyes out of respect.

"I dream of you often, little beast," Danu said. "And so does he." The Empress gestured towards Lir, watching her closely. A wolf hungry to pounce at a moment's notice.

Danu turned towards the Fae King, releasing the mortal queen from her regard.

"So, your mother's prophecy at last came to be. Did you know that? When you agreed to the union did you foresee your mother's prophecy fulfilling itself? Or did you intend to behead the mortal princess?"

Lir's eyes flashed like lightning. Sage storms thrashing behind his thick lashes.

Aisling held her breath. For Danu had asked the same question that'd plagued the mortal queen's mind since Peitho's revelation during their outing. One she herself desperately craved an answer to, an answer void of deceptions, spells, glamours, or lies.

"I knew," Lir said, before tightening his fists at his sides. Aisling whipped her head in Lir's direction, studying his tormented expression. "I knew of my mother's prophecy before the union."

"What prophecy?" Aisling blurted, the words spilling out of her mouth before she had an opportunity to stop them.

"Ash," Galad warned from behind, but Aisling shrugged him off. His words but a distant chime beyond the buzzing in her ears.

"He hasn't told you?" Danu asked, grinning from ear to ear. "Shame, Lir. Must I always be the one to tell the story? I suppose I'm best at it."

Aisling's head swiveled between the Empress and the Fae King. Her temples throbbing, her mouth going dry till her tongue was nothing but ash between her teeth.

"Before his mother and the people of Iod were cursed, she gave one last prophecy, for she was blessed with a *sight* like my own, a warning to her only son, the heir of the Greenwood. A promise that he'd be bound to not one but two *caeras*. And the second would be a love unmatched, a reckless, ruinous love capable of destroying kingdoms and plaguing the earth. A harbinger of great upheaval and certain death."

Aisling took a step back, wobbling on her weak knees. She couldn't look at Lir. Not now. One glance in his direction and she didn't know what would become of her. But she could feel the heat of his gaze on her. Cutting into her skin.

"Aisling," he said, his voice the thunder of a woodland storm.

His mother was cursed alongside her people. She gave one last prophecy to her only son.

Cathan's song. His tale the night after their union.

"Ina was punished by the Gods; both she and the entirety of her mountain kingdom cursed for all eternity. A kingdom doomed to a damned legacy. But before that, it's said she had one last vision. A prophecy she shared with her only son."

Aisling's tongue caught in her throat.

"Your mother was Ina, the Queen of the Mountains. Of Iod. One of the twelve original sovereigns," Aisling's chest rose and fell, reaching for breath but the air was thin. "Your father was Bres. The King of the Greenwood. You're the heir of two original sovereigns." Aisling lifted her eyes to Lir's. He watched her. Still as the pine on a windless day. Eyes harrowed. Rimmed with a silent sort of torture. A vein corded through his neck where his chest rose and fell to the rhythm of Aisling's own.

"Aye, he is," Danu answered for the Fae Lord. "The most powerful Sidhe sovereign known to this realm."

Lir's wings. He was a child of both the mountains and the forest. Why Castle Annwyn was carved into the mountain.

"What was the curse?" Aisling demanded, turning her gaze towards the Empress. Heat built in Aisling's palms as the *draiocht* began to feed off the mortal queen's anger. Aisling hushed it down, grinding her teeth to control it as best she could. "What happened to Ina and Iod?"

Danu leaned back, delighted.

"The Gods stripped her of her powers, of her wings, of her ability to summon the *draiocht*. They made her weak. Cursed her and all those belonging to Iod this way. And from that day onward, Ina and her people were destined to live less than a measly century, their long Sidhe lifespans stolen from their lungs."

"They were—" Aisling choked on the words.

"They were made mortal. Iod were the first humans and the ancestors of your kind."

Aisling shook her head, violet eyes as wide as violet moons.

"But you aren't quite like your kind, are you?" Danu continued, her silver eyes glistening with amusement. "You're something else now."

"What do you know?" Lir snarled, his voice laced with something that stripped Aisling's heart bare.

"Like your mother, she's the first of a new kind."

"What kind?" Lir demanded, snapping like a wolf.

Danu closed her mouth, smiling mischievously, leaning forward to dip her lichen-covered finger into the nearest pool.

"See for yourself," Danu purred, the still pond rippling from her touch. A finger that bloomed with toadstools and primrose.

Aisling faced the waters, stepping just near enough to see properly. Lir, Galad, and Rian followed, one eye on the pools and another on the Empress herself. Lir gripping the thread of starlight till Aisling believed it might turn to dust in his hand.

At first, the mortal queen only saw her reflection. The fair-faced mortal she'd known her whole life. Two amethyst eyes glaring back behind lashes as obsidian as the thick curls braided over her shoulder. But no longer was she the Northern mortal princess she'd met through the vanity in her Tilrish bed chambers. She was someone else now. Unrecognizable.

Thinner. Rougher. A stranger the mortal queen feared. More than she'd feared anything. For behind those purple eyes was something hungry.

Danu stirred the pool and Aisling's reflection vanished. The pond darkened until a single, violet flame burned within. Aisling craned her neck and squinted her eyes, doing her best to get a better look. But the image grew clearer and clearer until Aisling recognized that same stranger that glared back at her moments before, a woman dressed in a gown of glittering lilac pooling around her ankles. Her delicate features were lit by the fire brewing in her hands. The fire grew brighter and brighter. Larger and larger until it burst forth from her palms and spread down a mountain valley. Into a fleet of thousands of soldiers below.

The flames devoured every armored warrior like a bestial serpent. Pillaging the army until the sky was black and ash rained from the heavens.

Aisling's heart seized. The *draiocht* within her was aroused by the power it beheld.

"They will call you mage. Witch. Sorceress," Danu said. "Some will follow you. Many will hunt you. All will fear you."

Aisling shook her head, eyes burning until they leaked down her cheeks.

"And there will be others?" Aisling asked, her voice more level than she felt.

"Yes," Danu said. "There will be others like you. A rare few who will summon the *draiocht* as easily if not more powerfully than the Sidhe themselves."

"How is this possible?" Aisling continued, glaring at her hands held before her.

"You've awakened something, little beast," Danu said, narrowing her eyes towards the pool each of them surrounded. "Your very existence is an ill omen for the age to come." Aisling bit her tongue, sorting through the thoughts that swarmed her mind like an angry hive.

"The war, Danu. Who are those soldiers?" Lir asked, gesturing towards the bone and soot remains of hundreds, thousands, of warriors lying dead in the valley.

"I cannot tell. My visions are glimpses. Not lists of details or facts. This is all I can see."

"Then you don't know who will win the war?" Lir demanded, his expression growing more feral by the moment.

"The end will change little, Lir."

"With every given year, the Sidhe are thinning. The mortal sovereigns outnumbering our kind, exploiting our weaknesses with iron and fire, burning our land till the air echoes with the screams of the forest. A forest that the *Unseelie*, the dryads, call home. The end changes everything, gives us an opportunity to alter that which is not yet written," Lir growled, the muscles in his shoulders tensing. The surrounding dryads shrinking back from where they stood.

"Few if any have ever been capable of changing the course of my visions," Danu said, her voice deepening, "the Sidhe will continue to dwindle but they'll not grow extinct."

"And the mortals? What of them?"

"They will overtake this realm. With iron and fire, they'll carve the earth and return both Seelie and Unseelie into the realm of the Other."

Danu stirred the pool once more until another image took form. Fields and fields of forests were chopped down, burned, flattened, and trampled over by stone homes, thatched roofs, billowing chimneys, and corridors spilling over with mortal townsfolk. Villages, cities, empires built on the ashes of the kingdom before it. The Kingdom of Greenwood, the Kingdom of Mountains, the southern, western, eastern Sidhe territories. Images of men with iron weapons that explode with metal projectiles, men whose armies turn against one another and paint the deadened earth with their own blood.

"Mankind will dub us fairies, demons, spirits, Gods, monsters. Mankind will stifle us until we're nothing but a child's tale shared around the hearth."

"How long?" Lir bared his teeth, fangs flashing. "How long do we have?"

"I cannot tell. It could be another three millennia. A hundred years. A decade. It's impossible to tell—"

"How long?!" Lir yelled, his face twisting with fury.

"The Sidhe will lose this war, *mo Damh Bán*," Danu snarled in return, thorns growing from her flesh and serrating the curves of her once supple form. "If there is anything you can do to prevent it, the answers do not lie here."

Lir unsheathed his great axes, the sound of steel scraping against the scabbard echoing throughout the hollow. The dryads hissed, the earth beneath sprouting with weeds.

Galad stepped forward, placing a hand on the Fae King's shoulder.

"Instead of looking towards the morrow, look at today. You're powerless then but powerful now. Return to Annwyn. The Fire Hand is but a step in the right direction."

Lir growled, his fangs cutting his bottom lip.

"What must I do? Kill him? Serve his head on a pike? Will that end the war? Prevent what you've seen?" Lir said, his fists glowing with pale green light. The forest swung from side to side as though preparing for an oncoming storm. The shadows deepened and the earth grumbled as though irate itself. Aisling inhaled sharply, overcome with the maddened shrieks of the Northern feywilds building around them. The woodland responding to its Fae Lord.

The dryads cowered behind their trees, some sinking back into the branches of the willow.

"Return to Annwyn," Danu insisted, shutting her eyes and sinking back into her tree form.

"I command you to help me!" Lir shouted, his knuckles growing white around the hilt of his blades. But it was too late. No longer did the woman stand before them. Only the quiet ash whose roots snaked beneath it, lashing out like vipers and shoving the Fae King and his knights back. They were thrown into the pool. Aisling dragged along after them, pulled into the abyss by a tether of starlight.

Chapter XXVII

AISLING CLAWED UPWARD. SHE WASN'T CERTAIN how long she'd been submerged, swimming through darkness until she'd spotted the rays of light, penetrating the water like trails of a reed. Had it not been for her ability to breathe through the *draiocht*, Aisling would've drowned. Lost in some dark cavern where there was no north nor south. No west, nor east. Only black and the oily fingers of the pool, stroking her to sleep.

The mortal queen broke through the surface, gasping for air. The world spun or rather, the cavern in which she stood spun. No longer was she in the Isle of Mirrors amidst the dryads. No. She stood in a chamber of stone, a great corridor that stretched endlessly forward into an abyss. The only light, a hole in the ceiling further down the hall, glowing with the fresh rays of early afternoon. The stench of mold and mildew vegetating in the air. It was then Aisling understood she was underground.

Roots crawled along the stone walls, rising from the knee-deep water flooding the corridor, water she'd somehow emerged from, and surrounding the mortal queen from all sides.

Aisling watched them slither along the rocks. The way they

hugged the cool edge of every crease. Rubbing their bellies against the dampness of the passage. But beyond the roots, the vines, the moss sucking every stone, were twinkling gems. Colorful if it weren't for the filth of the subterranean tunnel. Every gem methodically hammered into the walls till it formed a mural.

Aisling pushed through the murky waters. Her leathers and tunic weighed heavy on her shoulders, sticking to her abdomen and back.

And as she tore at the vines, cautious as they snapped and hissed at her carelessness, she could feel the *draiocht* waking in this tunnel. Great magic swelling through the vast chamber, a perpetually crashing wave. Magic that brought these ancient murals to life. How long had they existed down here? Wherever *here* was, Aisling shook her head. Masterpieces of shattered, gleaming shards chronicling the conception of the world according to the fair folk.

The mortal queen peeled away the hair stuck to her face.

The narrative began with two faceless figures in the dark. All that existed were these two males radiating with celestial, white light. But amidst such blackness burned an ember. A red spark, flickering as Aisling traced the rubies with her fingertips. The mural brightened, spun into motion.

The two figures approached the ember, stoking it to life with their breath until it blazed greater and greater, hundreds of rubies hammered into the stone to reflect such a marvel. A marvel that came to be known as the Great Forge of Creation. Nothing else existed. Only the two figures and the Forge, churning its fires until the rubies transformed into blue mountains, seas, valleys, forests, islands, icy plains on the left. And on the right, the rubies became something else Aisling didn't recognize: a landscape she could scarcely behold, thanks to the roots tightly clasped over the mural at this end of the corridor. But what Aisling did see was enough. These were the two planes. That of the Other on the right and that of the world Aisling inhabited on the left, the mortal world Nemed had called it. Both Forged in the beginning of all things.

Aisling walked further down the wall, tearing at the stubborn lianas when she found a familiar image. Aisling stepped back, inhaling sharply.

It was a crowned male figure standing amongst eleven other sovereigns, both male and female. Each carrying a gift in their hands. And the first male, the one that'd caught Aisling's attention, wore a crown of gilded antlers. Carried Lir's twin axes in his hands. The blade she'd chosen at their union.

This was Bres. Lir's father. And further down, stood Ina, a female glittering in gold. But she was the only one of the monarchs who didn't boast a weapon. Her head was crowned by the image of a three-eyed owl, glaring back at Aisling and considering her in return. Ina's gift of *sight*.

Aisling's eyes devoured the mural, running down the walls of the corridor and into the darkness.

The fae sovereigns took ownership of the seas: flecks of kyanite embroidered with opals, multiplying and swirling around their merrow monarch; the great planes: sheets of cornelian splintering like rays of sun; the mountains: jagged mounds of amethyst piercing skies of moonstone; and so many more. The world took shape as the original two males stirred the Forge, a ruby growing larger with every churn. But it was the golden Ina rushing towards the city of emeralds that stole Aisling's attention, Bres impaled by another fae queen, one Aisling didn't recognize, and Ina weeping tears of kyanite as his gemstone dulled.

Enraged, the Forge overflowed, rubies tunnelling through Iod's amethysts until every gold-flecked subject of Ina was damned, writhing as their lights dulled as well. No longer as strong, as powerful, forced to live opposed to the world for which they were cast. No longer immortal.

Aisling stepped away from the mural.

"*I was among those who had voted against the union, considering it was practically an execution bound to exacerbate mortal and fae tensions. But alas, here we are. The mortal princess lives.*" Even Filverel hadn't known the truth. A secret Lir hoarded until Danu exposed it against his will. And now, the mortal queen was faced with the reality of her kind's heritage.

"*Man was born of nothing, but nevertheless born first.*"

Nemed was wrong. Mankind, the mortal queen's own blood, had been Ina's curse for her ill-fated love. Aisling had only lived in Annwyn for a short time. How many more lies, unspoken truths, and deceptions would she unravel in a lifetime?

"*They will try to deceive you. They will spin lies as easily as they spin their thread.*"

The mortal queen's mind was a tangle of disbelief. The world as she knew it was changing. No, it had always been this way. Only now her memory was corrupted by a newfound cynicism for the 'truths' she'd believed blindly. The doctrine she'd never questioned.

"*Return to Annwyn. The Fire Hand is but a step in the right direction.*"

Nemed wanted peace. Wanted the well-being of his kind. Wanted the mortals to thrive. He wouldn't jeopardize that after all Aisling's union had done to solidify the treaty. But even as Aisling rationalized her father's lies, the words did little to assuage the growing anxiety that'd taken root long before this day.

In the cold, her shoulders trembled. She held herself closer, tugging her drenched arms against her body. The tether of starlight hung from her wrist, frayed where she'd been torn apart from Rian, Galad, and Lir. The Fae King's expression as the thread snapped between them, flashing across her memory.

Aisling needed out of this cavern. However, the only

indication of the outside world was a circle of light located in the tunnel's ceiling.

Vines hung from the natural skylight. Surely one of them would be sturdy enough for Aisling to climb towards the top *if* she bore the strength to navigate so high, carrying the weight of her entire build.

Aisling wrapped her hands around one of the thicker roots, tugging to ensure it wouldn't spring loose the moment she entrusted it with her weight. It held. So, Aisling began climbing, pulling herself up with all her might.

Despite how thin she'd become over the last several months, she struggled to lift herself. Her arms burning, her hands, legs, and boots shaking and slipping thanks to the surrounding waters. Aisling managed to raise herself perhaps five feet before slamming back into the caverns. Hands ripped raw till her blood muddied the waters. And if it weren't for the vibrating of the tunnel, she might've tried again.

The dirt, moss, and worms flew from the cavern's ceilings, showering Aisling. The mortal queen cursed, her head whipping towards the darkness further down the passage.

Following the vibration was a growl. A deep, resonant sound that rattled Aisling's very core. Filling her ears till she thought they may pop. The growl persisted, growing louder. Closer. The snarl of some colossal beast followed by its wicked purrs and sighs.

Aisling's eyes widened, desperately peering into the gaping maw of black, more formidable by the minute. It was approaching. Dragging its body through the tunnels and towards Aisling.

The mortal queen launched herself at the hanging vine once more, straining to lift herself. The liana snapped at the top of the opening, sending the mortal queen flying back into the cavern. Aisling's heart pounded.

"*You may call me friend,*" the beast growled.

But Aisling ignored it, clenching her fists to stop their

shaking. She boasted no muscle nor brawn nor agility. But she did have magic. *Draiocht* she'd been practicing with Lir since that morning in the springs. So, Aisling wrenched her eyes shut, biting her tongue till she tasted the iron of her blood on the roof of her mouth.

Come, she called out into her void, the abyss where the *draiocht* waited patiently for its name to be summoned. Silence prevailed as it always did after Aisling hadn't called upon her creature in some time. But eventually, she heard its bones clicking. Waking. Poking its head from her internal dark and leaping forward.

It gathered in her lungs, her windpipes, her hands burning with a magical charge. Violet fires burst from her palms, crawling up her arms, her shoulders. A torch herself, the vines cowered from her, slithering up their walls and bunching in the creases. Away from the heat she exuded, heat that melted the dirt from the ceilings into mud.

And thanks to the light she now cast, a purple haze lengthened her line of sight amidst the darkness, the outline of a scaly aberration was taking form. Yellowed eyes narrowing into slits as it recoiled, cringing at the sight of her flames, baring its slender, wetted fangs.

More, the *draiocht* purred, coaxing Aisling. So, Aisling listened against her better judgment for she too hungered for more.

The mortal queen lit like a lilac star in the night. It was euphoric using magic like this. Letting that power grow, move through her veins, her muscles, her bones. Watching the faceless Unseelie shrink from her and return to the abyss from whence it came.

A smile stretched across Aisling's face as she indulged in the *draiocht* as she'd never allowed herself before. Magic that she loathed to think she'd been sheltered from all her life. For the way it made her feel was rapturous. So blissful Aisling hardly cared if it was good or evil. All she craved was feeling more. Having more.

From the top of the chamber, a crash shook the walls of the cylinder. Aisling whipped her head in its direction. Two figures eclipsed the daylight before bolting towards the bottom of the cavern with Otherworldly speed. One tall and slender. The other crouched on the first's shoulder, an armored ball of fur. They descended in a blur of color, splashing into the pool. But even such a splash, waters rippling and smacking the walls angrily, couldn't extinguish Aisling's growing flames.

"By the Forge." The mortal queen heard a familiar voice whisper over the crackling of her flames. Feminine, sweet, as crisp as the autumn air.

"Aisling," the other figure spoke, cautiously, stepping nearer to the mortal queen. "We're here to help you."

The backs of Aisling's eyes burned, and she hadn't realized how quickly her heart had been beating, how blurry her vision had become until it cleared enough for her to witness the two standing before her.

Gilrel watched Aisling, amazed. Perhaps horrified, her muzzle ajar so her fangs glinted in the mortal queen's light. She still wore her silver-plating. Her fur glossed by the light of the fire. And, from where she perched, stood Peitho. The fae princess was dressed in rich, finely cut armor. Sparkling chainmail and a crest Aisling didn't recognize. The seal of Niltaor, Aisling surmised. Her hair no longer bore its cornelian stones, flower buds, or sunset-hued beetles. No, it was tied in complex braids, falling down her back and ending at her waist. Her beautiful face twisted with alarm.

"Aisling," Gilrel spoke again, her eyes shifting with uncertainty. With fear, Aisling realized. "Exhale the *draiocht*," she said, holding out her paw.

Aisling glared at the lady's maid then her paw. Scars, calluses, burns peeking from where her leather sleeve ended at her wrist.

"Exhale the *draiocht*, Aisling," Gilrel said, her voice uneven, something more desperate gripping her throat.

"Gilrel," Peitho warned, reaching out to catch the handmaid as she scampered down the princess' arm.

"Please," Gilrel ignored Peitho.

Aisling looked at her own mortal palms then, wrapped in fire. Why was it so difficult to release the *draiocht*? It didn't want to let go either. It wished for Aisling to grow hotter, burn brighter. And Aisling desired nothing more in that moment than to let it have its way. Wanted to believe in the *draiocht's* promise. But there was no need anymore. The beast had slithered back into its inky den. She could let go.

"The Aos Sí say their magic comes from the Gods. There are no Gods. Whatever abilities they wield are aberrations. Perversities of nature. As they are themselves."

Something warm slithered out of Aisling's nose and into her mouth. Blood. Aisling wasn't breathing. Had been holding in the magic, pushing herself without realizing. She was supposed to breathe through it. Let it run through her. So why was it caught, begging for more?

At last, Aisling exhaled. The flames extinguished, nothing but tendrils of smoke feathering off Aisling and the stench of burnt Spidersilk permeating the air. Her tunic was nothing more than the charred scraps of what it once was, only her leathers remaining.

Both Gilrel and Peitho exhaled themselves, sharing a breath of relief as the mortal queen opened and closed her eyes drowsily. So, Aisling took Gilrel's outstretched paw, collapsing onto her knees. Bones dissolved to jelly. As though she herself was drained of blood and left ... lifeless. Such a contrast to the might she felt only moments ago.

Gilrel unbuckled a flask from her hip and lifted it to the mortal queen's lips with Peitho's help. Aisling choked on the sickly syrup before guzzling the entirety of the contents down till no drop remained.

"Where am I?" Aisling groaned, doing her best to will away the throbbing of her head.

"The aqueducts," Peitho said, screwing the lid back onto the flask. "They run beneath Annwyn."

"I was in the Isle of Mirrors before Danu—"

Peitho nodded her head. "She must have sent you here."

"And the others?" Aisling asked through uneven breath. "Galad? Rian? Lir?"

"The pools spat them out at the gorge"—Gilrel hesitated, searching Aisling's violet eyes—"two months ago."

Aisling shook her head, hands growing numb.

"The whole of Annwyn has been searching for you. There hasn't been a leaf or stone left unturned."

"I don't understand."

"Danu must've accidentally sent you forward in time. Sent you here."

Aisling stood on quivering knees.

"Or, you've been floating around down here in the aqueducts since the others returned."

Aisling took one look around at the murky waters, the fungus and mold growing between the cracks in the stones.

Peitho scoffed, inspecting the aqueducts herself. "It's unlikely. Racat would've eaten her by now."

"Racat?" Aisling repeated, "that bestial serpent?"

"You've seen it?"

Aisling nodded her head, glancing over Gilrel's shoulder to the darkness winding down the tunnels where Racat had loomed mere moments ago.

"He appeared shortly after I awoke. That's why I summoned the *draiocht*," Aisling said, glaring at her hands now pruning from such long exposure to the water.

Both Gilrel and Peitho hesitated before meeting Aisling's eyes once more. A glint lurked behind each of their expressions. One Aisling hadn't recognized before.

"He must've heard or sensed you. He's travelled through

the aqueducts, the underground waterways, the gorge, the caves since anyone can remember. Even the oldest amongst us claim he lived before them."

Aisling shivered, batting away the silhouette of his massive form.

"How did you know? To find me here?" Aisling asked, changing the subject as quickly as she was able lest she burst into flames again.

"We didn't. Not at first," Peitho and Gilrel exchanged another glance, inaudibly weighing a decision between them.

"What is it you're not telling me?" Aisling asked.

"You've been presumed dead for weeks now," Peitho spat bluntly.

Aisling flinched, the wind sucked from her lungs. The implications of such a presumption, catching in her throat.

Gilrel scolded Peitho in Rún before continuing.

"When Lir, Galad, and Rian emerged from the gorge, we thought perhaps you would too but when you didn't ..." Gilrel sucked in a breath. "Lir went mad. He searched the bottom of the gorge by sun and by moon, ordered every citizen and subject in his kingdom to do the same—every fox, bear, and badger with its nose on the ground—until you were found dead or alive. And when he'd memorized the bed of the gorge, he scoured the forests, every body of water within his territory. Even the aqueducts were searched, but if Danu sent you forward in time you couldn't have been found until now."

"Obviously," Peitho added, annoyance tightening her voice.

"Where is he?" Aisling blurted, eyes darting towards the light emerging from the hole in the ceiling as though the Fae King would be standing there, waiting for her.

"He's travelling towards neutral ground as we speak," Peitho said and again Gilrel scowled at the princess. "To attend my union," Peitho continued, her feline eyes sharpening with every word. Aisling's own eyes went wide. Of course. The union. Aisling had almost forgotten.

"By sunset this evening, Lir will inform the Fire Hand that his daughter was drowned by the Empress of the Dryads."

Aisling winced at the words. He couldn't. It would destroy, ruin, everything. Everything Aisling had sacrificed for.

"Filverel forced Lir to leave Annwyn for the sake of the Sidhe. He fought Filverel for weeks, for Lir believed you still alive, lost somewhere in between," Gilrel explained.

"With a new political union between our kind, there would be no better occasion to break the news to your father that you'd died. That and a council was already needed between our kind to discuss a certain princeling's correspondence concerning the Unseelie," Peitho smirked, eyes wandering towards the murals on the wall.

Gilrel searched Aisling's expression. "Lir only agreed to leave Annwyn if a party remained behind to continue the search for you until he returned. Peitho is still here—"

"Lest I lose what shred of sanity I still harbor. I was amongst those who believed your frail mortal bones disintegrated at the bottom of the gorge. Indeed, hunting a ghost is a fine distraction for tomorrow's dread."

Tomorrow? A single day was all that stood between Peitho and Dagfin's union.

"Myself and a handful of others planned to ride tonight and join Lir by morning," Peitho said, running her delicate fingers across the mural's stones.

"No," Aisling interrupted, her voice sharp. "We leave now."

Chapter XXVIII

SKALLA, THE AOS SÍ HAD WHISPERED AS GILREL and Peitho pulled Aisling from the well and out of the aqueducts.

Skalla, they'd chanted, the roar of their collective voices no different in sound than the susurration of the rustling forest craning their leafy heads to behold the spectacle.

The world had spun around Aisling; Annwyn had spun as her head swiveled, soaking in the hundreds of fair folk and their bipedal beasts surrounding her as she emerged. The hatred in their uptilted eyes only rivalled by their newfound fear, forcing mothers and fathers to pull their curious, rare children back into their homes, their giant, wooded hollows whose oaks and ashes and pines whipped nervously in the wind.

Skalla, the trees cursed.

"It means thief," Gilrel had told her as she bathed the mortal queen. As the magpies, as quick as angry bees, laced her black opal gown—cloaked in spider webs inlaid with petrified rain by the pixies—brushed her tangled ringlets, and painted her face with coal around her eyes and cherries on her lips. Lips that drank and ate as insatiably as the Aos Sí themselves.

"Danu's prophecy spread through the surrounding Unseelie like dandelion seeds, till even the Sidhe knew of her visions."

Aisling, Galad, Rian, and Gilrel tore through Annwyn's flagstone streets, into the surrounding woodland, and towards neutral ground with Peitho's bridal carriage following swiftly behind. Raced without reverence to the gathering fae spectators, leaning from their cottage doors, their canopies, their wind chimes, their shops, and chores to behold the raven-haired queen fleeing on an ivory stag. The afternoon sighs tearing at her curls, billowing behind her like ribbons of ink.

Did the others—Galad, Rian, Gilrel, Peitho, and the bears pulling her carriage—feel the energy coursing through the overcast sky, through the sweeping winds, the twisting trees, the beasts they mounted? Is that why Galad's knuckles grew white the tighter he gripped his reins? Why Rian fiddled with a charm on his necklace? Why Gilrel said not a word to Aisling as they rode as quick as the stags would carry them?

Aisling heard the drums before the forest thinned. The pounding of the fae instruments beat to the rhythm of the thunderous groans resounding overhead. The flashing of the lightning as it webbed throughout the sky.

Aisling held her breath. The cloak of the woodland was parting as she and the Aos Sí alongside her emerged from the wilderness and into the great verdant valleys. Fields shadowed by the steep cliffs of the northernmost mountains. And at their base, rested a circle of firelit torches, tents, and hordes of speck-like figures that grew as Aisling approached. Just as it had been the night of her union. Except then, Aisling had witnessed the world through a scarlet veil.

They were close. Her kind, they were moments away. Not a dream like she often felt they now were. The mortal queen's stomach sprung into her throat, pushing until she was unable to swallow. With every beat of the fae drum mirroring the staccato of her pulse.

Even from a distance Aisling could make out who was who; like a chessboard, the mortals wore their dimly hued tartans, the stench of iron carried on the Northern winds, and on the opposing side stood the Aos Sí mounted on their ivory stags. Mortal banners violently folding with crests and colors: the crimson flags of Tilren, the royal blue of Roktling, the bronze of Kinbreggan, and the ivory of Aithirn.

Her clann. Lir, they were all there. Beneath the shadow of the same stone giant.

"The Sidhe, Aisling," Gilrel had said as she'd followed the mortal queen down a spiral staircase back in Castle Annwyn. "The Sidhe believe you rose from the dead."

And as they drove their mounts into the sleeping field, the drums stopped.

Chapter XXIX

PETRIFIED, CLODAGH GAPED AT HER DAUGHTER, the harsh lines of her face loosening as her jaw went slack. A shock many of the surrounding mortals mirrored. A collective curse hung in the air between them all. Shared. Annind, Fergus, the King of Roktling who'd known her since she was a bairn, the Lady of Aithirn who'd gifted Aisling her first gelding on her 10th year.

"Sister?" Iarbonel, her second oldest brother, spoke first, against his own volition, Aisling could tell, for he himself appeared stunned the words had left his lips. But the cadence of his voice, his mortal accent, and the wave of familiarity its sound inevitably conjured weakened Aisling. Aisling did her best to rival the scowls of the other half of the mortals. Expressions, faces, features so different than the fair folk she'd grown accustomed to. The ones whose shock was only equaled by their glares of pure disdain. Of betrayal. Those belonging to Starn, Friseal who'd been her private tutor as well as her father's hand, and the King of Kinbreggan to name a few.

The mortal queen had anticipated experiencing relief, joy, excitement at being reunited with her own kind. But now only anger simmered in her belly. For how dare they narrow their eyes at Aisling as though she'd betrayed them? She who sacrificed herself, had sacrificed everything on their behalf? For the sake of their peace?

But there were others whose expressions Aisling found unreadable. Among them were her father and Dagfin.

Aisling's heart caught at the sight of her old friend. She hadn't expected to see him this soon. To witness him standing beside her clann, before the northern mortals, at his father's side, the shimmer of his stormy eyes incalculably alarming. Capturing her soul and pulling her beneath the Roktan seas. But what he thought, how he felt at the sight of her, he kept locked away deep inside the crypt of himself. A crypt that growing up, Aisling had often searched for the key to.

Aisling gripped Saoirse's reins. The stag prancing atop the invisible line Lir and Nemed had drawn between their kingdoms. The fair folk on one side and her clansmen on the other.

And as soon as Aisling's stag arrived beside Lir's, the Fae King tossed off his helmet and leapt lithely from his mount to approach her own. He offered Aisling a hand, a hand she accepted without thought as he lowered her to the earth, clasping her waist as he did so, his touch protective, desperate. The will to hold more than her mere hand, harrowing his red-rimmed eyes. Eyes riddled with the signs of sleepless nights and rumored mania.

She'd been wrong—accused him of planning her execution when he'd known all along. Known that which Aisling was ignorant to. The beat of Lir's heart knotted around her own as he held her hand possessively. The curve of his mouth flecked with tortured longing.

"Aisling," Nemed piped.

Aisling startled at the sound of his voice. How it strained, struggled to maintain its composure. Startled at the glazing of his eyes devouring the sight of her. The Fire Hand smiled, the scar across his face stretching. And it appeared *genuine*.

The others gaped at Aisling and the Fae King, devouring

the sight of them side by side. Dagfin's own expression at last cracking and revealing the fury of the Ashild beneath. The horror.

Aisling resisted the urge to squirm. Even the slightest of movements would reveal everything she felt towards her clann. A tuath who'd always been able to see through her, seemingly capable of reading her mind at will.

"Aisling, I—I can't express how wonderful it is to see you," her father continued, soaking in the sight of her alive and well after months, nearly a year, in a world of terrors and demons. Those he'd led her to believe were golems crouching in caves, sucking on the bones of children. "Come, come. Let me get a good look at you."

Aisling wasn't certain how to act, behave, feel, or think. Against her own volition, Aisling looked to Lir. But his tormented expression had shadowed, forewarning his bride of the monster she called her father. His twin axes winked back at her with a promise of violence.

So, Aisling inhaled, swallowing the bile gathering in her throat, and nodded towards the Fae King. And as soon as Aisling's hand slipped from Lir's own, she sensed him tense as a single step towards her clann became many and her father awkwardly rushed towards her, lumbering on his prosthetic legs. He wrapped his daughter in his arms and squeezed.

Aisling froze. The smell of him—of Tilrish spices, of fires crackling in the hearth, of the handmade soap Aisling's chambermaid botched the recipe for. Of home.

Tears pricked the backs of Aisling's eyes as she stood there. Motionless. Unable to move. Paralyzed by this distant dream rapidly manifesting around her. A reunion she never believed she'd survive long enough to experience. The hope of a day such as this was one of her only motivators during the first several weeks amongst the Aos Sí. And now that she was here, now that she was experiencing it … none of it was how she'd imagined, especially herself.

Nemed released her, beaming with all the warmth of home.

"You're in good health," he said, a question or a statement Aisling was unsure for the softness in his voice took her off guard. Perhaps he hadn't yet borne a moment of clarity to fully acknowledge the fae opals, the webs, the pixie dew draping Aisling's curves. Garments Aisling believed would drive him mad enough to estrange and condemn his only daughter to the gallows. But it hadn't.

"I am," Aisling spoke for the first time. Near wincing at the sensation of Lir's glare piercing her back as he forced himself to witness the image of Aisling and the Fire Hand embracing. For she herself struggled to make coherent sense of her feelings and everything unraveling like a thread pulled too soon from a tapestry.

One of the stags huffed amidst the silence, reminding Nemed of the fair folk before him. The image of these creatures, however, immediately sharpened the violet eyes he shared with Aisling. An edge of loathing he didn't shuffle away but rather embraced as he cleared his throat and addressed the crowd of Aos Sí and mortals alike.

"Tonight, we dine together for there is much to discuss between our kinds. A meeting between our leaders is overdue. And tomorrow we celebrate another interracial union, the purest of symbols for the newfound peace between mortals and Sidhe."

Sidhe. He hadn't said Aos Sí. Aisling hadn't heard of another moniker for their race until the day Galad had mentioned it. So why now did her father unveil a truth he never had before? Why now did he drop one of his many veils?

"In the time being," Nemed continued. "I hope the *Damh Bán* doesn't mind if I steal his bride away for the evening." His violet eyes flashed towards Lir. "And should you grow bored while she's away, Friseal, court advisor and hand to the High King, would be more than honored to begin debriefing the

Sidhe on the mortal perspective with regards to"—Nemed paused—"our relations both among ourselves and among others."

Aisling's glare darted towards her father, the urge to confront him growing with every breath she forced herself to take.

Lir's stag stomped behind him. "That's not possible. Our queen requires rest after her journey."

After having travelled through the Empress of the Dryads' mirrors and emerged in subterranean aqueducts months later, Aisling thought to herself.

"I assure you," Lir continued, "there will be more than enough time over the next several days to speak with your daughter." A feral inflection perverted his every word. That same mania she'd read in his eyes.

A vein appeared down the center of Nemed's forehead. A gesture she'd beheld far too often throughout her childhood. A gesture she'd come to fear. But it was also Dagfin whose eyes shifted to the Fae King with violent intent written across every fiber of his body.

"Aisling's own clann is more than happy to accommodate any of her needs," Nemed said. "She will both rest and find unparalleled sanctuary amongst her own kind. Her family," the Fire Hand challenged, his tone light but Aisling cringed at the venom she tasted in every word. The challenge he staked into the earth between himself and Lir.

Lir glared at the High King and Aisling knew he would rather be burned alive than surrender to the Fire Hand. So, the mortal queen stepped between them, raising her chin.

"I'll join you until dinner this evening," Aisling said to her father, hardening her expression so it exposed none of her inner turmoil. "After all, I've been dying to hear your response to my letter and what occurred to the raven, who not you but another returned to me."

Nemed's brows rose, eyes widening with surprise.

Perhaps he hadn't expected her to hold him accountable for never responding to her letters. Perhaps he'd forgotten about it himself. But his shock was short-lived. The Fire Hand swiftly collected himself, stealing away any emotion behind the thick walls of iron he'd built around vulnerabilities Aisling wasn't certain existed.

Aisling turned to Lir then, exchanging a look she hoped he'd understand. But she couldn't tell. His expression was one mortals had encountered on battlefields but never lived to describe.

Lir nodded his head at last, steadying his mount's growing anxiety.

The Fae King turned towards Galad, tipping his head in his direction. A silent command. And without hesitation, the fae knight stepped forward till he stood directly behind Aisling, hand on the hilt of his great sword.

"My first knight will escort her," Lir explained, returning Aisling's look with one of his own.

"I can assure you, there is no safer place for Aisling than amongst her own blood," Nemed argued, his voice as smooth as milk, the vein atop his forehead growing more prominent, his scar reddening.

"It's non-negotiable." The forest hushed in response to their lord's tone, a subtle growl deepening his every word.

Nemed considered for a moment, his knuckles burning white.

"Of course." Aisling's father bowed curtly to the Fae King, before spinning on his heels. His back now facing all the fair folk whose temper matched their savage sovereign's.

"Starn, escort your sister and her shadow to my private chambers. I'll join you all in a moment," Nemed said. Without a word, the sea of mortals parted to make way for their High King as the mortal sovereigns followed in his steps. The anxiety of turning their backs to the fair folk written across their mortal features.

Starn approached then, his countenance softening in the slightest. And behind him, Iarbonel, Annind, Fergus, and Dagfin waited for Aisling, gripping the hafts of their weapons. Still eying Lir who was already ignoring Friseal as he made his introductions to the Fae King; Friseal hadn't changed in the slightest since Aisling had last seen him. Instead, Lir focused his attention on Aisling, eyes glinting through the thickening haze.

"Keep your distance lest you answer in blood." Galad moved closer to Aisling, stopping Starn mid-stride.

Her eldest brother scoffed, turning to exchange glances with the rest of her kin.

"I wondered if I'd ever see you again." Starn beamed at Galad while squinting his charcoal eyes. Eyes he and the rest of Aisling's brothers had stolen from their mother.

"You know him?" Iarbonel asked, placing a hand on his brother's shoulder.

"Aye, he does," Galad answered for him, "we're well acquainted."

At his words, Aisling swatted away the image of the fae knight's mass branding. The vicious abuse her eldest brother had inflicted on the one who sought to free his *caera*.

"You've recovered well since the last I laid eyes on you, other than Aisling's union, of course," Starn continued. "In fact, you promised my head on a pike if ever again we met face to face."

"A promise I'm more than willing to uphold should you not quiet your tongue. After all, I need only wait for time to shrivel your bones and slow your beating heart."

"It appears this fae has a death wish." Fergus flushed with rage. "How dare you speak thus before the future High King of all Rinn Dúin?"

Starn rolled his neck, ignoring his younger brother. "There are stories that claim your iron scars still burn like the day they were dealt. So, tell me, fae, do yours still wake you in the night? Or is the memory of my face alone enough to bind me to your late-night horrors?"

Galad laughed but it was humorless. Hollow. Chilling the air they shared till Annind noticeably shivered.

"I harbor no late-night horrors, fleshling. I am the nightmare your clansmen fear when your dirt roads and your iron walls can no longer guide nor shelter you."

Aisling saw the loathing churning in Starn's expression. The veins cording his neck and painting his rounded ears red. But she felt no sympathy nor pity for her own blood. What he'd done was unforgivable in Aisling's eyes. There was reason and vengeance in death and destruction if committed in the name of their home, their clansmen, their futures. But what Starn had done was senseless hate. A wicked form of pleasure he'd satisfied with Galad's torment.

"Enough," Aisling spoke before any others could. "You're meant to be escorting me towards Father's private chambers, are you not?"

Starn reeled, facing Aisling for the first time. Aisling's heart twisted at the sight of him. For there was a lack of recognition in his eyes. They were an arm's reach away and yet, farther than they'd ever been before.

"Hello, sister." Her eldest brother extended the curve of his arm to Aisling. A mortal custom Aisling had forgotten, her brief, puzzled expression exposing her lapse in memory for her brothers and Dagfin, each exchanged knowing glances. She should've remembered such etiquette. It hadn't been that long since she partook in such customs. Yet, it felt like a lifetime.

At the gesture, Galad half drew his sword, pausing only for Aisling's touch on his arm, her violet eyes requesting he surrender this battle. For now. And so, he stood down, allowing Starn to guide his sister onward.

"It's good to see you." Iarbonel eyed Aisling, too afraid to touch her lest her fae shadow react once more.

By now, the Aos Sí had dispersed behind them, whispering *skalla* into the oncoming storm. So, Galad followed a pace behind her and her brothers. The intangible cord between herself and Lir tightened. But she dared not glance back at him as her brothers led her into the mortal camp.

Each of her brothers chatted idly amongst themselves. Starn's pointed expression eying Aisling from his periphery, an expression that, as children, had struck both fear and respect into herself, Iarbonel, Fergus, Annind, and Dagfin. Starn, the eldest of them all and destined to be High King before even Dagfin was to be king, carried an air of power. A shrewd, cold sense of authority since Aisling could remember. When Starn spoke, others listened. The strongest, quickest, mightiest of the Neimedh children.

Dagfin was the only one to keep silent, observing the mortal queen as though she might grow horns at any moment. And perhaps she would, Aisling thought to herself. But neither Starn, Iarbonel, Fergus, nor Annind were truly the Roktan Prince's brothers. Not by blood. But over the years he'd spent in Tilren, they'd become brothers. Played like brothers. Ridiculed one another like brothers. Fought like brothers. For one day, they'd all believed law would make them so if friendship couldn't entirely.

"We're glad you're alive, little sister," Annind chimed, a remark met with one of Iarbonel's glares of disapproval.

Something bitter stuck to Aisling's tongue. Something bitter and thick, eager to be swallowed. But before she could dwell on it further, the crowds dispersed, unveiling the labyrinth of mortal tents spread before her. Striped tents lined with both fiery torches and iron-clad sentinels alike. Humans, so many of them all in one place. All speaking in a tongue she understood. Foods, drinks, spices she could freely eat without fear of enchantment. Clothing styles she recognized. Fiddle, lute, harp strings, and medleys that washed over her in a wave of nostalgia for they were all tunes, melodies, and notes she'd heard since she was a bairn.

But the hospitality she'd once experienced, the respect from her people, was replaced with potent disapproval. Eying her as if she were a member of the fair folk themselves. Swatting their children's bottoms should they not rush indoors the moment she passed. Children who whispered to one another when they believed their mothers distracted.

"They say he's killed the Lady Aisling. Replaced her with a changeling," said one.

Another child shook their head. "I heard she exchanged her mortal soul in exchange for magic."

Aisling's stomach soured for where she once believed she'd find belonging here, at last meet a haven and sanctuary amongst these humans, but she'd never felt more like a stranger. Never felt more like an outlander than amongst her own kind.

Chapter XXX

NIGHT DESCENDED WITHOUT HESITATION, whisking the sun behind the veil of jagged cliffs and snowcapped mountains.

Two sentinels stood outside the mortal tent Aisling approached. Their suits of iron bronzed by firelight. Galad grabbed Aisling's wrist, lowering his mouth to her ear. A gesture met with the five prince's immediate apprehension, the instinctive reaching for their weapons.

"Keep your secrets," he whispered so only she could hear. And Aisling understood, briskly meeting Galad's eyes.

Wordlessly, the sentinels bowed to Starn and Dagfin as they passed between the canvas flaps, a custom Aisling had already grown accustomed to growing up. This considering, both Starn and Dagfin would eventually inherit crowns: Starn the crown of the High King of Rinn Dúin and Dagfin, the crown of the King of Roktling. Commoners, lesser nobles, servants, and guards would bow to these sons out of both tradition and ritual. But never had Aisling witnessed the sentinels considering Dagfin the way they did now, a glimmer of both respect and fear flashing in their rounded mortal eyes as he approached. Never had she witnessed trained guards hold their breath as her childhood friend neared. A similar reaction allotted to Galad as he passed but with more hate bent into the stiff lines of their mouths.

The inside of the tent was dimly lit. The perfume of Tilrish wool and blooming heather washed over Aisling in a potent wave. Scents that tasted of her childhood, of late nights peeking through keyholes to spy on Nemed's conferences. Those her brothers had infrequently been invited to but never she. No. Her perspective was always through the crack in the door, the floorboards, the midnight races back to her bed before her wetnurse would discover her mischief.

Her father no doubt slept here, a down feather bed draped in *olann* covers sat in another room of the tent. An extension that was large enough to be a Tilrish household in and of itself. But at the center of this room, the one she entered, stood a round table overrun with maps, scrolls, quills, and coins that, by the look of it, symbolized the mortal fleets scattered across the Isles.

Starn, Iarbonel, Fergus, and Annind dispersed around the room, unbuckling their bandoliers, setting down their daggers, and pouring themselves chalices of wine despite Galad's presence. Perhaps they supposed he'd not risk the unity between fair folk and mortals, especially when he was vastly outnumbered amidst their camp.

Dagfin, on the other hand, forewent disarming himself. What happened to the light-hearted boy she'd known as a child? This man who studied her through narrowed eyes wasn't the same boy she'd caught crying in the stables.

Aisling stepped further into the room. A gesture met by Dagfin's pointed glare, measuring her every step. Realization seized Aisling then: it wasn't only Galad he appraised but she as well. He didn't trust her. And although betrayal was a sickening fist in her gut, she couldn't blame him. If her tuath knew what she'd become, none of them would've robbed themselves of their defenses so easily.

"Can you sit in that gown?" Fergus asked, glaring up at his

sister from where he'd thrown himself into a wingback chair. One whose upholstery was fraying at the seams.

Aisling smoothed out the fabric of her opal bodice, sliding her fingers down the webbed skirts.

"Aye," Aisling said, cautiously stepping nearer to the disheveled table.

"Have you forgotten how to speak our tongue, little sister?" Annind asked next, flipping a coin he'd stolen from the maps. "You deign to speak unless necessary."

"So hostile, Annind," Starn smiled slyly, pouring five chalices of wine from a scarlet bottle. "Let her adjust. I can only imagine what she's been through." Both Starn and Iarbonel divided the half-filled glasses, handing a glass to each of Aisling's brothers. One for Iarbonel, one for Fergus, one for Annind. And where Aisling believed Dagfin next, Starn eventually approached Aisling, gesturing for her to accept the goblet.

"Tell us, what was it like?" Starn asked, ebony eyes glittering. "What was it like living amongst the fair folk?"

"I've never been allowed wine," Aisling blurted, looking to her brothers and Dagfin for an explanation as to the goblet offered now. "Nor mead, nor beer, nor ale." The only one not drinking was Dagfin. For initially, Aisling had thought the fifth glass reserved for the Roktan prince and not herself.

Starn exhaled a laugh. "You're no longer a child, Ash. Nor a commoner, nor noblewoman, nor a princess," he mocked her. "You're a queen now. You can do as you like."

Against her own volition, Aisling's lips curled. Those words, his tone. They acted as if—as if they respected her. For never had Aisling been allowed to do as she liked much less what she craved whilst within Tilren's stone keep. Before her union to Lir, she was scarcely permitted in the castle gardens without an escort. And now—now they handed her a glass of wine, a chalice nearly as forbidden to her as fae wine.

Aisling waited till the others gulped before doing so

herself, willing her hand steady as she accepted the chalice.

"Are you going to keep us in suspense? Tell us about your time with the Aos Sí," Fergus demanded, waving his arms dramatically.

"What would you like to know?" Aisling replied, taking another sip.

"Where do you sleep?" Starn asked first, leaning his elbow atop Iarbonel's chair.

"The dungeons?" Fergus chimed.

"She doesn't smell as if she's been sleeping in the dungeons," Annind leaned forward.

"Nor does she look it," Iarbonel added, each of them glaring at Aisling from head to toe. Iridescent in her raven-hued, dew drop encrusted gown. Nothing mortal hands could spin.

"No," Aisling said, eyes flicking to where Dagfin leaned against an antique chest, spinning a dinner knife artfully between his fingers. "I have my own royal chambers. It has a bed thrice as large as Clodagh's in Tilren. A balcony that hangs amongst the canopies. Songbirds that tie my hair and lace my gowns."

"And what did they have you do?" Iarbonel rested his head on his fist, already half-finished with his goblet.

"Did they starve you?" Fergus asked. "You're vastly thinner than we last saw you."

Aisling hesitated. Paused as if reluctant to spill more information than was necessary. But what did it matter? Of course, Galad stood a breath away from her, but her hesitation was born of more than simply being caught or overheard by a member of the fair folk. No. Her hesitation was deeper than that. A pang of guilt grew larger and larger the more she considered saying anything at all. As if it were a betrayal. But how could she betray the enemy? This—her brothers, Dagfin— they were her blood. Her tuath, Aisling assured herself.

"In my experience, the fair folk are skilled in nearly all of the arts," Aisling confessed, "including cooking and preparing *non*-enchanted meals for me to consume. So no, they didn't starve me. They did, however, bait me before a trow."

"A trow?" Fergus repeated without thinking, looking to Dagfin for an explanation. Aisling's eyes followed Fergus' line of sight, everyone's attention swiveling towards the Roktan prince. The shadows cast from the torchlight danced across his expression.

"A species of troll," Dagfin said, and everyone leaned closer to listen. "Trows typically reside west of Giant's Causeway, in which case, the Aos Sí must've hunted down and imported one from further north for their games." Dagfin flashed his eyes at the fae knight. A glare that both unnerved Aisling and riled Galad for the knight shifted behind her.

"So, the mortal prince has more uses than longing for a bride that isn't his own," Galad bit, unable to hold his sharp tongue, a personality trait Lir should've considered before sending him into a camp swarming with mortals. With those who'd branded the man's crest into his flesh. Those who'd imprisoned his Morrin. Or perhaps that was exactly why Lir had chosen Galad. Who else would unleash fiery retribution on the mortals if given the opportunity? One wrong move on behalf of the mortals and everything would be for naught, Aisling realized.

Dagfin straightened, meeting Galad's eyes.

"Watch your tongue, fae," Dagfin chided, halting the spinning of knives between his fingers. Hands void of markings, the fae tattoos Aisling had become so accustomed to over the past several months. And the malice in his tone ... Aisling had never known the Roktan Prince capable of such poison.

"Or should you watch yours lest you say more than you're permitted whilst in my presence?" Aisling blurted before she could think better of it. Dagfin's eyes shot towards her. "Lest you reveal the truth behind the mortals' elaborately spun veil?"

As if he'd been physically struck, Dagfin winced, eyes narrowing in response.

"You know nothing of what you speak," Dagfin replied, his voice laced with anger. Anger that boiled Aisling's blood for it was she who was entitled to such bitter resentment, the only one amongst them excluded from their secrets.

Dagfin had known about, was clearly well versed in, the Unseelie. Which begged the question: what else had they hidden from Aisling? Hidden from all the mortal commoners whose only refuge from the ghoulish aberrations, aberrations Nemed claimed were the fair folk, were their overcrowded cottages?

"No, that was before, before I was traded to the Aos Sí I didn't know of what I spoke. Now—" Aisling fumbled over the words, the rage, confusion, doubt these past several months mounting inside her, preparing to explode. "Everything is different now."

"Nothing's changed, Ash," Starn reassured her, stepping nearer. Galad tensed in response, for himself or Aisling she wasn't sure. Perhaps the urge to behead him in the name of vengeance was more potent now than protecting his mortal queen.

Starn shifted his gaze to Galad then, his lips curving into a lopsided grin before returning his attention to his sister. As if Galad had been one of the thousands Starn had tortured.

"You were young. A princess. More committed to breaking rules and mischief than harboring a difficult truth. A truth, the *elaborate* explanation of everything outside of Tilren's walls, was of no use to you."

"No use to me?" Aisling gripped the stem of her goblet till she believed it might snap. "Did you think it was of no use to me before I was handfasted to the King of the Aos Sí? He who my own blood would have me conceive an heir?" Aisling briefly closed her eyes, doing her best to dampen her anger.

"No, you claim you protected me, but such lies were spun in the name of distrust. You didn't believe me capable of safeguarding such secrets, did you?"

Silence spread between them as each of her brothers avoided her eyes, pretending as though the rings on their fingers, the mud on their boots, or the waxing candles harbored the answers to her questions.

Starn cleared his throat. "You were wild, Ash. Cheating at our games, lying to our father, tricking the guards to escape Tilren's law. But you were also only a child."

Aisling bit her tongue, collecting herself. Ground her rage into her teeth, opening and closing her fists. Cursing the *draiocht* that climbed out of its cavern and goaded to be used.

Hush, she hissed internally to the *draiocht*. Careful not to expose herself. For Aisling wasn't certain how much her brothers or Dagfin knew of fae magic. Specifically, how it was harnessed. But she knew Galad felt it, the *draiocht* pushing against Aisling's walls to be unchained, for he glanced at her, opening his mouth to speak and thinking better of it. That aura of magic so close to him, angry and eager.

"Father will arrive any moment now." Starn watched her closely. "He should be here for these conversations."

And as if summoned, the canvas curtains parted. Nemed entered the tent, his expression distorted by the dancing shadows spinning throughout the room. The evening gale, slipping in behind him and rustling the parchments, maps, and scrolls piled throughout the tent. Instinctively, Aisling snapped her mouth shut. Her back went rigid the moment the violet eyes only they shared fixed upon her.

"I think Aisling needs another glass of wine," Nemed said, limping towards Aisling. Starn snapped his fingers and Annind stood from his seat, fetching the scarlet bottle and pouring Aisling's glass near to the brim.

"Where's Mother?" Aisling asked, Clodagh's absence more potent by the minute.

"Your mother isn't feeling well," Nemed lied, Aisling knew, "she'll join us for dinner."

Aisling stilled. Paralyzed as the Fire Hand kissed the back of her hand before folding it between his own.

"I cannot express how wonderful it is to have you returned to your family." Nemed guided Aisling towards one of the chairs surrounding the center table. Starn pulled the seat back, its wooden legs sliding against the southern Centari rugs carpeting the grass beneath.

"Please, sit," Nemed said, but Aisling knew it wasn't a request. It was an order.

Aisling hesitated before, at last, swallowing her defiance. Galad followed closely behind, shadowing where she sat. But his unmatched loathing for Starn swiftly refocused on the calculated fury he felt towards her father.

"Your hands," Nemed began, "they feel different."

Aisling's heart sprung to her throat. But her father couldn't know, she reassured herself.

"They're more calloused. Scarred." He turned her fingers over.

Aisling released a breath of relief, studying her hands now returned safely to her lap. There were countless reasons to keep her newfound *draiocht* from her father. If she didn't already fear their rejection of her, their dismissal of her, the realization she was capable of practicing magic would sever any remaining ties she bore with her clann. To her kind. She'd be excommunicated from whatever life, bonds, relationships she'd cherished before her marriage to Lir. And although rage rattled her every bone, she couldn't lose them all. Couldn't bear the thought of her own family shunning her for an ability she hadn't asked for yet nevertheless treasured. Couldn't forsake this magic if she wanted to. And never, Aisling knew, would she want to. Even if magic was as perverse as her father believed, she found she didn't care.

Filverel feared Nemed would weaponize Aisling *if* he knew

she could char the forest. But Filverel's fear was irrational. Nemed would sooner banish Aisling than make use of her. After all, the only entity he loathed more than the Aos Sí was magic.

So, Aisling bottled the *draiocht* singing in her ears. So long as she told it no, it wouldn't lift its head from its primordial abyss. Only Aisling could release it if she so desired. And the mortal queen took comfort in that knowledge.

"Is this the topic that demanded such privacy? My hands?" Aisling bit, winning her the same lightning-fast flicker of both shock and anger from her father's eyes. Quickly concealed with soft laughter.

"I don't recall such a sharp tongue from you," Nemed sat in a chair of his own, reclining lazily as Annind poured Nemed's goblet. He didn't take her seriously. Considered her a rebellious child. So, Aisling scowled in return, resisting the urge to argue in response, a response that would only weaken her claims to strength, to power, to confidence.

"What do you recall of me, Father?" Aisling challenged, raising her chin as she locked eyes with the Fire Hand. She wouldn't shrink. She wouldn't cower before him as she'd done all her life. No, she couldn't, wouldn't, allow him to intimidate her.

The creases in Nemed's face deepened as his face stretched into an amused grin.

"I recall a princess of great potential: wild enough to be brave, clever enough to be wise, willful enough to be obedient, yet lured instead by temptation," he said, tilting his glass from side to side.

"Tell us, have you grown close with the Aos Sí?" Fergus interjected, picking through a platter of breads and cheeses Aisling hadn't noticed until now.

Aisling rolled her shoulders back, doing her best to ignore the rising tension around her neck. The sweat beading her brow. For every pair of eyes, brown, sapphire or, violet, was fixed upon her now, eagerly awaiting her response.

A few months ago, she would've wept on their shoulders, divulged everything and anything that had occurred yet now ... now she felt as if her lips were sewn shut. As if chronicling a single day amongst the fair folk was like pulling teeth from her jaw. Yet perhaps these questions were to aid in their pursuit of solidifying the marital alliance they'd already achieved with another of its kind. Nevertheless, a creature dark and heavy, weighed on Aisling's shoulders the longer her father awaited an answer.

Aisling's throat tightened, resisting the urge to meet Galad's eyes.

"For every time they put my life in danger, they also saved it," Aisling said, "such experiences aren't easily forgotten."

It was an honest answer. Perhaps more honest than Aisling had ever intended to be with her family in regard to her relationship with the fair folk. But she'd found herself incapable of uttering a mistruth. Of lying, or at the very least being convincing enough to deceive her father.

"How heartwarming," Nemed purred as every member of the tent save for Aisling and Galad exchanged quick glances. Glances Aisling wouldn't have noticed had she blinked.

"And the Fae King? Have you spent time with him?" Starn asked, crossing his arms over his chest. Dagfin's eyes shot towards Aisling, his hands tightening around the hilt of the dinner knives.

Nemed nodded his head at Annind, a silent command to pour Aisling more wine.

Aisling did her best to resist the assault of memories flooding her mind: Lir humming her to sleep when nightmares prevailed in the feywilds, translating his fae runes when Aisling grew bored on stagback, skinning a beast for her on a whim when he'd felt her shivering farther north. The foreign blood on his fangs, the sound of his axes unsheathing, the fear he perpetually instilled.

"Of course she has," Fergus said. "You heard what he called her: 'our queen.'"

Nemed nodded in agreement. "I'm assuming he took pride in showing you Annwyn? His people? Their way of life?"

Just as Aisling knew Galad had sensed her anger, oozing from the *draiocht* within her, she could feel his as well. The potent distrust swelling in each of his flexed muscles. How he bit his tongue to keep himself from lashing out, verbally or physically. He could slay them all if he wanted. Quickly. Easily. But with consequences. Immeasurable consequences for his own kind.

"I've answered enough questions," Aisling chewed the inside of her cheek as she glanced around the room. Her brothers watched her closely, Dagfin visibly fumed, and her father arched a knowing, inquisitive brow. "And I have plenty to ask of my own."

"Do you blame us? Our littlest sister's been living amongst barbarians for over a year now," Starn piped but not without looking to his father first.

"The Fae King, he's strange, isn't he?" Nemed pushed, shrugging off her protests.

"Strange is relative," Aisling replied. "And whether he is or not, whether I consider him to be or not, it makes little difference to you."

"I'd think it would be considering he's wed to my only daughter." Nemed grinned like a cat with a mouse between its teeth. "And considering another of our kind will be wed to a fae princess at dawn."

Aisling's eyes absently darted towards Dagfin.

"It's unlikely. The Sidhe can only be handfast if the correct blade is chosen or else—"

"Or else Dagfin will engage in combat to the death with his would-be bride," Starn finished for his sister. Annind poured Aisling more wine despite the glass being half full. Another goblet was also filled and placed before the Tilrish High King.

Aisling met Dagfin's eyes, searching those ocean depths. Surely, he wouldn't, couldn't, go through with this.

"He'll make the same choice you had, select the same axe?" Nemed inquired, leaning closer to her. So near, Aisling could smell his breath, the wine staining both his tongue and teeth.

Indeed, this custom was sealed in magic. If they weren't *caera*, one couldn't select the correct blade even if they knew which weapon belonged to their prospective suitor. Magic would guide their thoughts and body elsewhere.

"No," Aisling replied honestly, "by Peitho's own blade."

She eyed the glass warily, reluctant to sip before her father did himself. Galad's tension pushed down on Aisling as if she'd been submerged in water. But this was all harmless information. Aisling had sacrificed everything for such harmony. In which case, why would their queries be anything other than curiosity? But even as the thoughts passed her mind, the taste in Aisling's mouth turned bitter. She'd allowed her naivete to blind her in the past.

"Ah, of course," Nemed replied, rubbing his chin, "especially considering the Fae King appears rather attached to his axes."

Galad shifted and Aisling's heart seized for she knew if Galad chose to strike, to launch himself at the Fire Hand, it would occur in less time than it took any of them to blink.

"*Mo Lúra* has answered enough questions," the fae knight interjected, his voice no more than a growl.

"I've never seen him without those axes," Starn ignored Galad, never once releasing Aisling from his scrutiny, a response that made Galad imagine eleven different ways of slaughtering her eldest brother, Aisling knew. "Have you?"

The mortal queen stilled, eyes darting between her father and her eldest brother. They did not deign to divulge the entire truth; even after everything Nemed had praised her for, still, they didn't trust her enough to confide in her. After all, she was dressed in the trappings of the fair folk, wielding their *draiocht*. And despite the tender glint in her father's eyes, Aisling wasn't blind to Nemed's guile nor his propensity to cherish the mortal north above all else.

"I haven't," she confessed, suddenly aware of the stifling heat vegetating in the tented room.

"Surely, he doesn't sleep with them, eat with them, bathe with them, please his wife with them strapped to his back?" Annind pressed. He leaned forward in his chair till a candle nearly singed his black hair. And behind him, Dagfin rolled his neck from side to side, stormy eyes alive with thunder.

Aisling's ears buzzed, her stomach churning with a combination of both embarrassment and wrath. Pure, undiluted emotion she'd never felt before, never experienced. And it overwhelmed her. Made her lose feeling in her fingers digging into the arms of her chair, her feet crossed beneath her gowns, the pulsing of the headache that plagued her now, from minutes, or perhaps hours, of neglecting the *draiocht* clawing to be released.

Aisling inhaled. Exhaled. Concentrating on every breath before she spoke as smoothly as she was capable. "I've said enough. Did I not make myself clear the first time?"

Shock rippled through the room; this time, it wasn't so easily concealed. Each of them flinched at the claws alive in her violet eyes. As if every passing moment was a merciful one on her behalf. Whether they believed the might she donned in that moment, Aisling wasn't certain. Only that she'd silenced them all.

"More than the skin on your hands has changed, Aisling. Such change runs deep within you, doesn't it?" Nemed asked at last, shattering the awkward stillness swamping the canvas chamber.

Aisling resisted the urge to squirm beneath his regard, those violet eyes that dug deep below her flesh, unapologetically searching for the answers he sought. Not to mention, Aisling couldn't remember a time she'd been the subject of her father's undivided attention as she was now. The feeling of a thief caught in the night.

"Tell me, Aisling, what else happened whilst you lived amongst them?" Nemed pushed, leaned forward so his elbows rested on his knees.

"I chose to eat instead of be eaten," Aisling replied, and to her surprise, every word spilled from her lips as wickedly smooth as syrup, as silk, as fae sweet cream.

Nemed chuckled, taking another sip of wine. "Aye, you've done splendidly." He turned to Starn, Iarbonel, Fergus, Annind, and Dagfin one by one, meeting their eyes as he spoke. "It's because of Aisling's sacrifice to Tilren, to the North, to all of our kind that further bloodshed has been prevented. She brings us here today and she deserves our respect now. As a queen in her own right."

Aisling cursed the leaping of her heart. She'd feared they'd forgotten her, they'd forsaken her. But thus far, her anger rivalled their glowing praises. The child in her, the princess who'd desperately sought her father's approval, sweetened at the praise. For never had he complimented her so and now that he did, Aisling couldn't help but swell with pride. A fact she damned herself for internally for she knew it was, if not entirely, partially, smoke and mirrors.

"Yet you ignored my correspondence despite such sacrifices," Aisling said, chewing her father's charms and spitting them back out. "So, tell me, why keep the Unseelie a secret from the north? Why misrepresent the enemy? Why condemn libraries of knowledge that could've prevented the death of so many of our kind if only they knew? Knew what really lay beyond their mortal walls?"

Silence crashed into the room like ice in a storm, frosting everything it touched. The dripping of the candles was nearly audible in such potent quiet. But Aisling forbid herself from speaking further. From rambling on. From recoiling at her father's cryptic, horrid glare as even his fingers stopped their idle stroking of the fraying seams.

"You blame me for the brutality of the Aos Sí?"

"I question your intentions knowing of the brutality of the Sidhe and sending your only daughter regardless."

"What you did was an honor, a sacrifice the mortal kind has been blessed because of."

"Blessed by who? The Forge of Creation that never existed? The Gods that are nothing more than tales?"

Nemed stiffened, his smug expression collapsing into something darker.

"Ash—" Iarbonel opened his mouth to speak but Aisling ignored him.

"The Sidhe who devour our children, rape our women, live beneath the earth? Or the Unseelie that are never mentioned? The Lore that is forbidden?" Behind her, Aisling could feel Galad's own rage at such tales rippling from him. Centuries of hatred for the men who inhabited this tent were brought to the forefront and he could do nothing but stand as still as death.

All eyes darted between the mortal queen and her father, Nemed, whose veins snaked and bulged across the center of his forehead.

"I told you that—"

"That the Sidhe spin lies like they spin their thread? Yes, I remember. I remember everything you taught me. Everything that contradicts the world outside of Tilren's walls." Aisling levelled her voice. The rush of blood pulsing through the veins in her ears. "And all of you." Aisling turned to her brothers. She asked Dagfin, "you knew all of it, didn't you?"

The five princes hesitated, tongues catching in their throats.

Dagfin took a step nearer to her, a step met by Galad's sliding of his sword halfway from its scabbard. And in turn, the princes reached for their neglected weapons lest the fae knight unleash the chaos visibly storming from within.

"We were each informed some years ago, when we turned sixteen"—the Roktan prince confessed, guilt spreading across his handsome features—"told everything once we were of age to accept the throne should anything happen to either of our fathers or, in Iarbonel, Annind and Fergus' case, the direct lineage."

Years. They'd known for years.

Aisling's skin burned the longer she realized just how blissfully ignorant she'd been. So complacent, so stupid to have not sought the truth of her own accord. To have taken that agency and wielded it for herself. The power, the control she'd happily let slip through her fingers all these years, the thought of it maddened her. Made her hands blister with heat as she gripped the arms of her chair, scratching at its wood with her nails.

Iarbonel ran his fingers through his hair. "Ash, you were the youngest. The only northern princess, you were to be protected—"

"Protected and then sold at a price you deemed sufficient?" Aisling shook her head, tears threatening to spill from the corners of her eyes. She wouldn't let them. Wouldn't show them weakness. Wouldn't prove herself to be the volatile, naive, spoilt girl they believed her to be. So, she levelled herself but didn't calm the anger within her. Merely tempered it, chained it to the walls within herself, and commanded it to be obedient. To bite at her command and hers alone.

"I've never lied to you, Ash," Nemed said, schooling his expression, "you've merely allowed the fair folk to twist my words, to manipulate the past, to poison the truth. Clodagh warned me you'd be susceptible to their deceit."

Not now, she commanded the *draiocht*, pushing and pushing.

"Man was born first," Nemed continued, "was born of nothing, as I'm sure they've educated you." Born of a curse and not cast in a Forge. "Man *has* carved himself into the earth. The Aos Sí *are* aberrations, perversities of nature for they hold onto what's been stolen from man. And the Gods *are* nothing more than fanciful tales. They've abandoned all that they created. Left us to spill one another's blood while they sleep. They're gone, forsaken both Aos Sí and man alike."

In Aisling's periphery, Galad's knuckles grew white where they wrapped around the haft of his blade. A blade she'd witnessed him wield and knew the bloodbaths it'd tasted.

"There's more than one side to the tale, Ash. More than the account of the Aos Sí," Annind piped.

"And now you wish to teach it to me? Only now that I've been sold?" Aisling ground her teeth together.

"The information was useless to you until now," Annind snapped but the mortal queen was far past anger to listen to her brother's petty jabs. So, Aisling ignored him.

"I'm assuming no one other than the highest-ranking nobles are aware of these secrets. Do the common people, do they know any of it? The history, the truth of mankind's origins. That we are born of a curse? That we were once Sidhe? The truth of what lies outside the iron and stone walls of the mortal kingdoms? The Unseelie who not even the Aos Sí can fully control?"

Starn, Iarbonel, Fergus, and Annind each turned to one another, hesitantly trading glances.

"No," Dagfin confessed, his expression a muddle of anger and torment. None of which Aisling cared about given the fires clawing their way up her throat and demanding to be let loose. She wouldn't let them. Couldn't let her family witness her *draiocht*. So, Aisling twisted the skirts of her gown into her fists. Her cheeks flushing.

"The mortals are safe. What need is there to over-complicate matters? The Aos Sí and Unseelie are one and the same Ash and any tales they've told you of them being separate are lies, manipulations, half-truths. You've been told two halves of the full story, daughter. None complete and both misleading without their second half."

"So, while you wage war on the Sidhe, what of the Unseelie? What of the true threats to mortals that lie just beyond their cottages? Just beneath the rivers where they fetch their water? The woods where they're forced to hunt lest they starve as they're starving now?"

"That's why we have the *Faerak*," Nemed said, gesturing towards Dagfin.

"Hunters" in the mortal tongue.

Aisling's eyes betrayed her, following her father's finger until they found Dagfin.

"The Faerak hunt the Unseelie whenever issues arise. A pixie terrorizing children in their own gardens, demons feeding on mortal women's dreams as they sleep, dragons setting fire to settlements and stealing what little livestock we have, all hunted down and slaughtered by our Faerak. Expertly and thoroughly trained to eliminate the threats you speak of. Threats the fair folk allow to feed on mankind should innocent children or civilians wander too far from their homes."

Dagfin reluctantly met her glare. Melodies he'd played for her on the piano still echoing whenever she thought of him. Perhaps he had a chance against Peitho after all. Aisling's heart warred between relief and outrage.

Of all of them, Aisling hadn't expected this. Starn, Iarbonel, Fergus, and Annind were her elder brothers, each given reason by their father to look down upon their little sister. But Dagfin, Dagfin was a friend. He who'd sworn to never lie to her whilst they threw coins in the courtyard well. He was now a *Faerak*? So knowledgeable, so capable, so prominently aligned for power whilst Aisling was nothing. Left in the dark to rot until they could trade her as a pawn.

Aisling stood from the chair, the seat toppling over. There was truth in Nemed's words, Aisling could tell. A genuine desire for the well-being, strength, and prosperity of the mortals. All of which Aisling understood. Wished for mankind herself. Didn't she? For it dawned on Aisling here and now that Nemed was desperate to not only ensure the mortals were healthy, safe, and thriving but to ensure his side of the war won. That mankind lay waste to those who were stronger, older, more powerful than the fair folk through iron and fire. To demonstrate a curse couldn't make them powerless. What mattered was to eat and not be eaten.

Lir was right. Had always been right and Aisling too naive to understand.

"We are all beasts, slaves to desire. Mortals, Aos Sí, and all else driven by that which will sate our appetite. You must overpower that which sought to overpower you. Become the predator and not the prey."

"You wish to corrupt me."

"No. I wish to show you, you already are."

"Ash," Dagfin started but it was too late. Aisling buzzed with anger, controlling the writhing rage of the *draiocht* lest it master her. Aisling didn't think herself capable of such fury. Perhaps it was also the *draiocht*, feeding off her emotions and growing larger, stronger, more capable.

"Ash," Galad said next, placing a hand on Aisling's shoulder. But before she could address the fae knight at her side, he hissed in pain, drawing back his hand and glaring up at the mortal queen with wide eyes. Those sapphire orbs glittering with surprise as he devoured the sight of her.

"Forge help us," he cursed, collecting himself long enough for Aisling to look to the others for answers.

Their familiar faces beheld her in horror. And more than the dread, the horror, the confusion, was something else. Something far more painful to behold: a complete lack of recognition. As though Aisling were a stranger, employing their dead sister's body like a host. Perhaps that was exactly what she was, a creature of great power and thus evil, for Aisling had never beheld anyone with such strength use it for good. And why should they if they wished to rule and not be ruled?

So, Aisling held out her hands, confirming what she already knew to be true. Without having called upon it. Without having spoken its name. After having believed she'd successfully resisted its calls, the *draiocht* emerged, all the same, consuming her with fire till every pore on her body blazed in fiery, purple gems. She was a torch-lit star, hurtling towards the earth hungry for destruction, the *draiocht* using her instead, and she found she enjoyed it.

"What have you done?" Her father rasped, eyes wide, glazed over with tears. "What have you done, Aisling?"

Chapter XXXI

BY NOW, EVERYONE STOOD, INCHING AWAY from Aisling till their backs pressed against the canvas walls. All save for Galad who moved to face her, his fae features dappled in sweat from his proximity to her flames.

"Breathe, Aisling," Galad encouraged her, his face twisting with an uncertainty, an anxiety she'd never glimpsed from him before.

"You're not breathing, you need to breathe. It'll implode within you otherwise," he continued but Aisling had lost control, the *draiocht* bloomed within her, sealing her lungs shut. For so long as she couldn't exhale the excess magic, it would swell within her. Stretching until there was no more room. And Aisling could feel it, understand it, its insatiable desire to be unleashed. To consume and spread. Joyfully, euphorically writhing its way through her so the violet flames grew larger, rising to the steepled center of the tent and charring the drapery.

"Aisling," Galad said, his voice a croak of desperation. "Breathe," he commanded. The mortal queen met his eyes and shook her head. She couldn't. Could hardly hear him over the roar in her ears, as though the entire ocean was crashing around her and she herself was spinning, tossed, thrown, stolen away by a wave of pure desire. Of ancient, primeval need. And it hurt the longer it went on. So, Aisling reached inside herself, searching for that arcane creature, but it was nowhere to be found. No longer did it reside in its black pit. No. It'd escaped.

"*You must master it lest it master you.*"

It would destroy the mortal queen and everything that surrounded her before it surrendered the control it hung over her head now, Aisling realized. The mortal queen fell to her knees, her legs giving out. Unable to see, hear, feel through the fattening flames around her.

"Do something!" Nemed snarled, his head snapping towards where Dagfin stood, his expression harrowed with confusion. But once he'd been directly addressed, the moment was fleeting.

Dagfin's entire posture transformed as he unbuckled a thick, metal chain from around his belt. He spun it in the air five or six times, Aisling couldn't tell, before launching it at the mortal queen. The chain caught her left hand, and as she made to free herself its momentum spun around her right wrist, binding her. It was a bolas, Aisling realized to her own horror. An iron one, a lengthy chain whose ends held heavy weights to entangle its target. Aisling had witnessed the weapon be used on Tilrish training grounds before, mostly for educating townsfolk on how best to capture wild game. A comparison that maddened the mortal queen. But such rage was tempered, violently shoved back into the abyss within her, back into its dwelling along with the *draiocht*.

And at the touch of such potent iron, within its aggressive grasp, her eyes burned as if they'd been scalded with steam, her body felt heavier. It was nearly impossible to keep upright, her nostrils sparking with heat forcing her to curl in on herself. She'd never felt like this before. The way these shackles made her feel. As though she'd been placed in a box made of thorns and the walls closed in around her. Slowly. Her bones seemingly dissolving beneath her skin.

Aisling screamed but she couldn't fight. Struggled to see past the tears flooding her violet eyes. But the fires were gone. Nothing but smoke and scorched Centari rugs, grass, and furniture to expose the magic she'd wielded here on this night.

"Release her!" She heard Galad hiss and by the time she lifted her eyes, the fae knight had his sword pressed against Starn's throat, face twisted with white rage as he addressed Dagfin. "Release her or I'll slit your future High King's throat without a moment's hesitation." And kill him he would, Aisling knew. Knew Galad had been dreaming of spilling her brother's blood since he'd captured Morrin. Since he'd branded his chest with the mortal crest.

"Stand down, fae," Nemed barked, the veins in his neck bulging above his ebony collar. "We'll release her once we're certain she's not a threat. A threat to us as well as yourself, which I'm sure you well know."

Galad considered the High King, eyes flashing towards where Dagfin stood still as death, his fingers curled around the hilts of two throwing knives at his sides.

"Did you intend for her to kill us all? Was that the plan?" Starn seethed beneath the fae knight's pressure, his face reddening, purpling with every furthering second.

"She's of no harm to anyone now. The magic has drained her. She couldn't summon it again if she tried," Galad insisted, unwilling to surrender his leverage. "You should be more concerned that right now the Queen of the Sidhe is bound like an animal in your custody."

Nemed's lips spread into a thin line, losing their color. He considered Aisling slumped on her knees, the iron shackles around her wrists pushing her against the earth despite her efforts to remain upright. Her mind was dizzied by the smell of the chain's rust, its surface like needles to her. A substance that repelled magic, a magic that now flowed freely through her veins.

Nemed nodded to Dagfin. "Release her."

"Father, you can't possibly—She'll kill us all!" Annind shouted, bloodshot eyes darting between the Roktan Prince and his sister as Dagfin swiftly cut the distance between them.

"She won't," Nemed said, regaining a sliver of his composure, "she's been detained. I've witnessed the Faerak do it before on the Unseelie; such iron suffocates Unseelie and fae magic. And magic is where they derive their strength. The fae is right. No creature, Unseelie or Seelie, is powerful enough to nullify such a sedative."

Fergus opened his mouth as if to speak but one glance from his father and he snapped his maw shut, redirecting his attention to Dagfin carefully untying the bolo from around his sister's wrists.

"Is she Unseelie then? An Aos Sí?!" Iarbonel asked, his voice cracking mid-sentence.

"It's not feasible," Annind piped, rubbing his face with his hands, "one cannot simply become another race. There is no spell, no enchantment to perform such a feat. Unless"—Annind's face blanched—"unless she's a changeling."

"Impossible," Dagfin said. "We would've known." A hint of betrayal, of doubt betraying his expression, nonetheless.

"Fin is right," Nemed removed the crown from his head and set it on the table. "I witnessed Clodagh birth her and ever since she was kept within the close, attentive watch of Tilrish, mortal wetnurses. Never was there a moment she was left unattended or unobserved, precautions to prevent the Unseelie and their mischief from meddling with the royal clann."

"Then what is she?!" Fergus asked, eying his sister as though she might devour him whole if he so much as flinched.

"I'd like to know," Nemed said, lifting his fingers to silence each of them.

Dizzied, Aisling swayed from side to side, concentrating on regaining her self-control, rendered nearly ill by the storm blue eyes that circled around her, flashing like stars as they searched her expression.

"You'll be alright," Dagfin whispered, surprisingly calm. And once the shackles were fully removed, tossed across the room so their effects dwindled in her periphery, Galad shoved Starn from him, still scowling as the future High King collided against the center table, knocking half its contents onto the ground.

Dagfin lifted Aisling to her feet until she slumped against him; the smell of him was of salt and ocean air. Of the Ashild slapping against Castle Roktling. A cologne that sobered her. Rebuilt the melted bones beneath her flesh limb by limb. Dagfin was much taller than her now. Not like he'd been when they were children.

"What is she?" Iarbonel asked, standing in a puddle of his own spilled wine. "What have you done to her?!"

Galad ignored him, concentrating instead on sheathing his sword into his scabbard.

"What have you done to her?!" Iarbonel shouted again, this time louder, the white of his complexion greying.

"Nothing," Galad said, flashing his pointed canines. And it was the truth as far as even Aisling was concerned. No one was certain where such abilities originated or why. Not even Danu. Only that she now possessed them.

"Let's not be sparse for words," Nemed chided, clicking his tongue, "tell me what happened to my daughter or my Faerak will detain you next."

"You threaten me with a princeling?" Galad scoffed, shooting daggers at Dagfin from across the room. But the Roktan prince didn't notice, instead preoccupied with lifting Aisling's chin, so she glared up at him, tilting her face from side to side inquisitively. As if there were nothing more important than beholding her up close, this strange creature he'd once known. Was once intended for. As if he'd enjoy nothing more than to hunt her down like any other Unseelie.

Capture her. Bridle her.

"He's slaughtered creatures far bigger than you, fae." Nemed smiled uneasily, his purple eyes glinting with a string of madness. "Now, tell me; what happened to my daughter whilst she was in *your* custody?"

Galad considered Aisling, his expression softening in the slightest. But Aisling knew even the fae knight, even the Fae King, didn't know where she'd encountered the *draiocht* or why it whispered to her. Didn't know why or how or when. Only that it had. And while Aisling knew the fair folk would've gone to the ends of the Isles of Rinn Dúin to prevent the Fire Hand from discovering her abilities, it was already too late. She'd lost control and any dishonesty would prove destructive in securing continued prosperity within their delicate alliance. So, the fae knight licked his lips, shoulders slackening a hair as he opened his mouth to speak.

"I speak the truth: the Sidhe aren't responsible for the magic she now wields. And if we are, it is unbeknownst to even ourselves. In fact, these are all questions and answers we've sought as well."

"When did it first manifest?" Nemed demanded, turning from Galad and instead, ambling towards where Aisling rested her head against Dagfin's chest. Slowly regaining the strength to lift her neck, the stench of the iron fading.

"She was attacked, nearly killed by a Fomori. She saved herself by bidding the magic for the first time."

At the mention of such an Unseelie, Dagfin cursed, the volume of his vulgarity and the rumble of his chest startling Aisling.

"Is this how you protect your queen? How do you defend the treaty between our kinds? You're familiar with the bloodlust of the Unseelie so it is either ignorance or spite that she was so near to them at all."

"It was necessary," Galad replied calmly, "we needed an audience with the Unseelie and so we managed it."

"And since then?" Nemed asked, studying Aisling through narrowed eyes. His form loomed over her, shadowing Aisling from the candlelight. "When else has she used it?"

"Scarcely but when needed."

Cautiously, Nemed took one of her hands, turning it over so it faced palm up. And at the gesture everybody in the room tensed, eyes pinned to the flesh that had nearly cooked them all alive.

"Are there other mortals like her, Father?" Iarbonel asked. "Others who can use magic?"

"No," Annind answered for the Fire Hand, "it's not possible. Unheard of. A violation of the original curse."

"Fascinating," Nemed whispered, eyes still glazed with tears. Swimming with something Aisling had never encountered from her father, a man who was always calm. Collected. Even in the face of great horrors. But now, something stirred within him, slipping through the pores in his face till she could nearly smell it.

"What has become of you, my raven?" Her father asked just as Aisling fixed her eyes upon him. "You've stolen something that isn't yours, haven't you?" He smiled, his voice that of a father's reading bedtime tales. Gentle, warm, indescribably tender, a tone Aisling would've wrapped herself in as a child if she'd ever heard it.

"It wasn't stolen," Aisling managed, pulling herself up so Dagfin needn't hold her straight. "It was given."

To her surprise, Nemed laughed a laugh so gleeful it disturbed even his sons. Especially his sons. Aisling's lips parted, baffled. Desperately trying to make sense of her father's broad smile, brighter than any flames she conjured.

"You find this funny?" Aisling asked, tearing herself from the Roktan Prince. But Dagfin's grip lingered on her arm.

"No, not at all," Nemed replied, tears near slipping from his eyes and down his large scar. "I find it remarkable. I find you remarkable."

Aisling searched for the words. "But magic, magic is a perversity of nature. An aberration—"

"Because it was hoarded by the Aos Sí. Withheld, taken, *stolen* from the mortals because of the crimes of a single, foolish queen. That's why it's wrong. Because the Aos Sí and their Gods—for parents always have their favorites—have twisted it, bent it to suit themselves and be used against mankind." Nemed flushed with a strange sort of elation, the pitch in his voice rising the longer he spoke. And at his words, Galad ground his teeth, the desire to behead him and each of his sons swimming amidst the abhorrent sheen of his sapphire eyes, the grip on his sword, the curses he bid them beneath his breath.

"Yet you condemn the Forbidden Lore and all that is the Aos Sí—"

"Aye, aye I do. As should you. As I hope you still do. As our clann should always."

"I don't understand," Aisling confessed, meeting her brothers' distressed expressions. Heads recoiling as their eyes widened at the spectacle of their father *overjoyed*. Opening their mouths to speak but unable to find the words. Galad who stiffened each time Nemed neared Aisling, warily glancing at Dagfin, who never let Aisling out of his sight.

"Magic *is* diabolical at its core. A crooked, unnatural source of power. But with practice, with discipline, order, structure, you can learn to control it. To make it bend to your will. With control, you can use a very wicked thing, Aisling, for good."

"*There is no such thing as good or evil. Only power.*"

Nemed's expression brightened, the stillness of the room framing the frenzy potent in each of his jubilant steps, the wave of his arms, his trembling fingers.

"You're wrong, my daughter," Nemed cupped her face. "This magic was never given to you. You stole it," he said, eyes cutting into her center and prying her open. "You stole it back."

Chapter XXXII

EINRI, CATHAN, RIAN, AND GILREL SURROUNDed Aisling as she approached the tent. Designed to serve as a Great Hall, the canvas bastion was enormous, festively showered and lined with fae and mortal sentinels alike. Guards who eyed the armored bears and boards as much as they did the opposing races flooding into the tent for dinner.

Aisling, full on nearly a gallon of Leshy's tears, inhaled deeply, glancing at both Rian and Gilrel over her shoulder. Shortly after Galad had returned her to her tents, he'd fled in search of Lir and Filverel, leaving Aisling behind with Einri, Cathan, Rian, and Gilrel. The marten nodded her head encouragingly, her armor gleaming beneath the firelight. Equally as impressive as the red-haired knight beside her, dressed in such sleek armor from head to toe.

So, the mortal queen returned her attention to the tent's entrance. The panels of canvas spread apart by the mortal sentinels on either side, widening the maw of the chamber. Within, music roared; fae music, Aisling identified immediately. There would be no mistaking its rhythm, its pace, the sultry melodies that heated the flesh.

Chatter matched the volume of the music, both fae and mortal tongues whispering, gossiping, arguing over one another on their respective sides. For indeed, the fair folk and the mortals divided themselves down the center of the tent, scowling at the other, spitting at one another's feet, cursing one another's names if they met eyes from across the expanse. Even the food was split, meals made by mortal hands spilled over the lengthy tables on the right and those made by fae hands on the left, a precaution, Aisling knew, for despite the treaty, no trust dwelled between their races and poisons were common enough to access in either fae or mortal circles.

But unlike the Great Hall in Annwyn, no one danced in the air here. No wings flapped softly. Flowers didn't hang from the ceilings, nor did birds nor bats lace the edges of the room. No petals carpeted the floor nor did lightning bugs drift aimlessly like lanterns. Instead, guards stood every five or so paces from one another, iron chandeliers hung on thick chains, dripping wax down their candles' necks. The only enchantment alive in this so-called celebration was the music, the revelry of the fair folk.

So, Aisling wove through the dancers, Einri, Cathan, Rian, and Gilrel following distantly behind, smelling the familiar opiate she'd tasted at the *Snaidhm*. That beguiling, seductive spell, spinning her body through the ballooning gowns of the females, the sweat indecently glistening off the males, the stars lowering to join their capering and bathe their bodies in Otherworldly light. Wishing to partake herself, to indulge in their merrymaking as would the fair folk themselves. As they did despite the presence of humans, dulling the corners of the room, attempting and failing to extinguish their frenzy.

Without warning, male hands grabbed Aisling. Twirled her to the beat of the music, quickening to the pace of her pulse. Aisling spun and met familiar, pearly eyes.

Filverel.

He grinned, flashing his fangs unapologetically as he moved with her to the rhythm of the cords. Joy bubbled into the air with every string they plucked, every flute they blew, every drum they beat. She didn't know how to sway, to step, to match the energy as did the fair folk but it mattered little when such melodies lowered her inhibitions.

"I overheard there was an accidental fire in the High King's private chambers," the advisor purred, bringing her nearer until they were chest to chest. "One of his candles tipped over onto a pile of parchment. Tragic. Could've ended his life right then and there. How ..."—Filverel licked his teeth—*"poetic."*

Aisling stifled her annoyance.

"Careful what you speak," Aisling bit, "lest you manifest a similar fire in your own chambers tonight." For despite the anger she harbored towards her father, her tuath, her family, she wouldn't tolerate others speaking ill of him or wishing his demise. He was still her father. Once her High King.

"Is that a threat, *mo Lúra?*" He asked, eyes glittering with amusement.

"If you have to ask, it most likely is," Aisling quipped. She copied the movement of the fae females around her, studying the way they moved their hips, swung their arms, tossed their shimmering manes. Their every graceful, effortless movement was unique and dream-like.

Filverel laughed. *"Fearlies mern es na tu eas tresle hangus lao."*

Aisling's brows drew together. "What does that mean?"

"In that gown, you look as lethal as a nightmare and as feral as the dreams that follow." The advisor's moonstone eyes flashed wildly, studying her reaction.

"Is that a compliment?" Aisling asked and her voice bore the confidence she didn't yet feel.

"If you have to ask, it most likely is." He spun her three times, bringing her back towards himself at the song's cue. "It must be the magic, rippling through you, torching every mortal bone of yours each time you summon the *draiocht* or in your case, each time it summons you," Filverel lifted her into the air, lowering her in time for the pounding of animal skins. "With every flame you craft, a bit of your mortal self dies, doesn't it?"

Aisling recoiled, glaring at the fae advisor in horror. That wasn't true. No, it couldn't be. He was punishing her for revealing her abilities to the Fire Hand. Torturing her in a way he knew every word would carve through her muscles and into her heart.

"In fact, we can only begin to guess Nemed's next steps now that he's aware his daughter is his fleets' salvation. His very own child imbued with the essence of the enemy yet a wielder of his own hot poison."

"Fear doesn't become you, Filverel."

"And here again you sound like a mortal. Fear is useful: keeps the prey alive when the cards are seemingly stacked against them."

"Seemingly?" Aisling asked.

"There's a reason humans can no longer harness the *draiocht*. By nature, humans are greedier than either goblins or dragons, more spiteful than either banshees or brownies, and more naive than the Sidhe who choose to trust any one of them. The *draiocht* tasted your weakness and so, it conquered you. So, although the Fire Hand may have his tricks, I'm not concerned over whether he's aware of your abilities." Filverel licked his fangs and grinned. "After all, no one wants an arrow just as capable of shooting backwards as it is frontwards."

But Aisling had witnessed the hunger in her father's eyes, the joy when he'd beheld her use the *draiocht*. Knew the Fire Hand never bore merely one method of achieving his goals. And if any believed him to be as naive or as one-dimensional as Filverel believed him to be, they'd be made aware of such fatal assumptions soon enough.

"Hold your tongue, Filverel, lest I burn it from your mouth."

"I'd remind you whose allegiance you're bound to but then I realize your loyalties are tragically divided, aren't they? No, don't answer that. Answer this." Filverel smiled, snatching Aisling once more and elegantly dipping the mortal queen so her hair swept the grass beneath them. "If given the choice to return to your clann, would you?" he asked, unable to resist the cruel laughter that followed.

Bile rose in Aisling's throat as she desperately ignored the *draiocht* already reaching for more. Even when Leshy's tears still did their best to heal its damage.

"I can be both. I don't need to choose."

"No, Aisling," Filverel said, pulling her in close, "we may not know what you are: mortal princess, sorceress, *skalla*. But regardless of whatever the Gods are brewing in the Forge, you're part Seelie now whether you realize it or not."

Aisling's throat ran dry. He knew he'd caught her. A satisfaction she detested to witness him boast. As if the cleaving of her personal identity were entertainment to him.

But before Aisling could respond or stay true to her threats, the music changed, and the partners rotated. And so, another male grabbed her, spinning her towards him. Aisling thought to leave the dance altogether until she smelled this new dancer, the salt of the Ashild churning beneath a grey-clad sky.

Aisling's eyes darted towards her partner, glaring up at oceans for eyes. Eyes that cut into her and tore apart any resolve Filverel had hardened with his aggression.

"I don't have much time," Dagfin whispered, those shadows he'd grown over the years they'd been apart, thick and heavy as he spoke. "I know you're still angry with me, but I need you to listen closely."

"Lest you bridle me like a beast?"

Dagfin flinched as though he'd been physically struck, his brows drawing together. And the pain Aisling saw written across his expression threatened to undo her rage. A fact she cursed herself for.

"I was wrong not to tell you. I should've told you

everything as soon as I discovered the truth for myself. I regret not doing so and you can despise me for an eternity if you wish so long as you listen to me now."

The urgency in his voice caught Aisling off guard, startling her as the pace of their dance slowed. The Roktan Prince spun her on her heel—the feeling of him so close, the hardness of his chest, the sensation of his every breath against her neck, his heartbeat hammering against her ear as she turned to look up at him.

"Very well," Aisling surrendered, a slave to the bond they shared as children.

Dagfin released a breath of relief, guiding her through the rest of the dance. The music, the uproar, the laughter of the fair folk, cloaking their conversation from prying ears. Einri, Rian, Gilrel, Galad, Filverel, even Peitho, eying them through the crowds. And Aisling was certain there were others who watched as well, those she couldn't see and dared not search for.

"It was some years ago I was held captive in Lofgren's rise."

"Lofgren's rise?" Aisling repeated, quickly shushed by the Roktan Prince.

Lofgren's rise slumbered oceans away, a mountain range far into the wilderness of a foreign country whose mortal king was near as bloodthirsty as the fair folk themselves.

"What could've possibly taken you to Lofgren's rise?" Aisling hissed.

"There was an Unseelie I encountered whilst hunting for dwarven thieves near Giant's Causeway. A lady. She told me of a curse breaker, Ash. One that could give your father all he's ever craved, to restore the mortals' former glory and reclaim what the fair folk stole from us."

"That's impossible."

"I believed so too until I discovered exactly what lie within Lofgren's rise: a three-eyed owl and a weapon of unmatched power. Ina's gifts from the Gods."

"You're wrong. Ina never received a weapon as did the other fae sovereigns. Only Sight."

"A lie told by the Aos Sí to prevent the mortals from discovering a cure for Ina's curse existed at all."

"And you've seen this weapon with your own eyes?"

Dagfin hesitated, pulling her nearer to him as the song dissolved. "No. Never with my own eyes. Those mountains, Ash, are more heavily guarded than any fortress known to man or Aos Sí. They're hiding something and I believe that Unseelie when she tells me it's the curse breaker."

Aisling's mind spun, eyes darting between Dagfin's own.

"And what's more, the Unseelie who spoke to me, spoke of a mage. A witch. A sorceress. Words I didn't understand until I witnessed what you were capable of. Ash, if you truly don't understand what's happened to you, the answers may lie in Lofgren's rise. I need only take you there."

Aisling searched his expression for although the Sidhe couldn't lie, mortals could and did often. But what she found wasn't mischief or deception or trickery. It was hope. And if Dagfin was correct and answers indeed lie in Lofgren's rise, who Aisling was, why she obtained the *draiocht*, who she was becoming—Aisling couldn't refuse such an offer.

Lir would never allow it unless he journeyed with her. But Aisling knew his inevitable pursuit and race for the curse breaker would undermine her voyage.

"That's not possible," Aisling blurted, but the song was ending and Lir's knights were swiftly approaching. "You're to wed Peitho tomorrow and if you don't"—she hesitated, unable to speak the words aloud—"if you choose the correct blade, you'll be wed to a member of the Sidhe. The quest you speak of will be as improbable for you as it already is for me."

Dagfin reeled, baffled.

"In case you've forgotten, I've gotten us out of far more trouble before. I can do it again and again if that's what you ask of me, Aisling."

"Facing our fathers' wrath when we misbehaved somehow seems far preferable than toying with political unions on the cusp of reigniting worldwide feuds."

But even as Aisling spoke it, she felt the strange exhilaration of perhaps freeing herself the Sidhe's dominion.

Dagfin smiled, remembering the infinite examples of such misbehavior.

"Trust me, Ash. I'll find a way. I always do."

And with that, Dagfin released her, disappearing into the crowd of revelers.

Before the night was devoured by the rising sun, a council was to be held in a private extension of the Great Hall. And as if entering another realm, the music grew muffled by the canvas curtains, the light dimmer, and the room smaller.

At the center of the chamber, sat a round table surrounded by large, wooden chairs. Several places were already set, goblets filled to the brim. Human and fae sentinels alike stood around the circumference of the room; among them Aisling recognized Hagre, Aedh, and Tyr. Gilrel was the only bipedal beast in attendance, perhaps to not shock the mortals more than was necessary.

The other mortal sovereigns had yet to arrive, so Aisling, Lir, Galad, Filverel, and Peitho chose their seats. Aisling did her best to capture Lir's attention, but he evaded her. Standing near or watching from afar, but never allowing for a moment with her alone.

Gilrel placed herself behind Aisling's chair. A position closest to the exits should Aisling struggle to temper her *draiocht* once more. For now, that Nemed was aware of her abilities, none were certain what to expect of either him or the rest of the mortal sovereigns. And because the Fire Hand knew, Filverel was even more irritable than usual, his tongue sharper than any sword forged by either fae or mortal hands.

"Although the damage has already been dealt, refrain from expressing your *draiocht, mo Lúra*,"—Filverel's voice was as smooth as cream, but by now Aisling knew the venom it carried—"lest you slaughter every monarch in Rinn Dúin. Sidhe or human."

"You're in a bad temper, Fil," Galad taunted him, sipping the mortal wine, his smile vanishing the moment the liquid touched his tongue. He grimaced, setting the glass back down. "Don't try the wine. It'll only worsen your mood."

Both Filverel and Peitho opened their mouths to speak, but before they could utter a word, the curtains opened.

Aisling held her breath, watching the silhouette of a crowned man duck into their private extension. And once he was far enough into the room, the candlelight illuminated his features, gilding him.

Fínín Ó Bairr, the Bregganite King of the Southernmost Isle. Dressed in decadent robes, a bronze circlet sat upon his white head of hair. Hair that fanned around his shoulders and down his back, matching the impressive length of his beard. Two boars charging one another, embroidered across the Kinbreggan crest and sewn into his robes.

Lir, Filverel, and Galad rose from their chairs, so Aisling followed suit, unsure what the protocol for her role entailed. Peitho remained seated but perhaps that was because she was no queen yet. Only a princess until she married a mortal prince. Until she married Dagfin. Aisling shuddered.

He tipped his head towards Lir, meeting the Fae King's eyes. But before Fínín took his seat, his eyes flickered towards Aisling, flashing with something Aisling couldn't identify: fear? Uncertainty? Loathing? Nemed had already debriefed the other mortal chieftains on her newfound *draiocht*.

Feradach entered next, King of both Roktling and of the

most formidable naval fleets known to man; mortal soldiers who fought the aquatic Sidhe, merrows like Sakaala, Aisling now realized.

He wore an iron, naval crown surmounted with small replicas of Roktan ships, ships Dagfin had pointed out to Aisling off the coast of Roktling. Indeed, Feradach was a near mirror image of his son—stormy eyes, the same tousle of brown hair perfectly suited to bear a crown; only now Feradach's was speckled with white on either side. And as if Aisling had thought him into existence, Peitho snapped an ivory fork between her fingers, prompting Dagfin's entrance.

Both the Roktan King and Prince bowed curtly, their faces taut with severity. But Dagfin didn't so much as look at the Fae King. Instead, he locked eyes with Aisling. Eyes that Aisling now understood why they'd appeared so different from the boy she'd once known—there was violence there. Shards of the Faerak gauntlet.

"Aisling," he greeted her and only her. So as the Roktan Prince took his seat beside his father, Aisling didn't dare meet Lir's eyes. She didn't need to. She could feel the ire tightening his every muscle, darkening the room like a storm cloud. But to Aisling's surprise, Lir grinned, a terrifying sight to behold given the anger she felt brewing.

Aisling herself was irate with the Roktan Prince. For although she understood why he'd detained her, there was little that could forgive the stifling weight of iron trapping and choking her magic. Her temper was briefly distracted by the information he'd smuggled during their dance. The only grain of reconciliation between them, but to Aisling's horror she didn't trust him. The bond she'd once believed they shared was a ruse.

The Lady of Aithirn, Ciar, entered, dressed in an ivory gown, arm linked with her son. Aisling had met the Aithirnian Prince several times before: Sim Mac Dara. A boy whose pale, white hair rivalled not only his country's banners and flags but also the shade of his own mother's twisted locks. His once carefree jubilance was dulled by the realities of adulthood: war and the weight of knowing he'd one day be king. But only once his mother died. For in Aithirn, succession of the crown was performed after the death of a monarch and no sooner.

The two paid their respects to Lir and Aisling, light eyes falling on Peitho as had all the rest before them. The Aithirnian Queen regarded her with palpable disgust. Peitho's expression crooked with a contempt that rivalled Ciar's. That rivalled Clodagh's as she entered beside Friseal, Nemed a step behind, a Fire Hand who grinned from ear to ear, his ruby crown winking in the candlelight.

Starn, Iarbonel, Annind, and Fergus entered last, Starn and Galad locking eyes briefly before each brother took their seats in silence. And silence is what persisted for what felt like an eternity. The pouring of wine a crash in the quiet.

Aisling wondered then how often those who sat around this table had met face to face when not painted in one another's blood or on a battlefield. When they'd exchanged glances without a blade between them. But here they all sat, around a sole table, served the same spirits and lit by the same fires. Centuries of war, of violence, of burnt forests and ransacked villages, vegetating thickly in the silence, in the breath they all shared.

Chapter XXXIII

"IS THIS THE FAE WHORE OUR BELOVED PRINCE is to marry?" Ciar's pale eyes were sharp enough to cut.

Fergus choked on the fae lamb's leg he'd dived into, he and Galad the only ones interested in devouring their meals rather than nudging it with their ivory forks like the rest of them. Not that the fair folk used such utensils.

"I recognize her," Ciar continued, sliding her naked nails down the edge of her plate. "She was amongst those who pillaged Aithirn's Townsends when I was but a child. Although I must admit, her face has changed now that it's no longer painted with the purpled guts of my people."

"I'm glad you remember me so fondly," Peitho simpered, "and I you: the cowering princess shrieking till I nearly believed your fat head might pop. But please, now that we're on familiar terms, please refer to me as the Princess of Niltaor and mercenary for the Southern Sidhe armies."

Ciar hardened into stone, the only life in her otherwise still form was the loathing churning around her pupils as a single white curl fell from her tightly coiled braids.

"My name is Dagfin," the Roktan Prince piped, startling Ciar. He stood from his seat and bowed. "It's an honor, princess. I look forward to our union and the change it'll presage."

Peitho didn't move. Didn't so much as uncross her arms as she met his eyes. It was difficult to tell what the fae princess was thinking. Even Aisling wasn't entirely sure what to make of his greeting. The way he considered Peitho long after he'd taken his seat.

"Are you certain this is what you want Nemed?" Lir asked, leaning back in his chair as his ringed fingers toyed with the stem of his goblet.

"I was the one who requested another interracial union, wasn't I? It's for the best of both our kinds that we continue to blend our worlds. We won't know true harmony until that's a reality," Nemed said, the scar along his face still bright red from the excitement earlier on in the night.

"I don't think you've fully grasped just how rare the success of the first union was," Filverel interjected, brushing one of his white braids over his shoulder. "What you're asking for could incite more war should it not unravel the way you intend."

And what were the odds, Aisling thought to herself, that the Forge had knotted not one but two interracial unions by the same thread?

"You refer to the bonds you believe certain couples bear while others don't," Friseal spoke up. Aisling, alarmed by the familiarity of his voice, whipped her attention towards him. Her childhood tutor shot her a quick glance before focusing on Filverel once more. "We're aware of your customs. Whether we agree with them or not is another matter entirely."

"You can condemn our ways all you like but at the end of the day it'll be your prince's head rolling towards your feet."

"Savages!" Ciar stood from her seat, hands balled into fists. "You shall not touch him!"

"Sit down, Ciar," Nemed commanded. "We each agreed to this union knowing it was a risk. To build and foster a new age between man and Sidhe, sacrifices will be made, challenges faced, and risks waged. This shouldn't come as a surprise." The Fire Hand opened his arms wide, gesturing towards every mortal sovereign, flaith, and advisor seated around the table.

"Now, on to topics that haven't been overly digested," Nemed continued, ignoring Ciar as she slowly took back her seat. "Whilst we've agreed to this gamble of yours, a loss would indeed be disastrous." Nemed took a bite of red meat. "So, in order to ensure our gamble is worth this possibility, we ask for more in return: an offer of 'good faith' on behalf of the Sidhe."

Lir smiled casually at the Fire Hand, the image of cool, easy arrogance.

"What is it you want, Nemed?" The Fae King asked outright and as he spoke the tips of his fangs scraped his bottom lip. A detail neither Ciar nor Clodagh missed for their complexions paled.

"Your Unseelie are growing bolder, inching their way towards our villages, towns, cities, and, worst of all, our capitals. There are even those who've dared to scale our walls, breaching mortal territory. If I recall correctly, the terms of your union promised the Unseelie would abstain from preying upon our kind lest a human venture into their land. That was the agreement, so why hasn't it been upheld?"

"Isn't that why you have the Faerak?" Lir said coolly, "or are they as useless as they sound?"

A muscle flickered across Dagfin's jaw but he kept himself composed, stilling the ivory knives he perpetually spun between his fingers. And as a mortal barmaid scuttled around the table nervously, filling chalices with more ale, mead, wine, and ciders, Dagfin covered the top of his glass with his hand, refusing any alcohol for the second time that night.

"The closer the Unseelie venture into our borders— wyverns, golems, ogres, and selkies—the more they rouse suspicion," Finín said, his voice gravelly and aged. "There's already talk amongst our peoples that the fair folk and the

Unseelie are"—he considered for a moment, carefully searching for the correct words—"due a categorical separation."

"So, your lies are slipping through the cracks in your hands?" Aisling challenged, her heart pounding the moment the words fell from her lips, "tell the subjects you claim to adore the truth of who and what either the fair folk and Unseelie are. Print the Forbidden Lore for them to decide for themselves what they believe, what to think of the Gods."

Fínín glared at Aisling, an expression designed to melt the flesh from her bones.

"It appears your daughter has stolen more than just their *magic*," he spat across the table and as he did Aisling felt Lir darkening beside her. "She's adopted their boorish tongues as well."

"Settle down, Fínín. Aisling is an equal amongst the northern sovereigns now. Refrain from speaking to her with such disrespect," Feradach, King of Roktling, chided.

Over the years, Aisling had built a close relationship with Feradach. For one day, they'd all believed he'd be her father-in-law. A relationship that, although never concluded the way she'd anticipated, she was grateful for now.

"You speak of respect, Feradach?!" Ciar's complexion flushed with such potent acidity it soured the air around her. "She's no queen if all she's done is open her legs to the Aos Sí. I'd rather choke than honor her with such a title."

Aisling gripped the arms of her chair, willing the *draiocht* contained. But she wasn't the one imbuing the air with magic.

Amidst the silence, the Lady of Aithirn did choke; eyes like saucers, she gagged before erupting into a fit of useless coughs.

The table hesitated, confusion muddling every mortal mind.

"What do you think you're doing just standing there?! Get her some water!" Fínín barked at the barmaid, the sentinels, any who would listen.

But what began as one or two small coughs grew into a frenzy, the Aithirnian Queen standing from her seat, spilling Nemed's mead on Clodagh's lap, and clawing at her throat. Sim desperately slapped her back. But it wasn't until leaves spewed from her mouth, combined with her own saliva that all shook with horror. Thorns, small weeds and verdant grasses, even flower buds spat from between the Aithirnian Queen's shriveled lips.

"Speaking of boorish tongues," Lir purred, blithely cracking his neck from side to side.

And as the lianas fell onto the table, writhing like worms, Friseal whacked them with his fork.

"By the Forge," Iarbonel cursed, as each of his brothers fell out of their chairs and staggered back, weapons uselessly drawn.

"Make it stop!" Sim shouted, his voice cracking mid-sentence. But none could expel the enchantment save for the Fae King. For even the mortal guards and Dagfin knelt beside Ciar now; no potions, no weapons, no iron available could dampen Lir's *draiocht*.

"This is a direct offence to a mortal crown!" Finín boomed.

"I believe it was the Aithirnian Queen who initially began the offences," Filverel couldn't help but exhale a laugh, downing the last gulps of water from his glass.

Lir grinned murderously, leaning back in his chair. "I suggest you give the Queen of the Sidhe her due respect, lest your wish be granted."

All, now standing, turned to the Aithirnian Queen, hopelessly choking, panicking, her saliva rapidly dyed red. But Lir didn't move, didn't flinch, patiently waited until, at last, Ciar fell onto her knees. Until at last she pressed her nose against the Centari carpets beneath them and bowed to Aisling. Clodagh gasping with disgust or relief, Aisling couldn't tell.

"That wasn't so difficult," Lir said, and the Aithirnian Queen heaved a clear breath, congested no more.

Five or so mortal sentinels escorted Ciar from the council after Sim agreed to be her voice for the remainder of the night. But no mortal guard, advisor, flaith, queen, or king dared unleash their eyes from Lir. Every twitch of his lips, every smooth movement, every flick of his eyes, beneath their scrutiny.

"I'm willing to excuse your use of enchantments for now, *Damh Bán*, but another spell and my patience will've been exhausted," Nemed casually called the horrified barmaid over, gesturing for her to pour him another drink, frowning when she spilled cider across his plate.

Lir laughed but there was no humor in it. A sound that sent shivers down Aisling's spine and for a moment, she believed even her father hesitated at its cadence.

"By all means, lose your composure"—the corners of Lir's lips curled up—"as you mentioned earlier, it was you who requested this union. So, I suggest, High King, that lest this union slip through your mortal fingers, you avoid exhausting my patience and provoking me once more."

Aisling's stomach clenched; the dark authority the Fae King exuded effortlessly spread throughout the tent like ivy. Wrapping around all that it touched and squeezing till it tasted every dissenting breath and smothered it.

Nemed smoldered as he tipped his glass back, too proud to release the Fae King from his gaze.

"That won't be necessary," Feradach spoke up, "besides I'm more interested in the current stability of your relationship with the Unseelie, *Damh Bán*." All eyes turned towards the Roktan King.

"You see, I own over one thousand vessels spread throughout the Ashild and beyond. Every crewmate, captain, every stow away aware of those creatures that lurk in the deep. No one is ignorant to the risks of sea voyage, especially considering the territory lines, the walls, the divisions between Seelie, Unseelie, and mortal worlds that exist on land, are impossible to build or mark in the oceans. Unseelie encounters are, therefore, near inescapable at sea. But in the past several months, every one of my ships has had an encounter. Masts ripped to shreds, freightage lost, men either drowned or devoured, and entire carriers nothing more than splinters."

"Is there a specific Unseelie committing the aggressions or several?" Filverel asked, leaning to one side in his chair.

"You didn't answer my question," Feradach countered, a flash of irritation cutting across the Roktan King's bronzed features.

"You must first ask a question before it's to be answered, Your Grace," Peitho chimed.

Feradach levelled his temper. "Has your relationship with the Unseelie changed since Aisling's union or not?"

"Yes," Lir said rather bluntly, reminding Aisling of what he'd once told her:

"You believe we lie? It's possible but difficult for us. To tell a mistruth requires great concentration and even then, it is poorly told."

But Aisling was familiar with how cunning the Sidhe could be. How clever the Sidhe were regardless of their inability to outwardly lie.

"The Unseelie are chaotic in nature. For the most part, they lack moral dependency. Like the undomesticated animals and beasts your kind is familiar with, the Unseelie respond to social and instinctual cues far more than even the Sidhe. The chemistry and dynamics of a pack, a herd, a colony, a nest." Lir stretched his fingers, curled them in, then repeated the motion. The veins that protruded on the back of his hands near spellbinding to the mortal queen.

"Take away their food source, take away the hunt for your kind—hammered into their bones by the Forge—and they'll react, do anything in their power to steal it all back, beg their king to forsake the treaty. Devour the very princess who made such a union possible." All eyes shot towards Aisling. For indeed the trow, the Cú Scáth, the Fomorians had all attempted.

"Or," Lir continued, licking his fangs, "find another monarch powerful enough to seize their losses: the destroying of boundaries and the lawless, uninhibited hunting of mortals. Someone more aligned with their chaos than even the Sidhe."

The mortal sovereigns exchanged glances, as if speaking telepathically so none of the Sidhe nor Aisling could understand. And as the last words left Lir's lips, Filverel's entire form tensed. As if he'd deigned for his King to speak the truth, the whole truth. And for what reason? Lir cared little for his relationship with the mortals other than ensuring the benefits it awarded him. So, Aisling could only assume that the truth would get Lir whatever it was he desired.

"And is there another? One who is stronger, more powerful than you?" Sim asked, his pale hair falling into his eyes.

"No," Lir said simply, his axes catching the light of the fire. "Never has there been. Never will there be."

Aisling's skin shivered at his words. A flock of silver-eyed ravens flapping madly within her belly.

"The Unseelie then," the Bregganite King interjected. "They retaliate against your authority, Sidhe law, rejecting your sovereignty now that it no longer benefits them?"

Lir swallowed his annoyance, Aisling knew by the tightening of his jaw, silently nodding his head in response.

"What now, *Damh Bán*?" Nemed asked. "Our treaty explicitly agreed to new conditions amongst our kind, to the end of war, the burning of forests and Sidhe villages. All in exchange for the ceasing of Sidhe and Unseelie violence towards mankind lest they venture into your respective lands. Only then would such an agreement be revoked. But now, it appears your own kingdom turns their bloodlust against you, threatens to dethrone the *Damh Bán*, and the mortals suffer regardless of our alliance. I didn't exchange my daughter for nothing, and you've been unsuccessful in upholding your end of the deal."

"Negotiations with the Unseelie are still ongoing," Galad said.

"And how many more of my men, my ships, will be lost while you negotiate?" Feradach raised his voice, losing patience.

"Is it just me or does it appear more and more as if the Faerak truly are useless?" Peitho's lips curled, eyes fluttering mockingly in the Roktan Prince's direction.

But Dagfin didn't take the bait. "The Faerak hunt and slaughter the Unseelie to protect mortals and their livelihoods. Not to remedy the mistakes of Sidhe Kings." He met Peitho's smirk with a smug expression of his own, staking his knife into the table.

"Did you really believe the new law would be successful instantaneously?" Lir challenged. "That from the moment Aisling and I were handfasted, peace would reign throughout the land?" The Fae King scoffed. "I've been alive for three centuries now. Change—reformation is slow. Often painful. Heeds no man nor Sidhe nor Unseelie. Doesn't bow to the death of mortal sailors. You all knew the sacrifices, the lengths the treaty would demand before it was perfected. And perfection—even after your descendants rule, after death has claimed your frail hearts and you rot beneath the earth you burned, when I still rule—perfection will be far from within our grasp."

Nemed placed two fingers to his lips, considering for a moment. Just a moment before his mouth stretched into a cruel grin. One Aisling had witnessed on only a handful of occasions.

"Very well, *Damh Bán*," the Fire Hand spoke slowly,

indulging in every word. "The Mortal Sovereigns of Rinn Dúin will give you three years to adjust your leadership." At this, Clodagh immediately whipped her head to face her husband. Disbelief softened her sharp angles. "And if there has been no change in three years' time, consider the treaty null and void."

Aisling felt the *draiocht* pinch her fingertips. Aisling had sacrificed everything. Been traded like livestock only for Nemed to suggest negating it all. To threaten the treaty's nullification. To disband and render meaningless all she'd been through in the name of such a union. And here her father dangled it above the Fae King, as if it were another means to get what he wanted. Just as Aisling had always been.

Lir's anger matched Aisling's own, tightening his fists. The flaring of his nostrils as cold rage enveloped him. Terror thrumming through the room at the sight of his fingers moving. Dreading, anticipating the mad release of more magic.

"And before you make any rash decisions, *Damh Bán*," Nemed continued, relishing in the Fae King's vexation his words inspired, "in return for the advice you've just lent me, here is my own token of knowledge perhaps you've already become well acquainted with in your centuries." The Fire Hand took another large swig of wine. "The sins of the father often become the sins of the son. Passed down generation after generation. Growing more potent. The only curse breaker"—the last word like honey on his iron tongue—"the son who is strong enough to resist such sin. Such desire. But in your case, *Damh Bán*"—Nemed grinned—"I suppose it's the mother's sins you should be wary of repeating."

Chapter XXXIV

AISLING CLOSED HER EYES.

"There are few pleasures greater than having one's hair combed," Clodagh had once told a far younger Aisling, glaring at her daughter in the reflection of the mirror as her lady's maid tended to her tangled ringlets. And indeed, the sensation of Gilrel pulling a glass brush against the mortal queen's scalp was beyond pleasurable.

Gilrel's magpies busily organized the pins and ribbons she'd worn that night, tucking them away into small, colorfully painted clay pots. That same dreamy mist clouded the tent as it had on Aisling's wedding night, relaxing her as she smoothed out the skirts of her loose-fitted chemise.

It wasn't long before Aisling lay alone in the dark, swathed in both plush quilts, furs, and blankets but also the distant drawl of the festivities still burning the night away. The Aos Sí could dance for hours. Were more alive when stars hovered resplendently above.

One by one, Gilrel had extinguished the soft light warmly cooing within the surrounding flower buds: ample garlands draping the ceiling of the tent, her vanity, and speckling the floor with both petals and leaves alike. Until there was nothing but darkness. Black and the angry swarm of thoughts that kept

Aisling an arm's reach away from sleep. For tomorrow, either Peitho would be wed to the Roktan Prince or Dagfin would've passed on to the Other. Not to mention, Aisling feared her father's knowledge of her abilities would change the course of the future. Had Danu foreseen all of this? Did the Empress know what was to become of tomorrow?

Aisling rolled onto her side.

Still, she hadn't managed a moment alone with the Fae King. He eluded her, constantly immersed in more hushed conversations with Filverel and his knights. A fact that enraged Aisling for she too wished to understand, to know what the Sidhe planned, thought, argued if she were to live amongst them. But still, none trusted her. Still, she was a foreigner, a foreigner to all lands for she was seemingly the only one of her kind, a mortal able to wield the *draiocht*. Not quite human and not quite Sidhe.

Aisling stirred restlessly, waiting for Lir to enter but as the moon sipped the midnight hours, he never did. It wasn't until Aisling heard a bizarre hissing that she leapt from her sheets to peer at the creature. A small, black snake glared up at her from the grassy carpets below.

However, the serpent wasted no time, meeting Aisling's eyes before slithering back beneath the tent and into the outside world.

This way, it hissed as the last of its scales disappeared beneath the canvas.

Aisling didn't think twice, grabbing a cloak Gilrel had packed and rushing towards the entrance to her tent.

There were six or so sentinels guarding where she slept. And so, it occurred to Aisling: if these bipedal beasts were ordered to ensure none enter nor she leave her tent unescorted, which was most likely the reality, it was near impossible for Aisling to escape her chambers unnoticed.

Aisling stopped in her tracks, biting her bottom lip. There was an urgency hammering away within her. More than the snake encouraging her to follow. A tugging, a pulling that motivated Aisling onward.

So, the mortal queen concentrated, eyes darting about the room for an answer. But the answer came in the form of one of the sentinel's screams of agony. Aisling leapt at the sound, hurrying to the front entrance. And, from the thread-thin opening, she witnessed each of her guards drawing their weapons and leaping to the aid of he who was injured, cursing in Rún. He'd been bit. Attacked by a serpent who still snapped its fangs at any who dared approach next.

Aisling thought no more of it. She ran. Slipping past her chamber's threshold and into the night. Her cloak wrapped around her like the wings of a bat for she wasn't quite free yet. The Sidhe camp lit still with revelry, Sidhe dancing drunkenly between their tents, singing and chasing one another towards their individual rooms. Perhaps it was the stupor of their magic, the veil of night, or the fact none cared to search for a mortal queen who was not yet determined missing from her tent, but none noticed Aisling as she swept past them, a shadow bedizened with violet eyes.

And because Aisling wasn't certain where she was going, she listened to the rustling trees. For they spoke loudly tonight, debating amongst themselves, arguing, writhing back and forth as if amidst some great council. Indeed, once Aisling stepped between the oaks and the ash and the elms, they hushed themselves, each turning to get a good look at the mortal queen who'd interrupted their conversation.

Aisling wandered deeper than she'd ever dared wander alone before, her bare feet pricked by sharp stones, thorns, and splintering branches, wondering if this had all been a mistake. If she should return now before any discovered that she no longer slept well-protected—or imprisoned—by her guards. But it was then she spotted him.

Lir stood within a ring of trees of yore.

The gloom of evening cast the spectacle Aisling beheld in

shades of oblivion. A film of grim enchantment bathing the Fae King as the trees craned their great bodies towards him, groaning and reaching their branches to crown his head. As eager as the pools of fog crawling across the forest floor and running their wispy fingers along the contours of his hands, his arms, his legs. He, the heart of the woodland.

Aisling sat frozen, crouched behind a boulder, the gnawing sensation that her presence here was deeply forbidden quickening the pace of her heart. For the Fae King was confiding in this greenwood and they him. Speaking, listening, a language of arcane and bygone magic clotting the breath they all shared. So thick, Aisling could taste it on her tongue. Taste as the Fae King tasted the sap of these agrestal guardians. There was a darkness inherent within this spectacle. No, not darkness—a primal strength that surpassed mortal understanding of light and dark, righteous and unrighteous. It simply *was* and wished to *be* and would destroy all that wasn't.

"You're hurt."

Lir's voice echoed throughout the labyrinth. Aisling's heart seized at the sound of it, forgetting to breathe as all the forest whipped their attention towards her, whispering amongst themselves.

Lir's words rung true. Aisling's feet bled from the undergrowth, a reminder that despite her ability to wield the *draiocht* she was indeed still human or, at the very least, part human. For the natural world continued to reject her. Threatened her life with the ruthlessness of its keep, with infection, with pain, and suffering should she not protect herself with manmade crafts.

Lir having not moved, his back turned to her, had somehow known it was his bride hidden amidst the shadows. Had the trees given her away? The stones? The insects? The rodents scampering in the periphery?

Nevertheless he, at last, moved to face her.

Despite the black of night, the Fae King's feline eyes glittered. Shone with a predatory hunger that struck deep and unadulterated fear within Aisling, slipping through her veins in icy currents, frosting her bones and paling her complexion.

Wordlessly, the Fae King approached her. As nimble and quiet as a fox, never once releasing her from his gaze. And as though he'd bespelled her, Aisling was paralyzed. Nothing but the lurching of her heart as she fought to steady her breath, the drum of it echoing in the hollows of her ears. He moved nearer, the intangible string tightening between them, knotting deep in her abdomen and heating.

Aisling held her captor's regard, glaring up at emeralds for eyes. Absolute green pulsing with the spirit of the forest. Cutting into her and tearing her apart.

"You've been avoiding me." Her voice was mulled wine, nearly another's voice and not her own.

"Because you wield strange and cruel magic against me. You being near to me alone makes it difficult to think clearly."

There was something different about him, Aisling knew immediately; red circles rimmed his eyes and the anxious hunger that prowled there. The image of a starved wolf whose appetite made it desperate, manic, and truly mad. The glint in his fully dilated eyes was both bewitching and chilling all at once. The way he eyed the idle curls blowing across her face as if he wished to pull them away. To touch her but wouldn't allow himself. He was a physical manifestation of the energy Aisling felt coursing deep within him, the blackest shadows of the forest Forged into flesh.

"I hunted for you," he said, his voice as smooth as milk and as thick as blood. A harbinger of Sakaala's lawless magic. Charms Aisling found she admired. Understood and wished to harness herself.

"You believed me dead?"

A muscle flashed across Lir's jaw, his expression darkening.

"I believed you lost." Lost at the bottom of the Forge where Racat hoarded her bones.

"It hardly matters. We're both aware my death or my gone missing would prove beneficial to the Sidhe either way. No longer would you be bound to the fury of either Unseelie or mortal."

Lir considered her, narrowing his eyes.

"There was a time your death would've been gladly dealt by my hands."

"A time before or after I was proven to be the second *caera* your mother prepared you for?"

Lir reacted sharply to the word "mother," baring his teeth as he moved closer yet.

"Even then I considered it, watched you as you slept, convincing myself a dagger to your heart would prevent me—"

"From committing the same mistakes as your mother? From destroying your kingdom in order to preserve the breath of your"—Aisling tripped over her own words—"your superstitions."

"'Superstitions,'" Lir laughed, shaking his head. "You will always stand against the Sidhe and, with each day I do not kill you, the threat your breath symbolizes grows more powerful. Hangs more thickly over my head. For if it weren't only for the fact you undermined the Unseelie by handfasting me, but now you wield a weapon whose very nature heralds the end of our kind. An end I cannot allow."

Aisling shook her head.

"You live in fear, Lir, and it will eat you alive if you allow it."

"No, I live in the past, afraid to either fail you as I did Narisea, as I nearly did at the Isle of Mirrors, or commit the same crimes as my mother in your name. To either fail to protect you or fail to kill you."

Aisling bit her bottom lip, drawing blood. Her heart aching as though he'd indeed impaled her at her core.

"And now I'm found, alive and wreaking havoc on the alliance we both sacrificed to uphold."

"Did you intend to reveal your abilities to your father?" Lir asked, searching every twitch of her expression for signs of betrayal. Filverel must've done his best to convince the Fae King Aisling had indeed intentionally exposed the *draiocht* to the Fire Hand. But that was a lie. and the truth was far more concerning.

"No," Aisling said honestly, schooling her expression. "I lost control. I did my best to resist the *draiocht*. To ignore its begging and manage my emotions. Despite how it clawed and scratched and raved within me. But somehow," Aisling hesitated, gathering herself as her eyes burned with the memory. "Somehow the *draiocht* emerged without my permission. Held me prisoner and commanded me not to breathe."

For if anyone knew how to help Aisling gain control, to understand, to master her magic, it would be Lir. He'd taught her how to summon it and now he could teach her how to expel it.

"Will you teach me to master it? Control it? *If* indeed you wish for me to live with such magic and not die with it for the sake of Annwyn."

Slowly, the Fae King held her chin, tilting her face up, so she drowned more thoroughly in his sage pools.

He didn't answer her. Rather returned her query with a memory.

"You still owe me a dance." That lethal glint graced his eyes as he pulled her towards his ring of trees. Where magic churned like the boiling soup of a cauldron.

Aisling didn't answer but rather allowed the Fae King to gather her close, one hand possessively holding her waist and the other in his own. So, Aisling grasped his shoulder, completing the pairing.

He swept them into clouds of fog. There was no music, only silence. But such stillness was brief.

Lir's eyes glistened, the corners of his lips curling as he spoke a wordless spell into the breath between their lips. Aisling's body shivered, the *draiocht* writhing gleefully around her at Lir's command, popping her ears. Initially, only the brush of white noise surrounded them. Then a strange ringing. But at last, Lir's spell consumed her, filled her. They now danced to the rhythm and pace of a melody Aisling hadn't heard before this very breath. Couldn't discern before Lir allowed. That no mortal man nor woman nor child was permitted to glean. But should mankind catch a glimpse of its rapturous tune, by some scheming of fae or Gods, would spend their whole life searching if only to hear a single refrain once more. Indeed, Lir opened her ears to the voices of the woodland. Where every blackthorn, bramble, and alder hummed a haunting melody. A lullaby of pure sorcery. A voice given to the wind between leaves, the groaning of trunks, the cackles of birds, and the purling of creek beds. Where instruments lit no flame to the majesty that was the voice of the greenwood. Its song an opiate.

Aisling laughed, stunned by the beauty of Lir's enchantments. To enjoy what he must experience all his life: these songs, a ghostly reminder of the forest's screams that, Aisling imagined, one could never quite forget.

"Why do you wish to control the *draiocht*?" he asked at last, eyes darting towards her mouth.

"You once told me the *draiocht* seeks to master lest it be mastered."

"Aye, I did," he purred, his every word vibrating through his chest.

"To master, I must then control," the mortal queen conjectured, focusing now on the veins and fae markings coiling around his forearms, his long and elegant ringed fingers.

"You sound like a mortal."

"I am mortal."

"Are you?" He challenged, guiding her through the dance. The music, the uproar, the laughter of the beasts watching from their tree knots, hollows, and dens. Reflective eyes lighting the forest like a cave of jewels.

Aisling hesitated, opening her mouth to speak before snapping it shut.

"Galad told me how the princeling's iron affected you." At the mention of such iron, Lir's eyes considered her wrists, permanently scarred by such chains. Fury stormed his feral eyes as he held her closer. "The princeling is fortunate he still breathes."

"It must be the magic rippling through you, torching every mortal bone of yours."

"Because at that moment, the *draiocht* consumed me and the iron repelled it."

"Magic doesn't 'consume' mortals." Lir's eyes shimmered the way they did before he unsheathed his axes.

Aisling's face hardened, her heart beating wildly within her chest. He was wrong and so was Filverel. The mortal queen was born mortal and would die mortal for although she'd grown to adore this fae world and its savagery, she wouldn't, couldn't, betray her tuath. And to forgo one race to become another ... Annind had said it himself: it wasn't feasible. There was no enchantment nor spell nor charm to change one's blood or flesh or spirit. Yes, Aisling had adopted something strange and curious. An ancient creature the Sidhe dubbed the *draiocht* now lived within her. But she was still mortal. At the very least, something in between.

"You're part Seelie now whether you realize it or not."

"Tell me, princess," Lir spoke again, pulling her nearer to him as the song began to dissolve, "do you think I rule the Sidhe, the Unseelie, the Kingdom of the Greenwood through control?"

Aisling's brow pinched. "You rule through power."

Lir grinned, flashing the fangs that could disembowel her

if they liked.

"To control is to restrain, to limit, to bridle," he spoke slowly now, every word perfectly accentuated, "claws, fangs, horns are all to be exercised. Strength is to be exercised. A wolf is not made strong nor quick nor powerful shackled its whole life. It becomes weak, frail, sickly in captivity. But when allowed to roam free, it sharpens its claws and fangs, strengthens its muscles, makes nimbler its paws, and whets its appetite.

"What the mortals call savagery, inhumanity, barbarism, all make mighty the Sidhe. Are the bones with which our Sidhe world is made both feral and irresistible, what allows the Sidhe to become one with the world that rejects man. A world that forces humans into civilized shelters, into smoking cities, lest he die of starvation, of the cold, of the heat, of infection, of the appetite of one who is stronger, wilder, hungrier. Because mankind is weak. Because mortals insist on control. On the quelling of such base traits. And that is why they cannot survive in our world, Aisling. Not the way we do. You and I are predators. We rise up the hierarchy of natural beasts and man alike.

"So, you must allow your wolf to wander freely, to strengthen itself in the wild so that when you must call upon it, it is most powerful in your name. Strop your blade rather than dull it. Sharpen your claws and fangs and horns rather than let them waste away. And be prepared when you at last call upon your wolf. Make sure you yourself are wilder, more feral. More powerful until it is you who eats, you who wields, you who calls upon the weapon you challenged, instead of it you."

Chapter XXXV

BEFORE THE SUN ROSE, THUNDER CRACKED across the sky, showering the world in sheets of silver. Aisling woke alone, startled awake by Gilrel's magpies tugging her hair. She'd woken slowly that morning, weary after little sleep. Of late-night letters delivered to her childhood friend by the mouth of a serpent.

The magpies dressed her quickly, helping Gilrel slip another black gown over the mortal queen's head and structure its bodice, shoulders, and forearms with plates of fae armor. Glittering chainmail that hugged her form, cinched at the waist before draping over her ivy skirts. Immaculately forged, cut, cast in fae style, void of the iron worn on mortal sentinels and soldiers alike.

Aisling caught her reflection before she exited the tent. Eyes rimmed with charcoal, lips died with crushed cherries. The sharp angles of the armor were a striking complement to her pale complexion. Her violet eyes captured the light glinting off its surface. And although it appeared heavy, thick, impenetrable, Aisling barely noticed a difference between this armor's weight and the mortal corsets she once donned.

She was the image of a warrior. But not one of brawn nor skill with a blade or shield. One of rapacious, confounding sorcery rivalling the ferocity of the Sidhe themselves, how the Forbidden Lore described the fair folk: ancient, heroic warriors Forged with the blood of the earth in their bones. A sentiment, a resemblance that pricked the back of Aisling's eyes, for she too appeared of another age. An age of the Other where she was welcomed as one of its own.

"Come, *mo Lúra*," Gilrel called from between the canvas curtains, "the union is set to begin any moment now."

Aisling approached the ring of humans and fair folk alike. They stood surrounded by torches like rubies, flickering despite the morning storm descending upon the Isles. Parasols guarded the heads of most mortals while the fair folk braved the cloudburst, water drenching their richly colored locks, beading their skin, and soaking their dress.

Fae drums ricocheted off the bellies of the surrounding cliffs, booming into the mud, the grass, the wind, and through their bones. A rhythm joined by the charge of electricity webbing across the sky in flashes of white light.

As they parted the crowd, Gilrel followed Aisling a step behind. Four sentinels escorting their every step.

"*Skalla*," the fair folk whispered beneath their breath like rustling trees, their voices growing louder the nearer she approached the center of the circle, a large clearing where both the trooping fae and mortal clanns stood at the periphery. Not a single pair of eyes failing to land on Aisling, studying her as though she were Unseelie, Seelie, mortal, something in between. A beast. And perhaps she was.

Nemed was the only member of her audience who grinned as the crowds peeled back to make way for the mortal queen. His eyes glazed with such genuine pride, love, that Aisling felt her knees weakening. Never had her father regarded her so.

Her brothers, yes. Even Dagfin, who the Fire Hand considered a fifth son, but never Aisling. Clodagh, on the other hand, bit her bottom lip, eyes hollowing with horror as she beheld her daughter clad like a warrior. Like a fae knight. Her expression mirrored that of Ciar's, who stood clutching her son's arm so tightly Aisling believed Sim's limb might snap in two.

But it was Dagfin who unnerved the mortal queen most. Dressed in Roktan blue, he sported more weapons than Aisling could count, crossing his arms over his chest. Eyes flickering with something Aisling couldn't place but struggled to tear herself away from. Something like hope. Of unparalleled excitement. His brown hair curled around his ears as a result of the rain.

Lir caught Aisling's eyes as she approached. And while his cold, steely expression didn't change, Aisling could see the conflict harrowing his manic eyes the moment they shifted onto Aisling. The desire that dwelled there, unmet and unslaked.

Lir moved, lithely stepping towards Aisling; that same shivering of the heart each time his attention was fully fixed upon her was near overwhelming. And once he stood within reach, he extended his arm towards her and held out his hand. Those long slender fingers wrapped in fae interlace, symbols, knots. But she hesitated, the pounding of animal skins, mirroring the thumping in her chest.

Against her own volition, her eyes wandered towards her mortal clann. Watching her, her brother's callous expressions hardening the moment the Fae King neared her. Extended his arm towards her as if they were one and the same, she and the Barbarian King of the Greenwood. Intertwined like twin storms, destined to ravage all they touched. Nothing but sweet ruin lying in their wake.

Aisling inhaled sharply, placing her hand in Lir's. And even from her periphery, Aisling witnessed Dagfin shift. It was all that kept her from focusing on the cord between her and the

Fae King; it knotted tightly as she felt his every scar, smelled the wet leaves, heard the purling creaks, felt the monk's moss beneath her feet, tasted the wind weaving through the solemn forests, considering from afar. Woodlands that this morning were uncharacteristically quiet.

Lir smiled at his bride, a grin powerful enough to unbind the mortal queen lest she glare too long. Mercifully, there was no time. The Fae King guided Aisling towards their position around the circle, positioning her beside him. The predatory glint flashed in his Connemara eyes. Aisling still wasn't certain what Lir's intentions with her were. Just last night he'd confessed to not knowing himself. Described how he'd considered spilling her blood to rid himself of the encumbrance he believed her to be, torn between a supernatural bond and the responsibility to his kin.

Startled from her stupor, the drums stopped their beating.

Like ivory ships, three stags emerged from between the folds of mortals and fair folk, giant beasts, whose soaked pelts shimmered amidst the stormy haze, carrying their riders forward. Riders Aisling immediately identified as Blaine, Deidre, and Peitho at the center. The fae princess donned a similar beaded, crimson gown to the one Aisling had worn to her own union. Panels of sparkling stones and meshed lace. But where Aisling's hemline finished just below her slippers, Peitho's carried on, draping her stag in a cloak of red, plastering both its rump and thighs. And her veil, steeped in Northern rain, stuck to her face before hanging from her shoulders. A crimson goddess, gliding forth on her ghost.

Dagfin stepped into the circle. His eyes pinned to Peitho. But where Aisling believed she'd find terror dwelling amidst the contours of his handsome face, she only found resolve. Purpose and courage. The eyes of a hunter.

The Roktan Prince bowed his head, falling to one knee before Peitho's great stag, the fabric of his sapphire trousers now steeped with mud. It was then Aisling wondered why

Nemed had chosen Dagfin and not one of his own sons or even Sim to be married off in the name of Rinn Dúin. Why Feradach had ever agreed to this trade—Dagfin was the sole heir to the Roktan crown. If anything happened to him, Roktling would be left without a successor. The mortals were risking more than a princess this time. They were risking a crown.

This couldn't be happening, Aisling thought to herself. Her chest splintered with every passing moment.

Peitho, Deidre, and Blaine dismounted from their stags, splattering mud onto nearby gowns and trousers. One by one they drew their weapons and staked them into the earth. Blaine, a spear. Deidre, two short swords. And Peitho, a bronze greatsword. Aisling knew which blade was Peitho's; it was obvious enough by its autumn-hued splendor. But even if one was aware of which weapon belonged to the bride or groom, still they would be incapable of selecting it if they weren't *caera*. A phenomenon Gilrel had explained to Aisling several weeks after her union with Lir. Otherwise, Aisling would've been tempted to shout the correct response. To save her once-intended from an untimely death. But magic was particular. Magic was strict. Magic claimed what it desired and refused to compromise.

So, all Aisling could do was watch. Watch as Dagfin approached the line of weapons and considered each blade, tilting his head to the side as he inspected each finely crafted hilt, each sharply spun edge, every immaculate detail the Sidhe hammered into everything their graceful hands could craft. But he wouldn't touch a single haft until he'd made his choice. To touch was to choose.

Aisling grew numb to the rain showering from above, folding her hands into fists and digging her nails into her palms. She turned to Feradach, his expression as hard and cold as the Ashild, holding his breath as Aisling held hers. Ciar's teeth chattered as she embraced Sim. Clodagh wrapped in Iarbonel's jacket and shadowed by the parasol. But more than the anxiety of the royal clanns caught Aisling's attention. So too did the mortal sentinels unlatching their chains from their belts and unsheathing their weapons.

Aisling's head spun, her stomach vaulting up her throat.

But before Aisling could think more of these armed mortal sentinels, a sudden burst of commotion erupted from the crowd. Aisling whipped her head back to Dagfin.

He'd chosen.

Aisling's eyes grew wide as Dagfin's fingers closed around the heavy haft of the spear.

He'd chosen wrong.

Thunder clapped above. A boom that cloaked the maddened shrieks of Sidhe and mortals alike.

There were few seconds in Aisling's life that felt longer than those that passed now. More agonizing than the ones that slipped from her hands for she was powerless against what was to come. A beam swept Peitho's expression, visible even beyond her veil, as she lifted her greatsword from the wet earth and raised it above her head. She was quick. Quicker than any mortal sentinel, guard, knight, or soldier Aisling had ever witnessed. As though she hurdled a gold star whose tail of fire could cut. Could joyously sever Dagfin's head from his body.

Before Aisling could stop herself, she was stepping into the circle, reaching for Dagfin. But Lir caught her wrist and held her back. Just a step towards the Roktan Prince and Aisling knew, even without Lir's intervention, she hadn't been fast enough to prevent any of this from happening.

Dread as black as an inky swamp flooded her. Drowned her and filled her lungs as tears flowed freely from her eyes.

But quicker than Peitho, quicker than even her blade, was Dagfin.

The Roktan Prince fell to the earth the moment her sword was swung. She'd missed. Impossibly, she'd missed. And before Aisling could blink, Dagfin was on his feet, drawing three daggers from the bandolier strapped across his chest and tossing them towards the fae princess. One by one, like sparrows, they cleaved the rain, driving towards Peitho.

Aisling froze, paling as she processed what was unravelling. Desperately doing her best to move forward but Lir still held the mortal queen by the arms, preventing her from running towards the Roktan Prince.

But the daggers didn't find Peitho's heart. They found another's.

Galad stood before the fae princess, the knives stuck into his chest like a bloody star of undiluted iron.

Aisling fell to her knees. Lir still held her, pulling her away from the center of the circle.

Was he dead? Aisling thought to herself. For although such small amounts of undiluted iron could do little against a fae knight, how could one survive a dagger straight to the heart? A blade impeccably aimed and placed at the center of Galad's core?

The mortal queen shook as Lir at last released her, Rian taking his place. But Aisling was already on her knees, wiping away her tears as she processed what was happening before her eyes. So, Rian knelt beside her, holding her close.

Lir approached Galad, pulling the daggers from his chest one by one. The way his expression warped with cold, silent rage, bidding his fae knights a silent, wordless command to stay still. To not unleash bedlam just yet. To not rip the mortals to shreds where they stood and leave their entrails for the Unseelie to scavenge. For those were the desires painted across Galad's, Rian's, Filverel's, Hagre's, Einri's, Cathan's, and Gilrel's expressions. Every one of the fair folk simmering with white fury.

Peitho stood behind him, gawking, still clutching her blade in her hand. Galad had saved her life but her greatsword was still hungry. Still starved for the blood it felt it deserved. That the magic owed it. And once every shard of iron was removed from the fae knight's chest, he bent his neck side to side, cracking his bones.

Galad was fine.

Aisling choked out of pure relief.

"I believed this was a duel to the death." Nemed's expression darkened, meeting the Fae King's eyes. "With no interference from either race."

"Tricks," Clodagh spat, rolling her pale hands into fists, "tricks are all they know and all they'll ever be. You violated the sanctity of our agreement."

"'Sanctity,'" Lir mocked, the surrounding woodland groaning as they tossed violently in the storm, at last coming alive. "Do not speak of sanctity to me, mortal. Your Faerak was never meant to win. No mortal is meant to survive a duel of magic. It goes against the law of your kind. Your blood."

Lir had intended for Dagfin to die. Had wanted Dagfin to die.

Aisling shuffled through her emotions, desperately pushing them aside to see clearly through the veil of angry tears welling in her violet eyes.

"This was no duel then, was it? It was an execution of not only a mortal prince, but one I consider a son myself," Nemed laughed, stepping into the circle. "I can't say I don't understand. I would've done the same for Aisling had it come to it. Prevented her from facing the wrath of your enchanted blades. And your ensuing rage would be worth every law broken."

And at the mortal High King's words, all eyes turned back to Lir. The Fae King ground his teeth, his jaw flexing, as he spun Dagfin's daggers between his fingers. Never once unleashing Nemed from his gaze. From his irate scrutiny. From the loathing oozing from every Sidhe who gathered their weapons in hand and prepared themselves to fight. A miracle in Aisling's eyes they hadn't already unleashed their Otherworldly fury, dying this morning red.

"Your Faerak lost this duel the moment he accepted it," Galad spoke, sword already drawn and poised to fight if it weren't for Lir's command to stand down. "It may be true that the fair folk assumed Peitho would defeat the mortal prince easily, but even if she didn't, magic forbids a human victor."

Peitho shifted, eyes lowering to the ground in shame. They'd all believed this was no duel but certain death for Dagfin. Hadn't imagined the mortal prince was either Faerak or capable of matching the fae princess' prowess in direct combat. But he had. The shy boy Aisling had once known was now something else entirely.

"The magic will reclaim what it believes it is owed," Peitho said, eyes flitting towards Dagfin. "Your prince is cursed."

Dagfin didn't so much as flinch. Didn't move or shrink from both the fair folk and mortals who regarded him with disbelief. With terror.

Nemed grinned but there was doubt inherent within every twitch of his expression. He was determined to not be outwitted, outsmarted, outplayed by his enemy. For this was how the mortals had dominated the fair folk for so long despite the Sidhe's strength and *draiocht* and lifespans. Because the Fire Hand was cunning, clever, willing to make the choices no other King or man would to ensure the victory of his kind. To match the fair folk's mischief and devilry with pranks of his own. And somehow, to Aisling's surprise, Nemed had been outsmarted. Out maneuvered by the most cunning of creatures to exist. For despite the mortal victory Lir always knew magic would retaliate. When magic gives, it demands back

"What do you know of prophecies, Fire Hand?" Lir took several lethal steps towards Nemed, the air saturating with the Fae King's palpable bloodlust.

Nemed's violet eyes glittered with amusement. "That they are self-fulfilled."

Lir laughed, grinning like a wolf raising its head from carrion.

"There is a Lady who wastes away in a cave, century after century weaving. Every thread a thread of fate." The forest roared madly. "There are some who believe that once these threads are placed upon the spindle, woven and knotted together, there are none who can undo its tapestry. No mortal man nor Sidhe nor beast who can tear apart destiny and make of it that which pleases him. That we are all slaves to fate. Tell me, Fire Hand, do you agree?"

Aisling peered around the circle. Fair folk and mortals drenched in rain and hatred alike. And beyond their ring, were the mountains humming with energy, the fields flooding with rain, the forest thrashing from side to side. It was angry, echoing the wrath rippling off the Fae King. For either intentionally or unintentionally, the forest was growing, its trees rising from the dirt, snapping their roots, and moving closer. Larger. The greenwood shadows moving and taking form. Hundreds of eyes peering back from the darkness, beyond the veil of rain and storm. The mortal destriers grew inconsolable. Aisling's breath caught in her throat, choking on the words quickly becoming more than a nightmare.

The Unseelie. They were here. Lir had summoned them. Had already arranged for their arrival when she'd caught him the night prior amidst the pines. He'd planned for this. All of this. In the end, it hadn't been the mortals who'd betrayed the alliance as Aisling had braced herself for. It was the Sidhe.

This was an ambush. A cornering of every mortal sovereign: tiarna, chieftain, king, and queen. The Unseelie were here to destroy all the mortal Isles in one fell swoop. Their bipedal beasts—boars, bears, wolves, serpents— marching beside them, clad in complete armor and weaponry.

"No," Nemed confessed, aware or unaware of the trap Lir

had orchestrated, Aisling was unsure. Her tongue caught in her throat. Unsure whether she wished to snap her mouth shut or yell at the top of her lungs. "Man is indentured to no one and no thing."

The Unseelie would leave no man alive. All bones would be sucked clean. Still, there was a glimmer of hope: there were more mortal sentinels here than fair folk, each cloaked in undiluted iron—potentially among them, more Faerak. Hunters that Nemed claimed killed Unseelie for sport.

And despite the fragile bond between Unseelie and Seelie, Aisling knew their newfound support was founded on Lir's betrayal of the mortals. His deception, a declaration of the end to the treaty that had proven disadvantageous to the Sidhe's sister race. A promise to slaughter every mortal sovereign in the name of the Sidhe. To keep his kin from the brink of extinction and the Unseelie fed. A retaliation against Danu's prophecy.

"You will lose this war."

Words that had shattered the Fae King's world. The belief he'd lost Aisling as he'd once lost Narisea drove him further into madness. Had rendered any alliance or treaty or attempts at peace null and void. For where was the worth in risking his bond to the Unseelie for an alliance that would, according to Danu's prophecy, inevitably end in his loss regardless? And despite the boiling of Aisling's blood for his trickery, the very nature her father had forewarned, and she'd ignored, Aisling understood. Knew this war wouldn't end in coexistence but in dominion. The strongest to rule them all.

"For once we agree," Lir bore his fangs, eyes fixing upon Aisling with unparalleled triumph. The cord between them snapped to attention and nearly knocked the wind from her lungs. For there was a part of Aisling that felt no betrayal at all. That felt equal measure victorious because the Sidhe bore the advantage. The Seelie part of her rejoiced alongside the Barbarian King while the human part mourned, stretched between two loyalties.

But whatever the mortals could achieve in their attempts for retaliation were rendered obsolete once the hordes of Unseelie unmasked themselves from the forest's shadows. As the trees stretched and rose into the heavens with feral need. Fomorians mounted on Cú Scáth, dryads leaping from the trees, goblins hobbling from their caves, and stranger, more frightening creatures slipping into the rain and into the open. Creatures Aisling had never heard of or seen before. All imbued with the *draiocht* and prepared to bloody the emerald pastures in which they all stood.

And once Nemed had realized what Lir had done, how he'd indeed employed both mischief and trickery to obtain his wants, it was too late. His violet eyes widened the same moment Clodagh shrieked. The Unseelie stalked towards them from every direction, the growing trees, the groaning cliffs. Every mortal instinctively gasping, clutching their chests, fainting, or reaching for their weapons, backing away as their enemies surrounded them.

"Take the clann leaders and every woman and child!" Starn bellowed to a group of twenty or so sentinels, already ushering the High King and his Lady towards various destriers prepped and ready to ride. Immediately, Starn had shifted into the soldier his father had bred him to be.

Aisling caught her father's eyes as he was rushed away, Nemed's expression a combination of both horror and violence. Of shock and dread. His lips parted, still processing what was rapidly unspooling. He, the near victor of a war he'd surrendered in the name of peace, his daughter the pawn he'd deemed valuable enough to purchase such harmony. All for naught.

In a panic, many mortals ran. Aisling cursing their foolishness. Horses for the lower-ranking nobles were gathered and mounts haphazardly prepared amidst the discord. The circle, the union, was swiftly dissolving, every mortal counting their breaths until they were far from this place. Their mares stomping, whinnying, bucking.

And as the Unseelie trudged closer and closer, Lir said nothing, his lips curled at the edges.

Filverel laughed as the mortals trampled one another, Galad positioned himself beside his king, Peitho searched the crowd for Dagfin: every member of the Sidhe drawing their weapons and deciding on their victims.

The forest loomed over all their heads. It twisted its branches to break loose its roots and march onward. Among them, a beast so large, so ancient, Aisling knew its name. Could feel the *draiocht* move through every vein within its ghostly figure. Something birthed from the Forge, before the mountains, before the rivers, before the seas. A child the Gods named themselves. Had breathed with sighs of Northern winds, the reflection of deep pools, the jewels of the earth itself, and a brush of *draiocht*. A creature birthed and cast to protect the greenwood. To cure those who lived within its agrestal bastion.

Leshy.

A colossal, phantom of a giant made in the image of man. His beard and hair tufts of glittering clouds, braided through with the spirit form of flowers and thorns and leafy ferns. Every step, vibrating through the earth, unbalancing the mortals.

But it was hardly Leshy Starn cared for as he raced towards where Galad stood, his blade in hand. Iarbonel, Fergus, Dagfin, and Annind scattered throughout the bedlam either defending themselves or attacking. Iron against magic. Mortal blood against fae breath.

Aisling swiveled, doing her best to make sense of the chaos, the clash of blades and shields, shrieks of the injured or dying, the stomp of Lir's legions rising from the woodland, the tearing of the earth as his forest moved nearer. Mortals race for their lives on horseback only to be trailed and tackled by packs of purple-skinned trolls.

Aisling inhaled a breath, the *draiocht* pushing at her throat to be released. But she couldn't. Not here, not now. Her family battled around her and so did the Sidhe, a bloody mixing of her two worlds. To harm either would be to harm herself. For before her very eyes, Starn leapt into the air, lunging for Galad as the fae knight parried swiftly, the two of them locked blade to blade with violence in their eyes.

And if that weren't enough to tear Aisling's heart in two, Gilrel swept the feet of mortal sentinels with her small axe and brought them to their knees, Fergus jabbed at an armored bear who'd ridden with Aisling to the *Snaidhm*, Iarbonel tangled with Tyr, and Annind dodged Filverel's attempts, lifting his shield at the precise moment. But worst of all, Peitho held Dagfin pinned to the ground, her sword tracing a line of blood along the angles of his throat, both her boots nailing Dagfin's hands to the ground.

Aisling shook her head, witnessing the tragedy and unable to act. Helplessly caught between two worlds, for to harm the Sidhe would make her new world more an enemy than it already was, and to harm the mortals would be to betray her own blood. Her childhood. One half of her heart.

Peitho lifted her sword above her head, beaming from ear to ear. She was seconds away from beheading the Roktan Prince, at last, delivering to the magic what it demanded.

"No," Aisling whispered breathlessly, picking up her feet and racing through the labyrinth of metal and mud and bodies and blood.

The fae princess whipped her head in Aisling's direction the moment she emerged from the folds of battle, her temper flaring the moment their eyes met, and Peitho knew. Knew what Aisling had come to prevent. So Peitho drew a dagger with her free hand and flicked it in Aisling's direction.

Dagfin screamed something unintelligible, but it mattered not for the orchestra of battle muffled as the *draiocht* burst open its door and tore at Aisling until at last it was free.

Violet flames wrapped around Peitho's dagger. It fell to the earth, no more than dust. Peitho glared at Aisling with both loathing and alarm. But it was too late for the fae princess. Aisling was already guiding the *draiocht* towards her, its flames enveloping her hands and crawling up her arms.

Peitho screamed as she staggered back, swatting at the fire uselessly. Her sword was a forgotten memory atop the red-soaked fields.

Immediately, Dagfin leapt to his feet. Their eyes met briefly, sparking, before reality struck once more. The Roktan Prince knelt to the ground, retrieving whatever weapons he could from the bodies of the deceased piling around them, reaching for Aisling's hand and racing through the madness with her a step behind.

"There are destriers just within that crevice of the crags as well as three sentinels. I had horses saddled last night and bid our men wait till this evening unknowing ..." his words trailed off. Unknowing the Sidhe had prepared an ambush. Unknowing the Sidhe would fool them all into complacency.

But before Aisling could respond, a mortal man leapt for her. Dark eyes of abhorrence wielders of a sword of undiluted iron. He cursed her as mortals cursed the Sidhe, spitting on her gown as he made to deliver her soul to the Other. A Tilrish soldier Forge bent on eliminating the once princess of his tuath. In his mind, such a woman was dead and gone. Nothing but a sorceress left in her wake.

The mortal queen gasped in horror, summoning the *draiocht* in a panic just as Dagfin turned to block the onslaught. None of their attempts mattered, however, for the mortal guard was brought to the earth by great serpents for roots, coiling around his iron-clad body and crushing his bones one by one.

Aisling lifted her eyes only to meet Lir's from across the field.

His marvelous features were riddled with sweat, dirt, and the ichor of others. None of which rivalled the fury in his sage eyes that bid the grass below him to transform, to grow into a forest of its own. Giant yews sprouting between unassuming mortals and fair folk alike. This was impossible. Lir himself had deemed growing trees like this, growing a new forest, a dream but never reality. So how now, did he manage the strength to conjure so potently. To summon such wrath and vengeance, breathing it into the titan pines that burst from the earth. This was a new power. Something ancient. Something raw. Something Aisling and none of the Isles of Rinn Dúin had seen before.

"*Stay with me,*" the Fae King whispered across the expanse, yet Aisling heard it as if it were spoken directly in her ear.

"Aisling," Dagfin pulled her, his voice ragged with urgency as more trees burst from the earth, impaling mortal and Unseelie alike. But his voice was lost as he was tossed away from her, a new elm severing their hands and tearing she and Dagfin apart. For it was quickly becoming apparent Lir was forming a path. A path for her to walk towards him, undeterred by the mayhem around them. Rows of trees leading her towards the Fae Lord.

So, Aisling followed, defeating the distance that lay between them. Listening to the pull of the string, beckoning her closer with every beat of their hearts.

The forest knelt around her, arching their great backs, like a counsel of trees, eclipsing the only light able to percolate through the dense layer of canopy. Encouraging her onward.

And once she was near enough, Lir held his hand out to

her. A hand she accepted, despite her fury, every hair on her skin standing at attention.

"Some say the fair folk play tricks, spill mischief with a heavy hand," Aisling spoke first, searching his eyes. Glittering, red-rimmed orbs of feral, lethal intent. The sort of violent madness that only death can stifle. Madness and longing. An insatiable desire stirred within him the moment their eyes met. The moment they touched. For indeed, Lir had not only retained fountains of information but deceived his bride alongside all others. Enough to harden Aisling's heart and rue her naivete she'd so desperately believed no longer plagued her as it once had in Tilren.

"Those tales are all true," he confessed, his voice thick, warming her flesh. He pulled her nearer. Together they both stood in a realm of their own. Away from the pandemonium hovering just outside their periphery. Inching nearer.

He leaned towards her, the threat of a smile on his lips. "Return with me, Aisling."

"Our union was sworn in the spirit of an alliance, an alliance you've now betrayed."

"Your kind traded you to the enemy like a prize mare, unable to wield a dagger, unable to speak our tongue, and uneducated in the true Lore, helpless, defenseless, and ignorant. But it was the Sidhe and their *draiocht* that made you powerful. Opened your eyes to that which your clann kept hidden from you. Taught you to be predator and not prey." He wrapped his arms around her. "You belong amongst the Sidhe, Aisling. For you are no longer a princess of Tilren. You are something far more deadly."

Aisling glanced over her shoulder. Dagfin fought his way in her direction, cutting down goblin after goblin like a violent star hurtling towards her.

Lir tightened his grip at the sight of him, a muscle flaring in his jaw.

Aisling shook her head. "I don't belong anywhere. Not

amongst mortals and not amongst the Sidhe." She paused, considering before continuing. "There's someone or something that has mentioned the coming of sorcerers, of mages, of witches and wizards. Words I'd never heard spoken till they fell from Danu's lips. I must find this someone or something, discover what it is I've become or have always been."

Lir's expression hollowed, eyes glazing over, devoid of the sanity that tempered his rage. Danu's prophecy, Aisling's death having killed the stag and left the wolf to roam free.

"I must go."

For Aisling found she no longer cared for forgiveness. Forgiveness for either her family or the Sidhe. Whether they'd lied to her, traded her, used her as bait, insulted her, none of it mattered so long as she was powerful. So naturally, she couldn't find it in herself to relent what little power she'd been given nor discard an opportunity to embolden such might. For power, magic, the *draiocht* could give her everything and anything she'd ever wanted.

Aisling now knew such desires came at a cost whether it be cruelty, pain, or suffering and to pay them, to inflict them, was inevitable if she were to reign supreme. Ideals of goodness were as naïve as she was once herself. For there was no such thing as good or bad. Those who are powerful and those who are weak. Only those who eat and those who are eaten.

"Is this what you want?" His voice was calm, as ice-ridden as the highland woodlands.

Roots ruptured from the earth with greater zeal, showered them in mud, dirt, and grass. Darting towards the clouds with unmet rage.

"Aye, it is." Aisling nodded, witnessing his jadeite orbs morph into the beast she'd seen a handful of times. That vacant, wicked glint transforming him. "In time, we'll find one another once more. And perhaps then, we'll be equally matched."

For all that stood in the way of Aisling honing her newfound abilities, was knowledge of herself and her belonging. The legacy the Unseelie—the creature Dagfin claimed he'd encountered—had intimated she'd begin. She was on the cusp of power, and it drove her to such boldness. For once a taste was had, the appetite was insatiable.

"I swore an oath to you and such bargains amongst the Sidhe cannot be broken: a heart for a heart."

"By the Forge, I vow to you the first cut of my heart, the first taste of my blood, and the last words from my lips," Aisling remembered, the words lighting the cord between them till it branded their souls. Knotting, groaning, straining painfully.

Lir hesitated for a moment, searching her expression. What he found, Aisling was unsure. But it mattered little.

He brought his lips to her own.

His kiss was hungry. The taste of a single drop on the forest's tongue after years of drought. The cord between them unravelled, at last loosening, disentangling, slackening, as he wrapped his blood-stained arms around her and she him. The heat within her daring to flood the Isles of Rinn Dúin in waves of violet flame if she didn't pull away yet all the while Forge-bent on one more moment of this dark indulgence. For she felt his fangs against her tongue and knew he tasted her blood. Knew he wanted more but couldn't have it. Perhaps ever. A thought that maddened the Fae King. Made the *draiocht* coursing through him, spark her in return. Flow through her. A sensation she indulged. Relished. That overwhelming magic: primeval, old, all-knowing, and all-wanting. But the pocket of time they'd forged for themselves could no longer withstand the chaos that surrounded them.

So, Aisling at last tore herself away, summoning the *draiocht* as mightily as she was capable. Caring little for the guilt that would've once eaten her alive at the notion of embracing he who wished to slaughter her kind. Lir had been right. Had always been right. The strong rose on the failures of the weak. A fair game of strength, victory, and loss.

A wall of fire formed just as Lir reached out for her, unwilling or unable to release her.

"A heart for a heart," she repeated, through the veil of the torchlit wall. But Lir's expression spoke for itself, one that forced the rock-faced cliffs to their knees, re-energized the Unseelie, maddened the fair folk and their bipedal beasts. For he may have outwitted the mortals, ensnared much of her kind's most prominent leaders, but he hadn't won everything. And Aisling had. Relishing in the taste of her freedom, her agency apart from the ownership of others. Either Tilren's or Annwyn's.

"Stay," he whispered one last time.

In answer, Aisling stepped back, every step away from him fraying the cord between them.

She ran. Turned her back to her husband and sprinted towards her freedom. One day, they'd meet again, and she anticipated the day near as much as the day she learned of herself and her newfound fate. Her heart was bound to the Fae King either by magic spells, cords of destiny, or something else. Something greater, that much she knew. For Aisling and Lir's future were woven by the Lady. Intricate tapestries whose tales were knit tightly together. Needlework already sewn into the fabric of the stars.

So, she'd dream of him till once more they met.

And as though it were nothing more than a whisper. As though it were a voice in her own mind, Aisling heard him. Heard his voice slither through her as she ran farther into the bedlam.

"*Very well. Then I'll hunt you down.*"

Chapter XXXVI

AISLING PICKED UP HER SKIRTS AND FLED. Dagfin cut through yet another trow, breathlessly intercepting her and guiding her towards their escape.

It was possible she witnessed Gilrel impale a mortal amidst the chaos, beheld Rian skirt death, watched Filverel behead an ill-matched opponent, caught Galad's sapphire eyes. The Sidhe who battled the mortal sentinels till none remained. But it all could've been her imagination. Her mind making sense of the bodies she leapt over, the Unseelie swarming the verdant fields like floodwaters descending upon civilization. And ahead of her, her brothers waited for her. Sat on their mounts, yelling over the bedlam, until she arrived. Until she'd escaped the fae ambush none, not even Nemed, had been prepared for.

A creature Aisling had never encountered before lunged towards her, grabbing her ankles. For after a few moments it was clear the Unseelie were chasing her and no longer the fleeing mortals. Lir would stop at nothing before she was returned to him. Wouldn't allow her to slip from his grasp. And this demon, Aisling knew, was most likely a goblin.

It grinned as it latched its slimy green fingers around her ankle, pulling her onto the ground. In the blink of an eye,

Dagfin plunged a fae sword he'd collected along the way between the fiend's eyes. The goblin shrieked in pain, a sound that nearly rendered Aisling deaf.

With Dagfin's help, Aisling staggered to her feet, tripping on the hem of her gown now splattered with red and brown. Torn and fraying as she spotted Starn racing towards herself and the Roktan Prince on horseback, a spare horse following shortly behind. A pool of dread deepened within her as she wondered whether Galad had survived their clash.

With the flick of a wrist, he cut down two Fomori and three monsters Aisling didn't know the names of. One by one, they fell to the earth like birds shot from the sky, moaning as the Tilrish Prince's blades landed in their skulls. And once Starn was near enough, Dagfin lifted Aisling onto the spare destrier, joining her in front in one swift movement. Aisling wrapped her arms around his waist, bracing herself for the cool burst of wind cutting their faces, the gale as motivated to prevent the mortal queen's departure as Lir and his Unseelie were themselves.

But they weren't free yet.

Leshy stalked them from behind, reaching for their mare's hooves with his enormous hands. Wispy hands that could hold twenty men. And Aisling gasped as their mount nearly lost its footing. A result of Leshy's earth-shattering steps, as if rattling the world and turning it on its axis.

"Hold on," Dagfin whispered, lowering himself, driving the mare quicker. But the giant was too large, too quick to be outraced. Slamming his bare feet mere paces from the mare's rump.

"It's too fast," Aisling shouted.

She closed her eyes, concentrating on the *draiocht*, summoning garlands of fire before the giant's every step.

"Well done," Starn praised, racing beside them and eying where her fires wove across the earth like bestial serpents. Devouring all that was green and alive.

Leshy staggered awkwardly over the fires slowing his steps, buying them more time, but still, he loomed over them, regaining his balance.

So Dagfin ducked lower, weaving the mare through Leshy's legs. From his belt, the Roktan Prince unblocked a chain of iron.

"Hold your breath," he commanded Aisling, so she did.

After swinging the iron chain above his head, Dagfin released it, just as he'd done the bolo. One end he tossed to Starn, the other he kept firmly in his grasp. And together, they touched Leshy's ankle, simmering the giant's flesh. Still, it was not enough to bring the giant to its knees. But Dagfin wasn't done. He and Starn drove their destriers through the Unseelie's legs thrice more times, expertly guiding their mounts like needles, the chain as their thread. For once the Faerak and Tilrish Prince were done, they darted on ahead, still holding that chain tightly in their gloved fists. And the further they fled, the tighter the iron rope grew, cinching Leshy's ankles together where Dagfin and Starn had masterfully bound them together.

Leshy collapsed against the earth, flattening hordes of Unseelie racing just below him. A boom that echoed throughout all the Isles, perhaps even all the realm. The impact hurtled Starn, Dagfin, and Aisling into the air along with their horses. They slammed into the ground, the air knocked from Aisling's lungs.

"Ash!" Dagfin shouted, immediately rising from where he'd fallen and racing towards her. Aisling scrambled to her feet, catching his outstretched hand.

They ran. They ran quickly, sprinting for their lives as they'd done as children. Although now, it was no longer make-believe.

Chapter XXXVII

NOT TOO FAR OFF, IARBONEL, ANNIND, AND Fergus awaited both Aisling and Dagfin with fresh mares stirring beside them. They joined her brothers quickly, wasting not a breath of time.

"Took you each long enough," Fergus teased, as they each nudged their horses forward.

"You should know better than to doubt me," Starn quipped, offering Aisling his canteen of water. Normal water. Not Sidhe wine, Aisling realized, taking the bottle and downing its contents.

Aisling, her brothers, and Dagfin travelled both days and nights, glancing over their shoulders, sleeping with one eye open, their blades beneath their heads. Eating mortal foods that tasted of ash compared to the fae delicacies the mortal queen had become accustomed to. Even the air this far from Annwyn was stale. Duller, lacking in its fae luster. And the cord between herself and Lir grew taut. Grew angry. At times, waking Aisling to the sound of Lir's rage.

"It was Aisling we doubted," Annind woke Aisling from her reverie, eying his sister through slits for eyes.

"I admit I doubted when Dagfin first claimed you'd agreed to flee with us," Starn continued, leading their group forward.

"This is temporary," Aisling said, tempering her rage by squeezing the mount's reins. "Just until I reach Lofgren's rise."

"Father will be made aware of your plans one way or another." Iarbonel nudged his mount till it pranced beside Aisling's.

The mortal queen considered him. "It isn't I you should fear tattling." Her eyes flashed towards Starn, the Fire Hand's favored child.

"Nemed has already caught wind of a curse breaker. It's only a matter of time before he and the Aos Sí alike decide to pursue it. It'll be a race to Lofgren's rise." Annind gestured for the canteen.

"I'm not after the curse breaker." She needed answers. Needed to know who she was becoming and where she belonged.

"It's a perilous journey, Ash. One met by demons of the Other at every bend. I myself failed to enter Lofgren's rise on my first attempt," Dagfin chimed, his breath warming the top of her head, her cheeks, her neck.

"You cannot go alone; it's impossible—" Fergus began before Dagfin interrupted him.

"She won't be venturing alone. I'll be accompanying her."

"The Aos Sí will be after you near as madly as they'll pursue Aisling herself. You'll be outnumbered, chased, and challenged by all you encounter," Starn said, keeping his eyes on the highlands further North.

For indeed, if what the Sidhe spoke was true, Dagfin was cursed, destined to live the remainder of his years outrunning the very magic Aisling craved.

Aisling bit her bottom lip. Her brother's warnings meant little to her for there was nothing that would stand in the way of her pursuit for answers. She'd discover who and what she'd become whether it killed her to do so. At any cost.

"You'll need a capable fighter or four to accompany the both of you," Starn continued.

Dagfin turned his attention to the future King of Tilren. "A Faerak will more than compensate for those numbers."

"Perhaps but you lack reason and impulse control. Especially amongst the present company." Each of them glanced at Aisling from the corner of their eyes, Dagfin tensing behind her.

"Who do you suggest?" Dagfin continued rather desperately.

"I suppose I would do," Iarbonel responded. "I'm in need of a fine quest."

"As am I." Fergus raised his hand.

Annind shook his head. "And I suppose I'd feel rather left out if I didn't agree by now."

Starn grinned.

"There you have it."

Aisling looked between each of them, disbelief twisting her features.

"Don't look at us like that, little sister," Iarbonel said. "We left you to all the fun and adventure once. It won't happen again."

Aisling did her best to swallow but her throat had run dry. She'd believed they despised her and all that she'd become and perhaps they still did. Aisling wasn't so naive anymore to believe they wished to help her from the kindness of their hearts and no more.

"Father will never allow it. He'll command you to return to Tilren at once."

"After Dagfin shared your desire to escape at his side, I made arrangements. Feradach is fully aware of our intentions and has already begun preparing a ship for us to sail further North and towards Lofgren's rise. Father is under the impression we're helping Feradach secure his borders considering the Aos Sí will be in wild pursuit of Dagfin till further notice."

Aisling blanched, her mouth hanging open for she knew

not what to say. She couldn't deny the bitter cast of resentment that now cocooned her feelings for her brothers and all the love that lay beneath. It would take both time and trust rebuilt before she would allow any to warm to her. But if they wished to help her in her endeavors, to achieve her ends—ulterior motives or not—she was in no position to stop them. After all, her only weapon was a young fire and the Faerak riding behind her. If they could help her find answers, obtain what she wanted, she'd enjoy their company.

"I suppose we're headed for Roktling then," Aisling spoke at last, meeting Starn's raven eyes.

"Aye, to Roktling."

So, they travelled far and fast, hiding their identities from every port and city they crossed along the way, sticking to man-made roads and trails lest they be set upon by the Sidhe and Unseelie alike with fiery vengeance.

But no matter where Aisling slept or rode or stood, whether it be an inn or cottage or keep, she heard the woodland voices still. They screamed for her, writhing and rustling no matter how far she stretched the distance between herself and them. The cord within her yanking her back, tearing at her soul the longer she resisted, destroying a part of her she believed may never recover. And still the forest haunted her. Searched for her, vines crawling against her windowpanes, moss and algae tickling the stones she threw, flowers budding in unseemly places. All of which whispered her name again and again:

"*Aisling.*"

About Atmosphere Press

Atmosphere Press is an independent, full-service publisher for excellent books in all genres and for all audiences. Learn more about what we do at atmospherepress.com.

We encourage you to check out some of Atmosphere's latest releases, which are available at Amazon.com and via order from your local bookstore:

Twisted Silver Spoons, a novel by Karen M. Wicks

Queen of Crows, a novel by S.L. Wilton

The Past We Step Into, stories by Richard Scharine

The Museum of an Extinct Race, a novel by Jonathan Hale Rosen

Swimming with the Angels, a novel by Colin Kersey

Island of Dead Gods, a novel by Verena Mahlow

Cloakers, a novel by Alexandra Lapointe

Twins Daze, a novel by Jerry Petersen

Embargo on Hope, a novel by Justin Doyle

Abaddon Illusion, a novel by Lindsey Bakken

Blackland: A Utopian Novel, by Richard A. Jones

The Jesus Nut, a novel by John Prather

The Embers of Tradition, a novel by Chukwudum Okeke

Saints and Martyrs: A Novel, by Aaron Roe

When I Am Ashes, a novel by Amber Rose

Melancholy Vision: A Revolution Series Novel, by L.C. Hamilton

The Recoleta Stories, by Bryon Esmond Butler

About The Author

A.E. Jürgens grew up overseas as a diplomat's daughter, living in over nine different countries and five continents. She recently settled down in the United States with her South African husband and two sons. But that hasn't stopped her from exploring enchanted lands or fantastic realms through the pages of her favorite novels and the letters on her keyboard.

CPSIA information can be obtained
at www.ICGtesting.com
Printed in the USA
BVHW041451141022
649461BV00018B/1221/J